The Conspiracy of Words

Close Readings in Dickens, Hardy, and Others

Toru Sasaki

“This is exactly the kind of literary criticism I most admire, revealing the imaginative network behind the fiction.”

— John Carey, formerly Merton Professor of English Literature, University of Oxford

TORU SASAKI is Professor of English Literature at Kyoto University. He has translated Charles Dickens’s *Bleak House* and *Great Expectations*. He is a former President of the Japan Branch of the Dickens Fellowship and former President of the English Literary Society of Japan.

CONTENTS

III. OTHERS

Preface

This is a collection of my writings published in English in the UK and the USA, including journal articles, contributions to books, introductions to the books I edited. In the process of gathering them here, I have kept the revision to a minimum. The book title is a quotation from Nabokov, which I explain in Ch. 1. It nicely describes the "behavior" of the language of a rich literary text such as Dickens's or Hardy's. What I have been doing in my entire career is to study and analyze that behavior. For me it is the only approach that I can take as a Japanese scholar in order to say something original and relevant in the field of English Literature. We cannot read quantitatively more than native speakers because we are slow, but we perhaps tend to read more carefully for the very same reason. Because of this slowness, there may be things that English-speaking scholars have missed and I am able to spot. That is my belief and here is its outcome.

In reading, thinking, and writing in an acquired language, I have incurred many debts. Perry Meisel gave me inspiration when I was a graduate student. Norman Page warmly encouraged my study of Hardy. Since my interest turned to Dickens, Michael Slater has been the constant source of generous enlightenment. My thanks are also due to Malcolm Andrews, Edward Costigan, John Drew, Mark Ford, Philip Horne, Neil McEwan, and Andrew Sanders. I would be unpardonably remiss if I failed to acknowledge the friendly stimulations I received from the four departed masters: John Bayley, Barbara Hardy, Frank Kermode, and Tony Tanner.

Toru Sasaki, Kyoto, 2021

I. DICKENS

Ch. 1 The Conspiracy of Words in *David Copperfield*

Vladimir Nabokov remarks of Pushkin's *Eugene Onegin*: "there is a conspiracy of words signaling to one another, throughout the novel, from one part to another."[1] The Russian novelist's observation turns out to be perfectly apt for Dickens, whose words on the page constantly echo and resonate with each other, thereby generating significances that may be hidden unless carefully scrutinized, or that may be unintended by the novelist himself.[2] The idea of the "conspiracy of words" will be made clearer by juxtaposing Nabokov's comment with one from Edgar Allan Poe. In his review (*Saturday Evening Post*, 1 May 1841) of Dickens's *Barnaby Rudge*, a novel that begins with a mysterious murder, Poe claimed, having only read the first seventh of the whole novel, that he had seen through its tricks and could already tell who the culprit was. He also predicted some of the plot developments. Picking up, for example, the following passage of the novel, he said he had discerned Dickens's "evident design."[3] Here the mentally afflicted protagonist, Barnaby Rudge, is talking to Mr Chester about the clothes "hanging on [the] lines to dry, and fluttering in the wind":

> "Look down there," he said softly; "do you mark how they whisper in each other's ears; then dance and leap, to make believe they are in sport? Do you see how they stop for a moment, when they think there is no one looking, and mutter among themselves again; and then how they roll and gambol, delighted with the mischief they've been plotting? Look at 'em now. See how they whirl and plunge. And now they stop again, and whisper, cautiously together—little thinking, mind, how often I have lain upon the grass and watched them. I say what is it that they plot and hatch? Do you know?" (Ch. 10)

Suspecting something going on underneath the apparently inconsequential rambling of an "idiot," Poe argues:

> Now these incoherences are regarded by Mr Chester simply as such, and no attention is paid them; but they have reference, indistinctly, to the counsellings together of Rudge and Geoffrey Haredale, upon the topic of the bloody deeds committed; which

> counsellings have been watched by the idiot. In the same manner almost every word spoken by him will be found to have an under current [sic] of meaning, by paying strict attention to which the enjoyment of the imaginative reader will be infinitely heightened.[4]

Poe believed that later in the novel "the counsellings" would be revealed as actually having taken place, but he was to be disappointed. Then, after the serialization was completed, he wrote a second review (*Graham's Magazine*, February 1842), stating: "Upon perusal of these ravings we, at once, supposed them to have allusion to some *real* plotting; and even now we cannot force ourselves to believe them not so intended."[5] His dissatisfaction has some justification: as a detective novel *Barnaby Rudge* might have been better if it had gone along the lines he suggested. But in Barnaby's "ravings" there is "an undercurrent of meaning" that rewards the "imaginative reader's" careful attention. Consider the very words he utters. The "plotting" he sees amongst the fluttering clothes surely chimes with the "plot" (Chs. 24 and 51) Sim Tappertit is brewing with his secret society of "Prentice Knights, and ultimately chimes with the novel's main action, the anti-Catholic plot. Indeed, Barnaby's speech contains a number of story elements that are to come later in the novel, as if he were foreseeing the future: Gordon cannot breathe the air "filled with *whispers* of a confederacy among the Popish powers" (Ch. 37); his aide Gashford's "very shoulders seemed to sneer in stealthy *whisperings* with his great flapped ears" (Ch. 36); rioters enjoy "an extemporaneous No-Popery *Dance*" (Ch. 38); in the mob-ridden London "the *mischief* was . . . done" (Ch. 66); Barnaby himself is eventually "*whirled* away into the heart" of the riot (Ch. 48; all italics mine in this paragraph). One might say here Dickens's words themselves are plotting. This kind of "conspiracy" lying behind seemingly insignificant details is one of the features that make Dickens's novels so interesting, or, shall we say, intriguing.

The notion of the "conspiracy of words" is particularly fruitful when applied to *David Copperfield*, for the language of the novel expresses "an undercurrent of meaning" of great moment, related to Dickens's most profound personal anxieties. In his work during the period between *A Christmas Carol* and *David Copperfield* (1843-1850) the novelist repeatedly attempts to recover the emotion of his own past, "sinking a well into memory," as Kathleen Tillotson puts it.[6] Crucially in this context, in 1846 (4 November) Dickens wrote to his friend and future biographer, John Forster, referring to his own autobiography: "Shall I leave you my life in MS. when I die? There are some things in it that would touch you very much. . . ." The same letter reveals that the broaching of this idea was triggered by the composition of the early chapters of *Dombey and Son* (1846-48), especially the passage concerning Mrs Pipchin's establishment for boys and girls, which derives from his own childhood experience. From various sources it is inferred that in the course of the next two years—or earlier—he did write some portion of the autobiography. Forster printed it, or part of it (this is usually referred to as the Autobiographical Fragment), in his biography.[7] By comparing the Fragment with the relevant section of *David Copperfield*, namely, the fourth instalment of the novel (Chs. 10-12; published August 1849), we learn that Dickens drew heavily upon this material. His memorandum for the instalment in question includes a poignantly terse phrase, "What I know so well."

What he knew so well is the fact that, when a mere eleven years old, he was sent out to work at Warren's blacking warehouse for about a year, due to financial difficulties in the family.[8] Soon afterwards his father was arrested for debt and the family moved into the Marshalsea prison, leaving young Charles to live by himself. In the warehouse he "held some station," was called "the young gentleman" amongst "common men and boys," but was compelled to do what he deemed as degrading menial work. "No words can express the secret agony of my soul as I sunk into this companionship," he recalls.[9] The employment, the association with working-class surroundings, was kept a dark secret from everyone except his wife and Forster, until the latter revealed it in the biography two years after the novelist's death. Since then the blacking factory experience has been widely regarded as the single most decisive influence on Dickens's imagination. It produced in him "a trauma from which he suffered all his life," according to Edmund Wilson.[10]

The "conspiracy of words" in *David Copperfield* begins at the beginning. On the very first page the protagonist informs the reader that he "was born with a caul," a traditional sailor's charm (Ch. 1; 1).[11] Catching onto the nautical association, the language of the text foreshadows the vicissitudes of David's life by the movement, outside his house, of the "weatherbeaten ragged old rooks'-nests" swinging "like wrecks upon a stormy sea" (Ch. 1; 5). The talisman, though later sold off to someone else, turns out to be not without its effects on the hero. Towards the end of the novel, after the chastisement of Uriah Heep, David spends a night at Wickfield's; "I lay in my old room, like a shipwrecked wanderer come home" (Ch. 54; 670). The implication is that he has gone through some difficulties—at one point he speaks of himself as a "tempest-driven bark" (Ch. 38; 465)—but is now safe and well.[12] This "shipwreck" reference is placed in the chapter immediately preceding the one depicting "The Tempest," in which the shipwrecked Steerforth is drowned (Ch. 55), with a weighty contrast clearly intended. The hardship of life thus being linked with maritime disaster, it is natural that young David should imagine seeing Little Emily "springing forward to her destruction" from a timber protruding over the sea (Ch. 3; 31). Micawber characteristically offers a comic relief to these somber instances by saying, "I am a straw upon the surface of the deep, and am tossed in all directions by the elephants—I beg your pardon; I should have said the elements" (Ch. 49; 604).

All these nautical associations are fairly self-evident and easy to spot. More interesting, however, are the ways in which Dickens's words connect with each other in less obvious ways. As regards David's caul, his recollection of its sale is worth a careful consideration: "I was present myself, and I remember to have felt quite uncomfortable and confused, at a part of myself being disposed of in that way" (Ch. 1; 2). The phrase, "a part of myself being disposed of," curiously echoes the 1850 Preface to the novel: "an Author feels as if he were dismissing some portion of himself into the shadowy world, when a crowd of the creatures of his brain are going from him for ever." This, in turn, resonates with the final words of the novel: "so may I, when realities are melting from me, like the shadows which I now dismiss, still find thee near me, pointing upward!" Here in his address to Agnes, David is talking about his bidding a farewell to the characters ("the shadows") featured in his autobiography. Reading these passages in tandem, we are now in a position to see that the way David looks at his caul reflects the way Dickens looks at this novel, his "favourite child."[13] The idea of fathering, we ought to note, manifests itself in the very last sentence of Ch. 1:

> Betsey Trotwood Copperfield was for ever in the land of dreams and shadows, the tremendous region whence I had so lately travelled; and the light upon the window of our room shone out

> upon the earthly bourne of all such travellers, and the mound above the ashes and the dust that once was he, *without whom I had never been*. (Ch. 1; 11) (italics mine)

Apparently "the land of dreams and shadows" here denotes some nebulous world of pre-existence from which we are supposed to come; but considered together with the afore-mentioned self-reflexive references to fictional creation, it can signify the realm of the novelist's imagination, from which patrix all Dickensian characters are born.[14]

In the above passage we must pay heed to the phrase, "the earthly bourne of all such travelers." Dickens, through David, is alluding to *Hamlet*: the prince of Denmark says in the "To be or not to be" soliloquy, "But that the dread of something after death/ The undiscovered country, from whose bourn/ No traveller returns, puzzles the will".[15] The Shakespeare play is already present in the text when the reader is introduced to the meek Dr Chillip, who walks "as softly as the Ghost in Hamlet" (Ch. 1; 8). That the doctor who brings David to this world is likened to the father of the play's protagonist is part of the recurrent "fathering" motif in the novel.

Barbara Hardy discusses the above and other Shakespearian allusions with keen perception. She is undoubtedly right in stating that Dickens was "saturated in Shakespeare," and that he uses the playwright "most variously in *David Copperfield*."[16] Her observations are of interest, since she is not merely talking about direct quotations, but also alert to the "conflations, echoes and fragments" from the dramatist. For example, she finds in "The Tempest" chapter, in which Ham Peggotty prepares himself for a rescue operation, an allusion to *Hamlet* ("Readiness is all") even if Dickens "does not use Shakespeare's words."[17] Assuming that Dickens's mind was thus "saturated," I am tempted to suggest that when composing the Shakespearian phrase, "the earthly bourne of all such travelers," Dickens may have been remembering that Hamlet in the same soliloquy talks about "a sea of troubles" (3.1.60), a perfectly felicitous metaphor for his own hero's future life, which he was to go through without being drowned.

Shortly after the "caul" passage that triggers these maritime associations—and bearing a vital connection with it—the novel's most interesting eccentric makes her appearance. What is remarkable about Aunt Betsey is that she is not just quirky; there is "method" in her "madness." She has made up her mind that the baby about to be born is a girl and that she is to be her godmother. She desperately wants to make sure that "there must be no mistakes in this Betsey" (Ch. 1; 6): hence her extraordinary anxiety that night. David notes: "There was a twitch of Miss Betsey's head, after each of these sentences, as if her own old wrongs were working within her, and she repressed any plainer reference to them by strong constraint." Acting out this "constraint" with a curious gesture, she stops "her ears with jewellers' cotton" (Ch. 1; 8). Dr Chillip notices it, and queries:

> "Some local irritation, ma'am?"
>
> "What!" replied my aunt, pulling the cotton out of one ear like a cork.
>
> Mr. Chillip was so alarmed by her abruptness . . . that it was a mercy he didn't lose his presence of mind. But he repeated sweetly:
>
> "Some local irritation, ma'am?"
>
> "Nonsense!" replied my aunt, and corked herself again, at one blow. (Ch. 1; 9)

Aunt Betsey's "corking herself" is a piece of behavior wonderfully appropriate to such an eccentric character. But as a reader of this novel we must make a note of the fact that the *cork* harks back to the passage where David talks about the caul: there is only one "bidding" for it because "sea-going people . . . were short of faith and preferred *cork* jackets" (Ch. 1; 1) (italics mine). I have just said the cork "harks back," but what happens is that the significance of the caul (with its connections with the avoidance of maritime disaster) has been by association conferred on the cork, and that the recurrence of the cork brings with it that charged significance—the "caul" has, as it were, recruited the "cork" into the novel's semantic action; such are the workings of the Dickensian "conspiracy of words."

In addition, we must not overlook Aunt Betsey's corking herself "at one blow," the phrase suggesting the underlying violence, which motif, as we shall see, holds a key to our fuller understanding of the novel. The vehement physical force here is accentuated in what follows: when she finds out that the baby is a boy, "My aunt said never a word, but took her bonnet by the strings, in the manner of a sling, aimed a blow at Mr Chillip's head with it, put it on bent, walked out, and never came back" (Ch. 1; 10-11). Her comic violence has been emphasized also in her dealings with Ham, "a victim on whom to expend her superabundant agitation": "she shook him, rumpled his hair, made light of his linen, stopped his ears as if she confounded them with her own, and otherwise tousled and maltreated him" (Ch. 1; 10). This is a delightful farce, but far from a trivial one; it is closely related to the novel's central preoccupation.

The novel has begun with these words: "Whether I shall turn out to be the hero of my own life, or whether that station will be held by anybody else, these pages must show" (Ch. 1; 1). The hero's curious apprehension is understandable, for he is rather a bland figure, compared with the colorful people who surround him. Somerset Maugham bluntly puts it: "But he was surely a bit of a fool. He remains the least interesting person in the book."[18] Such an impression will arise, because David himself does not *do* much. In the novel other people act out David's repressed desire: Uriah Heep lusts after Agnes; Steerforth seduces Emily, and so forth.

On that point much has been written by modern critics from psychological or psychoanalytical perspectives.[19] Rosemary Bodenheimer, one of the shrewdest, speaks of "a dispersal and multiplication of subjectivity among various characters" and notes "David's multiple engagements with other characters who play out his own identity splits."[20] A pre-Freudian but entirely adequate explication, however, is already offered by Dickens in the novel itself. David says: "My aunt always excused any weakness of her own in my behalf, by transferring it in this way to my poor mother" (Ch. 19; 234). What Bodenheimer means by identity splits very much corresponds to this "transferring": projecting one's feelings and desires onto others.

Now we can see Aunt Betsey's behavior in a proper context; by the act of "corking" Ham's ears she is transferring her anxiety onto him. Also, in the description of her singular conduct ("she shook him, rumpled his hair, made light of his linen, stopped his ears"), we should be alert to the phrase, "shook him". This action has been nicely foreshadowed: "Ba-a-h!" said my aunt, with a perfect shake on the contemptuous interjection. And corked herself as before" (Ch. 1; 9). Shaking, too, we realize, is part of her transference. The idea continues in her treatment of poor Dr Chillip: "It has since been considered almost a miracle that my aunt didn't shake him, and shake what he had to say, out of him. She only shook her own head at him. . ." (Ch. 1; 10).

Indeed, Aunt Betsey's extraordinary behavior is nothing but a comic mirroring of the way David's anxiety or desire is transferred to other characters. Having made that point, we shall for the moment leave the eccentric Aunt "corking" and shaking Ham, with a promise to come back to her at the end of the essay. Let us now, in order to deepen our understanding of the "conspiracy," take a look at three notable scenes expressing the transference involving David; there, invariably, the "uninteresting" hero does nothing—he just stands still as a bystander.[21]

First, the chastisement of Uriah Heep (Ch. 52). When he becomes aware of Heep's desire for Agnes, David expresses his feelings thus: "I believe I had a delirious idea of seizing the red-hot poker out of the fire, and running him through with it" (Ch. 25; 326). With the hero bearing this sort of violent wish, a story, one expects, will end with his realizing it for himself. Yet David does not take any violent action at the denouement of this particular narrative thread; he "assists at" the occasion, as the chapter title tells us (meaning simply being present, as it turns out). David's desire to punish Heep is transferred to Micawber: "Mr Micawber, with a perfect miracle of dexterity or luck, caught [Heep's] advancing knuckles with the ruler, and disabled his right hand" (Ch. 52; 642). His ruler, referred to as "a ghostly truncheon" (Ch. 52; 641)—another allusion to *Hamlet*[22]—is a comic variation of David's "red-hot poker."[23] Heep's reaction here is remarkable. When he is surrounded by David's friends, with his scheme exposed, Heep shows anger at David's secretive operation: "If it had been *me*, I shouldn't have wondered; for I don't make myself out a gentleman (though I never was in the streets either, as you were, according to Micawber), but being you!" (Ch. 52; 641). The accusation of David's making himself out a gentleman is, as we shall shortly see, crucial; it is essentially this that causes our hero to be dumb and inactive.

Second, the scene in which the poor schoolmaster, Mr Mell, is dismissed, where David simply "stood beside him" (Ch. 7; 82). Here Mell becomes angry at Steerforth, who, from the teacher's point of view, has the temerity to "insult a gentleman" (Ch. 7; 83). Steerforth responds: "A what?—where is he?" (Ch. 7; 93). Steerforth goes on to call Mell a beggar, and informs Creakle, the principal, that Mell's mother is in receipt of relief. Mell admonishes the insolent student:

> "To insult one who is not fortunate in life, sir, and who never gave you the least offence, and the many reasons for not insulting whom you are old enough and wise enough to understand," said

> Mr Mell, with his lips trembling more and more, "you commit a mean and base action. You can sit down or stand up as you please, sir. Copperfield, go on." (Ch. 7; 83)

Mell's abrupt "Copperfield, go on" at the end gives us a slight pause. We do not know what Mell is ordering David to "go on" doing, as we are not told what he has been up to. Presumably, David has been tested about what he has memorized from the text book—Mell is holding "my book" (Ch. 7; 82). Be that as it may, this puzzling phrase, in an undemonstrative fashion, underscores the fact that David has been frozen.

The crux of this passage is Steerforth's accusation that Mell is pretending to be a gentleman. As we have seen, Uriah Heep accuses David of the same pretension ("making himself out"). The schoolboy David is always afraid that he might somehow give away his own lowly associations in the past: "Was there anything about me which would reveal my proceedings in connexion with the Micawber family?" (Ch. 16; 195). Steerforth's censure of Mell, in fact, hits David as hard as the schoolmaster. That is to say, to David, Steerforth's words seem, just like Heep's in the previous scene, to be thrown at him, which is why he is frozen in this scene. Ultimately, Mell's and David's anxieties are Dickens's own; they reflect the novelist's mental struggle with the blacking factory experience, the fall into the working-class life.

Finally, Rosa's attack on Emily (Ch. 50). Here David, not intervening, just watches it from the next room, with the pretext that only Mr Peggoty has the right to step in. The extreme violence contained in Rosa's verbal abuse of the poor girl is, again, class-related. In this context George Orwell's remark is suggestive:

> The "gentleman" and the "common man" must have seemed like different species of animal. Dickens is quite genuinely on the side of the poor against the rich, but it would be next door to impossible for him not to think of a working-class exterior as a stigma.[24]

This "stigma" manifests itself in a remarkable manner in the novel. When the boy David escapes from Murdstone and Grinby and reaches Dover, Aunt Betsey describes him thus: "He's as like Cain before he was grown up, as he can be" (Ch. 13; 168). This linking with Cain immediately conjures up a Biblical reference: "And the LORD set a mark upon Cain, lest any finding him should kill him" (Genesis 4.15). Behind Aunt Betsey's association of young David with Cain is a dark implication that upon the beautiful skin of the boy there is a "mark," namely, the stigma of the working class. It is the mark young David is keen to conceal from his fellow school boys and from Heep. Of crucial importance here is the fact that in the Autobiographical Fragment, describing the blacking factory days, Dickens speaks of himself as "small Cain."[25]

Earlier in the novel, Rosa has said: "I would have her branded on the face, dressed in rags, and cast out in the streets to starve" (Ch. 32; 402). To such a violent degree does she wish to be revenged on Emily, the woman who has stolen Steerforth from her. She wants to set a "mark" on Emily, as if in retaliation for the mark Steerforth has set on herself. The scar on Rosa's lip—"She has borne the mark ever since" (Ch. 20; 252)—is repeatedly mentioned in the scene in question. Jealousy is not the whole point, however. She wants Emily, who she thinks barefacedly pretends to belong to a better class, to wear an indubitable stigma of working class. That Emily appears to be "a very lady" (Ch. 50; 616) galls her.

Here David's wish to punish Emily is transferred to Rosa. David does have that wish, with all his sympathy for her, because of his bitter regret as regards Steerforth (if only she had not been there he would be still alive!), and significantly that feeling has much to do with class consciousness. Consider what he remembers about his childhood relationship to Emily: "As to any sense of inequality, or youthfulness, or other difficulty in our way, little Em'ly and I had no such trouble, because we had no future" (Ch. 3; 32). It is all in the past; the implication being "It was like that, but not so now." The grown-up David does feel a sense of inequality.[26] Although not to an equal extent, David at bottom shares Rosa's attitude; working-class people are "beings of another order" (Ch. 20; 251). At the same time, Rosa's taunting of Emily hurts David, just as painfully as Steerforth's insulting of Mell hurts him. Thus, David's double identification—with Emily on one hand, and with Rosa on the other—once again freezes him into passivity.

Taken together, these three scenes well illustrate how strongly the class issue is present in Dickens's imagination. The underlying violence common to them is arresting. At Heep's chastisement,

Micawber's ruler comically disguises David's burning poker. David, recalling Mell's confrontation with Steerforth, says: "I am not clear whether he was going to strike Mr Mell, or Mr Mell was going to strike him, or there was any such intention on either side" (Ch. 7; 83). Here, again, a displacement occurs, for instead of hitting the student, Mell strikes his desk: "It was my book that he struck his desk with" (Ch. 7; 82)—notice it is David's book, which reinforces the protagonist's psychological involvement here. When Rosa attacks Emily, she cries "with her clenched hand, quivering as if it only wanted a weapon to stab the object of her wrath" (Ch. 50; 616). The word "stab" indicates that the weapon Rosa wants is a knife. She herself is described by Steerforth as a cutting instrument; the "edged tool" (Ch. 29; 372), "all edge" (Ch. 20; 251).[27] There are a fair number of references to knives in relation to other characters, too. After being abandoned by Steerforth, the option left for Emily is either "a knife" or "the sea" (Ch. 46; 571—notice the maritime disaster again). Micawber threatens to commit suicide by a knife: "he begged me to send his knife and pint pot . . . as they might prove serviceable during the brief remainder of his existence" (Ch. 57; 690). But a more interesting comic variation comes from Aunt Betsey; her "making a distant chop in the air with her knife" (Ch. 13; 163) when David first sees her.

Rosa, as if with a knife, attempts to strike Emily, but the "blow, which had no aim, fell upon the air" (Ch. 50; 615). It is certainly a curious gesture, of which various interpretations have been offered. Barbara Black, for instance, argues that by this Dickens "emphasizes the purposelessness of such rage," in order to "limit the scope of these women's influence."[28] According to Rachel Ablow, the goal of Rosa's blow is "less to inflict damage than to insist on the distance between herself and the other woman."[29] Mary Ann O'Farrell speaks of "the mottled generosity of throwing a fit rather than a hammer, making a scene rather than a scar."[30] Perhaps literary criticism can be too sophisticated; Rosa may have simply realized that violence is futile. The focus of my present interest in her gesture, at any rate, lies elsewhere; it is upon seeing it in the context of the "conspiracy of words."

There is a striking moment where a character's rage actually explodes into physical action: David slaps Heep's cheek with his open hand, and when he tries to give another, "[Heep] caught the hand in his, and we stood in that connexion, looking at each other. We stood so, a long time; long enough for me to see the white marks of my fingers die out of the deep red of his cheek, and leave it a deeper red" (Ch. 42; 529). This is an exceptional instance, simply because the object of anger is the arch-villain. David has a hero's moment here, although, as we have seen, he is a bystander at the climactic chastisement. In this case, the changing colors of Uriah's cheek recall those of Rosa's lip—"it was the most susceptible part of her face, and that, when she turned pale, that mark altered first, and became a dull, lead-coloured streak, lengthening out to its full extent, like a mark in invisible ink brought to the fire" (Ch. 20; 252). Rosa's scar, turning pale, returns with the implication of violence in the scene where she attacks Emily; "I saw the scar, with its white track cutting through her lips, quivering and throbbing as she spoke" (Ch. 50; 613). Then, a few pages later, Rosa's blow vainly strikes the air. At this point we should recall Aunt Betsey, who "aims a blow" at Dr Chillip, the phrase suggesting that she does not actually hit him, either—another instance of brilliant comic mirroring.

We can now return to that redoubtable Aunt, in relation to the novel's protagonist. As we have seen, the boy David's constant worry is whether or not his past association with working-class life will not show itself. His secret is pried into and uncovered by the very last person whom he wishes it to be known by, namely, Uriah Heep. Heep is indeed adept at delving into a person's dark secret. Bodenheimer rightly points out Heep's "exposing role,"[31] and how he lays bare the unstable middle-class façade of David. I wish to back up her observation by looking into the Dickensian "conspiracy of words." When David visits Heep and his mother, the experience is vividly described as follows:

> A tender young cork, however, would have had no more chance against a pair of corkscrews, or a tender young tooth against a pair of dentists, or a little shuttlecock against two battledores, than I had against Uriah and Mrs Heep. They did just what they liked with me; and wormed things out of me that I had no desire to tell. . . . (Ch. 17; 219)

David here is comparing himself to a cork. The metaphor suggests that his dark secret is something put in a bottle, something he fears of being drawn out. It makes perfect sense that what he is trying to hide is his working-class experience, which in the novel is presented as the work at the wine cellar of Murdstone and Grinby:

> When the empty bottles ran short, there were labels to be pasted on full ones, or *corks* to be fitted to them, or seals to be put upon the *corks*, or finished bottles to be packed in casks. (Ch. 11; 133) (italics mine)

Furthermore, we may note that in the Autobiographical Fragment Dickens confesses, with pregnant resonance, that when he later came near to the blacking factory, he crossed over to the opposite side of the way, "to avoid a certain smell of the cement they put upon the blacking-*corks*, which reminded me of what I was once" (italics mine).[32] Again, we realize, David's anxiety painfully reflects Dickens's own.

All these associative threads come together in one of Aunt Betsey's distinctive remarks. She says to Uriah Heep:

> ". . . If you're an eel, sir, conduct yourself like one. If you're a man, control your limbs, sir! Good God!" said my aunt, with great indignation, "I am not going to be serpentined and corkscrewed out of my senses!" (Ch. 35; 442)

"To be *corkscrewed* out of my senses" is a wonderful piece of Betsey-speak, but after our probing, it is not hard to imagine what sinister association this expression carries for David, and Dickens. In addition, when we contemplate the above passage, we are forcibly reminded of another of her antics. Her corking herself, it will be recalled, is an action born of her "superabundant agitation"—an action that strikingly runs parallel to David's anxiously putting his secret in a bottle. What at first glance appeared to be a simple farce now turns out to have compelling significance.

Let Aunt Betsey have the last word. She speaks of Mr Dick's obsession with King Charles and flying a kite, in this manner:

> "That's his allegorical way of expressing it. He connects his illness with great disturbance and agitation, naturally, and that's the figure, or the simile, or whatever it's called, which he chooses to use. . . ." (Ch. 14; 175)

As an analysis of Dick's behavior, this is perhaps as good as any. To adapt Aunt Betsey's reasoning to our purposes, we might "allegorically" conclude: David Copperfield has corked his most profound anxiety, the wine-cellar experience, in a bottle, which leads to his fear of being corkscrewed; this inner process is projected onto Aunt Betsey's comic actions—first corking herself, and then Ham.

Aunt Betsey's perspicacity and Dickens's psychological penetration behind it were, one imagines, much appreciated by Freud himself. *David Copperfield* was a favorite read of his, a book close to his heart; the very first gift he gave to his future wife, Martha Bernays, was a copy of this novel. Intriguingly, one of the reasons why he was attracted to *Copperfield* is that he, too, was a child born with a caul.[33] It is highly doubtful, however, that the Viennese sage had an inkling of the novel's "conspiracy of words" involving the caul, which, I venture to submit, has not been unraveled till now.

(First published in *The Cambridge Quarterly*, 2020)

NOTES

1 Vladimir Nabokov, trans. *Eugene Onegin*, 4 vols. Rev. ed. (Princeton 1975) iii, 59.
2 Nabokov also speaks of "those strange subconscious clues which are discoverable only in the works of authentic genius." *Nikolai Gogol* (New York: 1944), 91.
3 Edgar Allan Poe, *Essays and Reviews* (New York: 1984), 221.
4 *Essays and Reviews*, 222.
5 *Essays and Reviews*, 237.
6 "The Middle Years from the *Carol* to *Copperfield*," in *Dickens Memorial Lectures 1970* (London: 1970), 11.
7 See Philip Collins, "Dickens's Autobiographical Fragment and *David Copperfield*," *Cahiers Victoriens et Edouariens* 20 (1984), 87-96; Michael Slater, *Charles Dickens* (London: 2009), 278-88.
8 According to Michael Allen, Dickens worked at the warehouse from September 1823 to September or October 1824. See *Charles Dickens and the Blacking Factory* (St. Leonards: 2011), 94. I discuss the novelist's imaginative engagement with this experience in Ch. 2 of this book.
9 John Forster, *The Life of Charles Dickens* (London: 1928), 27-29.
10 Edmund Wilson, *The Wound and the Bow* (1941; Athens, Ohio: 1997), 7.
11 All the page references, following the chapter number, are to the Clarendon

edition of the novel (Oxford: 1981).

12 David's drowning occurs only in a dream, in which he imagines Heep's "piratical expedition" on the Peggottys, "carrying me and Emily off to the Spanish Main, to be drowned" (Ch. 16; 202).

13 Preface to the Charles Dickens Edition of *David Copperfield* (1867).

14 The idea of "fathering" can be found, for example, in Dickens's refusal to "father" a "continuation of Pickwick" (Letter to Richard Bentley, 10 September 1838), his remark about Little Nell as "my child" (Letter to George Cattermole, 14 January 1841), and his editorial farewell in *Bentley's Miscellany* (February 1839), "Familiar Epistle from a Parent to a Child Aged Two Years and Two Months".

15 *Hamlet* 3.1.79-81. All the references are to the Norton Critical Edition of the play (New York: 2011).

16 Hardy, *Dickens and Creativity* (London: 2008), 145, 147. See also Valerie L. Gager's *Shakespeare and Dickens* (Cambridge: 1996), 226-9, 238-44.

17 Hardy, *Dickens and Creativity*, 151.

18 *Ten Novels and Their Authors* (London: 1954) 150.

19 Early examples include Mark Spilka, "*David Copperfield* as Psychological Fiction," *Critical Quarterly* 1 (1959), 292-301; E. Pearlman, "David Copperfield's Dreams of Drowning," *American Imago* 28 (1971), 391-403.

20 "Knowing and Telling in Dickens's Retrospects," in *Knowing the Past: Victorian Literature and Culture*, ed. Suzy Anger (Ithaca: 2001), 226, 229.

21 Of the last two of the three scenes Bodenheimer offers a sharp analysis from a perspective different from mine.

22 The ghost of Hamlet's father thrice walks past Marcellous and Barnardo "within his truncheon's length" (1.2.204). See Lionel Morton, "'His Truncheon's Length': A Recurrent Allusion to *Hamlet* in Dickens's Novels," *Dickens Studies Newsletter* (June 1980), 47-9.

23 Aunt Betsey provides another comic variation: she wishes Peggotty's husband were "one of those Poker husbands who abound in the newspapers, and will beat her well with one" (Ch. 13; 169).

24 "Charles Dickens" in *The Collected Essays, Journalism and Letters of George Orwell*, 4 vols. (London: 1970) i, 478.

25 Forster, *The Life of Charles Dickens*, 27.

26 When he goes to see Mrs Steerforth with Mr Peggotty, to inform her of her son's treatment of Emily, David is again silent, unlike Mr Peggotty who asks the sour lady to "raise [Emily] up" (Ch. 32; 400).

27 Again, Shakespeare's presence is felt: Hamlet talks about his "edge" (3.2.244) to Ophelia, and "speak[s] daggers" to Gertrude (3.3.387).

28 "A Sisterhood of Rage and Beauty: Dickens' Rosa Dartle, Miss Wade, and Madame Defarge," *Dickens Studies Annual* 26 (1998), 102.
29 *The Marriage of Minds* (Stanford: 2007), 36.
30 *Telling Complexions* (Durham: 1997), 98.
31 Bodenheimer, "Knowing and Telling in Dickens's Retrospects," 217
32 Forster, *The Life of Charles Dickens*, 35.
33 Lionel Trilling and Steven Marcus's "Introduction" to their edition of Ernest Jones's biography of Freud points out that "like the protagonist of his favorite Dickens novel, *David Copperfield*, he was born with a caul, the sign of a notable destiny." *The Life and Work of Sigmund Freud* (New York: 1961), ix.

Ch. 2 "Dickens and the Blacking Factory" Revisited

As is well known, when he was eleven years old Charles Dickens was sent out to work at Warren's blacking warehouse due to financial difficulties in the family.[1] Soon afterwards his father was arrested for debt and the family moved into the Marshalsea prison, but young Charles had to live by himself. "It is wonderful to me how I could have been so easily cast away," he confesses.[2] He felt "utterly neglected and hopeless" (AF, 26). Edmund Wilson famously argued that this experience produced in Dickens "a trauma from which he suffered all his life."[3] This psychological wound, in Wilson's view, holds the key to the novelist's creative activities: "For the man of spirit whose childhood has been crushed by the cruelty of organized society, one of two attitudes is natural: that of the criminal or that of the rebel. Charles Dickens, in imagination, was to play the rôle of both, and to continue up to his death to put into them all that was most passionate in his feeling" (14). While one cannot readily agree with Wilson's sweeping assertion,[4] there is no denying that the wound had a deep and lasting impact upon Dickens's imagination and this impact has been investigated by a host of post-Wilson biographers and biographically-oriented critics. But what is there to be learned from a more particular look at the language of Dickens's fiction?

Despite his resolute secretiveness and avowed revulsion—"I have never . . . raised the curtain I then dropped, thank God. . . . For many years, when I came near to Robert Warren's in the Strand, I crossed over to the opposite side of the way, to avoid a certain smell of the cement they put upon the blacking-corks, which reminded me of what I was once." (AF, 35)—Dickens often makes sly allusions to Warren's in his writings. The first biographer to notice it was probably Christopher Hibbert, who observes that Dickens "could not afterwards forbear to bring the name and advertisements which made [the factory] famous, into book after book."[5] More recently, Michael Slater picks up various references to blacking bottles and calls one of them, in the account of the "Great Walking Match" between James Osgood and George Dolby, "a grim little private joke of his own" that the novelist has smuggled in, almost expecting it to be recognised as such by later readers.[6] Robert Douglas-Fairhurst takes a similar line, concluding as follows:

> Dickens's habit of making fleeting references to Warren's Blacking in his writing starts to look less like a form of repetition compulsion than a running gag or creative itch he enjoyed scratching, like the cameo appearances of Alfred Hitchcock in his own movies.[7]

Rosemarie Bodenheimer also points out a ludic element in this practice. She quotes a passage from *David Copperfield*, where the hero, now a student at Dr Strong's school, looks back at his miserable days ("Murdstone and Grinby" substituting for Warren's)—

> I had become, in the Murdstone and Grinby time, however short or long it may have been, so unused to the sports and games of boys, that I knew I was awkward and inexperienced in the commonest things belonging to them. . . . My mind ran upon what they would think, if they knew of my familiar acquaintance with the King's Bench Prison? Was there anything about me which would reveal my proceedings in connexion with the Micawber family—all those pawnings, and sellings, and suppers—in spite of myself?[8]

—and comments:

> One such moment in *David Copperfield* stands out because it makes a direct link between Warren's and the problem of knowledge. . . . Having the wrong kind of knowledge is (at least partly) associated with shame; gentility and social acceptance depend upon hiding both the knowledge and the shame from the observation of others. Telling without telling that he's telling, the game Dickens played with his readers throughout his career, rehearses the simultaneous pride and shame in a knowingness that does not want to speak its name.[9]

These recent critics have identified a joke, or a gag, or a game. We might, however, try to look further than isolated references to blacking bottles or Warren's warehouse. I propose to examine the "conspiracy of words" in Dickens's writings, arising from the blacking factory experience.[10]

The novelist first seriously drew on his own childhood suffering in

Oliver Twist, a novel with an orphan of a tender age for its protagonist.[11] He took the name of the book's arch-villain from a fellow child-laborer who showed kindness to him at Warren's. This seemingly peculiar behavior is perfectly understandable: for him the boy Fagin was a threatening presence, just as the old fence is for Oliver. The boy's caring act was a seduction into the working-class life which the neglected young Dickens had to resist with the utmost rigor.[12] Regarding this good-natured boy, Dickens records a curious incident:

> Bob Fagin was very good to me on the occasion of a bad attack of my old disorder. I suffered such excruciating pain that time, that they made a temporary bed of straw in my old recess in the counting-house, and I rolled about on the floor, and Bob filled empty blacking-bottles with hot water, and applied relays of them to my side, half the day. I got better, and quite easy towards evening; but Bob (who was much bigger and older than I) did not like the idea of my going home alone, and took me under his protection. I was too proud to let him know about the prison, and, after making several efforts to get rid of him, to all of which Bob Fagin in his goodness was deaf, shook hands with him on the steps of a house near Southwark Bridge on the Surrey side, making believe that I lived there. As a finishing piece of reality in case of his looking back, I knocked at the door, I recollect, and asked, when the woman opened it, if that was Mr Robert Fagin's house. (AF, 30)

Dickens was surely recalling this episode when he had David Copperfield call at Miss Mills's house in order to ask Dora to marry him. David "was waiting at the door, . . . had some flurried thought of asking if that were Mr Blackboy's (in imitation of poor Barkis), begging pardon, and retreating" (460). The crucial detail here is the reference to Barkis: David is alluding to the fact that Barkis had a mysterious box with him all the time, the contents of which he kept strictly secret, and about which he invented a fiction that it belonged to "Mr Blackboy" (422). The color black, the jealously guarded secret, and the pretense of calling at the wrong house—in Dickens's memory these elements all hark back to his "blacking days" (AF, 28).

Interestingly, in "Full Report of the Second Meeting of the Mudfog Association," written at about the same time as Oliver's reunion with Mr Brownlow (Ch. 41), there appears a pub called "Black Boy and Stomach-ache."[13] When we recall that in the "Autobiographical Fragment" the strange pain which young Dickens felt and Bob Fagin was concerned about is described as a pain in his "side," it would not be difficult to see the stomachache here as a metonymic displacement of a side pain. The fanciful name of the pub again takes us back, through Barkis, to Bob Fagin and the blacking factory.

The "black boy" is reincarnated, assigned a different sex, in a later story, "Mrs Lirriper's Lodgings" (collected in *Christmas Stories*). The titular character does not like her servants to appear "with a smear of black across the nose" and confesses, "Where they pick the black up is a mystery I cannot solve." She is particularly irritated by a girl who is "always smiling with a black face":

> I put it to her "O Sophy Sophy for goodness goodness sake where does it come from?" To which that poor unlucky willing mortal—bursting out crying to see me so vexed replied "I took a deal of black into me ma'am when I was a small child being much neglected and I think it must be, that it works out. . . ." (507)

Mrs Lirriper calls this girl "Willing Sophy," which evokes the immortal phrase, "Barkis is willin'." Moreover, behind Sophie's wonderful expression, "that it works out," we sense Dickens's own anxiety about the blacking days (notice how he slips in the weighty causal phrase, "being much neglected"). At this point we might take another look at the *Copperfield* passage quoted earlier: what David is worried about—"Was there anything about me which would reveal my proceedings in connection with the Micawber family?"—is exactly the process Sophy calls "working out."

Sophy says she "took a deal of black into" her: the comical idea, in fact, expresses Dickens's primal anxiety. In a crucial sense this is the real threat Oliver Twist faces. The following passage contains the core of *Oliver*:

> In short, the wily old Jew had the boy in his toils. Having prepared his mind, by solitude and gloom, to prefer any society to the companionship of his own sad thoughts in such a dreary place, he was now slowly instilling into his soul the poison which he hoped would blacken it, and change its hue for ever. (133)

Fagin attempts to place Oliver in solitude and blacken his soul—indulging oneself in melodramatic fancy, one might say the poison Fagin intends to instill into Oliver's soul is shoe-blacking. To blacken is to tarnish, of course, but as Peter Ackroyd says of Dickens's childhood suffering, "Anxiety. Solitude. Defilement. Despair. Blacking. All these things come together"[14]: words related to this color, part of a network of pregnant associations, have a special resonance for Dickens which is felt throughout his writings.

Take for instance the chapter titled "An Opinion" in *A Tale of Two Cities*, in which Dr Manette, under emotional stress, reverts to shoemaking. Very much worried, Jarvis Lorry consults the doctor himself, on the pretense that he is making an inquiry about someone else:

> "The occupation resumed under the influence of this passing affliction so happily recovered from," said Mr Lorry, clearing his throat, "we will call—Blacksmith's work, Blacksmith's work. We will say, to put a case and for the sake of illustration, that he had been used, in his bad time, to work at a little forge. We will say that he was unexpectedly found at his forge again. Is it not a pity that he should keep it by him?" (205)

Shoemaking is displaced by blacksmith's work: an association at work on Dickens's part, from shoemaking, through blacking, to blacksmith. Suggestively, Manette goes on: "no doubt it relieved his pain so much, by substituting the perplexity of the fingers for the perplexity of the brain, and by substituting, as he became more practised, the ingenuity of the hands, for the ingenuity of the mental torture" (205). That the ingenuity of the hands relieves the mental torture is the kind of insight Dickens gained in the blacking factory.

The "ingenuity of the hands" in Dickens's memory is inseparable from the sense of shame: "Bob Fagin and I had attained to great dexterity in tying up the pots. . . . We worked, for the light's sake, near the second window . . . ; and we were so brisk at it, that the people used to stop and look in. . . . I saw my father coming in at the door one day when we were very busy, and I wondered how he could bear it" (AF, 34). The execrable feeling of being observed at work returns in *Great Expectations*, the novel immediately following *A Tale of Two Cities*. Right after becoming properly apprenticed to a blacksmith, Pip confesses: "What I dreaded was, that in some unlucky hour I, being at my grimiest and commonest, should lift up my eyes and see Estella looking in at one of the wooden windows of the forge. I was haunted by the fear that she would, sooner or later, find me out, with a black face and hands, doing the coarsest part of my work, and would exult over me and despise me" (95). The color black surfaces once again later when Pip makes a brief return to his old village in the middle of his gentlemanly training; before going back to London he says: "Good by, dear Joe!—No, don't wipe it off—for God's sake, give me your blackened hand!—I shall be down soon and often" (254). In spite of his declaration, however, he does not come down "soon and often." Even at the end Pip does not choose to go back to Joe's forge. Clearly his place is with Herbert in the moderately but steadily prospering Clarriker and Co. In a way Pip has managed to escape from Joe who, like Bob Fagin, presents the blackening threat. Seen in this light, Pip's great friend turns out to contain something of the villain of *Oliver Twist*.

Part of Fagin's plan is to take advantage of Oliver's "solitude." The boy's loneliness in the thief's den is most forcefully expressed in the following passage:

> There was a back-garret window with rusty bars outside, which had no shutter; and out of this, Oliver often gazed with a melancholy face for hours together; but nothing was to be descried from it but a confused and crowded mass of housetops, blackened chimneys, and gable-ends. (127)

Dickens gives us "solitude," a "garret" room; and objects associated with the color "black" (here chimneys): these elements keep recurring together in Dickens's writings, and one suspects the workings of childhood memories. It so happens that in the blacking period Dickens lived alone in a "back attic" (AF, 29) of a house in Lant Street. To be sure, children usually had rooms in garrets (or attics), and chimneys were usually black; but the repeated mention of them in close proximity, where a lonely figure is depicted with acute pathos, makes for significance. A few more examples; first, from *Nicholas Nickleby*:

> "Pooh! pooh!" said Tim Linkinwater, "don't tell me. Country! . . . Nonsense! What can you get in the country but new-laid eggs and flowers? I can buy new-laid eggs in Leadenhall Market,

> any morning before breakfast; and as to flowers, it's worth a run upstairs to smell my *mignonette*, or to see the double *wallflower* in the *back-attic* window, at No. 6, in the court."
>
> "There is a double wallflower at No. 6, in the court, is there?" said Nicholas.
>
> "Yes, is there!" replied Tim, "and planted in a cracked jug, without a spout. There were hyacinths there, this last spring, blossoming, in—but you'll laugh at that, of course."
>
> "At what?"
>
> "At their blossoming in old *blacking-bottles*," said Tim. . . .
>
> "They belong to a sickly bedridden *hump-backed* boy, and seem to be the only pleasure, Mr Nickleby, of his sad existence. How many years is it . . . since I first noticed him, quite a little child, dragging himself about on a pair of tiny *crutches*? Well! Well! . . . It is a sad thing . . . to see a little *deformed* child *sitting apart from other children, who are active and merry, watching the games he is denied the power to share in. . . .*"
>
> "It must be dull to *watch the dark housetops. . . .*"
>
> "His father lives there, I believe . . . and other people too; but *no one seems to care* much for the poor sickly *cripple*".
> (473-74; my italics)

In all likelihood Dickens has developed this scene from the Oliver passage already quoted. As far as the impact of Warren's is concerned this is the central passage, in that it contains all the crucial motifs: the tell-tale blacking bottle; the lonely, neglected child; the attic; the dark housetops (dark housetops forested with black chimneys); the deformity.

There are other scenes in which a lonely figure looks out from an attic. In *Little Dorrit*, Arthur Clennam is disillusioned after seeing Flora Finching for the first time in twenty years: "When he got to his lodging, he sat down before the dying fire, as he had stood at the window of his old room looking out upon the blackened forest of chimneys, and turned his gaze back upon the gloomy vista by which he had come to that stage in his existence. So long, so bare, so blank. No childhood; no youth, except for one remembrance; that one remembrance proved, only that day, to be a piece of folly" (168). Having suffered serious emotional damage, Clennam's mind reverts to his sad childhood, the memory of which includes the view of the blackened chimneys from his room—

we know from a later reference that this is a "garret bedchamber" (703). In *The Old Curiosity Shop*, Little Nell watches "the people as they . . . appeared at the windows of the opposite houses; wondering whether those rooms were as lonesome as that in which she sat. . . . There was a crooked stack of chimneys on one of the roofs, in which, by often looking at them, she had fancied ugly faces that were frowning over at her and trying to peer into the room". Afraid, she "felt glad when it grew too dark to make them out" (74). Nell's fear is expanded and elaborated in the famous view from Todgers's in *Martin Chuzzlewit*, in which "the revolving chimney-pots on one great stack of buildings seemed to be turning gravely to each other every now and then, and whispering the result of their separate observation of what was going on below. Others, of a crook-backed shape, appeared to be maliciously holding themselves askew, that they might shut the prospect out and baffle Todgers's" (126). Dickens gives us another view of spiteful chimneys in *Nickleby* (albeit with no specific observer in this instance):

> The very chimneys appear to have grown dismal and melancholy, from having had nothing better to look at than the chimneys over the way. Their tops are battered, and broken, and blackened with smoke; and, here and there, some taller stack than the rest, inclining heavily to one side, and toppling over the roof, seems to meditate taking revenge for half a century's neglect, by crushing the inhabitants of the garrets beneath. (148)

The chimneys are imagined to act aggressively towards the inhabitants of the "garrets," this time because they have been "neglected."

The attributes of the chimneys in these passages are striking: neglected, blackened, crooked—they are all suggestive of Dickens's miserable childhood. The aggressive anger arising from the feeling of being neglected is imputed to the chimneys, and onto them the fears of being blackened and of being crooked are projected. Crookedness is sometimes associated with moral deformity, which again is part of the novelist's anxiety: "but for the mercy of God, I might easily have been, for any care that was taken of me, a little robber or a little vagabond" (AF, 28). This is precisely the fear that lies behind *Oliver Twist*, and Dickens speaks of his intention to "paint [the criminals] in all their deformity" in the 1842 Preface to that novel.

In *David Copperfield* Mr Micawber, a character who is unmistakably connected with Dickens's blacking days, talks with maudlin grandiloquence about "being crushed out of his original form" (704). Though presented comically here, the combination of deformity and pathos is a serious matter to Dickens's imagination. Henry James's review of *Our Mutual Friend* does not do justice to the novel, but his comment on Jenny Wren contains an acute observation:

> Like all Mr Dickens's pathetic characters she is a little monster; she is deformed, unhealthy, unnatural; she belongs to the troop of hunchbacks, imbeciles, and precocious children who have carried on the sentimental business in all Mr Dickens's novels; the little Nells, the Smikes, the Paul Dombeys.[15]

It is not clear exactly whom James had in mind when he spoke of "hunchbacks," but Jenny is not one (she merely suffers from a severe back pain); nor is Smike.[16] Nevertheless James is pointing to an important aspect of Dickens's writings: hunchbacks in his novels are worthy of careful consideration. Crooked figures (people or things) can be threatening, but they can be pathetic: at times "deformity" and "sentimental business" are closely linked to a self-pity which originated in the blacking factory.

This is the case with the humpbacked boy of the central passage from *Nicholas Nickleby*, who appears only in that scene and is not mentioned again. And yet, there is much in him that demands unravelling. First, clearly he is doomed—like Smike. Indeed, this "poor sickly cripple" can be regarded as Smike's double.[17] In addition to the fact that Smike is also "sickly" (724) and "lame" (76), there are other points that connect them. It is Tim Linkinwater who fondly introduces the boy to Nicholas,[18] and it is he again who is later described as having become attached to Smike. Tim's account of the humpbacked boy begins, as we have seen, with a contrast between country and town: "Country! . . . Nonsense! What can you get in the country but new-laid eggs and flowers? I can buy new-laid eggs in Leadenhall Market." The same rhetoric is in operation when he is quite overcome with grief at the news of Smike's death in rural Devonshire. He pours out his feelings to Nicholas: "Poor fellow! I wish we could have had him buried in town. There isn't such a burying-ground in all London as that little one on the other side of the square—there are counting-houses all round it. . ." (731). Moreover, as if triggered by Tim's idea of burial in town, there appears a tremendous passage in the very next chapter, featuring a London burying-ground (though not as idyllic as Tim imagines), and once again stressing the boy's connection with Smike.

It is the sequence in Ch. 62, in which Ralph Nickleby walks back home after being told that he has helped to kill his own son, Smike. On his way he passes by a graveyard. Suddenly he remembers that interred here—"buried in town"—is a suicide whose inquest he has attended before:

> While [Ralph] was thus engaged, there came towards him, with noise of shouts and singing, some fellows full of drink. . . . They were in high good-humour; and one of them, a little, weazen, hump-backed man, began to dance. . . .
>
> He could not fix upon the spot [where the suicide is buried] among such a heap of graves, but he conjured up a strong and vivid idea of the man himself, and how he looked, and what had led him to do it; all of which he recalled with ease. By dint of dwelling upon this theme, he carried the impression with him when he went away: as he remembered, when a child, to have had frequently before him the figure of some goblin he had once seen chalked upon a door. But as he drew nearer and nearer home he forgot it again. . . .
>
> He . . . softly groped his way out of the room, and up the echoing stairs—up to the top—to the front garret—where he closed the door behind him, and remained.
>
> It was a mere lumber-room now, but it yet contained an old dismantled bedstead; the one on which his son had slept; for no other had ever been there. (735-37)

This powerful passage which, as Angus Wilson suggests,[19] possibly influenced Dostoevsky, is not just an effective piece of Gothic nightmare. Consider what happens here: a grotesque *hump-backed* man appears, and his image haunts Ralph for a while; struck by a horrifying memory from the period when he was a small *child*, he goes back to his house, and hangs himself in the *garret* in which Smike slept. The whole passage seems to invite the reader to recall bit by bit—or, to "articulate," in the manner of Mr Venus of *Our Mutual Friend*—that humpbacked child in the garret. So, with the recollection of that boy, the reader is left in Smike's old room at the end of the quotation. Then, consider what

Smike himself says about the room:

> "No," rejoined [Smike], with a melancholy look; "a room—I remember I slept in a room, a large lonesome room at the top of a house, where there was a trap-door in the ceiling. I have covered my head with the clothes often, not to see it, for it frightened me: a young child with no one near at night: and I used to wonder what was on the other side. There was a clock too, an old clock, in one corner. I remember that. I have never forgotten that room; for when I have terrible dreams, it comes back, just as it was. I see things and people in it that I had never seen then, but there is the room just as it used to be; *that* never changes".[20] (254)

A lonely, neglected child in an attic, once again: the humpbacked boy and Smike merge into one.

Dickens's sympathetic identification with a crippled character continues. When he was writing the later chapters of *Nickleby* Dickens thought of starting a weekly magazine to be edited by himself. The end result was *Master Humphrey's Clock*. The eponymous character, not often discussed by critics, is of great interest, for in him the extension of Dickens's creative engagement with the humpbacked boy can be observed. Master Humphrey confesses that he leads "a lonely, solitary life," suggesting that he suffers from a "wound" from the past (26). This wound has to do with his "deformed," "crooked figure": "the truth broke upon me for the first time, and I knew, while watching my awkward and ungainly sports, how keenly [mother] had felt for her poor crippled boy" (31-32). The sense of separation from other boys at games recalls Tim Linkinwater's account of the humpbacked boy: "to see a little deformed child sitting apart from other children, who are active and merry, watching the games he is denied the power to share in". This, in turn, recalls David Copperfield's observation, quoted earlier, about being "unused to the sports and games of boys," and his awareness that he "was awkward and inexperienced in the commonest things belonging to them": ultimately, all this goes back to Dickens's own childhood.[21] Forster reports what he must have heard from Dickens himself about his Chatham days:

> He was a very little and a very sickly boy. He was subject to attacks of violent spasm which disabled him for any active

> exertion. He was never a good little cricket-player. He was never a first-rate hand at marbles, or peg-top, or prisoner's base. But he had great pleasure in watching the other boys, officers' sons for the most part, at these games, reading while they played; and he had always the belief that this early sickness had brought to himself one inestimable advantage, in the circumstance of his weak health having strongly inclined him to reading. (3)

This is precisely the "violent spasm" that seized young Charles at Warren's warehouse. Forster also records the loneliness of Dickens's blacking days: "Still the want felt most by him was the companionship of boys of his own age. He had no such acquaintance. Sometimes, he remembered to have played . . . with Poll Green and Bob Fagin; but those were rare occasions. He generally strolled alone" (31).

Master Humphrey is not only intriguing from a biographical point of view, but also throws interesting light upon Dickens's animism. Bodenheimer argues that that has to do with the novelist's "fundamental fear of isolation": "Neither narrators nor characters can tolerate solitude; if necessary they will invent live presences made of houses, furniture, shadowy dark corners, ghosts or phantoms, and suffer horrors from them" (197). Certainly, Smike has a fear of things; but Master Humphrey has nothing to do with horror (Bodenheimer does not discuss him). His case is quite the reverse: "I have all my life been attached to the inanimate objects" (32). In fact, Smike and Master Humphrey make a nice contrast. Compare the ways in which they react to the clocks: as already quoted, Smike includes "an old clock, in one corner" in his horrified recollection of the attic; Master Humphrey regards the clock as his "comfort and consolation" (32).

Master Humphrey represents a novelist figure who has overcome loneliness by the power of imagination, crippled though he may be—or rather, by virtue of this very fact: "I know how all these things have worked together to make me what I am" (AF, 35). An artist triumphant over a traumatic wound, Master Humphrey does not boast of it; he speaks with quiet authority:

> What if I be [alone]? What if this fireside be tenantless, save for the presence of one weak old man? From my house-top I can look upon a hundred homes, in every one of which these social companions are matters of reality. In my daily walks I pass a

> thousand men whose cares are all forgotten, whose labours are made light, whose dull routine of work from day to day is cheered and brightened by their glimpses of domestic joy at home. Amid the struggles of this struggling town what cheerful sacrifices are made; what toil endured with readiness; what patience shown and fortitude displayed for the mere sake of home and its affections! Let me thank Heaven that I can people my fireside with shadows such as these; with shadows of bright objects that exist in crowds about me; and let me say, "I am alone no more".[22] (142)

Master Humphrey takes a sweeping view of London from his "housetop," which is just as panoramic as in the "Oh for a good spirit" passage in *Dombey*, where Dickens refers to Le Sage's story about "the lame demon" who takes off the housetops (623). That passage is often discussed—almost exclusively from the Foucauldian point of view in the past few decades—but read in conjunction with *Master Humphrey's Clock*, a different kind of significance emerges. Given that Le Sage's devil Asmodeus is a handicapped figure who uses crutches, it is tempting to suggest that Dickens, coming to *Dombey* after *Master Humphrey's Clock*, used another cripple as an authorial stand-in.[23]

"Trauma is recognizable . . . in the repetitive returns of memory fragments. There is no way to count the variety of metaphors, moods, or tones through which such fragments could be evoked by a writer like Dickens," Bodenheimer rightly points out (69). As we have seen, in Dickens's texts, compositional elements such as loneliness, black, cripple, garret, keep reappearing in varied combinations and ambiences. Thus the view from the housetop can be ominous, aggressive, pathetic, subdued—or comical, as in Dickens's last novel. Here is the description of Staple Inn where Neville Landless has "attic rooms" right across from Tartar's:

> Yet the sunlight shone in at the ugly garret-window, which had a penthouse to itself thrust out among the tiles; and on the cracked and smoke-blackened parapet beyond, some of the deluded sparrows of the place rheumatically hopped, like little feathered cripples who had left their crutches in their nests. (181)

The by-now-familiar elements of garret, blackened object, crutches, cripple—all appearing in the account of the humpbacked boy—are there. Furthermore, shortly afterwards, Tartar says to Neville, "I have noticed (excuse me) that you shut yourself up a good deal, and that you seem to like my garden aloft here. . . . And I have some boxes, both of mignonette and wall-flower, that I could shove on along the gutter . . . to your windows . . ." (187).[24] Tim Linkinwater mentions exactly the same flowers ("mignonette and wall-flower") in that central passage from *Nicholas Nickleby*: what is happening here with these rheumatic sparrows?

Dickens died in June 1870. In the last five years of his life he suffered from a foot problem (Forster, 837), probably gout. When the pain was severe he was not able to walk. An American clergyman, G. D. Carrow, who visited him in August 1867 at the *All the Year Round* office reports what the novelist said on the occasion: "I hope, my dear sir, you will pardon my apparent want of courtesy in not descending to receive you at the main entrance—I am quite a cripple as you will perceive."[25] This foot pain came and went. Since Dickens says in a letter of 11 May 1870 that the affection set in "last night," it started on 10 May that year. Forster records that Dickens read the installment of *Drood* covering Chs. 17 to 21 on 7 May (849). Therefore, when he composed the sparrows passage which appears in Ch. 17, Dickens was not suffering from the foot pain yet. That chapter was in all likelihood written in April. Dickens says the pain occurs "about once in the course of a year" at "wholly uncertain and incalculable times" (to J. B. Buckstone, 15 May 1870). But given that he had suffered from it in April, both in 1868 and in 1869,[26] it is not unlikely that he was expecting it that month in 1870: so, when writing about the "feathered cripples," Dickens quite possibly labored under the apprehension that he would become lame again any day; and sure enough, the pain attacked him shortly afterwards.

I have been arguing that Dickens sometimes sympathetically identified himself with crippled figures in his fiction, and he did so again when he playfully wrote about the handicapped sparrows, no doubt sensing the irony that life was catching up with his imagination. Here, we might recall Poll Green, another of young Charles's fellow-laborer. He was, Dickens reminisces, "believed to have been christened Poll (a belief which I transferred, long afterwards again, to Mr Sweedlepipe)" (AF, 26). When we find in *Martin Chuzzlewit* Poll Sweedlepipe likened to "the sparrow that builds in chimney-stacks" (396), it is hard not to feel that the comic description of the rheumatic sparrows hides a bitter memory of solitary captivity in "the prison of the blacking warehouse."[27] In *Edwin Drood* the imaginative return to Warren's warehouse was set in motion when Dickens felt himself into Neville's plight. The sentence describing the sparrows is immediately preceded by this: "An air of retreat and *solitude* hung about the rooms and about their inhabitant. [Neville] was much worn, and so were they. Their sloping ceilings, cumbrous rusty locks and grates, and heavy wooden bins and beams, slowly mouldering withal, had a *prisonous* look, and he had the haggard face of a *prisoner*" (181; italics mine). Dickens was going back to that painful past, taking the very route he had taken when he had created the humpbacked boy in *Nickleby*; hence the extraordinary reappearance of the exactly same compositional elements. Brought into existence just two months before the novelist's death, the rheumatic sparrows were the last of Dickens's "private jokes" about the blacking factory.[28]

(Originally a lecture delivered at the International Dickens Fellowship Conference, Portsmouth, 2012; first published in *Essays in Criticism*, 2015)

NOTES

1 Michael Allen's research shows that Dickens worked at the warehouse from September 1823 to September or October 1824. See Allen, *Charles Dickens and the Blacking Factory* (St. Leonards: 2011), 94.
2 This is taken from the so-called "Autobiographical Fragment" printed in John Forster's biography. See Forster, *The Life of Charles Dickens* (1928), 25. All subsequent quotations from this material are from Foster and indicated parenthetically, with the abbreviation AF.
3 Edmund Wilson, *The Wound and the Bow* (1941; Athens, Ohio: 1997), 7.
4 For a detailed assessment of Wilson's argument see Ch. 10 of this book.
5 Christopher Hibbert, *The Making of Charles Dickens* (Harmondsworth, 1983), 53.
6 Michael Slater, *Charles Dickens* (New Haven: 2009), 581.
7 Robert Douglas-Fairhurst, *Becoming Dickens* (Cambridge, Ma.: 2011). 38.
8 Dickens, *David Copperfield*, 216-17. All references to Dickens's fictional works are to Dent Everyman paperback editions (1993-2000).

9 Rosemarie Bodenheimer, *Knowing Dickens* (Ithaca: 2007), 19.
10 For this Nabokovian notion see Ch. 1 of this book.
11 Dickens has Grimwig remark, "the devil's in it if this Oliver is not twelve years old" (300); this is the age at which Dickens was working at Warren's.
12 John Bayley was the first critic to discuss this: "he must have hated the real Fagin for the virtue which he could not bear to accept or recognise in that nightmare world, because it might help to subdue him into it." See Bayley, "*Oliver Twist*: 'Things as They Really Are'," in John Gross and Gabriel Pierson (eds.), *Dickens and the Twentieth Century* (1962), 53.
13 Dickens, *Sketches by Boz and Other Early Papers* (1993), 540. All references to Dickens's nonfictional works are to the Dent Collected Journalism, 4 vols.
14 Peter Ackroyd, *Dickens* (1991), 88.
15 Henry James, review of *Our Mutual Friend*, in *Dickens*: *The Critical Heritage*, Ed. Philip Collins, (London: 1971), 470-71.
16 In spite of David Threlfall's memorable realization in the 1980 RSC production (adapted by David Edgar), there is nothing in the text to show that he is a hunchback; the description of him as "a tall lean boy" (73) indicates otherwise.
17 While arguing that in *Nickleby* Dickens attempts "to treat realistically one part of experience which is missing in *Oliver Twist*—the serious consequences of a bad childhood," Steven Marcus points out that Smike is "that part of the proto-hero, Oliver Twist, which is never allowed to reveal itself in Nicholas," and observes that this boy is Smike's alter ego. Marcus is a rare critic in paying even the smallest attention to this boy. See Marcus, *Dickens: From Pickwick to Dombey* (New York: 1985), 121, 123.
18 This crippled boy with a pair of tiny crutches is clearly a prototype of Tiny Tim. The latter's first name may be directly connected with Tim Linkinwater.
19 Angus Wilson, review of Michael Slater (ed.), *Nicholas Nickleby, The Dickensian* 74 (1978), 111.
20 Dickens describes a child's fear in the bedroom in "Travelling Abroad" in *The Uncommercial Traveller* in the way that recalls Ralph's nocturnal journey. He talks about grotesque crippled figures on a French hill (87), then about a dead man in the Paris Morgue who haunts him (90), and says, "The experience may be worth considering by some who have the care of children." He then goes on to speak of "a fixed impression" produced on a child: "If the fixed impression be of an object terrible to the child, it will be (for want of reasoning upon) inseparable from great fear. Force the child at

such a time, be Spartan with it, send it into the dark against its will, leave it in a lonely bedroom against its will, and you had better murder it" (91).

21 John Carey's comment on Master Humphrey is perceptive: "The odd choice of this fictional surrogate for a young, healthy, popular author suggests perhaps, Dickens's sense of his own blighted childhood, with its unmentionable horror of descent into the working class." Carey also argues that Dickens kept returning to Warren's in his writings, but his focus is on the image of the "bright, pure child in the mouldering house." See Carey, *The Violent Effigy* (London: 1973), 150, 149.

22 One might profitably compare this with a later story, "House to Let," in which a five-year old "lonely" boy living in a "back garret" (*Christmas Stories*, 291) plays at a charwoman, scouring the floor with "a mangy old blacking-brush" (292). When someone says to him, "you're the boldest little chap in all England. You don't seem a bit afraid of being up here all by yourself in the dark," the boy answers, "The big winder . . . sees in the dark; and I see with the big winder" (293). Again, unlike Smike, this boy has no fear of darkness. Cf. Bodenheimer, 166-67.

23 Previous to *Dombey*, Dickens alludes to Asmodeus in *The Old Curiosity Shop* (252), but there he does not mention the fact that he is a cripple.

24 The motif of "garden aloft" also appears in *Our Mutual Friend*. Jenny Wren is fond of the garden atop Riah's office. The view from that spot includes "a blackened chimney-stack over which some humble creeper had been trained," and "the encompassing wilderness of dowager old chimneys twirl[ing] their cowls and flutter[ing] their smoke, rather as if they were bridling, and fanning themselves, and looking on in a state of airy surprise" (296). Another configuration of the familiar elements. Also, the crippled sparrow with crutches in *Drood* can be considered a relative of Jenny Wren—her name being that of a bird—who uses a "crutch-stick" (462).

25 G. D. Carrow, "An Informal Call on Charles Dickens," *The Dickensian* 63 (1967), 114.

26 On 20 April 1868, before the final reading in New York, Dickens's doctor's statement was distributed in the hall that the novelist was "suffering from a neuralgic affection of the right foot" (*The Letters of Charles Dickens*, ed. Graham Storey et al, 12 vols. [Oxford, 1965- 2002], xii. 96n); in his letter to Georgina Hogarth (15 April 1869) Dickens reports that "the foot was bad all the way."

27 Edgar Johnson, *Charles Dickens: His Tragedy and Triumph*, 2 vols. (New York: 1953), 165. The phrase is Johnson's, but it may very well have arisen in Dickens's own mind.

28 Another ornithological "joke" might be found in *Nickleby*. Tim Linkinwater, who cares about both the crippled boy and Smike, also cares about a bird which he picked up when it was starving: the bird is physically disabled—blind, in its case. It is called Dick, and it is a blackbird (433). Given the Blackboy and the "black girl" we have observed, and the fact that Dick was one of Dickens's own nicknames (Slater, 296), this bird can be seen as an instance of the novelist's projection of his childhood suffering.

Ch. 3 Ghosts in *A Christmas Carol*: A Japanese View

My aim in this chapter is to examine *A Christmas Carol* from a Japanese point of view; first, very broadly in terms of its reception in Japan, and second, more specifically in terms of Dickens's presentation of the ghosts in the story. Since Scrooge's lesson in the *Carol* is initiated by his trip back to the past, it may be appropriate for us to start with a moment of retrospection into the Japan of approximately one hundred years ago. The scene we visit is a classroom in Tokyo University, which is, unlike that of the young Scrooge, packed with eager Japanese students. In front of them, at the lectern, stands Lafcadio Hearn, discoursing upon Dickens in his lecture series on the history of English literature. Defining Dickens as a gentle caricaturist, a painter of middle class life, Hearn says:

> [N]o more healthy, joyous, good moral books, were ever contributed to the literature of fiction than the novels of Dickens. Nevertheless I must tell you that they are not to be recommended in a general way to Japanese students. On the contrary I should advise you to read very little of Dickens for the present. Dickens can only be properly understood by a person who has lived a long time in England, and lived there from childhood. . . . I doubt extremely whether you could find any charm in his whimsical English middle-class life. It was for some time a custom to read "The Cricket on the Hearth" in Japanese schools; but I doubt whether a worse choice could have been made for the sake of Japanese students. Simple as the story appears to an English mind, it is utterly impossible for a Japanese student to understand it. No matter how much it may be explained, every paragraph in that little story treats of matters which do not exist in this country; even the picture of an English kitchen cannot be understood unless you have seen the real thing.[1]

Looking back at what he said, we cannot help feeling that circumstances have greatly changed since (Hearn taught at Tokyo University between 1896 and 1903). Things English are everywhere in Japan now. It is not difficult to find Twining's tea and Wedgwood teacups in a Japanese kitchen! In some ways, the distance that separates Dickens from us Japanese seems to be a great deal shorter than it used to be.

A Christmas Carol (known in Japan as "Kurisumasu Kyaroru" —we almost get it right, don't we?) is, to the Japanese, one of the most famous works of English literature, possibly in the same league with *Hamlet*, and its translation has a long and rich history. Roughly speaking, the translation of Western literature started one hundred and twenty years ago. Before that our country had been very much closed to the Western world. In Japanese history, there was what is called the Meiji Restoration in 1868, which marked the end of the feudal society, a structure dominated by Samurai lords, with the Shogun at the top of them. At the beginning of the Meiji period, they were eager to introduce what they thought were enlightened and advanced Western ideas. As part of this, a number of works of literature were translated, including some English novels, most notably those by Bulwer-Lytton (*Ernest Maltravers* and *Alice* in 1878, *The Last Days of Pompeii* in 1879, *Rienzi* and *Kenelm Chillingly* in 1885), and by Disraeli (*Coningsby* in 1884, *Endymion* in 1886, *Vivian Grey* in 1887). It must be added, though, that some of these novels were drastically abbreviated.

In those days many of the translations appeared in journals and magazines. In the case of Dickens, they began with some of the papers from *Sketches by Boz*. "The Contradictory Couple" in 1882, "The Steam Excursion" in 1886, and "The Black Veil" in 1893. Translations of the full-length novels started later, in the 1920s. As for *A Christmas Carol*, an adaptation set in contemporary Japan with characters' names changed to Japanese ones came out in book form in 1888. Later, in 1902, a complete translation appeared.[2] (This is roughly when Lafcadio Hearn was lecturing.) Up to the present, there have been approximately thirty translations, with four or five currently in print.[3] Simply in terms of the number of translations done, in the entire range of foreign literature, the *Carol* must be very close to the top of our list. Quite why there have been so many translations I do not pretend to know. Surely it is not that improvement was necessary every time. Perhaps what happened was that the demand was always there, and that when one translation went out of print, another publisher stepped in with a new one. At any rate, this brief survey of the translations will testify to the *Carol*'s lasting popularity among the Japanese.

Leaving aside an embarrassing question—why is the *Carol* so popular with the Japanese? (to which I can only answer "why not?")— I should like to move on to my second main topic, a consideration of the

Carol as a ghost story, in comparison with those of Japan.

I started with Lafcadio Hearn. An interesting thing about him is that he took a great interest in Japanese ghost stories. In 1904 he published a famous collection of his retellings of Japanese ghost stories called *Kwaidan*, which means "weird story," or more broadly "ghost story." Curiously, however, in his lecture on Dickens there is no mention of the *Carol*, nor in any of his writing was I able to find a serious discussion of Dickens's use of ghosts. Equally curiously, rather than the *Cricket*, he recommends "Mugby Junction"—"the wonderful railroad stories" which "could be tolerably well understood by any one familiar with railroad life"[4]—but does not mention that haunting story, "The Signalman." Although Hearn's collection, *Kwaidan*, contains a variety of Japanese ghost stories, I believe he was most attracted by the powerful, passionate relationship that obtains between the haunter and the haunted, whether it be of hatred, love, or friendship. Perhaps it is because he could not find this that Hearn did not take much interest in Dickens's ghost stories.

Here is a very rough sketch of Japanese ghost stories. The typical Japanese ghost appears, saying "Urameshiya," which means "I bear a grudge against you." This sounds rather matter-of-fact in English, but it is effective in Japanese. Ghosts are supposed to appear in this world because they want revenge. Of course there are exceptions, as in some of the famous *No* plays, where ghosts appear and solicit the attention of, for example, travelling Buddhist monks, and ask them to purify their souls so that they can go to heaven (or its equivalent). Notice, in this case, that it does not matter to whom ghosts appear. As long as their wish is granted, it does not make any difference. They usually appear at a certain place, and grab whoever is passing by, and if they are lucky, they come across a trained monk who can save them. Ghosts of this kind, however, are a minority; the majority are the ones who bear a specific grudge against specific people. A ghost who appears in order to save somebody, as Marley does, is rather unusual.

In Japanese studies of ghosts, a distinction is sometimes made between what we call "Yu-rei" and "Yo-kwai." Let us adopt, for the occasion, the terms "haunting humans" and "strange creatures," to correspond to this distinction. "Yu-rei" or "haunting humans" are former human beings (and appear more or less as they used to be), whereas "Yokwai" or "strange creatures" are not (though some of them might assume human-like forms). To apply this to the *Carol*, we have Marley on the one hand, and the three Spirits of Christmas on the other. The former, Marley, is in my terminology a "haunting human," and the latter are "strange creatures." Although Dickens does not differentiate between them—using the words "ghost" and "spirit" interchangeably, he refers to Marley and the Christmas Spirits both as "ghosts" and "spirits"— I think it is useful to make a distinction, because it enables us to see more clearly the twofold structure of Scrooge's change of heart. The first stage is where Marley, the "haunting human," appears, offering the chance of salvation. Scrooge, though strongly disturbed by it, does not fully grasp the importance of this event. The second stage is where we have the Spirits, the "strange creatures," and this is where the conversion really starts.

I shall come back to this question of ghost-types later. First, I should like to examine certain aspects of the language of the *Carol*, which, as I hope to show, have an important bearing upon Dickens's idea of ghosts in this story.

The *Carol* opens with the narrator's humorous musing on the simile of "dead as a doornail" (45).[5] Verbal jokes of this kind are found throughout the text, such as "[the rain and snow] often "came down" handsomely, and Scrooge never did" (46); "Scrooge had often heard it said that Marley had no bowels, but he had never believed it until now" (57), and so on. I believe they are important; they are not just frivolous jokes. They reflect Dickens's sheer joy in handling words, but at the same time, I suggest, they derive from the author's deep and serious engagement with his medium. These jokes might be regarded as an expression of the studied care that Dickens has brought into the telling of this story. For example, throughout the story, Scrooge is carefully defined with the metaphors of "hand."[6] "Oh! but he was a tight-fisted *hand* at the grindstone, Scrooge! a squeezing, wrenching, grasping, scraping, clutching, covetous old sinner!" (46). The Ghost of Christmas Past says to Scrooge, "What!... would you so soon put out, with worldly *hands*, the light I give?" (69). Even at the very beginning, we are told that "Scrooge's name was good upon "Change for anything he chose to put his *hand* to" (45) (all italics mine).

Discussing Dickens's use of "moral double" in the change of heart in his novels, Barbara Hardy observes that the "ghosts are not only aspects of Christmas, but in part at least aspects of Scrooge."[7] It is interesting to consider, in the light of this comment, the Ghost of Christmas Yet to Come, whose black garment "concealed its head, its face, its form, and left nothing of it visible save one outstretched *hand*" (110; italics mine). This ghost is nothing but a hand, as it were. This, then, is a reflection of the Scrooge Yet to Come, when only his covetous hand remains in existence. Hardy's point is important, and I should like to relate it to the examination of the twofold structure of Scrooge's change of heart.

Scrooge is not totally shaken by Marley, at the first stage of his conversion. He can crack a joke like "There's more of gravy than of grave about you" (59). He can also make a rebuttal: "Don't be flowery, Jacob" (63). This kind of comic defiance is still maintained at the beginning of Stave II. I now quote the relevant passage at some length, inserting comments:

> [Scrooge] then made bold to inquire what business brought him there. "Your welfare!" said the Ghost. Scrooge expressed himself much obliged, but could not help thinking that a night of unbroken rest would have been more conducive to that end. [A kind of subtly comic defiance here.] The Spirit must have heard him thinking for it said immediately: "Your reclamation, then. Take heed!" It put out its strong *hand* as it spoke, and clasped him gently by the arm. [Notice the reference to the "hand."] "Rise and walk with me." It would have been in vain for Scrooge to plead that the weather and the hour were not adapted to pedestrian purposes. [Another (indirect) suggestion of comic resistance.] . . . The grasp, though gentle as a woman's hand, was not to be resisted. He rose: but finding that the Spirit made towards the window, clasped its robe in supplication. "I am a mortal," Scrooge remonstrated, "and liable to fall." [Still a joke is possible.] "Bear but a touch of my *hand* there," said the Spirit, laying it upon his heart, "and you shall be upheld in more than this!" (69-70; italics mine).

This is the crucial turning point in the story. With this, they move back into the past, and there's no defiance on Scrooge's part any longer. The Spirit lays its hand upon Scrooge's heart. In the light of Hardy's observation, this can be seen as Scrooge examining his own heart himself, and this is the precise beginning of the second stage of his change of heart.

And when does this process end? At the end of Stave IV, where

Scrooge begs the Ghost of Christmas Yet to Come to let him sponge away the writing on his own gravestone:

> In his agony, he caught the spectral *hand*. It sought to free itself, but he was strong in his entreaty, and detained it. The Spirit, stronger yet, repulsed him.
>
> Holding up his *hands* in a last prayer to have his fate reversed, he saw an alteration in the Phantom's hood and dress. It shrunk, collapsed, and dwindled down into a bedpost. (126; italics mine).

Dickens thus rounds off Scrooge's change of heart, with various references to the "hands." Having now established the nature of the twofold structure and its verbal pattern, let us go back to the ghosts, the agents in the process of Scrooge's conversion, bearing in mind the distinction between "Yu-rei" and "Yo-kwai."

Graham Holderness once complained that not much attention had been paid to the problem of "ghosts" in *Carol* criticism.[8] His own argument, however, only deals with the "Spirits" of Christmas. He does not discuss the "haunting human," Marley, at all. This, it seems to me, is a strange omission, but I think I can understand why it happens. As we have observed, Scrooge's conversion starts in earnest with the Christmas Spirits: the twofold structure of the story does seem to indicate that in Dickens's imagination the Spirits are more important than Marley in the process of Scrooge's change of heart. It is worthwhile considering this implied gradation, or distinction.

In Stave II, the narrator says, addressing the reader directly, that the Spirit of Christmas Past stands as close to Scrooge, "as I am now to you, and I am standing in the spirit at your elbow" (68). Holderness emphasizes the importance of this identification of the narrative voice with the Spirit of Christmas, in relation to the saving power of Imagination. It is indeed important, I agree, but I also wish to draw attention to the fact that the identification is made at this particular juncture, with the Christmas Spirit in Stave II, and not with Marley's ghost in Stave I.

As I have said, Dickens seems to use the words "ghosts" and "spirits" interchangeably. And yet, consider the chapter headings: Stave I "Marley's Ghost," Stave II "The First of the Three Spirits," Stave III "The Second of the Three Spirits," and Stave IV "The Last of the Spirits." It appears that Dickens does make a distinction of some sort, and I wonder if this may not be reflected in the narrator's identification with the Spirit, rather than with Marley's ghost.

We have seen how Dickens carefully marks the beginning and the end of Scrooge's conversion with references to the "hands" of the Christmas Spirits. I am now coming to the main point of this essay: compared with the kind of involvement observed in the presentation of the Christmas Spirits, I find Dickens's creative engagement with Marley rather feeble. True, Marley is in a way conceived as Scrooge's "double": we are told that they are "two kindred spirits" (50), and that the people new to the business call Scrooge Marley. But I do not think this is worked out as convincingly as Scrooge's encounter with the Spirit of Christmas Yet to Come, with its hand. There is no comparable intensity.

Or consider this: in a remarkable scene, Marley shows Scrooge various ghosts who try unsuccessfully to help the people in this world. This is their punishment, Marley says. They want to help, but they can't. "The misery with them all was, clearly, that they sought to interfere, for good, in human matters, and had lost the power for ever," we are told (65). A question, however, arises here: why, then, can Marley intervene in Scrooge's fate when others can't? Dickens does not explain. Marley just says to Scrooge, "How it is that I appear before you in a shape that you can see, I may not tell" (63). I suspect that Dickens is fudging here, and it does seem to betray a somewhat weak imaginative hold on Dickens's part where Marley is concerned.

I may be being too scrupulous, and the reason for this is that I feel a little sorry for Marley. One assumes that, having saved Scrooge, Marley finally makes it to Heaven, but Dickens does not explicitly say so. In Japanese ghost stories, at the end, having achieved their purpose, ghosts are made to disappear from this world and rest in peace. It is true that this may not always be explicitly stated, but, as I have said, an instance like Marley, who tries to save someone, strikes us Japanese as unusual. This makes me pity him all the more, and at the same time makes me wonder why Dickens does not spare some more words for Marley at the end: a simple sentence, such as "Later on, every Christmas Scrooge thought of Marley," or something of this nature (Dickens, of course, would have done better). However, "[Scrooge] had no further intercourse with Spirits" (134) is all the novelist tells us. It might be argued that Dickens must include Marley as well when he talks about Spirits here. Half of me agrees with this view, but the other half keeps on wondering exactly where Marley stands in the picture evoked by this particular phrasing, given the implied distinction I have pointed out between Marley's ghost and the Christmas Spirits. For there is something dubious, something uncertain about this closing joke of the "Total Abstinence Principle" (134). Although it is structurally coherent that the *Carol*, having started with one, should end with a verbal joke, Dickens is here actually recycling the same joke he used previously in the story about Gabriel Grub in *The Pickwick Papers* (Ch. 29, "The Story of the Goblins who stole a Sexton"): "Let the spirits be ever so good, or let them be even as many degrees beyond proof, as those which Gabriel Grub saw, in the goblin's cavern."[9] There it was a good joke, because Grub had a drinking problem, but here in the *Carol* it is rather off the mark, since Scrooge is no drinker. The feebleness of this joke is the more disappointing if one regards, as I do, jokes of this kind as crucial components of the story. Although Michael Slater, in a splendid piece on the humor of the *Carol*, has recently referred to this joke as a "sublime pun,"[10] one might feel that it could have been better, if one looks at it from the angle suggested here. Perhaps I am asking too much, and yet this sense of Dickens's falling somewhat short of total creative engagement might be, I cannot help feeling, another symptom of his weaker conception of Marley, "the haunting human."

(Originally a lecture delivered at the Birkbeck College "Dickens Day," December 1993; first published in *The Dickensian*, 1996)

NOTES

1 Lafcadio Hearn, *A History of English Literature*, vol. 2 (Tokyo: Hokuseido, 1927), 577-78.
2 I am indebted to Masaie Matsumura's various studies of early Japanese translations of Dickens.
3 There is even an inventive translation by Shigeru Koike in the style of "Rakugo," traditional Japanese comic storytelling.
4 Hearn, 578.
5 All references to the *Carol*, appearing parenthetically, are to the Penguin edition (vol. 1 of *The Christmas Books*), edited by Michael Slater (Harmondsworth, 1971).
6 Robert L. Patten also picks up some of the "hand" references in the *Carol*.

He considers them, however, mainly in the light of Dickens's concern with the Christian theology in this story, and does not make the connections I make here. See his essay, "Dickens Time and Again," in *Dickens Studies Annual* 2 (1972), 163-96.

7 Barbara Hardy, *The Moral Art of Dickens* (London: The Athlone Press, 1970), 34-35.

8 Graham Holderness, "Imagination in *A Christmas Carol*," *Études Anglais* 32 (1979), 32.

9 *The Pickwick Papers*, ed. James Kinsley (Oxford: Clarendon Press, 1986), 444.

10 Michael Slater, "The Triumph of Humour: The *Carol* Revisited," *The Dickensian* 89 (Winter 1993), 191.

Ch. 4 Dickens in Confusion?: Discrepancies in the Dénouement of *Martin Chuzzlewit*

In the first paragraph of Chapter 4 of *Martin Chuzzlewit*, we are told that Pecksniff, after seeing Old Martin at the Blue Dragon, withdrew to his own home, and remained there three whole days. . . ." But in the very next paragraph we read: "During the whole of this interval, he haunted the Dragon at all times and seasons in the day and night. . . ." (43).[1] As Michael Slater observes in his Notes, this is "an oversight on Dickens's part" (792), for the two statements obviously contradict each other. Comparable minor errors can be seen in other passages, too. Margaret Cardwell points out, for instance, that the "goldfinch" (296) in Sweedlepipe's shop is later transformed into a "bullfinch" (713, 764). She also notes that "Insertions and deletions in manuscript and on proof can result in occasional minor discrepancies when related passages are not revised to correspond": for example, a reference to Pecksniff's turning red when Charity hints at his designs on Mary Graham was deleted in proof, but a few lines later he is described as "colouring again" (448). Those errors, she suggests, stemmed from "speed of composition and improvisation in small matters.[2] Inconsistency of another order has recently been detected by John Sutherland. He has found a chronological anomaly which involves Martin leaving England in winter and, after one year's stay in America, coming back in summer. Sutherland argues that "These anomalies witness less to any carelessness on Dickens's part, than to his Shakespearian confidence in making the elements do whatever it is the current mood and dramatic needs of his narrative require them to do."[3] There are thus various discrepancies in *Martin Chuzzlewit*, but those occurring in the dénouement seem hitherto to have escaped the notice of all commentators on the novel.

In Ch. 49 Martin and John visit Mrs Gamp, having agreed to approach Chuffey through her since she is nursing him: they wish to get confirmation of what Lewsome revealed to them about the death of Anthony Chuzzlewit. They find that Mrs Gamp has an appointment with Jonas "Tomorrow evenin' . . . from nine to ten" (715), and decide that Martin, playing the role of Mrs Harris, should go with her and confront Jonas. Then in Ch. 50 Martin, full of indignation, visits Tom "the next evening" (716). I draw attention to this phrase, for I believe it is another instance of Dickens's oversight.

Important events in the climactic chapters are Jonas's arrest and Pecksniff's punishment. It appears from the above ("Tomorrow evenin'") that the former takes place on the day after Martin and John visit Mrs Gamp. On the night of Jonas's arrest Old Martin, we are told, refuses to see his grandson "until tomorrow" (748) at Temple Bar. It follows that Pecksniff is chastised there the next day. Putting these events in chronological order we have: (1) Martin and John's visit to Mrs Gamp, (2) Jonas's arrest the next day, (3) Pecksniff's punishment the day after that.

Now, let us assume that Martin's angry visit to Tom in Ch. 50 takes place "the next evening" after his visit to Mrs Gamp, as the narrative has it. This, then, is the evening of the day on which Jonas is arrested. A little later in the same chapter (723), Tom and Ruth are described as having their breakfast the next day—that is to say, the day of Pecksniff's punishment—after which Tom goes out to his work at the Temple, and there he meets Old Martin, who reveals himself as his employer. This, however, is impossible.

One recalls that it is not—as was originally planned—Young Martin, but instead Old Martin who comes with Mrs Gamp to Jonas's house. The change is explained in Ch. 52: Old Martin "had sent for John Westlock immediately on his arrival; and John, under the conduct of Tom Pinch, had waited on him" (748). Presumably what happens is that after John informs him of Mrs Gamp's appointment with Jonas, Old Martin decides to go there himself instead of his grandson. There is, however, this difficulty: in order to participate in Jonas's exposure, Old Martin must employ Tom to get in touch with John; in order to be able to do so, he must first reveal himself to Tom. Accordingly, if the revelation occurs on the day of Pecksniff's punishment, as assumed in the preceding paragraph, then there is no time for Old Martin to get involved with Jonas's arrest, which by then has already taken place!

This contradiction could be resolved if, going back to the starting point of my discussion, we correct "the next evening" in Ch. 50 to "the same evening." This, however, would give rise to another difficulty. The occurrence of "the next" rather than "the same" is not simply a mistake due to haste: perhaps Dickens had a good reason for writing "the next evening." When the enraged Martin visits him in this chapter Tom is understandably perplexed by the sudden burst of anger of his friend. To be sure, a hint is dropped: Martin says, "I *cannot* believe . . . that it would have been in your nature to do me any serious harm, even though

I had not discovered by chance, in whose employment you were" (719)—though it is odd that Tom does not immediately ask Martin to make this remark clearer. At any rate, the explanation of Martin's behavior is held back until Ch. 52: at Temple Bar, after Pecksniff's chastisement, Martin says, "Oh, Tom! Dear Tom! I saw you, accidentally, coming here. Forgive me!" (761) That is, aware that his grandfather has a room there, he thought Tom was secretly working for the old man. In fact, Dickens has been carefully preparing for this development: in Ch. 48, shortly before he and John call on Mrs Gamp, Martin, who "had no lodgings yet" in London, "succeeded, after great trouble, in engaging two garrets for himself and Mark, situated in a court in the Strand, not far from Temple Bar," and then he "walked up and down, in the Temple, eating a meat-pie for his dinner" (702). Is Martin supposed to have seen Tom entering the Temple then? It must be so, if we substitute "the same evening" for "the next." He sees Tom, figures that he is working for his grandfather, then goes with John to Mrs Gamp, and visits Tom, all in the same evening. But this is hardly likely. Considering that it is dinner time when Martin is walking up and down in Temple Bar, Tom would have gone home already—according to Fips, Tom's working hours are "from half-past nine to four, or half-past four, or thereabouts" (579)—or at least he would have come out of the Temple, rather than gone into it (Martin says, "I saw you coming here."). Moreover, it is surely very strange that there is no indication of the disturbance this must have caused in Martin, when he visits Mrs Gamp with John soon afterwards. What all this seems to suggest is that when Dickens wrote the phrase "the next evening," he was primarily thinking of this particular narrative thread and allowing time for Martin to see Tom coming to the Temple in the morning, the day after his visit to Mrs Gamp.

There is another small discrepancy in the dénouement. Consider the last two paragraphs of Ch. 50, just after Old Martin has revealed himself to Tom:

> "Close the door, close the door. He will not be long after me, but may come too soon. The time now drawing on," said the old man, hurriedly: his eyes and whole face brightening as he spoke: "will make amends for all. I wouldn't have him die or hang himself, for millions of golden pieces! Close the door!"
>
> Tom did so, hardly knowing yet whether he was awake or in a dream. (p. 727)

Old Martin is clearly expecting Pecksniff at any moment, while Tom is completely baffled by his behavior (the time is about half-past nine, given Tom's working hours). As a matter of fact, there is a number division at this point, so readers of the serial, like Tom, were left in suspense. In the next (and the last) instalment, Jonas's arrest occurs in Ch. 51, and at the beginning of Ch. 52 we are told that "Old Martin's cherished projects . . . were retarded, but not beyond a few hours, by the occurrences just now narrated" (747). This refers back to the ending of Chapter 50, the passage quoted above, but does not accord with the rest. It should be recalled that Pecksniff's chastisement takes place the day after Jonas's arrest, at about "ten o'clock" (751). The delay then is not a matter of a few hours but of one whole day. Poor Pecksniff is held up by the plot machinery for twenty-four hours and when he is finally allowed to come to the Temple, he is caned by Old Martin! (Further slighting this brilliant creation, Dickens does not bother to explain how Pecksniff makes his appearance there conveniently just after all the others have gathered.)

When he was working on the last instalment, which required his "utmost exertions" (Letter to Mrs Gore, 11 June 1844), Dickens must have been confused about these details under the heavy pressure of bringing the complicated plot to a dénouement. In dealing with Jonas's arrest and Pecksniff's punishment, and in picking up the narrative thread involving Martin's mysterious anger against Tom, the novelist seems not to have realized that he had concentrated too many crucial events into a very short span of time. Also, in the final chapters Dickens appears to be concerned not so much with the titular hero as with his grandfather. This is reflected, for example, in his utter indifference to the manner in which the change of plan regarding Jonas's exposure is relayed to Young Martin. It may be that since Dickens was mainly interested in the precipitation (in the manner of God suddenly asserting Himself and overthrowing all evil) of Old Martin's "amends" and punishment of the two chief villains, the precise chronology of events was very much a secondary consideration.

In his edition of Dickens's "Working Notes" Harry Stone writes:

> Unlike the trial titles, which are abundant, the extant working notes for *Chuzzlewit* are meager. They consist of four early sheets of trial names (the fourth list associated with Number II) and two sheets of condensed memos, one for Number IV and one for

Number VI.[4]

These are the only things that survive, but that does not necessarily mean that there was nothing else. The accepted view, however, is that Dickens started making use of Number Plans with the next novel, *Dombey and Son*, and the discrepancies I discuss here may offer corroborating evidence in support of such a view. Even though he took pains, as he says in the Preface to the first edition, "to keep a steadier eye upon the general purpose and design of the novel" (xli), Dickens was most probably working without detailed Number Plans at this stage.

It is a tribute, at any rate, to Dickens's ability to sweep the reader along with his powerful narrative that nobody has noticed this particular confusion in the dénouement in the more than one hundred and fifty years since the novel's first publication.[5]

(First published in *The Dickensian*, 1998)

NOTES

1 This and subsequent references to *Martin Chuzzlewit* are to the Everyman Paperback edition (London: Dent, 1994), edited by Michael Slater.
2 See Margaret Cardwell's Introduction to the Clarendon edition of the novel (Oxford: Oxford University Press, 1982), xlv-xlvii.
3 John Sutherland, *Is Heathcliff a Murderer?* (Oxford: Oxford University Press, 1996), 47.
4 Harry Stone (ed.), *Dickens' Working Notes for His Novels* (Chicago: University of Chicago Press, 1987), 19.
5 For Dickens's confusion or seeming confusion, of more thematic significance, see Chs. 6 and 7 of this book.

Ch. 5 How Dickens Conceived Esther's Narrative: A Hypothesis

"In January and February, 1967, I gave a series of six Lectures at the Victorian Studies Centre of the University of Leicester, newly founded under the enlightened and energetic leadership of Professor Philip Collins," notes Sylvère Monod in his article (based on those lectures) titled "Esther Summerson, Charles Dickens and the Reader of *Bleak House*.[1] I should like to pay tribute to the Victorian Studies Centre, via Professor Monod (he and I are fellow translators of this novel, he into French and I into Japanese), by dealing with the same subject, Esther Summerson. Given the time restrictions, I shall limit myself to addressing one question: how did Dickens come up with the idea of using her as a co-narrator?

Bleak House is divided into two parts, one in which the "semi-omniscient," third-person narrator takes charge, and the other in which Esther carries out the task of narration.[2] Michael Slater calls this a "sensationally new narrative technique."[3] When the novel came out, however, the technical innovation did not create much excitement, as Philip Collins observed in his Critical Heritage anthology: "Dickens's experiment in [the dual narration] was little discussed."[4] From our point of view, with the awareness of modern narrative theories, this paucity of interest looks simply peculiar.

For, indeed, there was nothing like it before, or after. In novels with plural narrators the narration is invariably shared by characters, not by a character and a third-person narrator. As far as I know, *Bleak House* is the only instance of that type of sharing—except, perhaps, for John Updike's 1963 novel, *The Centaur*. But here, the narrative task is divided tacitly; the third-person narrator and first-person character alternate without recognizing each other. In *Bleak House* Esther knows she collaborates with someone else, for she speaks of "my portion" of the narrative (Ch. 3); the other narrator reveals his awareness of Esther's part, if very briefly, when he says, "While Esther sleeps" (Ch. 7). In fact, a fictional character making a contract of a shared publication with an author-like narrator is preposterous. In the fictional world a character is a flesh-and-blood human being, while the third-person narrator is a superhuman entity that knows everything and can go anywhere. Technically, as Seymour Chatman argues, the narrator belongs to the domain of "discourse" (expression) and a character to that of "story" (content); they belong to different dimensions.[5]

How, then, did Dickens hit upon such a singular idea? Michael Slater says, "We have no hint from Dickens as to why he chose this double narrative form," and offers a guess: "it is possible that in writing *Copperfield* he had found that combining satire with first-person narration where the narrator is supposed to be as ingenuous as the young David Copperfield posed a serious difficulty. In the case of a young woman narrator like Esther Summerson this difficulty would have been much increased, hence, perhaps, Dickens's decision to split the narration in this novel.[6] Since no evidence exists, we can only speculate.[7] What follows is my own hypothesis.

The first step, I propose, is to examine what was happening in Dickens's writing life, when he began to compose *Bleak House*. Judging from his letters, he started thinking about the novel in August 1851 (17 August: "I begin to be pondering afar off, a new book"). Next month his imagination had apparently warmed up (28 September: "I am in the first throes of a new book"), but in early October his creative engagement was disturbed because of the house-moving (9 October: "I am three parts distracted and the fourth part wretched in the agonies of getting into a new house. . . . I *can not* work at my new book"). Then, on 12 October, he drafted a preliminary advertisement for the new novel. Oddly enough, it merely refers to a "New Serial Work . . . In Twenty Monthly Numbers . . . with Illustrations by H. K. Browne," without the date for publication. In fact, this advertisement was never published, because, as the Pilgrim editors state, at this stage the writing "had not yet begun."[8] Presumably he was still distracted by the house-moving. Finally, settled in the new house in Tavistock Square, he reports on 17 November: "I am beginning to find my papers, and to know where the pen and ink are." We may safely infer that he commenced putting pen to paper shortly afterwards.

There is, I submit, an important key to the conception of the narrative form of *Bleak House* buried somewhere in early October 1851, when the novel was in gestation. In order to see this clearly, I suggest we look back a little in the novelist's creative life. In March 1850 he founded the weekly magazine, *Household Words*. With complete editorial control he printed articles on recent events in various fields such as science, politics, natural history, and geography; he used a number of contributors, but he edited every item and tried to ensure that the magazine would achieve coherence. He himself wrote, at the end of 1850, an article titled "A December Vision," where he talks about the miserable state of urban street children, a contagious disease arising from polluted air, and the malfunction of the legal system of equity. All these issues were to constitute important elements of *Bleak House*, as has been long recognized. I wish to explore, however, a different connection between the magazine and the novel.

A week after the publication of "A December Vision," there appeared, on 21 December, the "Christmas Number" of the *Household Words*. Dickens had already claimed Christmas as his own field, as it were, starting with the great success of *A Christmas Carol* back in 1843. That was followed by *The Chimes*, *The Cricket on the Hearth*, *The Battle of Life*, and after one year's hiatus, *The Haunted Man* in 1848. Since they had turned out to be very popular, it was natural that Dickens should have conceived a Christmas special issue of the *Household Words*, with a view to tapping further into this particular vein.

For the 1850 Christmas Number Dickens asked nine people to provide essays, stories or poems (to be published anonymously), each treating the seasonal theme, he himself contributing a piece called "A Christmas Tree." It was obviously a brilliant idea, and when the next Christmas came around in 1851, the year of *Bleak House*'s composition, Dickens thought he would do the same thing again. However, it was slightly different this time. In 1850 it had been a "Christmas Number," but in 1851 it was an "Extra Number for Christmas"—a separate issue, appearing on Christmas Day. Clearly it had become a more elaborate affair.

It is in this context that I now wish to examine a letter Dickens wrote to his sub-editor, W. H. Wills, dated 6 October. He says:

> On Saturday the 25th. we had better dine at the office—with Morley, Horne, and (I suppose) Forster—to decide upon the form and idea of the Christmas No. I think it would be well to let Morley and Horne know beforehand what we are going to meet for; as they might then have some suggestion to make. On second thoughts Monday the 27th. might be better.

Dickens, I take it, wanted to have a serious discussion on "the form and idea" of the Christmas Number on the 27th, presumably hoping to leave the matter behind, before starting the composition of the new novel.

Now, here is my speculation: sometime after 6 October 1851 (the date of the above letter), when he was reflecting upon the Christmas writing, an idea occurred to Dickens about the new novel, which inspired him to compose the preliminary advertisement on 12 October—at that time no word was written yet, but (I am guessing) he had the form. I suggest that whilst contemplating a collaborative composition of the Christmas piece Dickens came up with the idea of collaborative composition of a novel. Dickens, I submit, took an imaginative leap from writing with other people to writing with a fictional character; he decided to hire Esther as a contributor.

Esther, we will recall, speaks of her "portion" of the narrative (Ch. 3). This is a word Dickens the editor actually employed: "I should say [your work] might be spread into four portions—though more would be objectionable, as I conceive, to the fair reading of the story" (to Elizabeth Gaskell, 5 February, 1850); "It is clear to me that nobody might could would or should understand what [Horne's Diary] means, if we were to print this portion by itself, quite ignorant of what is to follow or when it is to come" (to W. H. Wills, 7 October 1852). Perhaps, much as the editor gives a certain portion of the magazine to a contributor, Dickens gave Esther half of his novel.

I have said that the idea of the omniscient narrator and a character making a contract is preposterous. It is so, from our standpoint. But obviously it was not the case in the nineteenth century. The reviewer of the *Eclectic Review* (December 1853), a notable exception to the contemporary indifference to the novel's narrative method, states:

> The tale is told by two parties, or rather distributed to the share of two parties;—one is the author speaking in his own person; the other is a female actor in the story. Thus there was requisite the diversity of style proper to the fictitious historian, and a gentle lady whose tastes cling to the narrow circle of home life. Yet, in this, he has admirably succeeded.

This reviewer has no problem with the categorical mixture of author and character, and their collaboration in narration.[9] In dealing with the "sensationally new" technique of *Bleak House*, perhaps we should forget about "sophisticated" narrative theories. An author having a contract with a fictional character may be absurd, but it would have been a real enough proposition for Dickens. I have used the word "leap" above—a leap from writing with other people to writing with a character—but for

Dickens it was not really a leap.

Dickens's daughter Mamie says he "turned his own creations into living realities, with whom he wept"[10]; according to his son Henry, the novelist declared, "when I am describing a scene I can as distinctly see the people I am describing as I can see you now"[11]; another son Charles says "[my father] lived two lives, one with us and one with his fictitious people, and . . . the children of his brain were much more real to him."[12] In the heat of imaginative creation Dickens literally saw his characters; he was in the same world with them, breathing the same air with them. In these quotations we have strong testimonies regarding that phenomenon. In addition, there is concrete evidence for it in the text of *Bleak House*, where Guppy and Jobling chance upon Krook who has spontaneously combusted:

> Here is a small burnt patch of flooring; here is the tinder from a little bundle of burnt paper, but not so light as usual, seeming to be steeped in something; and here is—is it the cinder of a small charred and broken log of wood sprinkled with white ashes, or is it coal? Oh, horror, he is here! And this from which <u>we run away</u>, striking out the light and overturning one another into the street, is all that represents him. (Ch. 32; underline mine)

When the two characters are frightened and take flight, Dickens the narrator, or Dickens the author, runs away *together with them*.[13] If he ran with Guppy, I am positive Dickens sat with Esther, showing her how to go about her "portion" of the narrative, or was able to imagine he had done so. No doubt Esther was an ideal contributor; unlike, for example, Mrs Gaskell, whom he later found too stubborn for his liking, Esther obediently listened to what he said.[14] And he did not have to pay.

(Originally a lecture delivered at the University of Leicester, November 2017; first published in *The Dickensian*, 2018)

NOTES

1 *Dickens Studies* 5 (1969), 5.

2 The adjective "semi-omniscient" is Dickens's own. In his talk, "*Bleak*

House through Binoculars" (Dickens Fellowship Conference, July 2002), Malcolm Andrews pointed out the relevance of "the Shadow"—"a kind of semi-omniscient, omnipresent, intangible creature," which Dickens proposes as a possible idea for the prospective periodical (see his letter to John Forster dated 7 October 1849). Dickens's description here is apt for *Bleak House* in that the roving narrator often pretends not to know everything.

3 *Charles Dickens* (New Haven: Yale University Press, 2009), 336.

4 *Dickens: The Critical Heritage* (London: Routledge and Kegan Paul, 1971), 273.

5 See *Coming to Terms* (Ithaca, Cornell University Press, 1990), Ch. 7, esp. 116-21. According to Chatman, the narrator is an agent of presentation, and need not be human.

6 *Charles Dickens*, 336.

7 Speaking of the possible connection between *Bleak House* and *Jane Eyre*, Ellen Moers suggests that "The very form of his novel . . . was perhaps conceived in a spirit of rivalry with Charlotte Brontë." See "*Bleak House*: the Agitating Women". *The Dickensian* 69 (1973), 22.

8 The preliminary advertisement and the editorial comment appear on p. 518 of the Pilgrim Edition of *The Letters of Charles Dickens, vol. 6*, ed. Graham Storey, Kathleen Tillotson and Nina Burgis (Oxford: Oxford University Press, 1988).

9 Nor does the reviewer of *Bentley's Monthly Review* (October 1853), who also notes the peculiarity of the narration.

10 Mamie Dickens, *Charles Dickens by His Eldest Daughter* (2nd ed. 1889; New York: Haskell House, 1977), 100.

11 Henry Fielding Dickens, "The Social Influence of Dickens." *The Dickensian* 1 (1905), 63.

12 Charles Dickens, Jr., "Reminiscences of My Father" (1934). Ed. Philip Collins, *Dickens: Interviews and Recollections* (London: Macmillan, 1981), 120.

13 It might be possible to read the last sentence of this passage as free indirect discourse representing Guppy and Jobling's consciousness, but the convoluted syntax strongly suggests the presence of the "semi-omniscient" narrator.

14 Compare Anny Sadrin's suggestion of "the likeness [Esther] bears to the Manchester lady novelist." See "Charlotte Dickens: the Female Narrator of *Bleak House*." *Dickens Quarterly* 9 (1992), 50.

Ch. 6 The Name of Barbary in *Bleak House*

A few years ago I noticed in a piece advertising the new BBC drama, *Dickensian*, that Lady Dedlock was introduced as Honoria Barbary.[1] This is of course an error, for in the novel Conversation Kenge reports of Miss Barbary that "her name was an assumed one" (Ch. 17) and Lady Dedlock herself says, "she [her sister] had renounced me and my name" (Ch. 29); we do not know Honoria's family name, as it is not specified in the text. I have, however, come across the very same error in several academic writings.[2] The reason for the misunderstanding is perhaps found in the passage, where on Esther's first visit to Krook's shop Miss Flite announces to him that he has wards of Jarndyce as his guests:

> "Jarndyce!" said the old man with a start.
>
> "Jarndyce and Jarndyce. The great suit, Krook," returned his lodger.
>
> "Hi!" exclaimed the old man in a tone of thoughtful amazement and with a wider stare than before. "Think of it!"
>
> He seemed so rapt all in a moment and looked so curiously at us that Richard said, "Why, you appear to trouble yourself a good deal about the causes before your noble and learned brother, the other Chancellor!"
>
> "Yes," said the old man abstractedly. "Sure! *Your* name now will be—"
>
> "Richard Carstone."
>
> "Carstone," he repeated, slowly checking off that name upon his forefinger; and each of the others he went on to mention upon a separate finger. "Yes. There was the name of Barbary, and the name of Clare, and the name of Dedlock, too, I think."
>
> "He knows as much of the cause as the real salaried Chancellor!" said Richard, quite astonished, to Ada and me.
>
> (Ch. 5)

Here "Barbary" appears right alongside "Dedlock." What confuses the reader must be the fact that the name Esther's aunt assumes is in the suit.

Gilian West, one of the very few who have taken the trouble to examine this matter, expressed her view in this journal.[3] Her conclusion is simply that it is "a mistake" on Dickens's part: "If Krook has heard the name in court, (for he cannot read), then *Kenge* would also have heard it, but Kenge does *not* know that Miss Barbary is in the suit" (164). Presumably, West has in mind the fact that, when Kenge comes to see Esther after Miss Barbary's death (Ch. 3), he does not say things like "Your aunt's name is Barbary, is it not? Do I understand that she is involved in that illustrious suit?" Instead, he merely states that Mr Jarndyce of the famed suit has taken pity on Esther and wishes to help her. To be sure, he does not mention any connection between the Jarndyce suit and the name of Barbary, but it does not necessarily follow that he is ignorant of that connection, as West believes—it may well signify that he is aware but chooses not to mention it.

Indeed, I do not think Dickens made a "mistake" here. His idea, as I imagine it, is that Barbary is a name of the family actually involved in the suit, and that Esther's aunt borrows it when she decides to bring up Esther. The novelist tells us: "Innumerable children have been born into the cause; innumerable young people have married into it; innumerable old people have died out of it. Scores of persons have deliriously found themselves made parties in Jarndyce and Jarndyce without knowing how or why; whole *families* have inherited legendary hatreds with the suit" (Ch. 1; italics mine). There are several families linked to the suit, Barbary being one of them. According to this scenario, Kenge, who knows the name of Barbary in relation to the suit, would deem it quite natural when Jarndyce asks him to visit a Miss Barbary; in the conversation with Esther he does not bring up the name's connection with the Jarndyce suit, perhaps sensing some delicate issue around Esther's illegitimacy.

There is, however, a bigger mystery in Esther's account of her first encounter with Krook: Esther must have been surprised to hear the name of Barbary from his mouth in connection with the suit—but in her account of the episode she does not say anything about her own reaction. This point has not been sufficiently explored by Dickens scholars. West, noting the problem, simply writes it off as Dickens's mistake, and, as far as I am aware, only three critics have attempted to find some significance here.

To examine their opinions chronologically, first, Lawrence Frank has this to say:

> The silence that so often accompanies the telling of her story

> suggests, not just a coyness bordering on the vacuous, but a failure to understand, a failure not fortuitous, but, in some way, willed. . . . In part, Esther's silence about the name *Barbary* is her attempt to deny the past, to shut out memories of her aunt's denunciations and bitter resentment.[4]

Although I agree with Frank's idea of Esther's willed silence, his reasoning begs a few questions: if Esther wants to deny the past with her aunt here, why does she speak about her elsewhere?; why is she not silent there, too?; why is she reticent about this particular part, and not others?

Joseph Sawicki, in his turn, qualifies Frank's argument from a narratological perspective, making a distinction between Esther the character and Esther the narrator:

> Esther remains silent at the mention of her godmother's name, an omission noted by Frank. . . . It is willed, but willed by the narrator who is clearly obliged to maintain silence here; the connection between her and Lady Dedlock must be hidden for a while longer because the reader must learn this only when the character does. What supports this reading . . . is that, in just a few paragraphs, Esther the narrator will mislead us by asserting that she is not connected to the suit: "*. . . and I was no party in the suit.*"[5]

Certainly Esther the narrator controls the narrative with some design of her own, but I do not think she is misleading us here. That she is "no party in the suit" is nothing but the truth. She is Honoria's daughter, but an illegitimate child. Therefore she has no legal rights; she has nothing to do with the suit.

Hilary M. Schor argues: "Although [Barbary] is a false name, it appears in the legal documents that link Esther and Honoria to the Jarndyce and Jarndyce suit. . . . [A]nd yet, Barbary is a name that John Jarndyce, who knew both Honoria and her sister years ago, did not recognise."[6] The problem Schor identifies in the first half of the quote will disappear if we assume, as in the above-mentioned scenario, that Esther's aunt has borrowed the name of a family related to the suit. The point Schor raises in the latter part mystifies me; I am not sure which place in the novel she is talking about. If she is referring to the moment when Jarndyce receives the letter from Esther's aunt, I would say he does recognize the name assuming that a distant relative involved in the suit is asking for help. My puzzlement deepens when I read Schor's footnote:

> The confusion cannot be explained away in purely verisimilar terms: I think Dickens both wanted "Barbary" to be Esther's mother, and knew it couldn't be, if John Jarndyce was to be unaware of Esther's familial connections. Or, put another way, it was so important to Dickens to get the name Barbary into the mock-Chancery of Krook's warehouse, and so before Esther's eyes, that he sacrificed "realism"—in part, I would argue, so that we can watch her suppress any knowledge of her "own" name. (222-23)

That Dickens deliberately sacrificed realistic logic in terms of plot construction, in order to present Esther in the act of suppressing her name, is a claim I find difficult to accept. Surely this is pushing Frank's idea of willed silence much too far.

No explanation offered so far for Esther's silence seems quite satisfactory. My view of the situation is as follows: Esther is surprised when Krook brings up the name of Barbary; but she has been vaguely aware that the name of Barbary has something to do with the Jarndyce suit, for when a person of that name (her aunt) dies, a lawyer comes to her and talks about that particular suit ("Is it possible that our young friend never heard of Jarndyce and Jarndyce!"), and she is called up to London by a missive from the same lawyer with the letterhead, "Jarndyce and Jarndyce," therefore when she hears Krook mention Barbary in connection with the suit, she is not exactly astonished, because it is something half-expected; however, she makes no mention of her response when writing about the event—because, I would argue, of her feelings about John Jarndyce.

In Dickens's novels we find variations of an "old man/young woman" couple. Sylvia Manning calls it, borrowing from Chaucer, a "January-May relationship"[7]; a strong tie between father and daughter (Dombey and Florence, Wickfield and Agnes, Dorrit and Amy, Reginald Wilfer and Bella), a marriage (the Strongs, the Bounderbys), or a possible marriage (Arthur Gride and Madeline Bray, Pecksniff and Mary). Jarndyce and Esther could be thought of as being in the group.

Their relationship, however, is particularly strange; noting which, Michael Slater hazards a biographical speculation:

> The whole affair seems very odd and strained and readers who are made uncomfortable by it are surely right in such a response. Dickens's personal preoccupations can, I believe, here be seen warping his art into some peculiar shapes. . . . There is absolutely no reason why Dickens could not have shown Jarndyce perceiving the growing mutual love of Esther and Woodcourt and encouraging it by all the means in his power. Why introduce the crisis of his improbable offer of marriage to Esther? Is this not an attempt to dramatize what Dickens felt was now happening in [Georgina Hogarth's] life?[8]

I am not prepared to produce a new theory about the reason for this plot development, but wish to explore its possible connection with Esther's silence.

At Krook's mention of Barbary in Ch. 5, what is stirred in the innermost recess of Esther's mind is, I suggest, her suspicion that John Jarndyce might be her father. She talks about her pondering that possibility in the very next chapter:

> My fancy, made a little wild by the wind perhaps, would not consent to be all unselfish, either, though I would have persuaded it to be so if I could. It wandered back to my godmother's house and came along the intervening track, raising up shadowy speculations which had sometimes trembled there in the dark as to what knowledge Mr Jarndyce had of my earliest history—even as to the possibility of his being my father, though that idle dream was quite gone now. (Ch. 6)

Here she says such a dream "was quite gone now" ("now" meaning "at that point in the narrative"), but it is Esther's characteristic understatement: what happens is that this "idle dream" has raised its head again at Krook's shop. However, she shies away from mentioning it when describing the scene, and touches upon it thirty-odd pages later.

Esther the narrator often resorts to this delaying tactic. A small example occurs at Krook's shop:

> [Miss Flite] stopped to tell us in a whisper as we were going down that the whole house was filled with strange lumber which her landlord had bought piecemeal and had no wish to sell, in consequence of being a little M. This was on the first floor. But she had made a previous stoppage on the second floor and had silently pointed at a dark door there.
>
> "The only other lodger," she now whispered in explanation, "a law-writer. The children in the lanes here say he has sold himself to the devil. I don't know what he can have done with the money. Hush!" (Ch. 5)

This passage shows in microcosm what Esther does throughout her narrative. The indirect mention of her own father (the law-writer, Nemo) is awkwardly delayed. It is only a matter of a few moments here, but the deferral is usually longer, as on several occasions relating to Woodcourt:

> I have forgotten to mention—at least I have not mentioned—that Mr Woodcourt was the same dark young surgeon whom we had met at Mr Badger's. Or that Mr Jarndyce invited him to dinner that day. Or that he came. Or that when they were all gone and I said to Ada, "Now, my darling, let us have a little talk about Richard!" Ada laughed and said—But I don't think it matters what my darling said. She was always merry. (Ch. 14)

In an extreme instance, she postpones the telling beyond the end of the novel: "What more the letter told me, needs not to be repeated here. It has its own times and places in my story" (Ch. 36). That is, she ends up without explicitly referring to what her mother's letter says.

In this fashion, Esther often resorts to delayed reports where her intimate feelings, familial or amatory, are concerned. Her feelings about Jarndyce are certainly a delicate matter for her, and they are at the bottom of her silence at Krook's remark. Consider once more the passage about her suspicion of Jarndyce being her father: "[My fancy] wandered back to my godmother's house . . . raising up shadowy speculations which had sometimes trembled there in the dark . . . even as to the possibility of his being my father." The quote tellingly shows the proximity of Jarndyce and Barbary (her godmother) in her mind.

Then, it will be interesting to examine a segment from the

"uncomfortable" sequence, dealing with Jarndyce's courtship of Esther:

> Supper was ready at the hotel, and when we were alone at table he said, "Full of curiosity, no doubt, little woman, to know why I have brought you here?"
> "Well, guardian," said I, "without thinking myself a Fatima or you a Blue Beard, I am a little curious about it." (Ch. 64)

Melissa A. Smith, in her analysis of the Bluebeard reference here, points out that "beard" is "barbe" in French, and argues that underneath the name of "Barbary" we hear the echo of "Bluebeard."[9] Her point is to stress the barbarousness of Bluebeard, but to my thinking, this is a fascinating detail that again reveals the proximity of Barbary and Jarndyce in Dickens's imagination, and by extension, in Esther's.

Thus, Krook's mention of the name of Barbary, the assumed name of Esther's aunt, in connection with the Jarndyce suit is not a mistake on Dickens's part. The novelist knew what he was doing. According to Dickens's scenario as I see it, Esther has been harboring the suspicion about Jarndyce being her father and Miss Barbary being given the task of raising her, so when she hears the name of Barbary at Krook's shop, she is struck but not exactly astounded by it. However, to write about that suspicion is itself a delicate matter, and the fact that Jarndyce is to court her near the end of the narrative she is composing makes it doubly delicate. Therefore she says nothing about it here, resorts to her habitual delaying tactic, and talks about it some thirty pages later in the next chapter.

(First published in *The Dickensian*, 2020)

NOTES

1 "Meet the cast and characters of *Dickensian*," *The Radio Times*, 26 December 2015.

2 See for example: Judith Wilt, "Confusion and Consciousness in Dickens's Esther," *Nineteenth Century Fiction* 32 (1977), 290; Susan Shatto, "Lady Dedlock and the Plot of *Bleak House*," *Dickens Quarterly* 5 (1988), 186; Chiara Briganti, "The Monstrous Actress: Esther Summerson's

Spectral Name," *Dickens Studies Annual* 19 (1990), 219; David Holbrook, "Some Plot Inconsistencies in *Bleak House*," *English* 39 (1990), 210; J. Hillis Miller, "Moments of Decision in *Bleak House*," *The Cambridge Companion to Charles Dickens* (CUP, 2001), 51; John Gordon, *Sensation and Sublimation in Charles Dickens* (Palgrave, 2011), 123; John Jordan, *Supposing Bleak House* (U of Virginia Press, 2011), 41.

3 "Some Inconsistencies in *Bleak House*," *The Dickensian* (Autumn 1991).

4 *Charles Dickens and the Romantic Self* (U of Nebraska Press, 1984), 101, 102.

5 "The Mere Truth Won't Do," *The Journal of Narrative Technique* 17 (1987), 213

6 *Dickens and the Daughter of the House* (CUP, 1999), 113.

7 "Dickens, January, and May." *The Dickensian* (May 1975), 67-75.

8 *Dickens and Women* (Dent, 1983), 167.

9 "When Fairy Godmothers Are Men." *Dickens Studies Annual* 44 (2013), 195-220.

Ch. 7 What Estella Knew: Questions of Secrecy and Knowing in *Great Expectations*

Great Expectations is filled with secrets: secrets kept from Pip, secrets shared with him, secrets that he himself devises. These secrets are not only accompanied by anxieties and fears about their disclosure, but sometimes by characters' inexplicable behavior, and by the language containing subtle reminders of details associated with the narrative's mysteries. A significant example of the type of puzzle at times found in the novel appears in chapter 44, when Pip, after realizing that the returned convict Magwitch has been his patron, journeys down to Satis House to see Estella. There he finds "Miss Havisham seated on a settee near the fire, and Estella on a cushion at her feet. Estella was knitting, and Miss Havisham was looking on. They both raised their eyes as I went in, and both saw an alteration in me. I derived that, from the look they interchanged." Estella pauses for a moment, then goes on knitting. Pip recalls: "I fancied that I read in the action of her fingers, as plainly as if she had told me in the dumb alphabet, that she perceived I had discovered my real benefactor" (268; Ch. 44).[1]

Recently this passage has been rigorously examined by Sharon Marcus, who states: "The scene begins with a typical configuration of the female dyad excluding the male spectator and climaxes when Pip finally succeeds in attracting each woman's gaze to himself alone." She notes the change of tense in the prose—the past progressive ("was looking," "pausing, "motioning") into the simple past ("both raised their eyes," "both saw")—and points out that this is "the last glimpse the novel provides of Estella and Miss Havisham together" (184-85). Marcus, however, does not stop to wonder—nor has any previous commentator on the novel, so far as I am aware—how peculiar the situation is as depicted by Dickens. Consider what happens: the moment he enters the room, Pip thinks that Estella perceives that he has become aware of the true identity of his benefactor. How can she manage such a feat?

An attempt at an answer might begin with an examination of Miss Havisham's reaction here. When Pip says, "I have found out who my patron is," and starts to talk about Jaggers, Miss Havisham sharply interjects: "His being my lawyer, and his being the lawyer of your patron, is a coincidence" (269; Ch. 44). Does this mean that Miss Havisham knows that Magwitch is Pip's benefactor? She certainly behaves as if she possessed that knowledge; she does not show any surprise at Pip's remark that the discovery of the real benefactor is going to cause him ruin and disgrace. But it is not possible, unless Jaggers has been indiscreet and divulged a client's secret. To be sure, he has earlier told her about Pip's great expectations and their ancillary conditions (123; Ch. 19), but he is fully aware how dangerous things can be for Magwitch, as well as for himself, if at this juncture he should pass on any information regarding his client to a third party. In answer to Pip's alarmed query, he takes care to talk only of a man who is in New South Wales (251; Ch. 40). No, we need not ponder the possibility of Jaggers's unprofessional conduct. In fact, Miss Havisham is not saying she knows the identity of Pip's benefactor. She is simply saying that Pip's benefactor, whoever it may be, is served by Jaggers, as she is. She shows no surprise at Pip's remark, because she (at this point) hardly cares: "Who am I . . . that I should be kind!" (269; Ch. 44). His explanation—"It's not my secret, but another's" (268; Ch. 44)—is enough for her to stop being curious.

Miss Havisham's reaction to Pip's mention of Jaggers is quick, because she has known from the beginning that there is a real benefactor other than herself. But what about Estella? To reiterate, Pip's words are as follows: "I fancied that I read in the action of her fingers, as plainly as if she had told me in the dumb alphabet, that she perceived I had discovered my real benefactor." His view is that Estella has "perceived" the truth at that very moment. For this to make sense, however, she has to be a clairvoyant: she has always thought Miss Havisham is Pip's benefactor presumably without any suspicion, and yet, merely by taking a look at him when he enters the room, she can see that he is distressed at the discovery of the truth. It is not humanly possible. Accordingly we have to understand that here Pip's agitated imagination is running wild; indeed, he "fancied" what goes on in Estella's mind.

Then, what is the actual state of things? The query, as the subsequent argument will show, is of great moment. Seeing that she shows no surprise at Miss Havisham's irritated interjection about Jaggers quoted above, we will assume that Estella already knows that Miss Havisham is not Pip's benefactor. Let us recall, however, what she says in her conversations with Pip after she comes up to London: "You had no idea of your impending good fortune, in those times?" (182; Ch. 29); "Two things I can tell you. . . . First, notwithstanding the proverb that constant dropping will wear away a stone, you may set your mind at rest that these people [the Pockets] never will—never would, in a hundred years—impair your ground with Miss Havisham, in any particular, great or small. Second, I am beholden to you as the cause of their being so busy and so mean in vain, and there is my hand upon it" (204; Ch. 33). So, Estella speaks of "your good fortune" and "your ground with Miss Havisham" to Pip, knowing full well that Miss Havisham is not Pip's benefactor. A cruel monster, indeed. But is she such a character? One doubts it, for here she remarks, in response to Pip's declaration of unchanging love: "I make a great difference between you and all other people when I say so much" (271; Ch. 44). So, what are we to make of the whole situation?

Given the circumstances, the most plausible scenario I can come up with is as follows: Pip erroneously fancies that Estella has perceived the truth at this moment; she has previously been ignorant but has only very recently come to know about Pip's real benefactor not being Miss Havisham; for some reason Miss Havisham herself has told her. This, however, does not make much dramatic sense, unless Miss Havisham's confession to Estella is motivated by something like Jaggers's telling her about Pip's new knowledge of Magwitch as the source of his great expectations—a most unlikely development for the reasons I have already indicated. Besides, even this scenario begs questions. For example, if she has been made aware of Pip's situation and, unlike Miss Havisham, cares about him (albeit in her own peculiar way), why does Estella not say something along the lines of "I didn't know, either, Pip"?

There are too many complications here, and one wonders if before putting pen to paper Dickens deliberated over the ramifications that have been detailed above.[2] Perhaps he did not think through what Estella knew? Or perhaps he was not aware how impossible Estella's perception was? It is pertinent here to recall Michael Slater's observation that "Dickens confuses us by not consistently presenting Estella: she is sometimes preternaturally passionless, and sometimes suddenly displays natural emotions" (*Women* 281). This view has been contested. For example, Robert G. Garnett says:

> But rather than a defect in her characterization, emotional ambiguity is Estella's character *as Dickens understands it*. . . . She descends from a well-established line of Dickensian women of "cold" passion—Edith Dombey, Lady Dedlock, Louisa Gradgrind. . . . (35, 36; italics mine)

Margaret Flanders Darby avers that Pip does not understand Estella:

> Pip's persistent blindness throughout the story of his romance *enables Dickens to complicate* conventional paradigms of moral growth. . . . [W]hat Pip finds heartless is her insistence on her own point of view, a perspective that is chilled, sardonic, unable to love, but ready to be friends. (215, 221; italics mine)

Whatever the merits of Garnett's and Darby's arguments may be, they are talking about Dickens's conscious intention. But, given our examination of what Dickens knows about what Estella knows, it is doubtful that we can confidently discuss his intention as if it had been clear and consistent. My reading of the text confirms Slater's view: Dickens confuses us—only, to a greater extent than Slater suspects—and he does so perhaps because he was confused himself.

It is, then, interesting to notice that there are similar confusions elsewhere in the text. For example, Magwitch's behavior on the boat down the Thames (324; Ch. 54): he says nothing at all about Pip's burnt arms and shows no surprise at the presence of a stranger on the boat, Startop. It is as if he already knew. One may hypothesize that Herbert has informed him of these matters, but even then it is strange that he does not express any concern about Pip's burn. Is it possible that Magwitch is too absorbed in their escape to notice these things? Hardly: Pip observes that he is "the least anxious" one on the boat (325). Also, consider how after Magwitch's death Pip collapses with a fever and Joe nurses him. How does he come to know of Pip's illness? Joe says that "the news of your being ill were brought by letter" (344; Ch. 57). The text fails to say who has written the letter. John Sutherland surmises that Jaggers has done so (170). Perhaps he is right. But asked by the fever-stricken Pip if he knows the real identity of the benefactor, Joe answers, "I heerd . . . as it were not Miss Havisham, old chap. . . . I heerd as it were a person what sent the person what giv' you the bank-notes at the Jolly Bargemen, Pip" (347; Ch. 57). How can he know about that person being Magwitch's messenger? To make an adequate reply, one would have to think of a highly convoluted chain of events.

Perhaps all this is simply a matter of hasty writing by a serial writer who had to produce his copy week after week.[3] But then again, there may be something to this pattern of "somehow they know what happens to Pip."[4] It is tempting to see the workings of the novelist's own psychology here. Indeed, an answer to the interesting question—why Dickens had Pip fancy such an extraordinary penetration on Estella's part—may be found through biographical speculation.

It was Edmund Wilson who famously found in Estella a projection of Ellen Ternan (57-60).[5] Modern biographers still tend to follow suit.[6] Claire Tomalin suggests that Pip's obsessive love derived from Dickens's feelings for Ternan (*Dickens* 323). Of course we can never know for sure, unless some new evidence turns up. But we do know that at the time of writing *Great Expectations* Dickens miraculously managed to draw a veil over his relationship with Ternan. All Tomalin can say is that he probably paid for the house in which she lived with her family in Ampthill Square (*Dickens* 307); "Secrets and lies threaded through the family's social arrangements" (*Dickens* 306).[7] Then we might recall Pip's words early in the novel when he realizes that he has provided the weapon that has been used in attacking Mrs Joe. He wonders if he should confess everything to Joe: "the secret was such an old one now, had so grown into me and become a part of myself, that I could not tear it away" (97; Ch. 16). Referring to this sentence, Peter Ackroyd observes: "The secrecy was a part of Dickens's being, too" (103; Ch. 17).

Secrecy, of course, is part of the stock-in-trade of melodrama. Dickens had used it as a plot device many times before, but in *Great Expectations* it is far more complex and urgent than in any of his previous novels.[8] This urgency, one might not unreasonably suggest, is related to the novelist's real-life situation. Pip's secrecy does seem to reflect Dickens's own. The novel is riddled with secrets. Pip has to keep his secret promise with the convict; he becomes the victim of a secret that his benefactor is a convict; then he has to keep the existence of this convict a secret. In due course fear arises in Pip, as no doubt it did in Dickens. Is it safe? What if someone is watching? What if someone should know about it? This anxiety, I would argue, finds expression in Wopsle's performances in Ch. 47 in a way that is truly remarkable.

Before exploring that point, however, I need to say a few words about the ways in which the language of *Great Expectations* works. In Ch. 46 Pip comes to see Magwitch in the house where Clara Barley, Herbert Pocket's fiancée, lives with her irascible father. After seeing Magwitch he leaves him at the top of the stairs: "Looking back at him, I thought of the first night of his return, when our positions were reversed" (283; Ch. 46). Here, through explicitly referring to his own thoughts, Pip invites the reader to look back at a past event, think about the difference from the present, and reflect upon its significance. But more often, the same task is performed silently, without the narrator's overt direction. For example, on the night of Magwitch's return, Pip describes the wet weather by noting "mud, mud, mud, deep in all the streets" and talks of how "the wind rushing up the river shook the house that night, like discharges of cannon, or breakings of a sea" (236; Ch. 39). The "mud" and the "cannon" hark back to the initial meeting of Pip and Magwitch: Magwitch is first described as "A man who had been soaked in water, and smothered in mud" (10; Ch. 1) and the "discharges of cannon" remind us of the warning gun about an escaped convict on the Kentish marshes (17; Ch. 2). The language of the novel is tacitly asking us to connect Magwitch's return with the convict's encounter with Pip years before.

There are a number of similar repetitions of phrases, images, and motifs in the novel, which have by now been well scrutinized by critics—yet not quite exhaustively. In Ch. 19 Pip, in his village, is preparing himself for London. He goes to Trabb's shop to purchase a nice suit, when he is confronted with the obnoxious boy. Trabb scolds the boy saying, "*Hold that noise . . . or I'll knock your head off*!" (118; Ch. 19: italics mine). Then, two pages later, after his visits to the hatter's, the bootmaker's, and the hosier's, Pip has a moment of inebriated celebration with Pumblechook. He says, "[Pumblechook] shook hands with me again, and emptied his glass and turned it upside down. I did the same; and if I had *turned myself upside down* before drinking, the wine could not have gone more direct to my head" (120; Ch. 19: italics mine). Now, consider how Pip records the very first words Magwitch utters in the novel: "'*Hold your noise*!' cried a terrible voice, as a man started up from among the graves at the side of the church porch. 'Keep still, you little devil, *or I'll cut your throat*!'" (10; Ch. 1: italics mine). Magwitch then turns Pip upside down, to empty his pockets. The italicized words in Ch. 19 bring to mind an earlier event in Pip's life. By making the connection between these two events, the text is hinting that Pip's upward move is bound to that momentous encounter in his childhood.

Of more importance is what happens in Wopsle's theatrical performances attended by Pip. As regards his *Hamlet*, I merely wish to draw attention to Pip's observation that Wopsle's "greatest trials were in the churchyard" (195; Ch. 31); as Daniel Belden argues, there is a link between this and Pip's own trial in the churchyard at the beginning of the novel (6).[9] My chief concern is the melodramas in which Wopsle performs, where more links of the same kind are found. Although these plays have received virtually no critical attention, they certainly ought not to be neglected. What is to be noted is that here we have an intriguing variation of the device of a play within a play (as in *Hamlet*). Ch. 47 of *Great Expectations* can be compared with Ch. 13 of *The Princess Casamassima*, where Hyacinth Robinson goes to see *The Pearl of Paraguay* (a fictional play concocted by James). Of this episode Adeline R. Tintner comments: "the play within the novel reenacts for our participants [the characters in the novel] a parallel drama which provides an analogy for their own life situation." On Wopsle's stage we find, to borrow from Tintner, a "correlative" of Pip's life (177).

There are two plays, and the second one is concerned with a sorcerer's apprentice. Wopsle is seen manufacturing thunderbolts under a master; he is later referred to as "the Enchanter" (287; Ch. 47).[10] A sorcerer conjures up an association with a witch: in Pip's story, the magical power of transformation is suggested by the name Mag*witch*, and Miss Havisham is at one point described as "like the Witch of the place" (69; Ch. 11). Here Wopsle, using magic, helps young lovers. The girl's father obstructs the way of true love, and assaults the boy in a peculiar fashion; "purposely falling upon the object . . . out of the first-floor window" (287; Ch. 47). The man's attack from above on a young lover curiously resonates with an occurrence in the immediately preceding Ch. 46, where Pip visits Magwitch at Clara Barley's house, which is presided over by an ill-humored father who is in the way of the young lovers. Pip tells us, "I was looking at [Clara] with pleasure and admiration, when suddenly the growl swelled into a roar again, and a frightful bumping noise was heard above, as if a giant with a wooden leg were trying to bore it through the ceiling to come at us" (281; Ch. 46). We must recall that this is the young couple Pip is secretly helping out with Wemmick's help (223-24; Ch. 37), using the same magic as Magwitch has used for him, by setting up great expectations for Herbert, which Pip has cryptically mentioned to Miss Havisham three chapters before (270; Ch. 44).

There is another violent scene on Wopsle's stage. In the ludicrous fight in the first play an "honest little grocer" knocks everybody down from behind, with a "gridiron" (287; Ch. 47).[11] The blow from behind with an iron implement is, as will be revealed six chapters later, what has happened to Mrs Joe; Orlick has attacked her from behind with "a convict's leg-iron" (97; Ch. 16).

Wopsle's first play is a maritime melodrama. People in Portsmouth are seen to celebrate the protagonist's marriage. Portsmouth, we have been told earlier, is the port where Magwitch has secretly landed after escaping from Australia (240; Ch. 39). The association of Wopsle's performance with that part of the story is strengthened when we notice in the second play Wopsle "coming up from the antipodes" (287; Ch. 47). The "antipodes" refers to the trap door of the stage, but we will remember that earlier Wemmick tells Pip, when he explains Jaggers's character: "'Deep,' said Wemmick, 'as Australia.' Pointing with his pen at the office floor, to express that Australia was understood, for the purposes of the figure, to be symmetrically on the opposite spot of the globe" (155; Ch. 24). Thus Wopsle's appearance from the antipodes, the trap door, hints at Magwitch's return from Australia.

In this connection, another point to be noted is the antagonist of the first play, "dark complexioned Swab" (286; Ch. 47). The word "swab" is tricky. The *Oxford English Dictionary* tells us that it is "a naval officer's epaulette," hence "a naval officer," though noting this usage is obscure (I. d); it is also said to be a term of contempt, signifying a swabber, one who uses a mop (II. a). On the issue of whether it means an officer or a sailor, annotators of the novel are divided.[12] I think Dickens means a sailor for two reasons. Firstly, he uses the word several times in his letters, and judging from the usage there the Pilgrim editors are surely right to take it for "a common sailor" (*Letters* 7: 285). Secondly, V. C. Clinton-Baddeley, in his discussion of Wopsle, draws attention to nautical dramas of the period (158), such as *The Pilot* (1825), *Black-Ey'd Susan* (1829), and *My Poll and My Partner Joe* (1835), and tellingly in the last-mentioned play there is a reference to a cook's mate as "the most disagreeable swab in the whole crew" (Booth 111). Tom Paulin, a rare critic who pays serious attention to this part of the novel, takes a different view. He argues: "The Swabs are the ship's officers and the scene shows a touching populist belief that somehow corrupt members of the ruling class can be swept away" (126). His interpretation is presumably based on the phrase, "the Swab family having considerable political influence" (286-87; Ch. 47). It is, however, most likely a comic exaggeration rather than a straightforward statement. Nevertheless, the fact that the swab antagonist is described as if he were from a good family is important. The villain of the piece who is (even as a joke) associated with a good social background; what this suggests is obvious. We will recall the trial scene where, in Magwitch's words, "what a gentleman Compeyson looked" (262; Ch. 42). We must also remember—and this is crucial—Compeyson is in the theatre, sitting right behind Pip. Ultimately, whether the swab is a sailor or an officer, what is of indubitable significance is that the protagonist and the antagonist in the play are shipmates, just as Magwitch and Compeyson have been "shipmates" in the hulks.

Thus, the language of the text would lead the reader to imagine Compeyson seated in the theatre, understanding the play's allusions to the swab and to Magwitch's return from the antipodes. Perhaps the villain gets the reference to Clara's father also, as he has been closely watching Magwitch. He may even be aware of Orlick's attack on Mrs Joe, as it is conceivable that Orlick has bragged about it to him. Somehow Compeyson knows everything, while Pip knows neither what is taking place on the stage nor that the man is right behind him.

Michael Slater considers *Great Expectations* a "highly personal" novel in that there is a significant similarity between Dickens and Pip; "a certain shrinking sensitiveness" bred in the novelist in the old blacking factory days (Slater, *Dickens* 492-93).[13] They are both fearful lest the "taint of prison" (202; Ch. 32) should be known. In addition to this innermost anxiety, at the time of writing this novel, Dickens had another skeleton he was desperate to keep in the closet. The play within the novel in Ch. 47 seems to highlight the question of "knowing" with which the novel is fraught, reflecting the novelist's own apprehension about people "knowing" his secret relationship with Ellen Ternan. This scene, it should be recalled, is preceded by Pip's agitation (Ch. 45) as a consequence of Wemmick's warning, which turns out to be about his house being watched by Compeyson.[14] Bearing these points in mind, one might profitably turn to Ackroyd's biography, where he notes Dickens's selfish preoccupation with his own concerns and feelings, which surfaced at the period of the novelist's separation from his wife, triggered by his involvement with Ternan. Ackroyd observes that "the reverse side of the self-concern is paranoia: everyone is watching me, everyone is talking about me" (877). Surely the paranoia would have generated the constant fear of exposure in the novelist's mind—what if everyone knows?—which sometimes turned into the apprehension that they must know. Anxiety of this kind, I suggest, led Dickens to create the scene in which Pip imagines Estella's impossible intuition. There Dickens was at one with Pip, so involved in the character's subjective reaction that he failed to give due deliberation to what is objectively happening in the dramatic situation. The very same anxiety led the novelist to put various "knowings" in the text, with the result that he was not aware they were too many to sort out: Compeyson knows everything, Joe knows this, Magwitch knows that, Estella knows—what?

(Originally a lecture delivered at the London Branch of the International Dickens Fellowship, 2014; first published in *Dickens Studies Annual*, 2017)

References

Ackroyd, Peter. *Dickens*. London: Minerva, 1991.

Axton, William F. *Circle of Fire*. Lexington: U of Kentucky P, 1966.

Belden, Daniel. "Dickens's *Great Expectations*, XXXI." *The Explicator* 35 (1977): 6-7.

Booth, Michael. *Hiss the Villain: Six American and English Melodramas*. New York: Benjamin Blom, 1964.

Clinton-Baddeley, V. C. "Wopsle." *The Dickensian* 57 (1961): 150-59.

Darby, Margaret Flanders. "Listening to Estella." *Dickens Quarterly* 16 (1999): 215-29.

Dickens, Charles. *Great Expectations*. Ed. Margaret Cardwell. Oxford: Oxford UP. 1994.

Dickens, Charles. *Great Expectations*. Ed. Charlotte Mitchell. London: Penguin, 1996.

Dickens, Charles. *Great Expectations*. Ed. Graham Law and Adrian J. Pinnington. Peterborough, Ontario: Broadview, 1998.

Dickens, Charles. *Great Expectations*. Ed. Edgar Rosenberg. New York: Norton, 1999.

Dickens, Charles. *The Letters of Charles Dickens*. Pilgrim Ed. vol. 7, *1853-1855*. Ed. Graham Storey, Kathleen Tillotson, and Angus Easson. Oxford: Clarendon, 1993.

Dickens, Charles. *The Letters of Charles Dickens*. Pilgrim ed. vol. 10, *1862-1864*. Ed. Graham Storey. Oxford: Clarendon, 1998.

French, A. L. "Beating and Cringing: *Great Expectations*." *Essays in Criticism* 24 (1974): 147-68.

Garnett, Robert G. "The Good and the Unruly in *Great Expectations*—and Estella." *Dickens Quarterly* 16 (1999): 24-41.

Guiliano, Edward and Philip Collins. *The Annotated Dickens*. 2 vols. New York: Clarkson N. Potter, 1986.

Kingsmill, Hugh. *The Sentimental Journey*. London: Wishart, 1934.

Marcus, Sharon. *Between Women*. Princeton: Princeton UP, 2007.

Paroissien, David. *The Companion to* Great Expectations. Mountfield: Helm Information, 2000.

Paulin, Tom. *Minotaur: Poetry and the Nation State*. Cambridge: Harvard UP, 1992.

Pionke, Albert D. "Degrees of Secrecy in Dickens's Historical Fiction." *Dickens Studies Annual* 38 (2007): 35-53.

Slater, Michael. *Charles Dickens*. New Haven: Yale UP, 2009.

Slater, Michael. *Dickens and Women*. London: Dent, 1983.

Sutherland, John. *Who Betrays Elizabeth Bennet?* Oxford: Oxford UP, 1999.

Tintner, Adeline R. "Henry James's *Hamlets*: 'A Free Rearrangement'." *Colby Library Quarterly* 18 (1982): 168-82.

Tomalin, Claire. *Charles Dickens*. London: Penguin, 2011.

Tomalin, Claire. *The Invisible Woman*. London: Penguin, 1991.

Welsh, Alexander. *Hamlet in His Modern Guises*. Princeton: Princeton UP, 2001.

Wilson, Edmund. *The Wound and the Bow*. 1941; Athens: Ohio UP, 1997.

NOTES

1 All page references to *Great Expectation* are to Edgar Rosenberg's Norton edition.

2 We have no clue as to how much the novelist thought about these things, for he did not compose working notes for *Great Expectations*, except for a few memoranda about the ages of the main characters, the tide, and the chief events in Chapters 54 through 58. See the Norton edition (480-87).

3 This is very much the case with the dénouement of *Martin Chuzzlewit*; see Ch. 4 of this book.

4 Another example may be found at the beginning of Ch. 58, where Pip comes back to his old town: "The tidings of my high fortunes having had a heavy fall had got down to my native place and its neighborhood before

I got there" (350; Ch. 58). It is, however, not unlikely that the "tidings" have been printed in newspapers. For example, the *Hampshire Telegraph and Sussex Chronicle*, a nineteenth-century paper published in Portsmouth, had a section titled "London" in which even fairly minor occurrences in the metropolis were reported.

5 Wilson's critical procedure of seeing Ellen Ternan in Estela, Bella Wilfer, and Helena Landless was, in fact, preceded by Hugh Kingsmill (195-97). Wilson is silent about his indebtedness, though speaking critically of Kingsmill (3).

6 Michael Slater is a notable exception. He submits, rather, that the creation of Estella has more to do with the memory of his former love, Maria Beadnell, who re-surfaced in his life shortly before (Slater, *Dickens* 492-93).

7 This is when Ellen Ternan became "invisible" (Tomalin, *Invisible* 128).

8 Focusing on Dickens's fictional strategies for distinguishing between acceptable and unacceptable forms of secrecy, Albert D. Pionke has examined *Great Expectations* in comparison with *A Tale of Two Cities*. He rightly points out the significant difference arising from the former's first-person narration, which, as I see it, greatly contributes to the urgency the reader feels, every secret being linked to Pip.

9 For significant discussions of Wopsle's *Hamlet* see Axton (110-36), French, and Welsh (102-39).

10 It is also to be recalled that Joe's original name was George Thunder, which, as David Paroissien points out, "connects him with the Roman Vulcan, the god of the forge, guardian of the fire, and manufacturer of thunderbolts" (35).

11 Joe mentions "gridiron" in discussing, with Pip, a possible present to Miss Havisham (90, Ch. 15).

12 Charlotte Mitchell notes that the swab means "a low seaman" (505); Graham Law and Adrian J. Pinnington, "sailor" (407); Margaret Cardwell, "sailor responsible for cleaning the decks" (502); Edward Guiliano and Philip Collins, "a sailor of low rank" (vol. 2, 1057); Edgar Rosenberg,"an abusive term for naval officer or sailor" (286); David Paroissien, "an officer" (362).

13 The phrase, "a certain shrinking sensitiveness," appears in Dickens's letter to John Forster (*Letters* 10: 98).

14 Pip, describing the "staringly wide-awake pattern on the walls" of the room in the Hummums, speaks of "this foolish Argus" (273-74; Ch. 45). It is patently a joke, but the reference to the ever-watchful creature reflects his anxiety, nevertheless.

Ch. 8 Translating *Great Expectations* into Japanese

In Japanese book publishing today there is a palpable interest in updated translations of literary classics, the "new" *Brothers Karamazov* making a best-seller list a few years ago. An offspring of this trend is my translation of *Great Expectations* (Tokyo: Kawade Shobo Shinsha, 2011), which, as you can see from the photographs below, comes out in two volumes. The cover of the Volume Two shows Pip "sadder and wiser."

This novel has been rendered into Japanese before. I am aware of a couple of versions published right after World War II; they are now rather obsolete, particularly in the dialogue. There is also one that appeared earlier this year by Professor Yoko Tanabe, who has heroically translated all Dickens novels, *Great Expectations* being the last to come out. In Japan it has always been called *Ooinaru Isan* (I have followed this well-established tradition), which signifies "great legacy." It is not possible in Japanese to express the meanings of "great hope" and "expected great fortune" in one phrase; the very title is already a problem!

* * * * *

Let me begin the account of my labors by quoting the beginning of *Great Expectations*:

My father's family name being Pirrip, and my christian name

> Philip, my infant tongue could make of both names nothing longer or more explicit than Pip. So, I called myself Pip, and came to be called Pip.

Then let us see how it looks in French, as Sylvère Monod renders it (1959):

> Comme le nom de famille de mon père était Pirrip et mon prénom Philippe, ma langue, dans ma petite enfance, ne sut rien articuler de plus long ni de plus explicite, pour l'un et l'autre de ces noms, que Pip. C'est donc sous le nom de Pip que je me désignai, et sous le nom de Pip que je vins à être désigné.

For my Japanese translation, take a look at the photograph below:

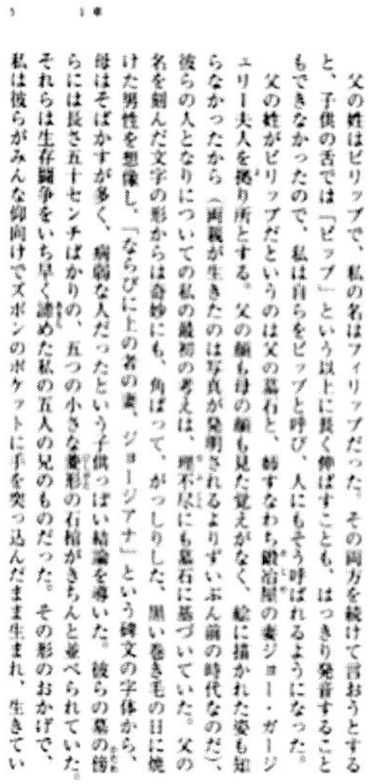

1章

父の姓はピリップで、私の名はフィリップだった。その両方を続けて言おうとすると、子供の舌では「ピップ」という以上に長く伸ばすことも、はっきり発音することもできなかったので、私は自らをピップと呼び、人にもそう呼ばれるようになった。

父の姓がピリップだというのは父の墓石と、姉すなわち鍛冶屋の妻ジョー・ガージェリー夫人を拠り所とする。父の顔も母の顔も見た覚えがなく、絵に描かれた姿も知らなかったから（両親が生きたのは写真が発明されるよりずいぶん前の時代なのだ）、彼らの人となりについての私の最初の考えは、理不尽にも墓石に基づいていた。父の名を刻んだ文字の形からは奇妙にも、角ばって、がっしりした、黒い巻き毛の日に焼けた男性を想像し、「ならびに上の者の妻、ジョージアナ」という碑文の字体から、母はそばかすが多く、病弱な人だったという子供っぽい結論を導いた。彼らの墓の傍らには長さ五十センチばかりの、五つの小さな菱形の石棺がきちんと並べられていた。それらは生存闘争をいち早く諦めた私の五人の兄のものだった。その形のおかげで、私は彼らがみんな仰向けでズボンのポケットに手を突っ込んだまま生まれ、生きてい

5　1章

It will be immediately apparent that, while there are noticeable similarities between English and French, Japanese is poles apart. The writing system is radically different: Roman letters are not employed, and it runs vertically and moves from right to left, mixing Chinese characters with our own syllabary. The grammar too is very different: among other things, the syntactic disparity that I most acutely feel as translator is the lack of the relative pronoun in Japanese. As a result, the structure of the translated sentence sometimes markedly diverges from the original; one long winding sentence may very well be divided into two or three terse sentences. Such differences of course lead to difficulties.

In general, puns are anathema to the translator. When the linguistic gulf is as wide as that between English and Japanese, the problem becomes troublesome to an inordinate degree. Where Joe says Mrs Joe is "given to government" and Pip wonders if "Joe had divorced her in favor of the Lords of the Admiralty," I have managed this by the use of homonyms, both pronounced *kanri*: one signifying "to govern," the other "a civil servant." This kind of breakthrough is, I stress, not the rule. Puns tend to evaporate in the process of translation; even here, I cannot do justice to the "given to."

Also hard to convey is the oddity of Joe's language. Generally I employ a version of stage rustic speech sprinkled with various irregularities, but faced with such brilliant specimens as his "architectooralooral" or "purple leptic fit," I feel I must somehow come up with equally sparkling expressions. Alas, it is nearly impossible. All I could do about the former was to lengthen one of the vowels of the Japanese word for a "building" (not very inspired, I admit) and as to the latter, to exploit the similarity of the sound of *hossa* ("fit") and *tossa* ("sudden") and hope for the best.

In addition to these obvious deep waters, difficulties may arise from very simple words: "heart," for example. In English this word can mean both the physical internal organ and the spiritual wellspring of love, so Miss Havisham can lay her hand on her breast and say there is a broken heart underneath, whereby reminding Pip of the young man who wanted to take out his heart and liver. In Japanese, however, we have two separate words to denote these matters. Consequently in my translation Miss Havisham talks about the fountain of love and Pip thinks of the biological organ. Here I have to perform a little cosmetic operation in order to make the conversation run smoothly.

Or consider the word "brother." In many European languages it could mean an older brother or a younger brother, but we have different words for each (in Chinese and Korean, too, I believe). We know Pip is the youngest of the sons, so when he refers to his five "brothers" I can translate it using the word for "older brothers," but when there is no indication (as in the case of Sally and Sampson Brass, for example) I simply must decide the relative ages of the siblings.

Indeed, age is an important factor in Japanese conversation: when dealing with someone senior, one is supposed to use polite expressions. But the system of politeness is so complicated that I am sometimes confused myself. It is not a simple matter of adding "sir" or "madam" at the end of each sentence; one has to choose the proper second person pronoun (from among various alternatives) and select a correspondingly appropriate verb form, judging the levels of politeness, respect, and familiarity that are involved in each case. Therefore in my translation Pip always uses polite language to Miss Havisham. With Wemmick, however, his politeness is modified, because their relationship is on a more familiar footing. On meeting him at Barnard's Inn, Pip speaks politely to Herbert at the start (Ch. 21), but once the latter proposes conducting the conversation on a first-name basis (Ch. 22) the language becomes informal—Pip now uses a different form of "you." The second person pronoun in Japanese is a tricky business. In conversation it is possible to omit it or use a substitute (we can say—supposing that I am talking to Joe—"What does Joe think?" instead of "What do you think, Joe?"). However, in written dialogue, complete omission may not be possible, and the simple substitution can look clumsy if one encounters half a dozen Joes in as many lines. This is a real problem for me, because I simply cannot imagine what kind of "you" Pip would use when addressing Joe! He is Pip's intimate friend, an equal, and also a senior person who ought to be respected. He is a gentle Christian man, I know, but he has given me a hard time.

I have been talking about the complications arising from the difference in the language systems. It would seem that translation between closely-related tongues, say, French and English, is much easier. But then, that may involve problems of a subtler kind. Monod, in the "Introduction" to his translation, expresses despair concerning the word "gentleman," noting how hard it is to find a French equivalent. He says he has employed various phrases for it—"monsieur" (most frequently), "gentilhomme," "home du monde," "honnête homme," "homme de bien" and only as the last resort, "gentleman," with a sense of defeat. I have, however, cheerfully rendered it as "gentleman," for we have imported that word, ours being a language that is very friendly towards foreign phrases, and it is already part of the Japanese (pronounced *jentoruman*, though).

* * * * *

In his characteristically shrewd review of the recent English translation of *Madame Bovary* (*London Review of Books*, 18 November 2010), Julian Barnes observes, employing a term in wine tasting, that "there is similar mouthfeel about translation." He goes on to say: "Its general development over the last century and more has been away from smoothness and towards authenticity, away from a re-organising interpretativeness which aims for the flow of English prose, towards a close-reading fidelity—enjoy those tannins!—which seeks to echo the original language." As a translator I have greedily aimed for both "smoothness" and "authenticity." I want my translation to be readable and faithful to Dickens at the same time. Of course that is an ideal, and in reality I have frequently to sacrifice one or the other.

When Pip speaks of "a comparatively pastureless" character of Herbert's room in Barnard's Inn, if I made a literal translation the Japanese sentence would be merely bizarre. Barnes judiciously cautions against this kind of "fidelity leading to perversity." Therefore, in this instance, I have tried to be faithful to the playful spirit of Dickens and concoct an amusing phrase that has a similarly affected flavor, by employing a quaint Chinese expression (our equivalent of Latinate phrase) which indicates the lack of pasture-like charm. For a novelist like Dickens, the translator repeatedly asks himself where fidelity ends and perversity begins.

In a few places I have taken liberties simply for the sake of readability. An interested reader might take another look at the photograph of the first page of my translation. There the first three lines of text (from the right) correspond to the Dickens passage I have quoted above. The little circles are our full stops, so you can see there are two sentences, and that the first sentence is shorter than the second, which is not the case with the original. I have rendered it thus, in the hope that it will, with a livelier rhythm, facilitate the reader's entry into the world of the novel.

So, all in all, have I succeeded in reproducing the Dickensian "mouthfeel"? Of course I am not the best judge, but I am vain enough to believe that my performance is at least better than Mr Wopsle's Hamlet—no orange-peel thrown at me so far.

(First published in *The Dickensian*, 2011)

Ch. 9 Chesterton's *Charles Dickens*

A number of Dickensians still consider Chesterton the best of all Dickens critics.[1] There have been countless books on Dickens, and much has been said since Chesterton's day that he did not say. But what he said brings the genius of the novelist into clear focus in a way no one can imitate. Commenting on Dickens's astonishingly fecund imagination he observes that any one of us might possibly have created a Guppy but "the effort would certainly have exhausted us; we should be ever afterwards wheeled about in a bath-chair at Bournemouth" (123).[2] Would that literary criticism were always such fun. Chesterton's remark—"all criticism tends too much to become criticism of criticism" (122)—seems particularly apt now when articles in "higher" journals very often simply refer to each other in a closed circuit. The reason for such tendencies, according to him, is that "criticism of creation is so very staggering a thing." "Real primary creation," he goes on, "calls forth not criticism, not appreciation, but a kind of incoherent gratitude" (122). To be sure, the best way of describing this book is to call it Chesterton's expression of gratitude to the staggering phenomenon that is Dickens. Fortunately, Chesterton being Chesterton, the result is far from incoherent.

Clearly, one of his chief strengths as critic is a wit that matches Dickens's own. The book is full of memorable expressions. To give a few examples:

> [Dickens's] art is like life, because, like life, it cares for nothing outside itself, and goes on its way rejoicing. Both produce monsters with a kind of carelessness, like enormous by-products; life producing the rhinoceros, and art Mr. Bunsby. (10)
>
> If Dickens learnt to whitewash the universe, it was in a blacking factory that he learnt it. (21)
>
> [Cruikshank's illustration] does not look merely like a picture of Fagin; it looks like a picture by Fagin. (57)
>
> Other people's lives may easily be human documents. But a man's own life is always a melodrama. (101)
>
> We know Toots is not clever; but we are not inclined to quarrel with Toots because he is not clever. We are more likely to quarrel with cleverness because it is not Toots. (131)

I could keep on quoting for pages, but that would be the laziest way of composing an introduction. Therefore, instead of doing so, I shall provide, first, a brief survey of Chesterton's writing career up until the publication of this book in 1906. While taking a look at several things he had written, we shall pick up certain threads that can be recognized in the study of Dickens and identify his continuing concerns. Then, after reviewing how Dickens's reputation stood around the beginning of the twentieth century, we shall examine some salient points of this book.

*

After two books of poetry, Chesterton published *The Defendant* (1901) and *Twelve Types* (1902), collections of miscellaneous essays that had already appeared in the *Speaker* and the *Daily News* (Dickens was the first editor of this paper, as mentioned on p. 91). Of the former book Sir Arthur Quiller-Couch remarked in his review: "The most ordinary occurrences in the world are marvelous in his eyes, and his optimism proceeds from a blessed contentment with a planet which provides so many daily miracles"[3]—a point we shall come back to later. Chesterton's dazzling journalism soon attracted the attention of, among others, George Bernard Shaw and Max Beerbohm, the famous caricaturist and drama critic. The former, after reading Chesterton's essay on Scott wrote to him asking who he was, "as he was evidently a new star in literature"[4]; the latter wrote, "Dear Mr Chesterton, I have seldom wished to meet anyone in particular: but you I should very much like to meet."[5]

Then, Chesterton was asked to write *Robert Browning* (1903), which was a great coup for a relative newcomer, for it was part of the prestigious "English Men of Letters" series, the line-up of contracted authors including Trollope on Thackeray, George Saintsbury on Dryden, Sir Leslie Stephen on George Eliot, and Henry James on Hawthorne (the Dickens volume was done by Adolphus Ward). Although the publishers were upset by the many misquotations in the manuscript they were obliged to correct—"I quote from memory both by temper and on principle. That is what literature is for; it ought to be part of a man," Chesterton later said[6]—the book turned out to be a great success. Chesterton emphasized Browning's optimism and the grotesque aspect of his art, prompting the poet Alfred Noyes to observe in his perceptive review: "It is the element of strangeness in familiar things, rather than that of beauty, that is most potent to bring Mr Chesterton into the heart of the world's mystery."[7]

Next came his first novel, a fantasy set in the future, *The Napoleon of Notting Hill* (1904). It begins in London of 1984 (any connection between George Orwell's book and Chesterton's is most probably coincidental), where the king is chosen, by lottery, from civil servants. By this system the crown comes to rest on a whimsical joker, Auberon Quin (partly modeled on Beerbohm), who orders the boroughs to build walls, raise militia, and dress the troops in medieval costumes. Adam Wayne, the provost of Notting Hill, takes this jest seriously and eagerly obeys the decree. When a plan to build a highway cutting through Notting Hill is proposed, Wayne opposes this by defending the area with his militia, and leads them to victory in the subsequent ferocious war. What lies behind the novel is the Boer War. Chesterton hated Joseph Chamberlain and his expanding imperialism (there is an ironic reference to him on p. 64 of *Dickens*). Chesterton was for the Boers and Little England—but he was not a pacifist, as can be gathered from the plot development outlined above (the reader may recall the martial tone of his oft-anthologized poem, "Lepanto"). *The Napoleon of Notting Hill* strongly reflects the author's idealization of the Middle Ages. In *Dickens* he writes: "Dickens had in his buffoonery and bravery the spirit of the Middle Ages" (81); he mentions Napoleon in connection with the idea of "the common man," one of his key notions (7).

Heretics (1905) is a gathering of polemical pieces. His targets are what he regards as modernity. He attacks the realistic literature of the late nineteenth century for its pessimism, and the idea of the Superman by Shaw who "cannot understand that the thing which is valuable and lovable in our eyes is man—the old beer-drinking, creed-making, fighting, failing, sensual, respectable man" (Ch. 4). H. G. Wells is also deemed guilty of a similar sort of hero-worship (Ch. 5). Chesterton argues that "Democracy is not founded on pity for the common man; democracy is founded on reverence for the common man" (Ch. 19), and in this context Dickens figures as a positive presence:

> All this means one thing, and one thing only. It means that the living and invigorating ideal of England must be looked for in the masses; it must be looked for where Dickens found it—Dickens among whose glories it was to be a humorist, to be a sentimentalist, to be an optimist, to be a poor man, to be an

> Englishman, but the greatest of whose glories was that he saw all mankind in its amazing and tropical luxuriance, and did not even notice the aristocracy; Dickens, the greatest of whose glories was that he could not describe a gentleman. (Ch. 15) [On this last point see (119).]

In the same year, Chesterton took objection to Shaw's view of Shakespeare, once more making a reference to Dickens (the *Daily News*, 15 April 1905):

> The moderns . . . are not used to seeing life exaggerated in the direction of life. That is why the moderns do not like Dickens. That is why Mr Bernard Shaw does not like Shakespeare. . . .
>
> In these undemocratic days we cannot grasp the possibility of the great man enjoying the same things as the ordinary man. Shakespeare enjoyed the same romance as the ordinary man, just as he enjoyed the same beer. . . . Mr Shaw may be quite as extraordinary a man as Shakespeare; but he is only an extraordinary man. Shakespeare, like all the heroes, was an extraordinary man and an ordinary man, too.

As we shall see later, this notion of the democracy in which the great man enjoys the same thing as the ordinary man reappears in his book on Dickens as an important theme (the very phrase, "to exaggerate life in the direction of life," appears on p. 46). In the meantime, Chesterton was thus in fair way of establishing his name as an upcoming man of letters: he was getting bigger. Around this time he was photographed by the later-to-become-famous Alvin Langdon Coburn. On this photo Shaw comments with an apt Dickensian quotation: Chesterton is "the young Man Mountain, a large abounding gigantically cherubic person who is not only large in body and mind beyond all decency, but seems to be growing larger as you look at him—'swellin' wisibly,' as Tony Weller puts it."[8]

*

In 1906 Dickens's reputation was in the doldrums, as a noted journalist-critic, R. Brimley Johnson (who was the publisher of Chesterton's *The Defendant*), observed:

> It can scarcely be questioned . . . that Charles Dickens has suffered more than any other eminent English writer from the arrogance of aesthetic criticism. His work has not merely been complacently dismissed as "bad art"; it has been cited again and again as a conspicuous example of degraded popular taste.[9]

Chesterton shares this view. "The disadvantage under which Dickens has fallen . . . is very plain," he says (10), and points out the rejections of the novelist by aesthetes, and by realists. But it must be remembered that he is talking about professional writers and readers. The case of the common reader is different. Dickens was always popular and constantly read, as far as we can judge from the sales figures of his books. It was "sophisticated readers" who tended to look down on Dickens. This condescending attitude was there already during the novelist's lifetime, and it became stronger after his death in 1870. The representative view of this trend was expressed by George Henry Lewes, the partner of George Eliot, in "Dickens in Relation to Criticism" (1872). His is very much the response of a "realist," he has a very strict standard of probability and finds Dickens's characters "merely masks . . . caricatures and distortions of human nature." In his concluding paragraph he writes:

> For the reader of cultivated taste there is little in his works beyond the stirring of their emotions—but what a large exception! We do not turn over the pages in search of thought, delicate psychological observation, grace of style, charm of composition; but we enjoy them like children at a play, laughing and crying at the images which pass before us.

Although Lewes chastises previous critics for having overlooked and undervalued "the great qualities which distinguished [Dickens]," his heart is clearly with the "reader of cultivated taste." His intellectual superiority shows itself where he recollects "the somewhat disturbing effect" produced by the sight of the books on Dickens's shelves when he visited the novelist soon after the completion of *Pickwick Papers*. "Compared with that of Fielding or Thackeray, his was merely an *animal* intelligence," Lewes complacently opined.

Another notable instance of this kind of condescension is the entry for Dickens in *The Dictionary of National Biography* (1888), which was written by the editor himself, Sir Leslie Stephen (the father of Virginia

Woolf). He declared:

> If literary fame could safely be measured by popularity with the half-educated, Dickens must claim the highest position among English novelists. It is said . . . that 4,239,000 volumes of his works [have] been sold in England in the twelve years after his death. The criticism of more severe critics chiefly consists in the assertion that his merits are such as suit the half-educated. They admit his fun to be irresistible; his pathos, they say, though it shows boundless vivacity, implies little real depth or tenderness of feeling; and his amazing powers of observation were out of proportion to his powers of reflection.

Here, and also where he points out Dickens's "exuberant animal spirits," Stephen's judgment echoes Lewes's, and it is not difficult to locate their real standing point, which is obviously not with "the half-educated." The intellectual novelist of this period whom they admired was George Meredith. George Eliot was also highly regarded for her portrayal of credible characters, psychological analysis, and the scope of her cultural reference. It was in this atmosphere that Chesterton's book made its appearance.

*

Chesterton's, however, was not a lone crusade. There were some voices raised for Dickens around the turn of the century, of which the most significant was that of George Gissing. His *Charles Dickens* (1898), a literary study with chapters like "Art, Veracity, and Moral Purpose," "Characterization," "Style" and so forth, is a fine book and, although not as exciting as Chesterton's, has a lot of sensible things to say. At the core of his interpretation is this notion: "So great a change has come over the theory and practice of fiction in the England of our times that we must needs treat of Dickens as, in many respects, antiquated." Himself a realistic novelist, Gissing calls Dickens's art idealism, as distinct from his own. His praise of Dickens, given this premise, is inevitably accompanied by qualifications. His own artistic inclinations lead him to value Dickens when he comes close to his standard of probability, or truthfulness. Thus he does not like Dickens's exaggeration and speaks very highly of the characterization of Dr

Marigold and George Silverman, little-known protagonists of his minor fiction. He is, however, not unaware, I suspect, that this is not really a proper response to Dickens, for in the end he confesses: "But there can be drawn only a misleading, futile distinction between novels realistic and idealistic. It is merely a question of degree and of the author's temperament."

To argue for Dickens was right, but Gissing was doing it the wrong way—that is how Chesterton felt. His book was very much conceived in opposition to Gissing. Sometimes he is blatant, as when he says Gissing does not understand the spirit of the age (5), or that *Little Dorrit* "bores Dickensians and especially pleases George Gissing" (116). While Gissing points out that "Dickens . . . seldom develops character through circumstance," Chesterton contends: "It was not the aim of Dickens to show the effect of time and circumstance upon a character; it was not even his aim to show the effect of a character on time and circumstance." For him Dickens was a mythologist rather than a novelist: "He did not always manage to make his characters men, but he always managed, at the least, to make them gods" (44). When he criticizes the condescending attitude of intellectuals towards Dickens, Chesterton includes Gissing among them. To be just, however, Gissing never says, as Chesterton claims he did, that Dickens "never made a working man, a poor man, specifically and highly intellectual" (128). Also, the point Chesterton raises in opposition to him—"It is not only true that Dickens seldom made a poor character what we call intellectual; it is also true that he seldom made any character what we call intellectual" (128)—is in fact made by Gissing himself.[10] The objection to Gissing's pessimism, too, is presumably a product of his impressions gained from Gissing's novels, for there is hardly anything in his study of Dickens that reflects this so-called pessimism. Chesterton's counterattack, therefore, is not quite accurate and a trifle prejudiced.

*

Chesterton's *Charles Dickens* is a "professedly personal judgment" (106). He has no intention of offering a well-balanced, objective assessment. He likes Dickens's early comic novels, particularly *Pickwick Papers*, which is "something nobler than a novel" (41). (His emphasis on the novelist's optimism and jolly humor has led to a quip that his is "the stout man's Dickens."[11]) For him Dickens is not a realist;

realists are merely those who wave "their documents" (10) like the mad Miss Flite. He glorifies Dickens's exaggeration, for "Exaggeration is the definition of art" (11). Chesterton's view is character-oriented: "Dickens's work is not to be reckoned in novels, but is to be reckoned always by characters" (41). Of Mrs Nickleby he says: "It is exquisitely characteristic of Dickens that the truly great achievement of the story is the person who delays the story" (58). Great Dickens characters are great fools; by being "taken in" they can "see the inside of everything" (50). They are impossible characters who do not change, so it is bad news when psychology enters—Jane Austen or George Eliot can do that sort of thing!

He was not free from making slips. For example, when he claims that Dickens originally wished the *Daily News* to be called the *Cricket* (91), he is confusing the newspaper with a weekly periodical Dickens was planning at that time. "His shortest postcard is often as good as his ablest novel," he says (109), but postcards did not come into use until after the novelist's death. These slips remain uncorrected, but he was made to put a few things to rights in later reprints. Shaw alerted him to a mistake about Dickens's announcement of his separation from his wife; Chesterton originally wrote it appeared in *Punch* instead of *Household Words*. As regards the sisters of Dickens's wife, Chesterton had written "he fell in love with all them" and that he "got hold of the wrong sister." Having read this, Dickens's daughter Kate got in touch with him and, whilst praising the book profusely, indicated that at the time of her mother's marriage her sisters were fifteen and under, the youngest a mere three. Chesterton was mortified, offered his apology in person, and changed the former sentence into "he fell in love with the chance of love" (34) and excised the latter.

His argument and the way he advances it are also not without faults. As Orwell pointed out, he presents Dickens as the spokesman of the poor "without showing much awareness of who 'the poor' really are."[12] Loving as he does to push back Dickens into the early nineteenth century, Chesterton does not fully realize "the impact of external changes on [Dickens's] work."[13] He is prone to make sweeping generalizations. His style, riddled with paradoxes and antitheses, can be irritating. "There is plenty to carp at in this man if you are inclined to carp" (13), Chesterton says of Dickens, and the same might be said of himself.

Nevertheless, as Dickens remained great for Chesterton, Chesterton remains great for us. There are more than enough compensations for his biases and shortcomings. We have touched on his wit. Consider his remark when noting that in Dickens the atmosphere is more important than the story: "The secrecy is sensational; the secret is tame" (85), or on Dickens's characterization: "he could only make his characters probable if he was allowed to make them impossible. . . . He was always most accurate when he was most fantastic (94). These observations are not merely witty, but shrewd enough to reveal some essential truth about the novelist. Besides, there is the remarkable asset of Chesterton's sympathetic understanding of Dickens, stemming, importantly, from the sense of wonder both writers find in childhood which they both believe must be treasured in adult life. In the autobiographical "A Child's Dream of a Star" Dickens writes of a boy and his sister: "These two used to wonder all day long. They wondered at the beauty of flowers; they wondered at the height and blueness of the sky; they wondered at the depth of the bright water; they wondered at the goodness and power of GOD who made the lovely world." He enthuses over the magic of *The Arabian Nights*, which he read as a child: "Oh, now all common things become uncommon and enchanted to me. All lamps are wonderful; all rings are talismans. Common flower-pots are full of treasure . . ." ("A Christmas Tree"). His attraction to "the romantic side of familiar things" (Preface to *Bleak House*) is obviously an extension of this sense of wonder. Chesterton, on his side, remarks in his *Autobiography*: "What was wonderful about childhood is that anything in it was a wonder." In *Orthodoxy* he says, "Ordinary things are more valuable than extraordinary; nay they are more extraordinary," and then speaks, in relation to the "elementary wonder" from which "all the fire of the fairy tales is derived," of "a certain way of looking at life, which was created in me by the fairy tales" (Ch. 4). It is natural, then, that for Chesterton the "last and deepest lesson of Dickens" is: "It is in our own daily life that we are to look for the portents and the prodigies" (132).

Chesterton's sympathetic understanding is most palpably felt in his perceptive remark on Dickens's days of drudgery, in which he locates the source of the novelist's creative imagination: "the whole secret of his after-writings is sealed up in those silent years of which no written word remains" (25). When he adds that "Those years may have given him many moral and mental wounds" (26), he seems to anticipate Edmund Wilson's book *The Wound and the Bow* (1941), in which, presenting the thesis that genius and some psychological wound are closely linked, the

American critic famously argued that Dickens's greatest art ultimately derived from the trauma of the blacking factory experience. Compare this with Somerset Maugham's view: "For my part, I do not believe that the experience caused him anything like the suffering that in after years, when he was famous and respectable, a social as well as a public figure, he persuaded himself that it had; and I believe even less that, as biographers and critics have thought, it had a decisive effect on his life and work."[14] It is fair to say that modern critics tend to side with Chesterton—"his sense of hopelessness was very genuine"; "a lost child can suffer like a lost soul" (19)—and Wilson, rather than Maugham.

However, while Wilson argues that this experience planted in the boy a deep resentment against society, Chesterton maintains that Dickens was given "the key of the street" (24):

> Herein is the whole secret of that eerie realism with which Dickens could always vitalise some dark or dull corner of London. There are details in the Dickens descriptions—a window, or a railing, or the keyhole of a door—which he endows with demoniac life. The things seem more actual than things really are. Indeed, that degree of realism does not exist in reality; it is the unbearable realism of a dream. (24-25)

Chesterton then alludes to the MOOR EEFFOC experience (the twelve-year-old Dickens reading the sign of the coffee room backwards) as "a perfect instance of how these nightmare minutiae grew upon him," adding that it illustrates the principle that "the most fantastic thing of all is often the precise fact" (25). His examples of the "demoniac life" in ordinary things—"the date on the door danced over Mr. Grewgious's, the knocker grinned at Mr. Scrooge, the Roman on the ceiling pointed down at Mr. Tulkinghorn, the elderly armchair leered at Tom Smart"—are not particularly nightmarish, but there is a terrifying instance of it in the view from the roof of Mrs Todgers's boardinghouse in Ch. 9 of *Martin Chuzzlewit*, where "the revolving chimney-pots on one great stack of buildings seemed to be turning gravely to each other every now and then, and whispering the result of their separate observation of what was going on below." The observer here is dominated by the things around him:

> Yet even while the looker-on felt angry with himself for this, and

> wondered how it was, the tumult swelled into a roar; the hosts of objects seemed to thicken and expand a hundredfold, and after gazing round him, quite scared, he turned into Todgers's again, much more rapidly than he came out; and ten to one he told M. Todgers afterwards that if he hadn't done so, he would certainly have come into the street by the shortest cut; that is to say, head-foremost.

Chesterton does not mention this passage, but he seems to describe its essence in his study of Browning, in whose works he perceives a similar animism (interestingly Jorge Luis Borges detects Chesterton's leaning "towards the nightmarish" and relates it to his fascination with "two great gothic craftsmen, Browning and Dickens"[15]):

> Now this sense of the terrible importance of detail was a sense which may be said to have possessed Browning in the emphatic manner of a demoniac possession. Sane as he was, this one feeling might have driven him to a condition not far from madness. Any room that he was sitting in glared at him with innumerable eyes and mouths gaping with a story. There was sometimes no background and no middle distance in his mind. A human face and the pattern on the wall behind it came forward with equally aggressive clearness. It may be repeated, that if ever he who had the strongest head in the world had gone mad, it would have been through this turbulent democracy of things. (Ch. 7)

This is terrifying indeed, and what particularly strikes us in this nightmare is Chesterton's phrase, the "democracy of things."

As noted earlier, democracy is a key concept for Chesterton, and it often appears at crucial points in his work. According to him, the "first principle" of democracy is "that the essential things in men are the things they hold in common" (*Orthodoxy*, Ch. 4). Based on the same conviction he declares, in *Charles Dickens*, that "Dickens was destined to show with inspired symbolism all the immense virtues of the democracy" (36) and that the source of "the great popularity" of the novelist was the fact that he expressed "the things close to the common mind" (55). A comparison is made between Scott's kind of democracy where all men are equally sublime and Dickens's "grotesque democracy" (126) where all men are equally interesting. Then there is a reference to "the whole superiority of the democracy of Dickens over the democracy of such a man as Gissing" (128)—the bête noire again. And it is of course democracy that Dickens wanted to find in America.

As Chesterton spends so much time on early Dickens, the chapter on America (Ch. 6) comes at the center of this book. This may not be without significance, for the American experience, in his view, is of central importance, in that it is an incident "so typical of Dickens's attitude to everything and anything" (65). His account of Dickens's disappointment with America is brilliant. "The Yankees enraged him at last, not by saying different things, but by saying the same things. They were a republic; they were a new and vigorous nation . . . ; but it seemed maddening that they should say so to each other in every car and drinking saloon from morning till night" (69). This was unbearable to Dickens, because "variety" (126) was the heart of his "grotesque democracy." Chesterton envisions the whole experience as "the great optimist" confronting "a horrible nightmare of optimism" (75). This is YCARCOMED, one might say; the democracy rendered in the moor-eeffoc fashion at its eeriest.

Dickens turned from American extremity, because he was not a "man who likes extraordinary things wildly." He "liked quiet ordinary things; he merely made an extraordinary fuss about them" (65). That is what Chesterton means when he says the American experience shows the novelist's essential characteristic, "the conjunction of common sense with uncommon sensibility" (64). A little later, observing in Dickens "the union of a general wildness approaching lunacy, with a sort of secret moderation almost amounting to mediocrity," Chesterton sees this "dualism" as "the whole crux of his character" (111). The key to Dickens is this coupling of the common and uncommon. Indeed, Dickens's greatness lies in the way he describes the wonder of the common with uncommon sensibility. Chesterton prepares for this central concern of the book in the first chapter where he talks about greatness, democracy, and "an ecstasy of the ordinary" (7). What may seem to be a slow beginning, in fact, contains the crucial elements of this highly interesting and very persuasive argument.

The chapter that follows the account of the novelist's encounter with America, "Dickens and Christmas," is also stimulating. Chesterton begins by talking about Dickens's Italian sojourn with a provocative paradox, "He never travelled out of England"—"His travels are not travels in Italy, but travels in Dickensland." Of a puppet play in Genoa and of a Punch and Judy show in Lincoln's Inn Fields Dickens made exactly the same fun. There is a sense in which Dickens's imagination was not really responsive to foreign cultures as such. Again, although he did like tales of travels and adventures in exotic lands, the ultimate source of that pleasure was his nationalistic pride in the heroism of British explorers. Chesterton has a point when he says Dickens was "as English as any Podsnap" (78). Then, ingeniously connecting travelling in distant lands with travelling in distant ages, he remarks of *A Child's History of England*, a book Dickens wrote for his children, that "the child is the writer and not the reader." Here, too, he is perceptive about the novelist's limitation due to his being a sturdy English radical, the "besetting sin or weakness of the modern progressive, the habit of regarding the contemporary questions as the eternal questions" (81). He does not mean to be critical, however, because Dickens's very Englishness led him to the "great defense of Christmas" (82); at the bottom of this festivity Chesterton recognizes a sense of comfort peculiar to England (and his favorite idea of medievalism).

Dickens was of course extremely influential in institutionalizing the English Christmas, and no doubt *A Christmas Carol* was the chief vehicle. In his discussion of that story, it ought to be pointed out, Chesterton shows no interest whatever in Tiny Tim. I have earlier spoken of the sympathy between Chesterton and Dickens as regards their ideas of childhood, but a qualification has to be added; he does not respond to the sentimental attitude of the novelist. This is most clearly seen in his view of little heroines such as Nell, Florence, and Agnes. He feels they are definitely lacking in something very important: "whatever charm these children may have they have not the charm of childhood. . . . The beauty and divinity in a child lie in his . . . not being like Little Nell" (62).

We have noted above that this book was written at the time when Dickens had a very poor reputation. We must bear that in mind when we come to its concluding chapter, where a prophecy is made that Dickens's "place in nineteenth-century England will not only be high, but altogether highest" (146). Today no one doubts the correctness of this verdict. Chesterton had wisdom as well as wit in a large measure.

*

Aside from this book, Chesterton wrote much on Dickens, starting with "Literary Pictures of the Year: Shakespeare, Tennyson, Dickens," a joint piece with J. E. Hodder Williams (the *Bookman*, June 1900). Of these writings, most significant is the collection of introductions to the Everyman edition of Dickens, *Appreciations and Criticisms of the Works of Charles Dickens* (1911). It is particularly valuable for his comments on later novels and other pieces that he does not adequately deal with in this book. He says, for example, *Bleak House* is "Dickens's best novel, though not the best book" (that honor goes to *David Copperfield*). In *Hard Times* "even [Dickens's] sympathy is hard." Despite his lack of love for *Little Dorrit*, he is sharp enough—possibly sharper than any previous critics—to see that "The people of *Little Dorrit* begin in prison; and it is the whole point of the book that people never get out of prison" (when he says "people," presumably he is not just talking about the Dorrit family). On the whole, *Appreciations and Criticisms* is, if a touch less exuberant, as interesting as this 1906 study, and well worth perusing. In addition to writing on Dickens, Chesterton several times gave speeches and lectures about the novelist as a member of the Dickens Fellowship, and when it organized a mock trial of John Jasper on the charge of the murder of Edwin Drood in 1914, he presided over the occasion as judge (Shaw was foreman of the jury). He was elected president of the Fellowship in 1921.

*

As I have said at the outset, Chesterton is often regarded as the greatest Dickens critic, and I feel certain that the reader will find in this book ample warrant for such a judgment. I feel equally certain that one does not come across books of this kind very often where two geniuses encounter so interestingly.

(First published as an "Introduction" to G. K. Chesterton, *Charles Dickens*, Wordsworth, 2007)

NOTES

1 T. S. Eliot's praise, "There is no better critic of Dickens living than Mr

Chesterton" (*The Times Literary Supplement*, 4 August 1927) is still relevant.

2 All references to Chesterton's *Charles Dickens* is to the Wordsworth edition.

3 The *Bookman*, February 1902. *G. K. Chesterton: The Critical Judgments Part 1*. Ed. D. J. Conlon (Antwerp: 1976), 38.

4 Shaw, "A Generous Opponent," *The Mark Twain Quarterly*, 1 (Spring 1937), qtd. in William B. Furlong, *Shaw and Chesterton* (University Park: 1970), 4.

5 Letter of 4 May 1902. *Letters of Max Beerbohm*, Ed. Rupert Hart-Davis (London: 1988), 25.

6 The *Daily News*, 28 September 1912.

7 The *Speaker*, 13 June 1903. Conlon, 68.

8 Maisie Ward, *Gilbert Keith Chesterton* (1944; London: 1958), 116.

9 "The Genius of Dickens," *Book Monthly* 3 (1906), 235, qtd in George H. Ford, *Dickens and His Readers* (1955; New York: 1974), 201.

10 *Charles Dickens: A Critical Study* (London: 1898), 101.

11 Ford, 242.

12 "Charles Dickens" in *The Collected Essays, Journalism and Letters of George Orwell*, 4 vols. (London: 1970) i, 476.

13 Humphry House, *The Dickens World* (Oxford: 1941), 135.

14 *Ten Novels and Their Authors* (London: 1954), 129.

15 *Other Inquisitions*, trans. Ruth L. C. Simms (1952; Austin: 1964), 84.

Ch. 10 Edmund Wilson's "The Two Scrooges" Reconsidered

According to Lewis M. Dabney, Edmund Wilson's recent biographer, "The Two Scrooges" is "his most widely read literary essay."[1] This comes as no surprise, for it is indeed a remarkable piece of writing. George Ford and Lauriat Lane, Jr in their selection of representative studies of Dickens in 1961 regarded it as "undoubtedly the most important critical statement on Dickens of the last twenty-five years."[2] Some fifty years later Paul Schlicke declared it to be "unquestionably the most influential single study of Dickens of the 20th century."[3] There will be little dispute about these claims: the importance of Wilson's study in the history of Dickens criticism is firmly established. That being the case, I believe it is worth our while to scrutinize this celebrated essay once again, and bring its strength and weakness into sharp focus.

Wilson first broached his ideas about Dickens as a lecture in the summer school at the University of Chicago in 1939 (this is the reason why his essay is dedicated to the students there). He then published them in the form of three magazine articles; "Dickens: the Two Scrooges" (*The New Republic*, March 4 and March 11, 1940), "Dickens and the Marshalsea Prison" (*The Atlantic Monthly*, April 1940 and May 1940) and "The Mystery of Edwin Drood" (*The New Republic*, April 8, 1940). Put together, they became a chapter called "Dickens: the Two Scrooges" in *The Wound and the Bow: Seven Studies in Literature* (1941).[4]

This book as a whole has a running theme, which Wilson identified by reference to Sophocles's *Philoctetes*, where the eponymous hero, a Greek warrior, is, on his way to the Trojan War, bitten by a snake, and the wound begins to emit such a terrible stench that he is marooned on an island. Philoctetes, however, possesses the invincible bow which is necessary for the conquest of Troy. In the end he is persuaded to join the war again, kills Paris, and ensures victory for the Greeks. Wilson sees this story as a parable of artistic creation, suggesting that genius and some psychological wound are closely linked.[5]

"The Two Scrooges" is an application of this notion to Dickens. The "wound" in his case was the fact that at the age of eleven he had been sent to work in Warren's Blacking Factory,[6] almost simultaneously with his father's imprisonment in the Marshalsea: "these experiences produced in Charles Dickens a trauma from which he suffered all his life" (7).[7] Wilson attempts to trace the effects of this trauma through the novelist's career. Here is a brief summary of his argument.

Dickens's dark obsessions, according to Wilson, make their presence felt even in the ostensibly comic *Pickwick Papers*, notably in one of the incorporated tales about "The Queer Client," which deals with the revenge of a man put in the Marshalsea prison for debt. Even in the main story Mr Pickwick has to go to prison towards the end, and before the writing of this novel was finished, Dickens started a new story about an orphan born of a good family but consigned to a workhouse, which is virtually a prison. Wilson writes:

> For the man of spirit whose childhood has been crushed by the cruelty of organized society, one of two attitudes is natural: that of the criminal or that of the rebel. Charles Dickens, in imagination, was to play the roles of both, and to continue up to his death to put into them all that was most passionate in his feeling (14).

In the early Dickens identification with the "criminal," particularly "the murderer," is noticeable, as can be observed in the powerful passages about the flight of Sikes, or Jonas Chuzzlewit's murder of Tigg Montague and its aftermath. The two themes involving the rebel and the criminal are combined in a peculiar way in *Barnaby Rudge*, the climax of which is the destruction of Newgate Prison by the mob, with Dickens apparently reveling in the event. In Dickens's middle period the identification with the rebel becomes predominant. This is seen in the increasing severity of his social criticism and the indictment of "the self-important and moralizing middle class" (26). *Dombey and Son* is the first serious attempt at an anatomy of society—"always through the observed interrelations between highly individualized human beings rather than through political or economic analysis" (29). *Bleak House* realizes "this intention to perfection" (29). *Little Dorrit* shows a new depth of psychological characterization and social criticism, reflecting Dickens's unhappy marriage and "social maladjustment" (42). His gloomy view of society continues and deepens in *Great Expectaions*, culminating in *Our Mutual Friend*, where the novelist shows his utter disillusion with middle class values as represented by Podsnap. Dickens always had difficulty in combining good and bad in one character, but he finally rose to the challenge in John Jasper. In *The Mystery of*

Edwin Drood, the social criticism disappears and psychological interest predominates. With the theme of "the rebel" gone, the theme of "the criminal," "the murderer," is pursued to an unprecedented degree. But Dickens died leaving it unfinished, without resolving this confrontation between good and evil.

Such is Wilson's main argument. He believed that "literary criticism ought to be . . . a history of man's idea and imaginings in the setting of the conditions which have shaped them."[8] Here his performance lived up to that ideal; he delved into the psychology of Dickens the man and connected it with the age that produced him, and at the same time provided a clear picture of his artistic development. Against the then prevalent view of Dickens as primarily a comic novelist, Wilson wanted to assert his significance as a serious social critic. Thus he was among the first fully to appreciate the later "dark" novels. One of the most important of his contributions to Dickens criticism was the discussion of the novelist's symbolism at a far deeper level than ever attempted before; above all, his analysis of the prison symbol in *Little Dorrit*, which was truly epoch-making.[9] We must remember that this novel was long regarded as a sad failure. In 1870, when Dickens died, the *Saturday Review* remarked in its obituary notice: "With the single exception of *Little Dorrit* there is not one of his numerous stories that has not touches of the master-hand and strokes of indisputable genius".[10] This was very much the standard view for a long time, and even if there were some isolated defenders of it, such as George Gissing and Bernard Shaw, it was left to Wilson to demonstrate Dickens's artistic success in concrete details:

> The main symbol here is the prison . . . but this symbol is developed in a way that takes it beyond the satirical application of the symbol of the fog in *Bleak House* and gives it a significance more subjective. . . . The Clennam house is a jail, and they are in prison too. So are the people in Bleeding Heart yard . . . ; so is Merdle . . . imprisoned . . . in the vast scaffolding of fraud he has contrived, who wanders about in his expensive house . . . afraid of his servants. . . .
>
> . . . [T]he Dorrits, accepted by Society, still find themselves in prison. The moral is driven home when old Dorrit, at a fashionable dinner, loses control of his wits and slips back into his character at the Marshalsea. . . . Arthur Clennam, ruined by

> the failure of Merdle, finally goes to the Marshalsea himself; and there at last he and Little Dorrit arrive at an understanding. . . . The whole book is much gloomier than *Bleak House*. . . . The murk of *Little Dorrit* permeates the souls of the people. . . .
>
> . . . [T]he fable is here presented from the point of view of imprisoning states of mind as much as from that of oppressive institutions. This is illustrated in a startling way by *The History of a Self-Tormentor*, which we find toward the end of the book. Here Dickens, with a remarkable pre-Freudian insight, gives a sort of case history of a woman imprisoned in a neurosis which has condemned her to the delusion that she can never be loved. (44-47)

This is brilliant literary criticism, and his elucidation of the prison symbolism has since become part of the critical consensus. In addition, the overall view of Dickens as a tormented genius, developed by Edgar Johnson's monumental biography, *Charles Dickens: His Tragedy and Triumph* (1953), is still with us. Our idea of Dickens remains very much a creation of Wilson's. His argument, however, is not without its problems.

Wilson's keen biographical interest sometimes leads him to make a rather facile connection between life and art. This tendency is observable in his treatment of Ellen Ternan. Given that he was writing immediately after the explosion of the great scandal—Thomas Wright's *The Life of Charles Dickens* appeared in 1935 and Gladys Storey's *Dickens and Daughter* followed in 1939—it was natural that his view was strongly affected by it. Eagerly swallowing Wright, Wilson argues that Dickens based his late heroines on Ternan.[11] He admits the paucity of information about her, but observes: "We do, however, know something about what Dickens thought of her from the heroines in his last books who are derived from her" (59). Estella is frigid, Bella (before conversion) is intent on money, therefore Ellen must be a person with these qualities—this is a typical Wilson move. In a similar fashion he speculates about Catherine Dickens: "Dickens' terrible gallery of shrews who browbeat their amiable husbands suggests that she may have been a scold" (39). Concerning such critical procedures of Wilson's, Vladimir Nabokov wrote:

> The method he favors is gleaning from my fiction what he supposes to be actual, "real-life" impressions and then popping

> them back into my novels and considering my characters in that inept light—rather like the Shakespearian scholar who deduced Shakespeare's mother from the plays and then discovered allusions to her in the very passages he had twisted to manufacture the lady.[12]

Wilson was not always as crude as this, but he was prone to fall into the trap of the biographical fallacy.

As its title indicates, the core of Wilson's essay lies in Dickens's dualism, but his treatment of this central theme is curiously vague. It is first brought out as follows: "The world of the early Dickens is organized according to a dualism which is based . . . on the values of melodrama" (51). There are bad people on one side, and good people on the other; comic characters here, "straight" characters there, and so on. The only complexity Dickens was able to manage, in Wilson's view, is to make a noxious character wholesome, and Scrooge is the prime example of this. Now he moves from the fictional world to its creator: "Scrooge represents a principle fundamental to the dynamics of Dickens's world and derived from his own emotional constitution. It was not merely that his passion for the theater had given him a taste for melodramatic contrasts; it was rather that the lack of balance between the opposite impulses of his nature had stimulated an appetite for melodrama. For emotionally Dickens was unstable" (51-52). It is this psychological feature that Wilson sees in both the novelist and the character:

> Shall we ask what Scrooge would actually be like if we were to follow him beyond the frame of the story? Unquestionably he would relapse when the merriment was over—if not while it was still going on—into moroseness, vindictiveness, suspicion. He would, that is to say, reveal himself as the victim of a manic-depressive cycle, and a very uncomfortable person.[13] (53)

Next, we are quickly back in the fictional world again: "This dualism runs all through Dickens. There has always to be a good and a bad of everything. . . . Dickens' difficulty in his middle period, and indeed more or less to the end, is to get good and bad together in one character" (53-54). Then, after an interval, we hear about the theme in relation to *Edwin Drood*: "The duality of high and low, rich and poor, has evidently here given place to the duality of good and evil" (82).

This "duality of high and low, rich and poor," however, has not been explained at all. We are left to presume that he means something about Dickens's social criticism and unease about his own class identity. In the discussion of these topics, we are not made aware that Wilson is treating them in connection with the dualism in question. Also we wonder what all this talk about dualism has to do with "the rebel" and "the criminal" themes (a point to which I shall return at the end).

This lack of clarity is related to the structural problem.[14] As I have pointed out, Wilson's study is made of three magazine articles that were published separately. The essay as it stands now starts with what used to be "Dickens and the Marshalsea Prison," which deals with the childhood trauma, the rebel/criminal theme, and the prison motif. Then it is followed by what were originally "Dickens: the Two Scrooges" and "The Mystery of Edwin Drood," these two mainly treating the dualism in Dickens, with the "criminal" theme surfacing in the latter. In my view, the synthesis of the three is not entirely successful. Wilson's argument tries to follow Dickens's novels chronologically and trace his development, but after dealing with *Little Dorrit* (the end point of "Dickens and the Marshalsea Prison"), it goes back to *A Christmas Carol* (the beginning of "The Two Scrooges"). The main topic of Dickens's dualism is not mentioned at all in the first third; its discussion begins with the *Carol*, and then continues in the hazy fashion I have noted, until it comes to be the focus in the last third of the piece. Scrooge, though featuring in the title, appears to be sandwiched by the discussions of the rebel/criminal theme, having nothing to do with it himself.

The book version we have today contains some additions to the original articles, but these added materials are not the stronger parts of his essay; they include, for example, a notorious judgment of *David Copperfield* as "not one of Dickens' deepest books" and "something in the nature of a holiday" (37). The hurried dismissal of this novel in one paragraph—"David is too candid and simple to represent Dickens himself" (37)—tells us where the critic's most urgent concern is: it is as if the novel were not important because it does not reveal anything significant about the author.

"The Two Scrooges" is weakest in its conclusion. In dealing with a writer's career, Wilson, like the good journalist that he was, tended to form it into a well-shaped story. For example, in "The Kipling That Nobody Read," he notes that "It is striking that some of the most authentic of Kipling's early stories should deal with children forsaken by their parents and the most poignant of his later ones with parents bereaved of their children," thus suggesting a neat symmetry in the author's creative life.[15] Again, towards the end of "The Ambiguity of Henry James" Wilson says that although the novelist was buried in America, "one occasionally finds references to him which assume that he was buried in England. . . . [E]ven Henry James's death has been not without a suggestion of the equivocal"—a nice finish to the whole argument about "ambiguity."[16] A similar desire for a tidy ending (but with an unfortunate result) can be observed in "The Two Scrooges." Here, the fact that Dickens was not able to complete *Edwin Drood* is seen as a reflection of the novelist's inability to resolve his internal conflict:

> But now the Dickens who had been cut off from society has discarded the theme of the rebel and is carrying the theme of the criminal, which has haunted him all his life, to its logical development in his fiction. He is to explore the deep entanglement and conflict of the bad and the good in one man. . . .
>
> . . . The protest against the age has turned into a protest against self. In this last moment, the old hierarchy of England does enjoy a sort of triumph over the weary and debilitated Dickens, for it has made him accept its ruling that he is a creature irretrievably tainted; and the mercantile middle-class England has had its triumph, too. For the Victorian hypocrite—developing from Pecksniff, through Murdstone, through Headstone, to his final incarnation in Jasper—has finally come to present an insoluble moral problem which is identified with Dickens's own. . . .
>
> In this last condemned cell of Dickens, the respectable half of the divided John Jasper was to be brought face to face with the other half. But this confrontation . . . was never, in fact, to take place. For Dickens in his moral confusion was never to dramatize himself completely, was not even in this final phase of his art to succeed in coming quite clear. He was to leave *Edwin Drood* half-finished, with the confession just around the corner. (81-85)

In this extract there are several problems. Wilson says "Dickens had been cut off from society," but what basis is there for this judgment? To be sure, he has talked about the termination of Dickens's public readings, but immediately before the above quotation, he gives an account of the novelist's dinner engagement (among the guests was the

Prince of Wales) two weeks before his death which he *kept* in spite of the "neurotic foot" (81). Perhaps "society" in a wider sense is meant? Even then, the discussion so far only touches upon Dickens's change of class allegiance in *Our Mutual Friend*—"Shrinking from Podsnap and Veneering, he falls back on that aristocracy he had so savagely attacked in his youth" (66)—which is an entirely different matter from social isolation. The fog becomes thicker when Wilson contends that in the "protest against self" Dickens was defeated by "the old hierarchy of England" and found himself "irretrievably tainted." Since shortly before the above passage he quotes Sir Henry Fielding Dickens's account of an occurrence at a Christmas party in 1869, the year before Dickens's death—in the middle of a word-list game suddenly Dickens interjected the words, "Warren's Blacking, 30, Strand" (80)—I suppose by the word, "tainted," we are meant to remember the point made at the beginning of his essay: that Dickens's humiliation at the blacking factory was "a trauma from which he suffered all his life." John Gross's remark that "Of all modern writings on Dickens, Edmund Wilson's essay . . . is the most dramatic"[17] is true enough, but all these phrases here—"cut off from society," "protest against self," "the triumph of the old hierarchy of England," "irretrievably tainted"—are close to being melodramatic exaggerations, and do not bear critical scrutiny. I cannot help feeling that they are introduced to satisfy Wilson's desire for a showy ending.

Using a theatrical metaphor himself, Wilson declares that "Dickens in his moral confusion was never to dramatize himself completely" and that he did not "succeed in coming quite clear"—"*not even in this final phase*."[18] This is puzzling, for twenty pages or so before, discussing *Our Mutual Friend*, he has said: "Dickens has here distilled the mood of his later years, dramatized the tragic discrepancies of his character, delivered his final judgment on the whole Victorian exploit. . . . Dickens' line in his criticism of society is very clear in *Our Mutual Friend*, and it marks a new position on Dickens's part. . . . Dickens has come at last to despair utterly of the prospering middle class" (61-63). There seems to be a self-contradiction regarding whether or not Dickens managed to dramatize the discrepancies in his character. Presumably, Wilson is suggesting that Dickens was clear about his attack on the mercantile middle class in *Our Mutual Friend*, but that when he came to write *Edwin Drood* he was not certain as to where he was morally. This theory of Dickens's "moral confusion," however, is not convincing.

Wilson wants to see Dickens identifying himself with Jasper:

"Jasper is, like Dickens, an artist. . . . Like Dickens he is a skilful magician. . . . Like Dickens he is an alien from another world; yet, like Dickens, he has made himself respected in the conventional English community" (83). If Jasper is "a dual personality" (76), so is Dickens. One might follow Wilson this far. His next move is questionable. He argues that Jasper, a Thug, commits the murder in the name of the goddess Kali, so that his act can be pardoned, even praised, in a morality that is different from that of Victorian England. Granted that one might draw from this a conclusion that Jasper is both innocent and wicked, but is this really an "insoluble moral problem"? More crucially, does this lead to a "moral confusion" on the novelist's part? Surely to create a morally ambiguous character and to be morally confused are two completely different things. Although it can be said that Dickens was in his imagination two persons, good and evil, there is no evidence that indicates his confusion between them: as Philip Collins observes, "throughout his fiction and journalism, Dickens regards murderers as unequivocally and entirely wicked men."[19] Collins also states that the alleged resemblance between Dickens and Jasper "does not strike [him] as impressive" (312). Dickens may have had an unstable social identity up to the very end, but Wilson connects that with moral uncertainty in the novelist—this is where I have the strongest reservation about his argument.[20]

In the assessment of "The Two Scrooges," we ought not to reckon without Philip Collins, who has offered a most sustained and learned critique not only of Wilson's reading of *Drood*, but his idea of Dickens as a whole.[21] His magisterial book, *Dickens and Crime* (1962), which amply demonstrates the complexity (inconsistencies and contradictions included) of the novelist that appears in his opinion on public issues, was largely an attempt to redress the image of Dickens Wilson helped to create; "a Dickens increasingly clear-sighted in his radical opposition to the structure and ideology of his society" (22). Several years later, in the anniversary issue of the *Dickensian*, "Dickens and Fame," Collins had occasion to make his point succinctly:

> The recurrent tendency in [Edgar] Johnson and in most American (and much British and other) discussion of Dickens is to exaggerate the extent and the clarity of his reaction against his time. Edmund Wilson gave the lead—taking a hint, no doubt, from Shaw (but then no-one should take such Irish statements literally). "Of all

> the great Victorian writers," wrote Wilson, "he was probably the most antagonistic to the Victorian Age itself." Dickens, heaven knows, is a remarkable writer, however one understands and judges him; but surely it should have struck Wilson, and those who followed his lead, that it would have been more than remarkable—it would have been incredible—that an author so antagonistic to his age should have been the age's darling for a third of a century, and then posthumously thereafter? However would he have got away with it?[22]

Then Queen Victoria's testimony is brought in: she "wasn't clever" but what she says "strikes something near the right note." At Dickens's death the Queen records: "He is a very great loss. . . . He had a large loving mind and the strongest sympathy with the poorer classes. He felt sure that a better feeling, and much great union of classes would take place in time. And I pray earnestly it may."[23] Collins concludes: "People really antagonistic to their age don't get that kind of concurrence from queens" (155).

This is certainly a most forceful objection to Wilson's important point. For the further consideration of this issue—our last point of examination—it is instructive to turn to George Orwell, whose equally famous study of Dickens was conceived exactly at the same time as Wilson's.[24] Interestingly, Orwell, too, regarded the novelist as a rebel, using the very same word: "even if Dickens was a bourgeois, he was certainly a subversive writer, a radical, one might truthfully say a rebel." And his thinking seems to go along the line of Collins's criticism just quoted:

> In *Oliver Twist*, *Hard Times*, *Bleak House*, *Little Dorrit*, Dickens attacked English institutions with a ferocity that has never since been approached. Yet he managed to do it without making himself hated, and, more than this, the very people he attacked have swallowed him so completely that he has become a national institution himself. . . . Dickens seems to have succeeded in attacking everybody and antagonizing nobody. Naturally this makes one wonder whether after all there was something unreal in his attack upon society. Where exactly does he stand, socially, morally, and politically?[25]

Orwell answers this self-imposed question, first by pointing out what Dickens was not: namely, he was not a "proletarian" writer; he was not a "revolutionary" writer; he was not destructive in any sense. What he wanted was not social, but moral change (21-22). The central secret of the novelist's popularity, in Orwell's view, was his native generosity, his tendency to support underdogs. This type of mentality, he goes on, is one of the marks of western popular culture, like Mickey Mouse and Popeye. His conclusion runs as follows:

> Nearly everyone, whatever his actual conduct may be, responds emotionally to the idea of human brotherhood. Dickens voiced a code which was and on the whole still is believed in, even by people who violate it. It is difficult otherwise to explain why he could be both read by working people (a thing that has happened to no other novelist of his stature) and buried in Westminster Abbey. (55)

This is how Dickens "got away with" the attack on his age: so Orwell would have countered Collins's objection to Wilson. As far as the idea of the novelist as rebel is concerned, Orwell may have been a touch shrewder than Wilson in seeing the matter in a highly generalized fashion: Dickens was broadly "in revolt against authority"; "his radicalism was only of the vaguest kind" (54).[26]

Certainly Wilson made too much of the novelist's hostility towards his age. Collins's criticism is just: "[Dickens's] vision of capitalist society was less complete, coherent, and hostile than [Wilson] claims" (*Dickens and Crime*, 308).[27] The keen journalist in Wilson was, I suspect, very much responsible for the stark, provocative view. He could have avoided this trap, however, by reading his own piece more carefully and following through its logic to the end. Earlier I have said we wonder—since it is never made clear—what all the talk about dualism has to do with "the rebel" and "the criminal" themes under discussion. If, as Wilson maintains, "This dualism runs all through Dickens [he means, we have seen, both the novels and the man]," there is bound to be the "opposite impulse" (51) of the "rebel," which would be related to the conservative side of the novelist. Then, the "two Scrooges" one imagines in the logical extension of that might point to the kind of Dickens Collins has in mind. In this sense one might say Wilson's argument is more perspicacious than the critic himself realized.

In spite of its problems, Edmund Wilson's study remains a monumental achievement. It is well worth re-reading, or worth taking issue with. "I nag at [Wilson] in this way, not because I lack respect for him (on the contrary: I pore over him with continual delight and benefit)," says Collins (*Dickens and Crime*, 307)—my sentiments exactly.

(Originally a lecture delivered at the International Dickens Fellowship Conference, Amsterdam, 2006; first published in *The Dickensian*, 2008)

NOTES

1 *Edmund Wilson: A Life in Literature* (New York: Farrar, Straus and Giroux, 2005), 266.
2 *The Dickens Critics* (Ithaca: Cornell University Press, 1961), 180.
3 *Oxford Reader's Companion to Dickens*, ed. Paul Schlicke (Oxford: Oxford University Press, 1999), 590.
4 Wilson afterwards made some minor alterations in the text of this essay (but no substantial revisions); see Note 18.
5 In the play there appears a character named Neoptolemus, whom Greeks send, with Odysseus, to persuade Philoctetes. According to Leon Edel, this figure "becomes a kind of archetypal critic" in Wilson's vision: see his "Introduction" to Edmund Wilson, *The Twenties: From Notebooks and Diaries of the Period* (New York: Farrar, Straus and Giroux, 1975), xli.
6 Dabney speculates that Wilson "enters into young Dickens's sense of abandonment at the blacking factory, drawing on his relationships with his own parents" (*Edmund Wilson*, 22).
7 This and the subsequent references to "The Two Scrooges" are to *The Wound and the Bow: Seven Studies in Literature* (Athens: Ohio University Press, 1997).
8 This is from the dedicatory words to Christian Gauss in *Axel's Castle* (New York: Charles Scribner's Sons, 1931).
9 See Philip Collins, "*Little Dorrit*: the Prison and the Critics," *TLS*, 18 April 1980, 445-46.
10 *Dickens: the Critical Heritage*, Ed. Philip Collins (London: Routledge and Kegan Paul, 1971), 509.

11 Wilson's idea of seeing Ellen Ternan in Estela, Bella Wilfer, and Helena Landless was preceded by Hugh Kingsmill, *The Sentimental Journey* (London: Wishart, 1934), 195-97. Wilson is critical of Kingsmill (*The Wound and the Bow*, 3) but silent about his indebtedness.

12 Originally a letter to the editor, *The New York Times Book Review*, 7 November 1971; reprinted in Vladimir Nabokov, *Strong Opnions* (New York: Vintage Books, 1990), 218. Wilson's other contribution to Dickens studies was to suggest to Nabokov, when there was a friendly relationship between them, that he teach *Bleak House* at Cornell. The Russian novelist's highly interesting lecture can be read in his *Lectures on Literature*, Ed. Fredson Bowers (New York: Harcourt Brace Jovanovich, 1980).

13 The idea of Dickens as manic-depressive was taken up by an eminent neurologist, W. Russell Brain, in his "Authors and Psychopaths," *British Medical Journal* (December 24, 1949), 1427-32.

14 The structural problem is also noted in Janet Groth, *Edmund Wilson: A Critic for Our Time* (Athens: Ohio University Press, 1989), which contains a useful chapter on "The Two Scrooges."

15 *The Wound and the Bow*, 145.

16 *The Triple Thinkers: Twelve Essays on Literary Subjects* (1952; Harmondsworth: Penguin, 1962), 140.

17 "Dickens: Some Recent Approaches" in *Dickens and the Twentieth Century*, Ed. John Gross and Gabriel Pearson (London: Routledge and Kegan Paul, 1962), ix.

18 The 1997 reprint I am quoting from is exactly the same as the 1978 Farrar Straus Giroux, or the 1970 Oxford University Press printing. In earlier printings—for example, the 1947 "New Printing with Corrections" (OUP) and 1952 W. H. Allen "Revised Edition"—the text reads "never in this last phase." In that case, it may just be possible to regard "this last phase" as designating the period relating to *Drood* only. Then there is no contradiction involved. The phrase after the revision, "not even in this final phase," seems to preclude such a possibility.

19 *Dickens and Crime* (London: Macmillan, 1962), 305.

20 More locally, I find Wilson in a muddle about Captain Hawdon, whom he conceives as "the reckless soldier, adored by his men, beloved by women, the image of the old life-loving England, whose epitaph Dickens is now writing." The Captain, he says, "has failed in that world, has perished as a friendless and penniless man, and has been buried in the pauper's graveyard in one of the foulest quarters of London, but the loyalties felt for him by the living will endure and prove so strong after his death that they will pull that

world apart" (34-35). If by "the loyalties felt for him" pulling "that world apart" he means Joe's spreading his disease (surely not anything done by Lady Dedlock or George), he is overstating the case.

21 Not to be forgotten, either, is Q. D. Leavis's intemperately expressed, yet not wholly ill-judged remark on "amateur psychologists" led by Wilson. See her Note to the Preface, *Dickens: the Novelist* (1970; Harmondsworth: Penguin, 1972), 14-20.

22 *The Dickensian*, No. 361 (Spring 1970), 154-55. As Collins points out, Wilson owes much to Shaw. This is obvious and he would have been the first to admit it. But what about Chesterton? Rating Gissing higher, he has little time for Chesterton as a critic of Dickens (4), but the latter, in fact, seems to have anticipated some of his key notions. Of Dickens's blacking factory days Chesterton says, "Those years may have given him many moral and mental wounds, from which he never recovered. But they gave him the key of the street"; he also notes "dualism in Dickens . . . constitutes the whole crux of his character". See *Charles Dickens* (1906; London: Methuen, 1946), 35, 157. See also pp.93-94 of this book.

23 Quoted from *Letters*, 1862-78, ed. G. E. Buckle, 1906, ii, 21.

24 As I have said, Wilson gave his Dickens lectures in 1939. Quite independently, across the Atlantic, Orwell wrote his essay that year, and published it in *Inside the Whale* (1940). They reviewed each other, however. Orwell (*The Observer*, 10 May 1942) buys the "Two Scrooges" argument and says, "One is forced to believe in a sort of split personality" of Dickens. He submits: "[Wilson] overstresses the element of symbolism in Dickens's work and understresses the mechanical side of commercial story-writing. But this aside this is the best essay on Dickens that has appeared for some time." He does not forget to add that "Mr Wilson at times writes clumsily, even vulgarly" (this has some truth, as we have seen). This review is reprinted in *The Complete Works of George Orwell* Vol. 13, *All Propaganda is Lies*, Ed. Peter Davison (London: Secker and Warburg, 1998), 314-16. Wilson, in his turn (*The New Yorker*, 25 May 1946), says: Orwell's study, though "original and interesting," suffers from "a tendency to generalize about the first-rate writer . . . without following his development as an artist . . . and from a habit of taking complex personalities too much at their face value, of not getting inside them enough. Orwell does not see, for example, that Dickens was more attracted than repelled by horror and violence." This review is reprinted in *From the Uncollected Edmund Wilson*, Ed. Janet Groth and David Castronovo (Athens: Ohio University Press, 1995), 306-12.

25 "Charles Dickens" in *The Complete Works of George Orwell* Vol. 12, *A Patriot After All*, 21.

26 One should remember, however, that, as Collins points out, in Dickens's "inability to sympathise with established authority" there is "the conspicuous exception of the New Police and, overseas, of those who resolutely disciplined the turbulent natives" (*Dickens and Crime*, 47).

27 Sharp as it is, Collins's criticism of Wilson in this book does not seem fair when he observes that "More of [Dickens's] greatness resides in his comedy than Mr Wilson ever recognizes" (308). Wilson was aware of the novelist's comic genius; he was simply not dealing with it, for he says: "I shall make no attempt to discuss at length the humor of the early Dickens. This is the aspect of his work that is best known, the only aspect that some people know" (13).

Ch. 11 Major Twentieth-Century Critical Responses to Dickens

At the beginning of the twentieth century Dickens did not enjoy a high reputation among literary critics (this state continued till the thirties). After Dickens's death there had been a noticeable tendency to regard him merely as a jovial novelist for the half-educated. In this climate George Gissing raised a supportive voice (1898)[1]. However, as he was a novelist working in the age of realism, Gissing valued Dickens where the latter approximated this literary ideal. G. K. Chesterton (1906) felt it was a misguided defense. He praised Dickens's exaggeration and glorified the fecundity of his comic imagination. In his opinion, "the units of Dickens, the primary elements, are not the stories, but the characters who affect the stories—or, more often still, the characters who do not affect the stories."[2] Five years later Chesterton gathered his Introductions for Everyman's Library editions of Dickens in one volume (1911), in which we have his extended views on individual works—"*Bleak House* is not certainly Dickens's best book; but perhaps it is his best novel"—and more of his sharp observations, such as: "[Dickens] did not dislike this or that argument for oppression; he disliked oppression. He disliked a certain look on the face of a man when he looks down on another man."[3]

The last remark is approvingly quoted by George Orwell (1940) in his discussion of Dickens as a rebel. In the 1930s some critics saw Dickens as a revolutionary, proletarian writer (most notably, the biased but perceptive T. A. Jackson),[4] but Orwell did not agree. He points out that "Dickens's criticism of society is almost exclusively moral," and that he "sees the world as a middle-class world, and everything outside these limits is either laughable or slightly wicked." Like Chesterton, Orwell thinks the novel form is at odds with Dickens's genius: "Significantly Dickens's most successful books (not his *best* books) are *The Pickwick Papers*, which is not a novel, and *Hard Times* and *A Tale of Two Cities*, which are not funny"; "Dickens is obviously a writer whose parts are greater than his wholes. He is all fragments, all details—rotten architecture, but wonderful gargoyles—and never better than when he is building up some character who will later on be forced to act inconsistently."[5]

Meanwhile Edmund Wilson (1941) was developing his own theory of Dickens as a rebel. On the premise that his father's imprisonment and the drudgery in the blacking factory "produced in Charles Dickens a trauma from which he suffered all his life," Wilson argues: "For the man of spirit whose childhood has been crushed by the cruelty of organized society, one of two attitudes is natural: that of the criminal or that of the rebel." According to Wilson, while the theme of the criminal is prominent in early novels, in the middle period the identification with the rebel becomes predominant, which is seen in the increasing severity of his social criticism. In the very last novel "the Dickens who had been cut off from society has discarded the theme of the rebel and is carrying the theme of the criminal, which has haunted him all his life, to its logical development in his fiction." Despite his claim that Dickens was driven by an "unstable" dualism, Wilson very much foregrounds the rebellious side of the novelist. This view, as it turned out, was so influential that the jolly Christmas Dickens was virtually eclipsed. Wilson also made a significant contribution to Dickens studies by conducting the first substantial analysis of his symbolism, particularly that of the prison in *Little Dorrit*.[6]

Humphry House's was the first book-length study of Dickens written by an academic (1941). His purpose was to show "the connexion between what Dickens wrote and the times in which he wrote it," and his examination of the novelist's views on economy, religion, and politics remains in many ways unsurpassed. He demonstrates that Dickens's social criticism (which was inconsistent) lay in attacking abuses that were already matters of the past—the novelist was following, rather than leading, public opinion—and that due to the "continued habit of drawing on his own past," Dickens "tended to push his stories back in time," thereby often producing anachronisms. House's interest led him to become the first critic to pay serious attention to Dickens's social journalism.[7]

In his ambitious and influential attempt at establishing the canon of English fiction (1948), F. R. Leavis observed that Dickens was merely a "great entertainer," and since "[t]he adult mind doesn't as a rule find in Dickens a challenge to an unusual and sustained seriousness," he deemed the novelist unworthy of inclusion in his "great tradition." However, in the Appendix, he made an exception for *Hard Times*, conceding that in this novel Dickens "is for once possessed by a comprehensive vision," the "confutation of Utilitarianism by life."[8]

Dorothy van Ghent (1950) focuses on the way Dickens treats living beings as if they were things, and things as if they were alive.

This reciprocity is "wrought out of the broad common intuition of the connections between moral and physical phenomena." "Coincidence," van Ghent declares, "is the violent connection of the unconnected; but there is no discontinuity in the Dickens world, either between persons and things, or between the private and the public act"; it is "a thoroughly nervous universe, whose ganglia spread through things and people alike." Its central expression is the view from Todgers's, "with its baffling labyrinths, its animated chimneys, its illicit bacillary invasions, its hints of a cancerous organization"—"a world in which significance has been replaced by naked and aggressive existence."[9]

J. Hillis Miller (1958), too, conceived the "world" of Dickens. He postulates that Dickens's novels form a unified totality: "Within this whole a single problem, the search for viable identity, is stated and restated with increasing approximation to the hidden center, Dickens' deepest apprehension of the nature of the world and of the human condition within it." In his view, the characters' drama becomes the author's own, and their experiences reflect his exploratory search and personal development. Miller traces "a movement from dependence on the child-parent relation as an escape from isolation to a dependence on the more adult solution of romantic love" in the early to middle period. Later novels show society as evil and explore the difficulties arising from love, until *Our Mutual Friend* shows in Bella and Rokesmith "an attitude which recognizes that value radiates not from any thing or power outside the human, but outward from the human spirit itself."[10]

Robert Garis (1965), aiming to "restore something like the popular understanding of Dickens," argues that we should not judge him by the same standards we use when reading George Eliot or Henry James. He makes a distinction between theatrical and non-theatrical art: the latter is the mode adopted by Eliot/James, in which the focal point is the character's inner life; Dickens employs the former mode, in which "the centre of our attention . . . is the artificer himself." It was, he argues, "an essential part of [Dickens's] genius that kept him, as a rule, so strangely innocent of the spiritual exercise which we think of as natural to the serious dramatic artist."[11] (Barbara Hardy, though sympathizing with Garis, still reads Dickens as a moral novelist, who has his "peculiar crudity, a crudity that is both essential to him and valuable in literary experiment.")[12]

Since New Critics, in their concentration on the words on the page, tended to exclude history from their consideration, Philip Collins brought out his books on Dickens in relation to crime (1962) and education (1963) to redress the balance, the former being largely an attempt to modify the image of the novelist that had been built up since Wilson; "a Dickens increasingly clear-sighted in his radical opposition to the structure and ideology of his society".[13] Collins also offers interesting testimony regarding Dickens's critical reception: "it was not until around 1960 that an admiration for Dickens altogether ceased to have a taint of endearing eccentricity in literary and academic circles."[14]

Reaction to New Criticism can also be detected in Steven Marcus's study (1965) of the first half of Dickens's career, a synthetic effort from the critical, biographical and socio-historical perspectives. The master theme he discerns is the father-son relationship; the theme of careless or cruel fathers and neglected children, deriving from the novelist's childhood experiences. In his view, while in the early novels heroes are passive and the main impulse is "a deliverance from society," the novels of the middle period (from *Barnaby Rudge* through *David Copperfield*) "contain an attempt to achieve an accommodation within society." By the time of *Dombey and Son* Dickens was divided between the life of aggressive will and change on one hand, and the life without will, the life of simplicity and affectionate feeling, on the other. Marcus submits that "part of Dickens's genius was to see that society itself suffered from similar contradictions."[15]

Alexander Welsh (1971) examines Dickens's thinking about death. Dickens, he argues, associates death with the city (the City of Destruction) but the Christian alternative (the Heavenly City) is not directly present in his novels; instead, Dickens locates one's immortality in the memory of the people who survive one. Welsh's "search for a religious centre in Dickens" leads him to the hearth, where the heroine stands against death (that she often plays the role of wife, sister, and daughter all in one embodies the "timelessness of the female principle").[16] The literary value of the heroines as characters, however, does not concern Welsh. It is extensively dealt with by Michael Slater, who argues that in the period from *Dombey* to *Little Dorrit* the novelist's imagination was deeply engaged with women, creating passionate, intelligent figures—Betsey Trotwood being "the finest flowering."[17]

F. R. Leavis (1970), now regarding Dickens as a serious novelist worthy of ample treatment, pronounces that "*Little Dorrit* confronts the technologico-Benthamite world with a conception of man and society to which it is utterly blank," and places him in the company of Blake and

Lawrence; "the vindicator[s] of the spirit—that is, of life." Q. D. Leavis on her part provocatively argues: in *David Copperfield* Dickens tries to create, not his autobiographical reflection, but "a typical male history in that age," *Great Expectations* is not a snob's progress; sometimes (for example, where Mr Peggotty's love for Little Em'ly is concerned) Dickens "wrote to be read in two ways"—on one level he offered "a harmless sop to the Meagles section of his reading public" and on the other undermined their smug morality.[18]

Duality, indeed, is at the center of John Carey's study (1973)—for him the most important aspect of Dickens is his ability to see things from two opposed points of view (as instanced in his fascination with violence and order)—but unlike most critics he pays no attention to Dickens's moral concerns and social criticism, stressing his comic genius instead: "We could scrap all the solemn parts of his novels without impairing his status as a writer. But we could not remove Mrs. Gamp or Pecksniff or Bounderby without maiming him irreparably." Again, contrary to the majority of critics since Wilson, he dismisses Dickens's symbolism, because his "sharp-edged" imagination "fills his novels with objects that vividly loom—locks, graveyards, cages—intensely themselves, not signs for something else".[19] Garrett Stewart (1974) also explores, in a highly idiosyncratic but stimulating manner, Dickens's imagination as it manifests itself in his style and his characters, chiefly those sharing their creator's power of fancy, from Sam Weller ("the most complete hero") through Dick Swiveller to Jenny Wren, whom he calls—borrowing from Jane Austen—"imaginists."[20]

The last three decades of the century might be called the age of theory, and the signs of the times were palpably felt in Dickens criticism. Hillis Miller, now under the influence of Jacques Derrida, thinks there is nothing outside language, and he brings that philosophy to bear upon his reading of *Bleak House* (1971). This novel, in his view, "is a document about the interpretation of documents," and its ultimate villain is not the Court of Chancery or the corrupt Victorian society, but "the act of interpretation itself, the naming which assimilates the particular into a system, giving it a definition and a value incorporating it into a whole." Esther seeing herself as part of a flaming necklace offers "a fit emblem for the violence exercised over the individual by language and other social institutions."[21]

If Hillis Miller sees man as trapped in the system of language, D. A. Miller (1988), drawing on Michel Foucault, sees man as under the dominance of power. For him the nineteenth-century novel is a disciplinary discourse, policing the subjectivities of its readers. His reading of *Bleak House* is an attempt to illustrate the complex operations of this social control. For example, the novel shifts focus from the Jarndyce suit to the Tulkinghorn murder case because the Court of Chancery, "to make itself tolerable, produces a desire for the detective story," something that can be interpreted and brought to termination. In his view, "despite or by means of its superficially hostile attitude toward bureaucracy, a novel like *Bleak House* [with its own extraordinary length and complexity] is profoundly concerned to train us . . . in the sensibility for inhabiting the new bureaucratic, administrative structures."[22]

Indeed, in the political turn the recent criticism has clearly taken, Foucault's thinking about power and discourse has been most influential. Catherine Gallagher (1985), concerned with the ways in which Victorian social-problem fiction was permeated by various discourses on industrialization circulating at that time (she examines a range of texts including Parliamentary Bluebooks, journalism, manuals on labor relations and domestic felicity, stories in working-class magazines), argues that *Hard Times*, with its ending where the novel seems to retreat from social considerations into the purely private sphere, exposes a dilemma inherent in the contemporary discourse based upon the "society is a family" metaphor.[23] Mary Poovey (1993) looks at *Our Mutual Friend* in relation to "a series of legislative measures that culminated in the establishment of limited liability" between 1844 and 1862 and the ensuing speculation mania, probing the implications of the same "structure of wishful projection" underlying financial investment and men's assignment of virtue to female nature.[24]

In a pivotal text in gender studies, Eve Kosofsky Sedgwick (1985) considers Dickens's last two novels as his contribution to the political naturalization of homophobia about men. Central to her analysis of *Our Mutual Friend*, "*the* English novel that everyone knows is about anality," is the triangle involving Lizzie, Eugene, and Bradley, whose only mode of grappling for power is "sphincter domination." In *Edwin Drood* Dickens recasts this triangle into that of Rosa, Jasper, and Edwin; here "the denied erotics of male rivalry are discussed more sentiently" and the socially crucial signifying function is performed by race, instead of class as in the previous novel. Neither of the female characters, Sedgwick notes, is a real object of love; each of them is merely used "as a counter in an intimate struggle of male will."[25]

Thus in the twentieth century Dickens invited a wide variety of critical responses. And he continues to do so. Currently scholars tend to examine the novelist in relation to such issues as gender, sexuality, empire, race, visual culture, politics, economics, and science. The "Dickens industry," led notably by Rosemarie Bodenheimer (2007) and Sally Ledger (2007), is thriving, indeed.[26]

(First published in *Charles Dickens in Context*, Ed. Sally Ledger and Holly Furneaux, Cambridge University Press, 2011)

NOTES

1 George Gissing, *Charles Dickens* (London: Blackie, 1898).
2 G. K. Chesterton, *Charles Dickens* (Ware: Wordsworth Editions, 2007), p. 42. See Ch. 9 of this book.
3 G. K. Chesterton, *Appreciations and Criticisms of the Works of Charles Dickens* (London: Dent, 1911), pp. 148, 46.
4 T. A. Jackson, *Charles Dickens: The Progress of a Radical* (London: Lawrence and Wishart, 1937).
5 George Orwell, "Charles Dickens" in *The Complete Works of George Orwell* Vol. 12, *A Patriot After All*, Ed. Peter Davison (London: Secker and Warburg, 1998), pp. 22, 31, 50, 51.
6 Edmund Wilson, "Dickens: The Two Scrooges" in *The Wound and the Bow: Seven Studies in Literature* (Athens: Ohio University Press, 1997), pp. 7, 14, 81, 52. See Ch. 10 of this book.
7 Humphry House, *The Dickens World* (Oxford: Oxford University Press, 1960), pp. 14, 21.
8 F. R. Leavis, *The Great Tradition* (London: Chatto & Windus, 1948), pp. 19, 228, 236.
9 Dorothy van Ghent, "The Dickens World: a View from Todgers's." *The Sewanee Review* 58 (1950), rpt. in *Dickens*, Ed. Martin Price (Englewood Cliffs: Prentice-Hall, 1967), pp. 29, 31, 38, 29.
10 J. Hillis Miller, *Charles Dickens: The World of His Novels* (Cambridge: Harvard University Press, 1958), pp. 329, 331, 333.
11 Robert Garis, *The Dickens Theatre* (Oxford: Oxford University Press, 1965), pp. 5, 15, 62.
12 Barbara Hardy, *The Moral Art of Dickens* (London: Athlone Press, 1970),

p. xi.

13 Philip Collins, *Dickens and Crime* (London: Macmillan, 1962), p. 22; *Dickens and Education* (London: Macmillan, 1963).

14 Philip Collins, "1940-1960: Enter the Professionals," *The Dickensian* 66 (1970), 144.

15 Steven Marcus, *Dickens: from Pickwick to Dombey* (New York: Norton, 1985), pp. 255, 255, 356.

16 Alexander Welsh, *The City of Dickens* (Oxford: Oxford University Press, 1971), pp. 141, 157.

17 Michael Slater, *Dickens and Women* (London: Dent, 1983), p. 275.

18 F. R. and Q. D. Leavis, *Dickens the Novelist* (London: Chatto & Windus, 1970), pp. 273, 274, 51, 121-22.

19 John Carey, *The Violent Effigy* (London: Faber & Faber, 1973), pp. 64, 130.

20 Garrett Stewart, *Dickens and the Trials of Imagination* (Cambridge: Harvard University Press), pp. xviii, 84.

21 J. Hillis Miller, "Introduction," Charles Dickens, *Bleak House* (Harmondsworth: Penguin, 1971), pp. 11, 22, 24.

22 D. A. Miller, *The Novel and the Police* (Berkeley: University of California Press, 1988), pp. 73, 89.

23 Catherine Gallagher, *The Industrial Reformation of English Fiction* (Chicago: University of Chicago Press, 1985).

24 Mary Poovey, 'Reading History in Literature: Speculation of Virtue in *Our Mutual Friend*' in *Historical Criticism and the Challenge of Theory*, Ed. Janet Levarie Smarr (Urbana: University of Illinois Press, 1993), pp. 48, 65.

25 Eve Kosofsky Sedgwick, *Between Men* (New York: Columbia University Press, 1985), pp. 163, 169, 181, 181.

26 Rosemarie Bodenheimer, *Knowing Dickens* (Ithaca: Cornell University Press, 2007); Sally Ledger, *Dickens and the Popular Radical Imagination* (Cambridge: Cambridge University Press, 2007).

Ch. 12 Modern Screen Adaptations of Dickens

Ever since the cinema came into existence, Dickens's works have been continually adapted to the screen. It is no doubt partly due to his popularity, and partly to the close affinity between his novel and this art form: the plastically visible characters, melodrama, montage, orchestration of sensuous details, which were brilliantly observed by the Russian director Eisenstein.[1] As the films are numerous,[2] I must be highly selective in my discussion, in which I adopt Linda Hutcheon's view: "an adaptation is a derivation that is not derivative—a work that is second without being secondary."[3] A film adaptation should be judged on its own terms, rather than on whether it is "faithful" to Dickens (whatever that may mean).

The first Dickens film was, as far as we can ascertain, *Death of Nancy Sykes* (1897). It is unfortunately lost, and the oldest of the preserved films is *Scrooge; Or, Marley's Ghost* (1901). The most famous, and perhaps most interesting, adaptation of the silent period is *Oliver Twist* (1922). It features Lon Chaney, and the child star Jackie Coogan who in the previous year had a brilliant success in Chaplin's *The Kid*. This film manages to pack in much of the novel in about an hour, and in several places it anticipates David Lean's version (see below): the Punch and Judy show in the background of the "Stop thief" sequence; the subjective shot when Oliver loses consciousness at Fang's court; the use (if clumsy) of Bull's Eye at Sikes's murder of Nancy; the shot of the tightened rope suggesting Sikes's death by hanging.[4]

Two early talkies stand out, both sumptuously and meticulously produced by David O. Selznick in 1935; *David Copperfield* and *A Tale of Two Cities*. The former—directed by George Cukor—is valuable as a series of superlative filmic incarnations, such as Lionel Barrymore's Mr Peggotty, Basil Rathbone's Murdstone, Edna May Oliver's Betsey Trotwood, and Roland Young's Uriah Heep (W. C. Fields as Micawber is an interesting idea, but his line reading does not do justice to "the old roll" of that character). Since Dickens conceived *A Tale of Two Cities* as "a *picturesque* story,"[5] the novel seems particularly suited for being brought to the big screen. Here that process is greatly helped by Ronald Colman who expresses Carton's melancholy and dignity extremely well, as in the scene in which he stands in front of Lucy's house in the falling snow, and the one in which he calmly ascends the guillotine.

The 1940s saw the best adaptations of Dickens; the two films by David Lean. Excellently cast, and presented with a stylistic vigor worthy of the Inimitable, they amply reward close viewings. *Great Expectations* (1946) begins with a shot of the book with its first page opened. We hear the voice of the adult Pip reading it. Then a wind blows the pages over, and they dissolve into a shot of a boy running in a lonely marshland under lowering clouds. He comes to a village churchyard. The rustling of the wind creates a sinister effect. The boy, frightened, turns back, and there suddenly appears a fierce-looking convict. This is a terrific start. Lean recalls: "I went to the press show and as the boy ran into the convict, the whole audience went back in a wave and I knew I was in business. It was lovely. It really worked."[6]

The film immediately impresses us with the beauty of its black and white images—especially the contrast of light and shadow, which is most noticeable when Joe and Pip join the army squad on the recapturing expedition; first the soldiers, and then Joe and Pip, emerge in stark silhouette against the sky. This leads effectively to the scene in which Jaggers appears with the news of Pip's great expectations. Here Lean first shows the shadows on the wall. They are those of Pip and Joe working at the forge. On the wall there is a door between these shadows, through which Jaggers enters. Thus the point is visually made that the lawyer is intruding from a different world; we see him in person facing us, not as a shadow. Lean adds emphasis by repeatedly placing Jaggers between Joe and Pip in this sequence.

Lean is often criticized for removing Orlick, thereby losing an important aspect of Pip's dark psychology. However, in rendering a novel of this length and complexity into a film of two hours, a substantial compression is inevitable. It would be critically more productive to note that in compensation Lean's film has created interesting complications of its own, which manifest themselves, again largely by visual means, in climactic moments.

After he becomes aware of the identity of his patron, Pip goes to see Miss Havisham at Satis House. Estella is there (Lean skillfully conflates a few scenes of the novel into this one). Notice here how our attention is drawn to "the hand." Four times Lean's camera captures, in the same frame, in medium close shots, Estella's hands busy knitting and Miss Havisham's left hand resting on the arm of her chair. Estella, before going out to see Drummle, says to Pip, "Don't be afraid of my being a blessing to him. Here's my hand." Left alone with Miss Havisham Pip says to her, "Estella is part of my existence" (John Mills, who is rarely praised for this role, is particularly fine here), and after urging her to think better of giving Estella to Drummle, he leaves the room. Immediately afterwards Miss Havisham's clothing catches fire. Trying to save her, Pip burns his hand. The film, then, deals with his attempt to smuggle Magwitch out of the country. It fails, Magwitch is sentenced to death, and Pip goes to see him in the prison infirmary. In a moving scene, informed of his child's survival and Pip's love for her, Magwitch brings Pip's bandaged hand to his lips, and dies peacefully. Thus the deaths of the two people who had a hand in Pip's destiny are visually united.

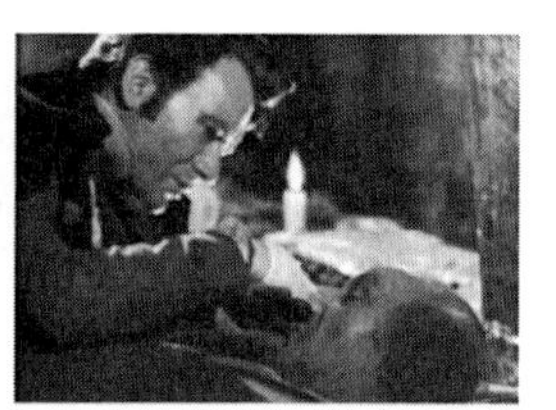

Lean's handling of Miss Havisham's death by fire is of great interest. Pip goes out of her room angrily and shuts the door. The next shot shows a burning coal dropping from the hearth onto the bottom edge of Miss Havisham's dress. Soon she is devoured by fire. Thus Pip appears to be, if unwittingly, responsible for her death. This montage can suggest that his suppressed anger has somehow brought it about, thus anticipating Julian Moynahan's idea of "an analogy between that part of Pip which wants Miss Havisham at least punished, at most removed from this earth for which she is so profoundly unfit, and the destroying fire itself".[7] There may be little evidence to support this in the novel, but she has after all wrecked Pip's life and it would be possible to imagine that deep down he harbors resentment against her—and it is such a psychology that Lean hints at.[8] This is perhaps an exemplary instance where a screen adaptation functions as an adjacent (not simply derivative, parasitic) text, offering an intelligent reflection upon (not necessarily a "faithful" rendering of) the original.

Lean makes up for the loss of Orlick by amplifying the significance of Miss Havisham. In the end Estella identifies herself with Miss Havisham; jilted by Drummle (an interesting alteration of the plot), she just sits in the darkness of Satis House, believing that the former mistress of the house is still there. Pip is determined to save her from this dismal fate. "I have come back, Miss Havisham!" he cries, and breaks the old witch's spell by tearing down the curtains and bringing in sunlight. Brian McFarlane sees this as "a metaphoric letting in of light on British life at large after the rigours of the war years."[9] This is a possible reading, but at the same time, it should be recalled that Pip's action here visually matches his pulling off the table cloth when Miss Havisham catches fire, thereby strengthening Miss Havisham's presence at the ending.

In the final scene we have Pip and Estella going out of Satis House hand in hand. Lean has prepared for this ending by using a shot from the reverse angle earlier, when depicting their childhood—though on that occasion only Estella is seen trotting, and now they both are.

Oliver Twist (1948) amply realizes the cinematic possibilities Eisenstein saw in this novel, and Lean's visual storytelling is again remarkably forceful. Most impressively, the sequence of "Oliver asking for more" is pure cinema with no dialogue: the drawing of the lot; Oliver chosen; the awed faces of the children; the sound of their running away; Oliver left alone in a circle of light; the meal begun; every one staring at Oliver; his walk towards the cook. Immediately after he begs for another helping, Lean shows, in quick succession, the surprised faces of the cook, Mrs Mann, Bumble, and the Board of Guardians. The film opens with a pregnant woman walking in a violent rainstorm. The pain she is suffering is reflected in the form, caught in close-up, of the briars bent by the wind. There is a high-angle shot of the workhouse boys so that the spikes of the wall are seen to threaten them. Upon Oliver's entrance into London at a busy market, the cut-away from our hero to the cattle driven about signifies the boy's present circumstances, and the placing of him in the same frame with a caged bird foreshadows his future predicament. When the Artful Dodger leads Oliver to Fagin's den, the shaking screen suggests the hero's anxious state of mind.

Fine touches abound. When dealing with Noah Claypole's reaction to Sowerberry's caning of Oliver, Lean first shows Noah's sadistic smile, and then lets the camera linger to record his face changing from smug satisfaction to awe at Oliver's holding back his tears. In presenting the murder of Nancy, Lean expresses the horror of it by the frantic behavior of the frightened dog. After the deed Sikes is dazed, and when the sunlight pours in from the window he comes to himself. Then there is a series of montages of Nancy's face, Fagin's face, Sikes hitting him, Fagin falling to the ground, and his corpse changing into that of Nancy. This suggests Sikes's regret that it was not the loving Nancy but the duplicitous Fagin that he should have killed. Lean can also extend the Dickensian humor. In order to reveal the unhappy state of Bumble's marriage, he places the enormous Francis Sullivan (who played Jaggers two years before) in a tiny chair, where he finds himself uncomfortably sitting on his wife's knitting needle.

The film leaves us with indelible images of some faces. The boys in the workhouse all look convincingly hungry, and Frederick Lloyd's Grimwig is amazingly appropriate. John Howard Davies shines as Oliver when Brownlow (at a loss to find that the name of the boy he has helped is not Tom White) says, "Some mistake"—Davies counters this with a smile that speaks of his innocence far more eloquently than any words could. The most striking face of all, however, is that of Fagin. Unfortunately, Alec Guiness's heavy make-up based upon Cruikshank's illustrations incurred the charge of anti-Semitism. Because of this, the film was not shown in America until three years later, after a number of cuts of his scenes. So, as Juliet John observes, "Fagin on screen has seldom subsequently been both very Jewish and very evil."[10]

Of all Dickens's works it is *A Christmas Carol* that is most often filmed (Fred Guida lists up more than 150 film and TV versions made between 1901 and 1998).[11] These adaptations show an amazing variety:

Carol for Another Christmas (1964; an antiwar allegory), *Mickey's Christmas Carol* (1983; Disney), *Scrooge's Rock 'n' Roll Christmas* (1984; a rock musical), *The Muppet Christmas Carol* (1992), *Ebenezer* (1998; a western), and *A Diva's Christmas Carol* (2000; a musical featuring Vanessa Williams as Ebony Scrooge). The definitive version, however, is *Scrooge* (1951). What is striking about this film is that, unlike many of its predecessors, the tone is often dark and somber. It features the children "Ignorance" and "Want," the poor people on the street of London, and the humble miners in a distant industrial area. The social background is solidified by an introduction of the character called Jorkin, who is an aggressive businessman "in this age of machine and the factory." This man invites Scrooge to come to work for him when he was a clerk at Fezziwig's. Initially he declines the offer, saying money is not everything. Interestingly at this moment the film shows Scrooge in the office room with a small reflection of himself on the glass door, thereby expressing his divided response.

We see him next working under Jorkin with Jacob Marley, a fellow after his own heart in business competitiveness. This film is also notable in its psychological investigation of the hero: Scrooge's father hates him because his wife died giving birth to him, which parallels Scrooge's own aloofness from his nephew Fred because his beloved sister Fanny died in childbirth. The script—by Noel Langley of *The Wizard of Oz* fame—is also witty in the spirit of the Dickens of the tale: when on Christmas Eve Bob Cratchit says, "They [his family] put their hearts into Christmas, as it were, sir," Scrooge retorts: "Yes, and put their hands into my pockets, as it were, sir." Above all, this film owes its success to Alastair Sim, who superbly expresses the protagonist's wide range of emotions from sarcastic glumness to wild ecstasy.

While on the whole black and white films serve Dickens better, Christine Edzard's *Little Dorrit* (1987) cannot be overlooked.[12] Consisting of two parts—the first telling the story from Clennam's point of view, and the second from Amy's—and running close to six hours, it is an ambitious attempt but only a qualified success. The film painfully reveals that it was made with a limited budget, moves at a slow pace, and is visually unexciting. Its strength is in the wonderful performance; Alec Guiness perfectly embodies Dorrit's vanity and selfishness, and Miriam Margolyes's Flora, Max Wall's Flintwinch, Roshan Seth's Pancks are outstanding portrayals of Dickensian eccentrics.

I have touched on the *Carol*'s various metamorphoses, but there are some other retellings in which Dickens stories have been transplanted into contemporary contexts. *Tempos Difíceis* (1988), for example, is set in a dreary industrial town of the present-day Portugal. The world of this film, caught in black and white cinematography, is very bleak, as there is no positive principle operating in it other than Sissy (Sleary is absent and the circus not shown). The last shot, a close-up of Louisa's bitter, unhappy face, is unforgettable. In the South African film, *Boy Called Twist* (2005), Oliver, a black boy brought up in a rural orphanage, and mixed up with a juvenile gang in Cape Town, turns out to be an heir to the fortune of a wealthy Muslim living in the affluent part of the city. Visually more interesting is *Great Expectations* (1998), which concerns Finn, a boy from Florida with artistic talent, who is brought to New York by an anonymous benefactor. The film begins with a voice-over: "I'm not going to tell the story the way that it happened. I'm going to tell it the way I remember it." This point, as Michael K. Johnson argues, is reinforced through the ingenious use of Finn's drawings. In the most sensual scene of the film, in which Estella poses as a model for Finn, "we do not see Estella so much as we see Finn's version of her—as revealed in his sketches."[13] When Joe and Lustig (a mafia hit man, the counterpart of Magwitch) reappear from the past, they are shown against Finn's portraits of them; thus we are made aware of the discrepancies between Finn's story and reality.

(A few words about the movies made for television. Longer than feature films, they have more room in which plot and character can be developed. For example, the recent BBC *Bleak House* (2005) consists of a one-hour opening episode followed by fourteen half-hour episodes. And by being shown twice weekly with cliff-hanger endings, it succeeded in reviving the feel of a Victorian serial. Judged as a whole, however, the well-appointed 1985 BBC production of the same novel, with a fine cast led by Denholm Elliott and Diana Rigg, remains the most satisfying TV adaptation.)

Dickens's unfailing popularity will ensure the continued production of film adaptations in one fashion after another, the most recent *Carol* (Disney, 2009) showing that the 3D technology has quickly caught up with the Great Inimitable, the novelist the cinema has most often imitated.

(First published in *Charles Dickens in Context*, Ed. Sally Ledger and Holly Furneaux, Cambridge University Press, 2011)

NOTES

1 Sergei M. Eisenstein, "Dickens, Griffith and Ourselves". *Selected Works, Vol. 3: Writings, 1934-47*, Ed. Richard Taylor, trans. William Powell (London: BFI Publishing, 1996), pp. 193-238.

2 For detailed filmographies, see *Dickens on Screen*, Ed. John Glavin (Cambridge: Cambridge University Press, 2003); *Charles Dickens on the Screen*, Ed. Michael Pointer (Lanham: Scarecrow Press, 1996).

3 Linda Hutcheon, *A Theory of Adaptation* (London: Routledge, 2006), p. 9.

4 For a thorough discussion of the Dickens silent films, see Graham Petrie,

"Silent Film Adaptations of Dickens" Parts 1-3, *The Dickensian* 97 (2001): 7-21, 101-15, 197-213. The DVD *Dickens Before Sound* (BFI) contains *Scrooge and Oliver Twist* here mentioned.

5 Letter to John Forster, 25 August 1859.

6 Kevin Brownlow, *David Lean: A Biography* (New York. St. Martin's Press), p. 225.

7 Julian Moynahan, "The Hero's Guilt: The Case of *Great Expectations,*" *Essays in Criticism* 10 (1960), 77.

8 Curiously enough, Moynahan finds Lean's treatment of this scene "All wrong." See his article, "Seeing the Book, Reading the Movie" in *The English Novel and the Movies*, Ed. Michael Klein and Gillian Parker (New York: Frederick Ungar, 1981), p. 150.

9 *Novel to Film* (Oxford: Oxford University Press, 1996), 111.

10 Juliet John, "Fagin, The Holocaust and Mass Culture: or, *Oliver Twist* on Screen," *Dickens Quarterly* 22 (2005), 213.

11 Fred Guida, *A Christmas Carol and Its Adaptations* (Jefferson: McFarland, 2000). See also Paul Davis, *The Lives and Times of Ebenezer Scrooge* (New Haven: Yale University Press, 1990).

12 For a fine detailed study of this film, see Joss Lutz Marsh, "Inimitable Double Vision: Dickens, *Little Dorrit*, Photography, Film," *Dickens Studies Annual* 22 (1993), 239-82.

13 Michael K. Johnson, "Not Telling the Story the Way It Happened: Alfonso Cuarón's *Great Expectations,*" *Literature/Film Quarterly* 33 (2005), 69.

Ch. 13 We Ask for More: A Note on Polanski's *Oliver Twist*

Leon Litvak reviewed Roman Polanski's *Oliver Twist* for the *Dickensian* and the *Dickens Quarterly*.[1] Although the conclusion of the latter piece is accompanied with more qualifications, on both occasions he expresses a favorable opinion, praising the film's interior design and performances, especially that of Sir Ben Kingsley: "It is, in many ways, true to the spirit of Dickens's original, but enhances it with a fresh approach that should satisfy casual movie-goers and serious Dickensians alike."[2] My view is less enthusiastic, and I wish to offer some more detailed observations, prompted by the recent release of the DVD of the film.

In the interview included in this DVD Polanski says he wanted to make "a film for my children." This wish on the director's part may have been largely responsible for the film's colorless, unexciting style, which I think is a great mistake for *Oliver Twist*. Indeed, what is most disappointing about this new film is that it is lacking in the kind of excess that we associate with Polanski; something that made films like *Repulsion* (1965), *Macbeth* (1971), *Chinatown* (1974) and *The Tenant* (1976) so memorably unique. One wonders if that distinctive texture now belongs wholly in the past for him. While there was still the fascination with tortured psychology in *Bitter Moon* (1992) and *Death and the Maiden* (1994), they were visually indifferent. The most highly regarded of his recent films, *The Pianist* (2002), was, given the subject matter and its personal resonance, strikingly restrained. Perhaps this change can be seen to have occurred when he adapted Hardy's *Tess* (1979), in which some of the melodramatic elements of the original novel were conspicuously absent: the wagon-horse Prince's death, Angel's sleepwalking, Alec's sudden appearance from the tomb, etc. Unfortunately, the method adopted for *Oliver* is very much a continuation of this approach.

In the interview Polanski does not refer to David Lean (Carol Reed's *Oliver!* is the only other version mentioned), but the comparison is inevitable, and nearly fatal. Dickens on film needs a vigorous, heightened style and Lean's 1948 version amply possessed it. The cinematic possibilities Sergei Eisenstein saw in the novel are expertly realized, for example, in Oliver's entrance into London.[3]

Polanski's film, though crafted with highly competent

professionalism, has none of this flair, and comparisons of the same scenes almost always show Lean to advantage. Take, for example, Noah's reaction to Sowerberry's caning of Oliver. In both versions we have Noah's sadistic smile, but Lean's camera deftly lingers to record his face changing from smug satisfaction to awe at Oliver's choking down his tears. In presenting the murder of Nancy, while Polanski is content to have the effect (mostly aural) of blood splashed towards the barking Bull's Eye, Lean conveys the horror by the frantic behavior of the frightened dog. Polanski says he has taken care to preserve Dickens's humor, but if we simply consider the treatment of Bumble, Lean's superiority is apparent. In order to show the unhappy state of the parochial officer's marriage he has the enormous Francis Sullivan sit on a tiny chair, where he finds himself uncomfortably sitting on his wife's knitting needle, which he immediately throws away in a miff—a brilliant touch I'm sure Dickens would have loved.

It must be added, however, that Polanski's film is not without interesting elements. A case in point is the scene in which the children in the workhouse try to decide who is going to ask for more. Here the lots are made of shreds of oakum, and the one who draws the shortest loses. This is a neat pun on "picking out the oakum"—there is an earlier scene which shows this is what the boys do there. Also, one is pleased

to note that the chimney sweep Gamfield (who did not figure in the Lean film) makes an appropriately grotesque appearance.

Litvak no doubt speaks for all in commending Sir Ben Kingsley's performance. In his view, unlike Alec Guiness, "Kingsley humanises the character" and "there is some genuine warmth" in the relationship between Fagin and Oliver.[4] To be sure, this Fagin attends to Oliver's wound, giving some sort of "magic" ointment. The boy thanks him for his "kindness," and at the final encounter in the condemned cell says to him, "You were kind to me," which leads to their embracing each other. What is interesting, though, and admirably conveyed by Kingsley, is the duplicitous nature of this "kindness." (In saying that Fagin gives Oliver "one of the film's central moral lessons"—about ingratitude being the greatest sin—Litvak may be right, but he rather simplifies matters.[5])

When Sikes says he is going to kill Oliver so that he will not squeal, Fagin agrees that "It's for the best." His "kindness" derives from his thinking that if he should get caught Oliver will speak for him. In his attempt to evacuate his den after Nancy's murder is disclosed, Fagin desperately gathers his property and runs out, leaving the sleeping Oliver behind. Then he does a double-take and comes back for the boy. (Litvak says Fagin "is continually seen from Oliver's point of view,"[6] but the last two scenes mentioned above show that he is not quite accurate.) This is a curious moment, but I believe it is meant to indicate Fagin's calculating nature, for soon after when his gang is besieged, he says of Oliver, "He's our bargaining tool."

In contrast to this, Polanski presents the kindness of a pure nature. Oliver, after escaping from Sowerberry's, encounters an old woman, who helps him out of benevolence. This character appears in Ch. 8 of the book: "the old lady, who had a shipwrecked grandson wandering barefoot in some distant part of the earth, took pity upon the poor orphan, and gave him what little she could afford. . . ." As far as I know, Polanski is the very first filmmaker who puts her on screen. I venture to guess that he does so because he has taken to heart the passage which describes this woman and another kind soul, "a good-hearted turnpike-man": "In fact, if it had not been for [them], Oliver's troubles would have been shortened by the very same process which had put an end to his mother's; in other words, he would most assuredly have fallen dead upon the king's highway."

To back up this conjecture, I want to draw attention to the streamlining of the plot in this film. Like Lean, Polanski drops the entire Rose Maylie strand of the story. He even goes so far as to eliminate Monks, with the result that Brownlow is no relation of Oliver's at all. This, I take it, is crucial for the director's vision: Oliver survives only because total strangers help him. With this understanding, one begins to see a significant continuity between Polanski's *Oliver Twist* and its immediate predecessor, *The Pianist*, in which exactly the same point is made with a helpless Jew for the protagonist. Watching the latter film one gets the impression, as Clive James did, that the titular character manages to avoid the holocaust, not so much thanks to his musicianship as from sheer luck.[7] And in *Oliver*, too, Polanski reinforces this feeling by repeatedly showing the hero in luck at critical junctures; he twice escapes from the evil hands of Sikes—once when a running carriage obstructs him, and once when the thief happens to slip and fall into the river.

Thus, to see this film in conjunction with *The Pianist* allows another dimension to our appreciation. To recognize this, however, is not to deem Polanski's as a successful adaptation of the Dickens novel. I, for one, firmly stand by the Lean version for its cinematic brilliance.

(First published in *The Dickensian*, 2007)

NOTES

1 *The Dickensian* (Winter 2005), 252-55; *The Dickens Quarterly* (December 2005), 261-67.
2 *Dickensian*, 255.
3 For Eisenstein on Dickens and Lean's film of *Oliver*, see Ch. 12 of this book.
4 *Dickensian*, 255
5 *Dickens Quarterly*, 266
6 *Dickensian*, 255.
7 *The Times Literary Supplement*, 31 January 2003.

Ch. 14 Listening to Dickens

There is a charming passage in Henry James's autobiography, describing an incident in his childhood (he must have been six years old), when an elder cousin of his

> had begun to read aloud to my mother the new, which must have been the first, instalment of David Copperfield. I had feigned to withdraw, but had only retreated to cover close at hand, the friendly shade of some screen or drooping table-cloth, folded up behind which and glued to the carpet, I held my breath and listened. I listened long and drank deep while the wondrous picture grew, but the tense cord at last snapped under the strain of the Murdstones and I broke into the sobs of sympathy that disclosed my subterfuge.[1]

This is a most memorable record of one of the ways in which Dickens was enjoyed in his century: Victorians read his novels aloud at home. Listening to Dickens was a vital part of their appreciation of his art.

It would be very far from the truth to say that reading aloud is actively practiced in our household today. We can, however, still enjoy listening to Dickens by means of "books on tape," also known as "audio books." The audio book market, which originally targeted at the blind, has been steadily growing, and it seems to be thriving with blockbusters like Stephen Fry's (utterly delightful) reading of the Harry Potter series (Fry's Dickensian connection has been sadly limited—I can only think of an appearance in *Blackadder's Christmas Carol*—but he would be an ideal reader of *Martin Chuzzlewit*). People listen to recorded books mostly as accompaniment of various house chores, or as in-car entertainment. As a matter of fact, I was first made aware of the idea of listening to Dickens, nearly twenty years ago, by the American novelist John Irving—whose novels such as *The World According to Garp* and *The Cider House Rules* are distinctly Dickensian—when I read in an interview that he was listening to *Bleak House* in his car. Not a driver myself, I do the listening while commuting on foot. The Sony Walkman was invented for me.

*

What is an ideal style of reading Dickens aloud? We know the novelist's own method. "He does not only read his story; he acts it. . . . Each character . . . is as completely assumed and individualized . . . as though he was personating it in costume on the stage," a reviewer said of his performance.[2] Emlyn Williams observes that "impersonation" was the key to Dickens's histrionic talent.[3] In short, Dickens's reading style was that of Sloppy, "doing the police in different voices." I believe this is the way his novels should be read. It is by no means an easy thing to do. First of all, it demands a wide-ranging, flexible voice. Moreover, it must involve an act of interpretation, for Dickens is not always specific about a character's voice or delivery. To be sure, we have some memorably idiosyncratic instances: Creakle's "no voice," Vholes's "low, inward voice," Jasper's "deep and good" voice, Littimer's "peculiar habit of whispering the letter S so distinctly," and Sleary's asthmatic voice "like the efforts of a broken old pair of bellows." We also have fairly predictable descriptions: Bumble has a "majestic" voice, Scrooge "grating," Bounderby "brassy," Gradgrind "inflexible, dry," Mrs Clennam "strong, low," Charlie Hexam "hoarse and coarse," Rose Mailie "sweet," etc. But in many other cases where no indications are given, one simply has to take an educated guess on the basis of characters' other attributes and then imagine how they sound.

In my view, Martin Jarvis is the great master of the Sloppy method; his readings of *Great Expectations* and *David Copperfied* (both published by Cover to Cover) are superb. His Miss Havisham is properly weird and mysterious ("Love her, love her, love her" lingers in the listener's ear), Magwitch gruff ("Tell us your name"), Mrs Joe irascible ("You young monkey"), and Joe simple and sweet ("Pip, old chap"). Jarvis showcases his versatility when he does the voices of Joe, Mrs Joe, Wopsle, the Hubbles, and Pumblechook at the Christmas dinner. As far as impersonation is concerned, he is equally good at men and women, but he does not always manage a deep voice well. When such a voice is required (for example, with Jaggers or Murdstone), he often resorts to a nasal one. That is my only qualm about this talented reader. Jarvis has also recorded complete readings of *A Tale of Two Cities*, *Hard Times*, and *Oliver Twist* for Chivers—all highly enjoyable.

Cover to Cover is the leading company of books on tape (they also produce Timothy West's wonderful Trollope readings). They only do unabridged recordings; an admirably sound policy. In addition to

Great Expectations and *Copperfield* by Martin Jarvis, their Dickens catalogue contains *Oliver Twist*, *Nicholas Nickleby*, *A Christmas Carol*, *Domby and Son*, *Bleak House*, *Hard Times*, *A Tale of Two Cities* and *Our Mutual Friend*. Miriam Margolyes reads *Oliver* and *Carol*, and what a fine mimic she is! (This is surely no news for anyone who has seen her marvelous one-woman show, "Dickens' Women"). Not only can she do the innocent boy Oliver convincingly, but also she does Bumble extremely well—she can use a deep voice—and his courting of Mrs Corney is made wonderfully funny. When the scene moves to London, one is impressed by her dexterous handling of cockney accents. All in all, I have simply the highest regard for Margolyes as a reader. There is, however, something problematic about a woman doing the Dickensian narrative voice. The sophisticated literary theory may tell us that the narrator of the text has no gender, but Dickens's presence is so strong in his novels that if his voice is done by a woman it is a trifle strange—to me, at least. (By the same token, I would have reservations about a male reader for Jane Austen or George Eliot.) Hugh Dickson, who reads *Bleak House*, is also remarkable, impersonating the gallery of characters, from poor Jo to haughty Sir Leicester. If his rendition of the narrative voice could have been slightly more forceful, he does Esther with exquisite delicacy. *Hard Times* is read by Steve Thorne with his beautiful baritone. His Bounderby sounds like the bully that he is, and he skillfully adopts the working-class accents for Stephen and others. Richard Pasco, too, has an attractive voice, which he puts into excellent use for *Two Cities*. I do not think, however, I can say the same for David Troughton (*Mutual Friend*) and Alex Jennings (*Nickleby* and *Dombey*). They are both highly competent readers, but their voices are somewhat thin and bland.

The competing American company is Blackstone, whose catalogue lists, impressively enough, every one of Dickens's novels, plus *Carol* and *Christmas Stories*. Now, in addition to the gender question, I have a view as regards pronunciation. At the risk of sounding like Podsnap, I maintain "with a dignified conclusiveness" that Dickens must be read with a British accent. Fortunately, the best reader of Blackstone, Peter Davidson, is British. His reading style, though, is rather mannered, which makes his *Dombey*, vivid as it is, a little tiring to attend to. Davidson's skill is turned to great advantage in *Chuzzlewit*. He overdoes Pecksniff, but it is a role that can accommodate exaggeration. This *tour de force* performance is worth a listen.

A company that surpasses Blackstone, in terms of its coverage of Dickens, is Complete Readers. This is a very small outfit based in Yorkshire, with only one reader, Anthony Homyer. He reads everything in their catalogue, which amounts to 50 titles, including all the Dickens novels, *Christmas Stories*, and the whole *Christmas Books*. Although this comprehensiveness is good news, their production value is low: the cassettes come with cheapish labels and covers; the sound quality is poor. Homyer has a pleasant voice, but annoyingly he neglects to read the chapter divisions, and his occasional mispronunciations are distracting—for example, Lammle becomes "Lamalle" with an accent in the rear, Wegg "Wedge," and Grewgious "Greegious".

Assembled Stories (UK) has published *American Notes*, the only title from Dickens's non-fictional writings on the market. Peter Joyce's reading starts in a ponderous fashion, but once Dickens lands in America it improves considerably. Taken as a whole, this is a fine audio book. I have a minor complaint to make, though. On the tapes Joyce changes the words "the reader" in the original text to "the listener." This is no doubt meant well, but I would say it is an unnecessary tampering. Interestingly, listening to this travelogue, one is made to realize the powerful effect of the list of runaway slaves that appears towards the end. When reading, you may be tempted to skip (for at a glance you can see the monotonous-looking list go on for a few pages), but there is no way of doing so when you are listening (theoretically you can, by fastforwarding the tape; but you wouldn't know where to stop, so you don't). The cumulative force of the list has a physical impact on the listener.

So far we have been dealing with unabridged recordings. Now we move on to abridged ones. These, I cannot help feeling, are meant for the uninitiated, and not for seasoned Dickensians. Just imagine: the Cover to Cover *Copperfield* runs 34.5 hours, whilst both Naxos and Penguin (the two big companies in this market) versions run less than 6 hours—which means that approximately five-sixths of the novel is missing! You are bound to be frustrated to find your favorite bits mercilessly cut. Of course, on the other hand, abridged recordings are less expensive.

Naxos's tapes have high production values. (Their CDs come with an information sheet which clearly indicates how the tracks are divided, which allows the reader to move easily in the book.) Given that they are created by a music company, it is not surprising that their sound quality is superb. And their audio books are always accompanied with well-chosen classical music. I would, however, rather have more words instead. Their Dickens catalogue consists of *Pickwick*, *Oliver*, *Nickleby*, *Carol*, *Copperfield*, *Hard Times*, *Two Cities*, and *Great Expectations*; all read by Anton Lesser (*Carol* is unabridged). Though I am willing to admit that Lesser is an able performer, his soft voice is, to my taste, not an ideal vehicle for the reading of Dickens.

Penguin also offers several abridged titles: *Copperfield*, *Oliver*, *Bleak House*, *Two Cities* and *Great Expectations*. (There were more, but these are the ones available at present.) I wonder why they only give three hours to *Great Expectations*, when all the other novels get six. It is the more regrettable because Hugh Laurie is a very good Pip and shows an adroit command of many voices, if a little weak on female characters. Nathaniel Parker, also a deft hand at the Sloppy method, reads *Copperfield* with vigor. A possible criticism is that his Steerforth is a bit on the heavy side. To be sure, David imagines that J. Steerforth has "a rather strong voice" from the carving of his name, but we are not told whether he guessed right or not. Martin Jarvis makes him sound bright and breezy, which I think is right. Besides, Parker's Rosa Dartle is not malicious enough, and Heap not mean enough. Compared to Jarvis, however, Parker can manage a deep voice better, and he uses it effectively for Murdstone and Micawber. On the other hand, his employment of a similar voice for Creakle, who should "have no voice" and speaks "in a whisper," is completely wrong. This is no doubt due to the fact that the passage describing his voice was cut. For the same reason, Littimer's dissstinctive ssspeech habit is gone. This is a pitfall of the abridgement. Like Naxos, Penguin makes an exception of *Carol*, which comes in its entirety. Geoffrey Palmer's reading is very good, if a touch subdued on the whole. He manages Nephew Fred's hearty laugh admirably, but sounds not quite at ease when doing the voices of women and children.

Carol, ever a popular title, is read by various distinguished actors. Paul Scofield has a delivery which tends to be too flowing, but he nicely captures the sudden shifts in mood of this volatile narrative (HarperCollins; unabridged). The transition from a gloomy London to the merry moments in Scrooge's past—the con brio rendition of Ali Baba's appearance and Fezziwig's Christmas dance—is outstanding.[4] John Gielgud's nuanced reading (Hodder & Stoughton), though only an hour long (that is, about one-third), is a delectable listen. Arguably the greatest voice of the twentieth century is particularly resonant when doing Marley's ghost. He reads out the adjectives describing the two children Ignorance and Want ("wretched, abject, frightful, hideous, miserable") with beautiful cadence. Patrick Stewart's performance (Simon & Schuster) is in its way quite lively. He has a powerful voice that carries the listener along. But his imitation of the sounds of bells, clocks, or Scrooge's snoring, and his gratuitous rendering of Tiny Tim's singing, are ill-judged. *Carol* is also part of Simon Callow's ambitious attempt to re-create Dickens's public readings, just like that of Emlyn Williams in the 50's. "An Audience with Charles Dickens" (Hodder and Stoughton) includes, in addition, his performance of "Bardell and Pickwick," "Doctor Marigold," and "Sikes and Nancy," all using Dickens's reading texts. Callow too often pulls out all the stops and plays his voice at full volume. Listening to him, I am constantly reminded of Henry James's phrase for Dickens's performance in 1867: "the hard charmless readings."[5] His theatricality, however, finds a happy outlet in "Doctor Marigold," and it is excellently done. For this alone the cassettes are worth purchasing.

*

Reading is not the only way of enjoying Dickens. Listening to his works adds another dimension to our appreciation of the Great Inimitable. As there are a number of good audio books around, I say with Squeers, "Here's richness"!

(First published in *The Dickensian*, 2005)

Addendum

David Timson's reading of *Dombey* is truly distinguished. His is a voice with vigor and malleability, and he puts it to highly effective use. He can deal with grotesques such as Major Bagstock and Mrs Skewton, can re-create the timidity of Perch, the boyishness of Rob the Grinder, and the likeable dottiness of Cousin Feenix. I am particularly impressed by the way he handles Toots, for I have always thought this is one of the most difficult Dickens characters to impersonate. To be sure Timson is not so sure-footed on Toot's first appearance when he accosts Paul "in a voice so deep, and a manner so sheepish, that if a lamb had roared it couldn't have been more surprising." Admittedly this is a hard thing to realize, but he exudes confidence from there on, and is particularly fine at the end of Ch. 44, where Toots asks Susan if Florence can reciprocate his romantic feelings (starting with "Do you think she could—you know—eh?" and ending up with his everlasting "It's of no consequence."). Elsewhere Timson's versatility is notably felt in the sequence involving the vibrant confusion at Staggs's Gardens, Florence's losing her way, and the dramatic appearance of the Good Mrs Brown (Ch. 6), Dombey's death-ridden train ride (Ch. 20), and Captain Cuttle's series of encounters with Toots, Rob, Bunsby, and Mrs MacStinger, every single character beautifully individualized (Ch. 39).

The first ten seconds of *Pickwick Papers* is enough to assure us, with its palpable buoyancy, that we are in capable hands. Although the reader of a Dickens novel always has to have an especially flexible voice for many characters and various moods, this book offers a particular challenge, in that he or she has to sustain, at almost a dozen points, the tonal change for the duration of an inset story. Yet this does not give Timson any problem at all. Nor does Sam Weller's cockney speech—whose u/v transposition John Sutherland discusses, citing the following example:

> "I had a reg'lar new fit out o' clothes that mornin', gen'l'men of the jury," said Sam, "and that was a wery partickler and uncommon circumstance vith me in those days. . . . If they wos a pair o' patent double million magnifyin' gas microscopes of hextra power, p'raps I might be able to see through a flight o' stairs and a deal door; but bein' only eyes, you see, my wision's limited."

Sutherland addresses his reader: "You can read it, you can translate it, you can laugh at it, but can you hear it?"[6] Vell, Dawid Timson's 'ere to 'elp us.

(First published in *The Dickensian*, 2010, 2013)

NOTES

1 Henry James, *A Small Boy and Others* (1913) reprinted in Frederick W. Dupee (ed.) *Autobiography* (Princeton: Princeton UP, 1983), 68-69.
2 *Courant* (Edinburgh), 28 November 1861; quoted in Philip Collins's Introduction to *Charles Dickens: The Public Readings* (Oxford: Clarendon Press, 1975), lix.
3 Emlyn Williams, "Dickens and the Theatre" in *Charles Dickens 1812-1870: A Centennial Volume*, Ed. E. W. F. Tomlin (London: Weidenfeld and Nicholson, 1969), 191.
4 Scofield has also recorded a sizable number of Dickens's novels, but they are drastically cut (down to a mere three hours) and his readings rather monotonous.
5 James set down his recollection on 29 March 1905; see *The Complete Notebooks of Henry James*, Ed. Leon Edel and Lyall H. Powers (Oxford: Oxford University Press, 1987), 238.
6 *The Dickens Dictionary* (London: Icon Books, 2012), 196.

II. HARDY

Ch. 15 Viewer and Victim in *Desperate Remedies*: Links between Hardy's Life and His Fiction

Early in *Desperate Remedies* there is a striking scene in which the heroine, Cytherea Graye, sees her father accidentally fall to his death. Robert Gittings has drawn attention to the similarity of this scene to a passage in Hardy's autobiography where the novelist recalls the experience of watching a hanging with the aid of a telescope. I should like to examine this similarity further, paying close attention to Hardy's language. *Desperate Remedies* is much more interesting than is commonly assumed in that it contains passages uniquely alive with a linguistic vitality which stems from Hardy's imaginative involvement, and, as happens in his greater works, this vigor of creative engagement is often most apparent where the subject is death.

What happens in the scene in question is this: Cytherea is in the Town Hall, and through one of its windows she can see the spire of the neighboring church, at the top of which her father is supervising architectural work. Watching him, she whispers to herself:

> "I wish he would come down. . . . It is so dangerous to be absent-minded up there." When she had done murmuring the words her father indecisively laid hold of one of the scaffold-poles, as if to test its strength, then let it go and stepped back. In stepping, his foot slipped. An instant of doubling forward and sideways, and he reeled off into the air, immediately disappearing downwards. (44)[1]

Upon this Cytherea loses consciousness. She has to be carried home, arriving there just after her father's body has been taken in.

The passage in Hardy's autobiography describes an event in 1858, when he was still studying with a view to becoming an architect. It concerns a young man called James Seale who was hanged at Dorchester Gaol for the murder of a young girl:

> An unusual incident occurred during his pupilage at Hicks's which, though it had nothing to do with his own life, was dramatic enough to have mention. One summer morning at Bockhampton, just before he sat down to breakfast, he remembered that a man

> was to be hanged at eight o'clock at Dorchester. He took up the big brass telescope that had been handed on in the family, and hastened to a hill on the heath a quarter of a mile from the house, whence he looked towards the town. The sun behind his back shone straight on the white stone façade of the gaol, the gallows upon it, and the form of the murderer in white fustian, the executioner and officials in dark clothing and the crowd below being invisible at this distance of nearly three miles. At the moment of his placing the glass to his eye the white figure dropped downwards, and the faint note of the town clock struck eight.
>
> The whole thing had been so sudden that the glass nearly fell from Hardy's hands. He seemed alone on the heath with the hanged man, and crept homeward wishing he had not been so curious. It was the second and last execution he witnessed, the first having been that of a woman two or three years earlier, when he stood close to the gallows.[2]

Although he does not go into details, Gittings says of this passage that "it is surely the basis" for the scene of Mr. Graye's death, and that "These two scaffold scenes . . . are described in almost the same way."[3] Clearly some notable correspondences can be seen in the rendering of the real-life episode and the fictional one. There is the careful noting of the conditions of the sunlight and its dramatic effect: in the novel, the accident is closely associated in Cytherea's mind with the "white sunlight shining in shaft-like lines from a rift in slaty cloud" (44), while in the *Life* Hardy recalls that "the sun behind his back shone straight on the white stone façade of the gaol, the gallows upon it. . . ." There is also the strong contrast in the appearance of the human figures, that of the victim isolated by its singularity: in the novel, "four in clothes as white as the new erection beneath their hands, the fifth in the ordinary dark suit of a gentleman" (43); and in Hardy's memory, "the murderer in the white fustian, the executioner and officials in dark clothing." Most importantly, there is the device of setting the crucial events within a frame[4]: in the novel, "an illuminated miniature framed in by the dark margin of the window" (43), and in the *Life*, the circular frame of a telescope's lens. In view of these parallel features, Gittings's claim that "there is no doubt Hardy was remembering the hanging when he wrote the novel" (35) is justified.

This raises the more problematic, and more interesting, issue of the implication of this connection. In order to investigate it, the significance of the actual event for Hardy has to be considered. Gittings comments:

> What may well seem so strange about this narrative is the almost total lack of horror at the hanging itself, and the fate of the hanged man. Hardy is disturbed not by the event nor the moral and social ideas connected with it, but by his own sensations at the moment, and his own isolation. "He seemed alone on the heath with the hanged man" suggests almost a pleasant kind of horror, and he only half-heartedly rebukes himself for having been so "curious"—itself a monumental understatement for his eager early-morning dash out on the heath. (35)

Was it, I wonder, really "a pleasant kind of horror"? As Gittings himself is well aware, in the *Life* passage there are a few points—"monumental understatements" or otherwise—which we cannot possibly take at face value. Hardy says that this incident "had nothing to do with his own life," but in spite of this light dismissal—or indeed because of it—it seems that a genuine horror is being suppressed. I suggest that by trying to define the specific nature of this horror, a clearer account of certain essential qualities of the two "scaffold scenes" will be gained.

For this purpose, it is instructive to turn to another eye-witness account Hardy left us of a hanging—"when he stood close to the gallows"—which the quoted passage from the *Life* mentions. On that occasion, two years previous to Seale's execution, the person hanged was a middle-aged woman called Martha Brown, who in a rage of jealousy had murdered her husband, nearly twenty years younger than herself. Hardy's account (in his letter to Lady Hester Pinney, 20 January 1926) runs as follows:

> I remember what a fine figure she showed against the sky as she hung in the misty rain, and how the tight black silk gown set off her shape as she wheeled half-round and back.

Gittings discusses this, too, and notes its "distinctly sexual overtones" (33). A similar comment is made by Judith Wittenberg in her analysis of the "voyeuristic moments" in Hardy. Both find the sexual implications to be a common denominator in the two eye-witness accounts of hangings.[5] Rightly so, but there is also an important difference to be noticed. That Seale was a young man (not a mature woman) must have had special significance for Hardy, then eighteen years old. Actually Seale was about twenty, though he looked, according to a contemporary broadside, "three years younger."[6] Despite the suggested casualness in the report of his own behavior—"just before he sat down to breakfast, he remembered that a man was to be hanged"—it is highly likely that Hardy would have been well aware of the main facts concerning Seale, particularly of the closeness of the man's age to his own. This, I believe, underlies the strong feeling of disturbance in Hardy's reaction on that occasion.

Gittings maintains that Hardy was upset because of "his own isolation." I would argue that the disturbance was aroused by Hardy's curious sense of identification with Seale. It is very hard to accept Gittings's suggestion of an "almost total lack of horror . . . at the fate of the hanged man" on Hardy's part. Rather than a sensation of "a pleasant kind," what Hardy would have felt is, one might venture to suggest, something very close to Henchard's feeling near the end of *The Mayor of Casterbridge* when, seeing what he takes to be a corpse in the river, he "perceived with a sense of horror that it was himself" (Ch. 41). Indeed, it is this sense of identification that crucially lies behind the similarities which connect the passage in the *Life* with the scene in *Desperate Remedies*.[7] This view, I shall argue, is supported by a close examination of Hardy's language.

"Thomas Hardy's prose is the prose of a poet, and his poetry is the poetry of a story-teller," observes Raymond Chapman.[8] Certainly the language of Hardy's fiction deserves the kind of meticulous attention we usually reserve for poetry. Of course a number of critics have been sensitive to this, but as far as I know, John Bayley is the only one who has seriously addressed himself to the language of "the scaffold scene" in *Desperate Remedies*.[9]

In the novel Cytherea has come to the Town Hall in order to attend "the much talked-of reading from Shakespeare" (41). She is soon absorbed, however, in another kind of performance: she becomes "engaged in watching the scene that [is] enacted about [the spire's] airy summit" (43). Meanwhile we, in turn, are made to see the entire scene from another perspective, attending a linguistic drama "enacted" in the author's medium itself. For the language here is dramatically active, words and phrases interacting with each other in a quite striking fashion.

In his remarks on this scene, Bayley has suggested that there is a special cohesiveness in the description of character and the presentation of action:

> Violent movement recalls the aspect of Cytherea singled out by Hardy—"the oscillations and whirls for the preservation of her balance"—and connects with her father's "doubling forward and sideways" before he "reeled off into the air." (127-28)

Bayley is drawing attention to the passage immediately prior to the account of her father's death where Cytherea has been described as follows:

> Indeed, *motion* was her speciality, whether shown on its most extended scale of bodily progression, or minutely, as in the uplifting of her eyelids, the bending of her fingers, the pouting of her lip. . . . In infancy, a stone or stalk in the way, which had been the inevitable occasion of a *fall* to her playmates, had usually left her safe and upright on her feet after the narrowest escape by oscillations and whirls for the preservation of her balance. (41-42; italics mine)

Here the word "fall" clearly anticipates her father's death, and "motion," mentioned as an intrinsic part of Cytherea's makeup, is also important, for it is in keeping with this that she becomes agitated when she sees her father stand "motionless" (44) on the scaffold.

As Bayley says, "the oscillations and whirls" are connected with her father's "doubling forward and sideways." His reading, however, leaves an important question unanswered: what exactly is the significance of this "connection"? I would suggest that the implication of the parallelism is that Cytherea, as it were, re-enacts or "doubles" her father's fall. Indeed, this is precisely where we should locate the most significant link between "the scaffold scene" in the novel and the actual one it is based on: the sense of identification between the subject seeing and the object seen.

In the novel, further details reinforce the parallelism. Up on the scaffold, Mr. Graye "retired as far as the narrow footing allowed"

(43) and then "stepped back" (44), whilst Cytherea, standing "upon the extreme posterior edge of a tract in her life" (a metaphor not only characteristic of Hardy, but also wonderfully operative), "stepped" (43) from there into the labyrinthine experiences. Just as he is in the midst of a "spirit-like silentness" (43), so she, upon his fall, "could utter no sound" and then "fell to the floor" herself (44). Finally, she is carried into her house, closely following her father's body, described as "another and sadder burden" (44): again the two are seen in equal terms. Altogether, Cytherea is figuratively placed in a similar position to her father's, and then made to take the same action. Given this strange identification between Cytherea and her father, what this scene ultimately conveys is the horror of witnessing one's own death.

Hardy's language is worth further scrutiny. Regarding the fall of Cytherea's father, Bayley observes:

> There is no doubt it is an accident, but Mr. Graye is in deep financial trouble, as his son and daughter soon find out, and he is the first of Hardy's characters to have his dilemma and his nature externalised in a striking tableau. . . . In terms of the spirit-like picture, Mr. Graye could easily, it appears, have vanished upwards, and the macabre emphasis upon the inevitable direction of his descent suggests both something like a Kafka-type execution (the four white and one black figures) and the switch from the passive contemplation of the aesthetic to the brute irruption of fact. (127)

Mr. Graye's financial trouble, as Bayley suggests, is indeed relevant. Before the accident, we have been told, Mr. Graye "had endeavoured to regain his standing by the illusory path of speculation" (45). This in itself is an unremarkable sentence, but it contains echoes of Cytherea's "standing" at the edge of the "tract," and then his own "standing" motionless on the "footing," thus giving appropriateness to the fact that in losing his balance—failing to "regain his standing"—he should fatally slip from this "illusory path."

Also notable is the somewhat tautological phrasing of Mr. Graye's "immediately disappearing downwards" (44), in which Bayley finds a "macabre emphasis." This, too, can be related to an earlier phrase, describing how Cytherea's presence in the Town Hall on that dull day is "prevented from dropping into the oblivion" (43). The word "drop" here, in resonance with phrases such as "disappearing downwards" and an "occasion of a fall to her playmates," generates a sinister downward trajectory in the metaphorical structure of the text.

If, when he speaks of a Kafka-type "execution," Bayley means "capital punishment" rather than "rendering,"[10] his suggestion has an added dimension, in view of the association of this scene with the hanging. If we return to that passage in the *Life*, we may observe a similar patterning of language, if on a smaller scale, generating once again a downward trajectory (with the "macabre emphasis upon the inevitable direction" that Bayley notes):

> At the moment of his placing the glass to his eye the white figure *dropped downwards*, and the faint note of the town clock struck eight. The whole thing had been so sudden that the glass nearly *fell* from Hardy's hands. (italics mine)

These words, coming as they do in quick succession, create a kind of echo. There is a sense of interaction between the victim and the viewer, with one verb describing Seale, the other Hardy. If we read the telescope which nearly dropped as a synecdoche for the viewer himself, there is almost the same effect as the one noted in the other "scaffold scene," the observer doubling the action of the observed. In a sense, Hardy's autobiographical account is a skilled story-teller's reconstruction and therefore as much a narrative text as his novels. When he came to write this passage as an autobiographer, Hardy's imagination might have been working in the same way as when, as a novelist, he created the scene involving Cytherea.[11]

The most powerful parts of *Desperate Remedies*, where there is greatest vitality of language, occur when death is the main focus of attention. Bayley, in his discussion of "the scaffold scene," makes a penetrating observation as to how it "involves us in a kind of intimacy with author and heroine, of a kind unique to Hardy":

> True, [Cytherea] does not stay wholly with us, the novel is too much for her, though she is still very much a part of its response to impressions and oddities of sight and sound. But she is too involved in Hardy's own perceptions, as those successfully sustained heroines, Elfride and Bathsheba, are not; and the dream-like lack of effort in the arrival of her personality is made

> more common-place towards the novel's end by a real dream in which she is being attacked with a whip by Manston, as a demon bridegroom. . . . (128)

This can be usefully amplified by considering the dream that is mentioned here. It occurs at a time of crisis, just before her scheduled wedding with the villain Manston:

> During the dilemma she fell into a troubled sleep, and dreamt that she was being whipped with dry bones suspended on strings, which rattled at every blow like those of a malefactor on a gibbet; that she shifted and shrank and avoided every blow, and they fell then upon the wall to which she was tied. She could not see the face of the executioner for his mask, but his form was like Manston's. (245)

This may be a "common-place" Gothic nightmare, conjuring up a cheap kind of horror, but its key feature is, it seems to me, not the whipping, but the association with a gibbet, then by extension, with a hanging. This is a telling detail if Cytherea is, as Bayley claims, "too involved in Hardy's own perceptions." It is also interesting, in this respect, to observe that Cytherea is "about eighteen" (41) when she witnesses her father's death, which was Hardy's own age when he saw Seale's execution.

Including this nightmare, the entire course of Cytherea's association with Manston is thoroughly death-ridden. Their first meeting affects her thus:

> "Oh, how is it that man has so fascinated me?" was all she could think. Her own self, as she had sat spell-bound before him, was all she could see. Her gait was constrained, from the knowledge that his eyes were upon her. . . . (159)

"Her gait was constrained." This means that her natural "motion" is checked, which is a danger signal: just before her father's fall, "she moved herself uneasily" (44). This restriction of her "motion" is emphasized in the scene where she finally succumbs to Manston's charm: "The only wish the humidity of the place left in her was to stand motionless" (234-35). It culminates in the image of her on her wedding day: "She seemed to stand more like a statue than Cytherea Graye" (250). In the heroine's relationship with the villain, fascination with death (her wish to "stand motionless" signifying nothing less) and sexual desire are intertwined, very much as they are in Hardy's own reaction to the Martha Brown hanging.

Manston's attitude, too, has morbid associations. When he faces difficulties in wooing Cytherea,

> Turning aside, he leant his arms upon the edge of the rainwater-butt standing in the corner, and looked into it. The reflection from the smooth stagnant surface tinged his face with the greenish shades of Correggio's nudes. Staves of sunlight slanted down through the still pool, lighting it up with wonderful distinctness. Hundreds of thousands of minute living creatures sported and tumbled in its depth with every contortion that gaiety could suggest; perfectly happy, though consisting only of a head, or a tail, or at most a head and a tail, and all doomed to die within the twenty-four hours. (227-28)

The reference to the sunlight is arresting. Very often when Hardy meticulously notes the condition of sunlight, the scene is emotionally highly charged, as J. B. Bullen persuasively demonstrates.[12] The "scaffold scenes" discussed above are cases in point. We will notice that in addition to the "staves of sunlight", some other elements in those scenes return here. There is the sense of identification: Manston is to remark immediately after the passage quoted, "Damn my position! Why shouldn't I be happy through my little day, too?" (228). There is also the circular frame created by the top of the rainwater-butt; here it is as if the telescope were replaced by a microscope.

Later, Manston, contemplating the disposal of his wife's body, sees "the reflected image of his own face in the glass-pale and spectre-like in its indistinctness" (354). This is close to the situation where a living person sees his own corpse, almost a crude prototype of Henchard's experience on the bridge.[13] It is not in the least surprising to find that Manston dies by hanging himself in the prison cell. The turnkey finds his body, inevitably it seems, "with the early sun ashining in at the grating upon him" (373). As Wittenberg rightly observes, "Manston's death has explicit links both to that of Cytherea's father and those witnessed by the adolescent Hardy" (159). The novel's preoccupation with death is directly projected in Manston's extraordinary words:

> I am about to enter on my normal condition. For people are almost always in their graves. When we survey the long race of men, it is strange and still more strange to find that they are mainly dead men, who have scarcely ever been otherwise. (377)

This is his Will, presented in the text with the caption "Last Words." They are practically the "Last Words" of the novel itself, which has been so governed by the idea of death.

*

When *Desperate Remedies* was reissued in 1889, Hardy added a "Prefatory Note":

> The following novel, the first published by the author, was written nineteen years ago, at a time when he was feeling his way to a method. The principles observed in its composition are, no doubt, too exclusively those in which mystery, entanglement, surprise, and moral obliquity are depended on for exciting interest; but some of the scenes, and at least one or two of the characters, have been deemed not unworthy of a little longer preservation. . . . (35)

We shall not have much difficulty in identifying the scenes Hardy feels confident about. Surely "the scaffold scene" is one of them. Although Bullen argues that as the visual property of this scene is not thematically integrated, Mr. Graye's fall is "important only for the development of the narrative" (33), I would say that "the scaffold scene" is the central expression of the preoccupation of the whole novel, and that it is, as Bayley says, "one of the most astonishing [scenes] in any of [Hardy's] novels" (127).

When we ask ourselves whom Hardy has in mind when he speaks of "one or two of the characters," our answer must be Cytherea and Manston. True, their portrayal lacks in psychological depth. Yet to them undoubtedly belong the novel's stronger passages.[14] Perhaps in this "Prefatory Note" Hardy's feeling is, consciously or unconsciously, that Cytherea and Manston are worth preserving because they embody his innermost obsessions. There is, of course, no way of ascertaining this, but I would suggest that the vitality and personal resonance of the language of "the scaffold scene" and the other passages discussed here constitute a telling argument in favor of such an interpretation.

(First published in *The Thomas Hardy Journal*, 1994)

NOTES

1 This and subsequent references are to the New Wessex (hardcover) edition of the novel (London: Macmillan, 1976).
2 *The Life and Work of Thomas Hardy*, Ed. Michael Millgate, (Athens: University of Georgia Press), 32-33. Hereafter referred to as the *Life*.
3 Robert Gittings, *Young Thomas Hardy* (London: Heinemann, 1975), 35.
4 As has been pointed out, Hardy uses this kind of "framing" device throughout his novels. See, for instance, Norman Page, *Thomas Hardy* (London: Routledge and Kegan Paul, 1977), 79-80; J. B. Bullen, *The Expressive Eye* (Oxford: Clarendon Press, 1986), 33.
5 Gittings, 34; Judith Bryant Wittenberg, "Early Hardy Novels and the Fictional Eye," *Novel* 16 (1983), 151.
6 "The Dreadful Murder at Stoke Abbot," rpt. in *The Thomas Hardy Yearbook* 1 (1970), 93.
7 For a different, Freudian interpretation, see Wittenberg, 157-58.
8 Raymond Chapman, *The Language of Thomas Hardy* (London: Macmillan, 1990), 141.
9 *An Essay on Hardy* (Cambridge: Cambridge University Press, 1978).
10 John Bayley privately confirmed that this was the case.
11 Hanging also figures in *Tess of the D'Urbervilles* and *Jude the Obscure*, but only tangentially. It is perhaps more central in "The Withered Arm," but then it is not visually realized at all.
12 Bullen, 4-5; 40-42.
13 Cf. Norman Page, "Visual Techniques in Hardy's *Desperate Remedies*," *Ariel* 4 (1973), 68.
14 A good example, apart from those already examined, is the passage where in the London crowd Manston observes: "Each and all were alike in this one respect, that they followed a solitary trail like the inwoven threads which form a banner, and all were equally unconscious of the significant whole they collectively showed forth" (311-12). That an extraordinary perception

of this kind is placed in the consciousness of Manston, rather than that of the hero Springrove, is intriguing.

Ch. 16 *The Hand of Ethelberta*: An Introduction

With *The Hand of Ethelberta: A Comedy in Chapters* (1876) Hardy made "a plunge in a new and untried direction," for he "had not the slightest intention of writing for ever about sheepfarming," as he tells us in his autobiography, *The Life and Work of Thomas Hardy*. In 1872 he had published *Under the Greenwood Tree*, aptly subtitled "A Rural Painting of the Dutch School," which caught the attention of Leslie Stephen, the editor of the *Cornhill*. In the same year he asked Hardy to write a serial story for his magazine, and the novelist responded with *Far from the Madding Crowd*, which turned out to be a popular and critical success, and made his name as a promising writer of rural novels. Pleased with its reception, Stephen asked Hardy for another serial. The result was *The Hand of Ethelberta*, a social satire with a largely urban setting.

Hardy models the novel after a comedy of manners of the kind performed in the Restoration and eighteenth century theatre. The chapter-headings designating the scenes of action, the arch naming of characters (Neigh, Ladywell, Menlove, and so on), and the plot which depends on unexpected arrivals of characters and other similar contrivances, all directly reflect this conception. The subtitle, "A Comedy in Chapters," is a variation on that of a play, such as "A Comedy in Five Acts." It is, then, not surprising that Hardy in the *Life* mentions Congreve and Sheridan in connection with the novel. But it would be a mistake to regard *Ethelberta* as a straight imitation of the stage genre. Ethelberta is by no means a stage-type heroine, and Hardy, with his characteristic iconoclasm, deliberately upsets conventional expectations we may have. The reader is decidedly not given a story in which a proud heroine finally learns her lesson and marries the patient humble hero, on the pattern of *Far from the Madding Crowd*.

In his writing Hardy often takes some elements from his previous work which he then examines in a different light. In *Far from the Madding Crowd* there was Bathsheba, and in Ethelberta he continues his study of a woman of marked independence, giving a different kind of complexity to the characterization of the heroine. For one thing, Ethelberta has strong social ambition. This appears in what she says to Christopher in a letter: "the undoubted power you possess will do you socially no good unless you mix with it the ingredient of ambition"

(Ch. 9). At the same time, however, she can make an extraordinary declaration like this:

> "Life is a battle, they say; but it is only so in the sense that a game of chess is a battle—there is no seriousness in it; it may be put an end to at any inconvenient moment by owning yourself beaten, with a careless "Ha-ha!" and sweeping your pieces into the box. Experimentally, I care to succeed in society; but at the bottom of my heart, I don't care." (Ch. 17)

Ambition, then, is not of the utmost importance to Ethelberta: she is not a social climber in the manner of Becky Sharp. Indeed, this "experimental" attitude, here expressed in terms of the detachment from her own ambition, is a significant part, and the most interesting feature, of her make-up. This attitude can be observed in her relationship with Christopher. To be sure she has a tender regard for the young man, and when she tells him that they are to remain as friends only, "[t]ears were in Ethelberta's eyes" (Ch. 24). But later when Picotee asks her if she would have married him had it not been for her, Ethelberta coolly answers: "It is difficult to say exactly. It is possible that if I had no relations at all, I might have married him. And I might not" (Ch. 43). She can cope with the loss of Christopher, not so much because she knows that he, signally lacking ambition, is not suited to her, as because she is at bottom detached from her own emotions—more so than from her social ambition.

Notice, however, that when the point is reached where, true to her "experimental" principle, she should sweep her pieces into the box with a careless laugh, she does not do so:

> To calmly relinquish the struggle at that point would have been the act of a stoic, but not of a woman, particularly when she considered the children, the hopes of her mother for them, and her own condition—though this was least—under the ironical cheers which would greet a slip back into the mire. (Ch. 28)

The novel hinges on the question: whom will Ethelberta choose for a husband? In making this choice she considers her family, her ambition, and her romantic feelings—in that order. On the whole, her action is not to be regarded as selfishly motivated, for she is admirably concerned about the survival of the family more than anything else. Nevertheless, perhaps because she herself is detached from her emotions, one does not feel involved with Ethelberta, in the way one does, for instance, with Tess. She invites a unique response from us: she is different from Hardy's other heroines in some important respects. Fate has relatively little to do with her: she is too much in control of herself. Crucially, she is not gripped by sexual love, which she substitutes with reason and will-power. Her first marriage, cursorily described in the first paragraph of the novel, is practically non-existent: her "boy husband" (Ch. 10) soon dies "from a chill caught during the wedding tour," and she "seemed a detached bride rather than a widow." (Ethelberta is compared to the biblical virgin Abishag in Ch. 45: it is interesting to note Hardy's continued use of female figures associated with King David, following Bathsheba in the immediately preceding novel.) Christopher is plainly not a sexually strong male like Alec d'Urberville, a man to whom Ethelberta might succumb with tragic consequences. He is only a factor among her possible choices, and is unable to affect her seriously. In this regard, he is not much different from other suitors. Hardy was apparently aware of all this, for he says, referring to the subtitle of the novel, in a letter to Stephen (21 May 1875): "My meaning was simply, as you know, that the story would concern the follies of life rather than the passions, & be told in something of a comedy form, all the people having weaknesses at which the superior lookers-on smile, instead of being ideal characters." The reader, then, is meant to maintain a sense of distance from the characters, even from Ethelberta. The novelist, another detached "looker-on," is here being "experimental" himself, placing the uniquely strong heroine in a comedy without providing sexually dangerous men.

The prevailing detachment, I suspect, is paradoxically related to the fact that Ethelberta is a deeply personal novel, with Hardy projecting much of himself, particularly his class anxiety, into the protagonist. For example, Ethelberta's secret marriage ceremony is not unlike Hardy's own, where Emma's uncle was the only guest, since the two families were hostile to one another. Indeed, the novelist and the heroine have the same class background, their family members and relatives consisting of servants, carpenters, and schoolmistresses. On Hardy's mother's side there were people in service. Since his mother's maiden name was Hand, one wonders if Hardy might not have been wryly amused by a private resonance in the novel's title. (Emma Hardy, who probably did not know the whole of her husband's background, disliked the novel, because, she is reported to have said, there is "too much about servants in it," and the inscribed copy Hardy gave her remained uncut.) With its contrast between the country and the city, the novel centers on Ethelberta's encounter with London society, very much reflecting Hardy's own experience at the time of its composition, when he was just beginning to socialize with the metropolitan literati. The novelist, like the heroine, made his way into this new territory by the profession of writing, also with anxieties about his social background. Their artistic careers follow the same course: Ethelberta starts as a poet, and then becomes a story-teller in order to make a living, while Hardy himself wanted to be a poet, but turned to novel-writing to "keep base life afoot," as the *Life* informs us. The sense of detachment one may feel in the portrayal of Ethelberta is perhaps partly due to a careful distancing by means of which Hardy objectifies himself, and partly to his "experimental" attitude towards the novel.

Class awareness, the novel's major preoccupation, is most strongly expressed in Ch. 46, where Sol accuses Ethelberta of being "a deserter of [her] own lot." "Look at my hand," he says (a pregnant gesture for Hardy?), pointing out that there is something wrong with him, with his ugly hand, becoming a brother to a viscountess. Ethelberta responds with, "Whether you like the peerage or no, they appeal to our historical sense and love of old associations." Here is a clear symptom of what one might be tempted to call Hardy's "d'Urberville complex," a conflict between the dignified solidarity with country laborers and the irrepressible yearning for an ancient aristocratic lineage. This conflict appears in many of Hardy's novels in various forms. He had earlier attempted a class-conscious autobiographical probing in *A Pair of Blue Eyes*, where a poor architect falls in love with a social superior, a rector's daughter, but in the novels up to this time the class issue is nowhere so pronounced as in Ethelberta—except for his very first work of fiction, which we may surmise had some close links with this one. Hardy's statement that with Ethelberta he made "a plunge in a new and untried direction" may need qualification: in a way he went back to the unpublished *The Poor Man and the Lady* (finished in 1868). The manuscript of this work is lost, and we have no way of knowing its exact content, but according to the *Life*, it was "a striking socialistic novel," the targets of its "sweeping dramatic satire" including "the squirearchy and nobility, London society, the vulgarity of the middle class," and "the most important scenes were laid in London." *Ethelberta* is by no means a "socialistic" novel, but it deals with a serious issue which is of central importance to Hardy's artistic career. We should not be blinded by the novel's oddity (the urban setting, comedy, and so on) and overlook its continuity with his other fiction.

Today Hardy's reputation as a novelist mainly rests upon what in the "General Preface to the Wessex Edition of 1912" he calls the "Novels of Character and Environment." His other novels, however, are by no means negligible. They are undoubtedly stamped with the genius of the great novelist. In different modes, and with different degrees of commitment, all Hardy novels deal with his central preoccupations: sexual love and class. Hardy was intrigued by women, and observing them with a remarkably keen eye, he depicted the pain and joy of the relationship between the two sexes with deeper penetration than any of his contemporary novelists. He belonged to what Merryn and Raymond Williams call "the intermediate class," a precariously mobile group between laborers and the petit bourgeoisie, consisting mainly of farmers, artisans, and tradesmen. The Wessex novels amply demonstrate the ways in which this class, both as a sector of the economy and as the bearer of a culture, was put under pressure in the growing capitalist industry of nineteenth century England.

Ethelberta, with *Desperate Remedies* and *A Laodicean*, is put in the category of "Novels of Ingenuity," or "Experiments," which "show a not infrequent disregard of the probable in the chain of events" ("General Preface"). The truth, however, is that Hardy does not care much about probability even in his "major" novels. These "Novels of Ingenuity" simply display this attitude in a marked degree. By the same token, the class issue is boldly "experimented" with in *Ethelberta*, where the novelist presents an extreme case of a marriage between a viscount and a servant's daughter without involving the heroine in sexual complications. When he wrote the novel Hardy was perhaps not yet prepared to grapple with the issue in a more realistic mode. The "comedy" was in a way a safeguard, whereby he could say, as in the 1895 Preface, that "there was expected of the reader a certain lightness of mood" in dealing with this "somewhat frivolous narrative."

One strong merit of *Ethelberta* as a novel is that it starts very well, and keeps going, without losing much of its narrative momentum, through to the exciting final chapters. This sounds like a blurb, but it is a point worth making: Hardy was fully aware of the importance of narrative interest—"A story must be worth the telling," he repeatedly says in the *Life*—and he knew how to arouse and sustain it. The novel also contains powerful and uniquely Hardyan writing. As usual, the novelist's touch is sure in the depiction of country scenery, but here he shows that he can write about the city just as well: the scene in Ch. 18, where Picotee takes a walk across Westminster Bridge as the "lights along the riverside towards Charing Cross sent an inverted palisade of gleaming swords down into the shaking water," is a case in point. Also strikingly memorable is the horrifying description of Neigh's estate, Fanfield Park, in Ch. 25, with decrepit horses which "seemed rather to be specimens of some attenuated heraldic animal, scarcely thick enough through the body to throw a shadow: or enlarged castings of the fire-dogs of past times." The strength of the writing, however, does not lie in these isolated descriptive passages alone. Hardy's is a highly cohesive language which produces echoes and makes thematic connections, thereby creating a richly resonant texture. And the novelist combines this resource with his gift for creating memorable, dramatic scenes.

Consider the title: the "hand" of Ethelberta. Not only is her "hand" sought by various suitors, but also the heroine plays her "hand" in a game of life: "I have the tale of my own life—to be played as a last card" (Ch. 13); "I am a rare hand at contrivances" (Ch. 28). It is in keeping with this that Lord Mountclere's brother observes that she "has played her cards adroitly" (Ch. 45). This series of metaphors energize seemingly simple gestures in other places. Sol's showing his "hand" to Ethelberta in Ch. 46, to which I have referred, is one such instance. Also interesting is one involving Ethelberta where, her escape being thwarted, she "lift[s] her hand for a thrust" in a desperate attempt at pushing Lord Mountclere into a ditch (Ch. 47).

Ethelberta's feet, too, are worth admiring. At the beginning of the novel, when her attention is caught by a wild-duck being chased by a big duck-hawk,

> Ethelberta impulsively started off in a rapid run that would have made a little dog bark with delight and run after, her object being, if possible, to see the end of this desperate struggle for a life so small and unheard-of. Her stateliness went away, and it could be forgiven for not remaining; for her feet suddenly became as quick as fingers, and she raced along over the uneven ground with such force of tread that, being a woman slightly heavier than gossamer,

> her patent heels punched little D's in the soil with unerring accuracy wherever it was bare, crippled the heather-twigs where it was not, and sucked the swampy places with a sound of quick kisses. (Ch. 1)

Hardy is often very good at providing a dramatically arresting moment at the start of a novel. Henchard's selling of his wife in *The Mayor of Casterbridge* and Cytherea's witnessing of her father's fall in *Desperate Remedies* readily come to mind. Not so sensational but equally effective is the passage cited above. For here we have, as it were, a microcosm of the whole novel, important themes and metaphors densely combined. The novel is a record of Ethelberta's determined effort for survival, which is here projected in the flight of a duck, and the ensuing Darwinian struggle. That she is a detached, curious observer of this struggle is a reflection of her "experimental" attitude towards life. The idea of sexual pursuit is suggested also, and not by the use of the word "kisses" alone. A few pages earlier, a conversation between an hostler and an aged milkman is reported, in which the latter covetously speaks of her beauty, causing the other to reply, "Michael, a old man like you ought to think about other things, and not be looking two ways at your time of life. Pouncing upon young flesh like a carrion crow—'tis a vile thing in a old man." This has prefigured the hawk's chase after the duck, which in turn looks forward to old Mountclere hankering after Ethelberta who is represented as a small bird: "Was ever a thrush so safe in a cherry net before!" (Ch. 39).

These metaphorical networks are further extended, via Ladywell's hunting ducks and his voyeuristic spying on Picotee in Ch. 3, to another sexually charged chase scene in the story Ethelberta tells in Ch. 13:

> "He came forward till he, like myself, was about twenty yards from the edge. I instinctively grasped my useless stiletto. How I longed for the assistance which a little earlier I had so much despised! Reaching the block or boulder upon which I had been sitting, he clasped his arms around from behind; his hands closed upon the empty seat, and he jumped up with an oath. This method of attack told me a new thing with wretched distinctness; he had, as I suppose, discovered my sex; male attire was to serve my turn no longer. The next instant, indeed, made it clear, for he exclaimed, 'You don't escape me, masquerading madam,' or

> some such words, and came on. My only hope was that in his excitement he might forget to notice where the grass terminated near the edge of the cliff, though this could be easily felt by a careful walker: to make my own feeling more distinct on this point I hastily bared my feet."

The focusing upon the feet of the heroine at the end carries us back to Ethelberta's own, treading the ground with the sound of kisses, and the duck's struggle for life which immediately follows. This connection, reinforcing as it does the point made about sexual pursuit in both scenes, leads us to notice that Ethelberta's fantastic story is, again, a reflection of her own situation. The heroine's masquerading as a man corresponds to Ethelberta's concealment of her class origin. Like the man in the story, Lord Mountclere finds out about Ethelberta's humble background underneath the disguise. When at the end Ethelberta is in need of rescue (which she, like her heroine, previously thought unnecessary) Christopher ineffectually comes in, just as he intrudes upon her story-telling at this point, rather foolishly taking the story for an account of a real event.

The heroine's "baring" her feet, together with the placing of the action on a cliff, reminds us of that erotic scene in *A Pair of Blue Eyes* involving Elfride and Knight. The point about Ethelberta, however, is that sexuality remains somewhat "outside" her. It is all there in the eyes of the beholders, such as the milkman, Mountclere, and others. Despite her attractive body, which is "slightly heavier than gossamer," she is indifferent to her own sexuality and not really troubled by it.

Throughout his career Hardy explores problems of class and sexuality. In *The Hand of Ethelberta* he presents these problems without humanizing them, as he does in *Tess*, for example. No serious suffering is involved here. The novel is essentially an experiment. The detached treatment of Ethelberta and other characters, and the artificial mode of the whole novel, are deliberate. Whatever the reader might make of it, Hardy knew exactly what he was doing. If this is, as one Victorian reviewer (in the *Morning Post*, 5 August 1876) observes, "a decidedly clever book," then the novelist himself was not fooled by its cleverness.

(First published in *The Hand of Etherlberta*, Ed. Toru Sasaki, Everyman Paperback, 1998)

Ch. 17 *The Hand of Ethelberta* and Critics

Since its immediate predecessor, *Far from the Madding Crowd*, had been a great success, *The Hand of Ethelberta* was reviewed in more than a dozen journals and newspapers. Most reviews find both weakness and strength in the novel: faults are said to lie in inauthentic dialogue, stylistic clumsiness, the improbability of the whole situation, and in the characterization, particularly, of Ethelberta. On the other hand, the novel is considered amusing and entertaining, and there are tributes to Hardy's "power" and "originality."

The *Saturday Review* (6 May 1876) is typical: "one lays down the book with a mixture of feelings"; Hardy is "capable of making himself a place in the first rank of novelists," but this novel, "amusing as it is, is hardly worthy of its author's powers." The reviewer notes Hardy's "besetting faults of giving incongruous dialogue to his characters, and going far out of his way for laboured similes," "a certain air of improbability which runs through the book," and the failure "to inspire a reader with any strong belief in Ethelberta's existence." R. H. Hutton in the *Spectator* (22 April 1876) declares, "A more entertaining book than *the Hand of Ethelberta* has not been published for many a year." No one will read the novel "without being aware from beginning to end that a very original and a very skilful hand is wielding the pen." However, "while Mr. Hardy has enough superficial knowledge of human nature to give an air of plausibility and life to all he paints, he has not enough,—or at least, seldom shows enough,—to engrave individual figures on our minds as figures which take leave to live in our memories." Ethelberta is "so much of a riddle to us, and so little of a living figure," and other characters, too, are "vivacious shadows, who amuse us without impressing us." The *Graphic* (29 April 1876) says, "This book is unquestionably the work of a true artist and humourist, and yet both the art and the humour somehow miss their effect." The art is employed in building up a series of situations which are "well-nigh extravagantly improbable" and the characters who are "for the most part unreal beings" (Ethelberta is "throughout a puzzle to us"), while the humor evolving out of such creations, "amusing as it is, we yet feel to be unsatisfactory." The reviewer goes on:

We take it ill of Mr Hardy that he should have abandoned that

> rustic life which few can portray—for George Eliot concerns herself with farmers, not with farm-laborers—for London drawing-rooms and "good society," ground on which he seems much less at home. His "society" talk is clever, but apt to seem strange and unnatural. The wits and the unwise people talk too much alike. . . . However, in so far as Mr Hardy may have aimed, first of all, at amusing his readers, his book is a brilliant success, for its interest is strong and well sustained to the end.

There are, however, a few points where we find opposed judgments. While some criticize Hardy's style, George Saintsbury in the *Academy* (13 May 1876) notes a "stylistic improvement" (that is, less labored eccentricity) in this novel, and the *Atlantic Monthly* (August 1876) says:

> the style everywhere gives token of a sensitive personal touch from the author, where the words . . . continually freshen in the quiet dew of thought that the author lets fall upon every detail. . . . Everything is given in pictures, so far as it may be, and these are always delicately drawn, with a spiritualized force of language, which seems to us uniquely Mr Hardy's among all English novelists.

Hardy's attempt at "a new direction" in *Ethelberta* was, one suspects, strongly motivated by his wish not to be categorized as a follower of George Eliot. In spite of this effort, when critics blame Hardy for deserting the rural background, or failing thereby to give credible portraits of people, the ghost of Eliot still often hovers behind their judgment. In the *Times* (5 June 1876), where this novel is reviewed side by side with *Daniel Deronda* (then running as a serial), Eliot's genius for "making everyone in creation, from a Duke to a Dogberry, figure as himself, and not as a puppet" is invoked to make a contrast with Hardy. Yet, the *Westminster Review* (July, 1876), where again the novel is reviewed together with *Daniel Deronda*, considers Hardy equal to Eliot. There is a remark that "It is fortunate, perhaps, for him that it was published before "Daniel Deronda," or else ill-natured critics would have declared that his principal character was only a copy" (Gwendolen Harleth is also beautiful and strong-minded, entertains an idea of becoming a public performer—a singer—marries without love, and has to face the fact that her husband kept a mistress). But this reviewer is clearly not "ill-natured," for *Ethelberta*, it is observed, "will sustain Mr Hardy's reputation," and "He may again, as in 'Far from the Madding Crowd,' divide the honours with George Eliot." After instancing convincing little touches found in lines given to Picotee and London characters, the reviewer says, "The talk, too, of Mr Hardy's clowns is, we think, more natural than" the *Madding Crowd*, and positively declares that "the masterpiece in the book is undoubtedly Ethelberta."

Another interesting area of mixed reactions concerns the question of genre in relation to the "improbability" of the novel. The *Athenaeum* (15 April 1876) rather condescendingly says:

> Mr Hardy seems, after a preliminary trial of several kinds, to have finally chosen as his branch of fiction that which, for want of a better name, may be called the modern-romantic. That is, he takes the present for his time, and such people as move among us at the present for his characters; but he makes his characters do things, and puts them into positions, which, if not impossible, would at least be thought very remarkable, and worthy of a leading article in every daily paper, if they had really been reported by a living witness. This must be called the second order of fiction, as it is distinctly inferior, in an artistic point of view, to that which produces its effects solely with the materials of everyday life: but in the hands of a master, who is capable of seeing how people might probably act and speak in improbable circumstances, it is by no means unsatisfactory.

The *Examiner* (13 May 1876) takes a directly opposite view:

> Improbability has been the main fault alleged against the "Hand of Ethelberta" in current criticisms of the story. Now we have always been among the enthusiastic admirers of Mr Hardy's work, recognising in it the very highest artistic purposes and something not far short of the highest powers of execution, and we venture to think that this accusation of improbability as a fault proceeds upon a misapprehension of the writer's intentions. . . . If the novelist did not intend his story to be a reflex of real life, he cannot be blamed if it is not, unless we are to lay down a close adherence to the probabilities of real life as an indispensable condition of novel-

> writing. Mr Hardy seems to us to have deliberately disclaimed being tried by a rigid standard of probability when he adopted as the sub-title of his work "a comedy in chapters."

This, the reviewer goes on, is "what may be called ideal comedy, in which fancy is permitted to range beyond the limits of real life." *Ethelberta* is an admirable success, for "[f]rom whatever point of view we regard the work, we find deliberate artistic aims and unflinching fidelity of execution." The novel "shows no falling off in intellectual force," as compared with its predecessor. The review concludes with this observation: "We doubt whether *Ethelberta* possesses the popular interest of some of Mr. Hardy's previous novels . . . but it is more masterly as a work of art—it reveals a progress in technical excellence which makes us look forward with curiosity to his next publication."

The *Examiner* reviewer was certainly right in expressing doubt about the fate of the novel, for in critical studies of Hardy of the following decades, *Ethelberta* was most of the time disregarded, or dismissed as of little significance. Albert J. Guerard (*Thomas Hardy*, 1949) typically observes that this novel, like *A Laodicean*, is "generally regarded as a complete failure."

Modern critics repeat more or less the same charges against the novel as Victorian reviewers. If anything, they tend to be severer on the comedy: Irving Howe (*Thomas Hardy*, 1966), referring to the subtitle of the novel, tersely comments that "the chapters are more noticeable than the comedy." Joseph Warren Beach (*The Technique of Thomas Hardy*, 1922) says, "After the grave and beautiful work of art of *Far from the Madding Crowd*, Mr Hardy diverted himself with an essay in comedy of rather dubious effectiveness." Suggesting that here the novelist was aiming at something like Meredith's *Evan Harrington* or *Sandra Belloni*, he points out the failure of Hardy's comedy:

> There is no one to correspond to the Countess de Saldar or to the Pole sisters—no one so funny. Ethelberta is not funny at all, in spite of her comic role of social climber. She is merely the object of an irony that misses fire. It misses fire because, somehow, the author makes us take her seriously, though without arousing deep interest in her. . . . There is only the most perfunctory suggestion of her being subjected to an ordeal and being found wanting. We cannot feel for her the admiring sympathy we feel for Evan

> Harrington in his tardy triumph over snobbery, nor the amused scorn we feel for Wilfrid Pole when he succumbs to the seduction of a weak sentimentalism. (111)

A few critics, however, have dealt more sympathetically with the comedy. Richard H. Taylor (*The Neglected Hardy: Thomas Hardy's Lesser Novels*, 1982), also refers to Meredith, particularly to his essay on "The Idea of Comedy and the Uses of the Comic Spirit" (1877), where it is said that "the test of true comedy is that it shall awaken thoughtful laughter," and declares that *Ethelberta* "passes this test well." He then quotes the letter Hardy wrote (8 August 1927) to J. B. Priestley, who had just published a book on Meredith:

> Meredith was, as you recognize, and might have insisted on even more strongly, and I always felt, in the direct succession of Congreve and the artificial comedians of the Restoration, and in getting his brilliancy we must put up with the fact that he would not, or could not—at any rate did not—when aiming to represent the "Comic Spirit," let himself discover the tragedy that always underlies Comedy if you only scratch it deeply enough.

In the novel, Taylor goes on, "we do not have to scratch very deeply to discover the potential tragedy; only the author's perspective preserves the comic mode." In his view, whether employing comic (as in *Ethelberta*) or tragic strategies (as in *Jude the Obscure*), Hardy's fundamental vision remains the same: "the tragedy (if we conclude, as I think we may, that in a real moral sense Ethelberta's success is a tragedy) in each of these novels originates in that most consistent of Hardy's preoccupations: class division."

According to Paul Ward ("The Hand of Ethelberta", in *The Thomas Hardy Yearbook*, 1971), neither the Victorian reviewers nor the modern critics seem to have grasped that "what the book really has to offer is a fascinating commentary on the relationship between the tragic and comic masks, and on the technique of the artist in establishing and exploring his genre." Pointing out that a given situation can be treated either comically or tragically, depending upon the manner in which the situation is presented and the character of the persons involved, Ward suggests that here the novelist resolves a potentially serious Hardyesque situation into the comic mode by the use of disinterested observers and inessential details, and through the characterization of the heroine. With regard to the last point, quoting Ethelberta's remarks about life as a game of chess in Ch. 17, he argues:

> Where other major characters in Hardy really risk themselves in their encounters to win the highest prize or to lose all, Ethelberta is content to play for smaller stakes. The metaphor of the chess game is significant: where for many of Hardy's characters the pieces are vital parts of their inner souls, for Ethelberta they are façades or poses—not insincere, but as she calls it "experimental." What irritates the unsympathetic critics into dismissing the novel as trivial is their inability to accept that with certain people, as with certain buildings, the façade may be the most beautiful or interesting part. (42)

Michael Millgate (*Thomas Hardy: His Career as a Novelist*, 1971) argues that most of the comedy "can be related, in one way or another, to the question of appearance and reality which provides one of the novel's continuing themes: Faith's truth to herself is not matched by Neigh the knacker's heir, nor by other characters who set store by their social pretensions." He, too, considers the characterization of Ethelberta in relation to the comedy of the novel:

> Hardy seems to have been especially fascinated by the perpetually merging layers of reality and unreality implicit in the pattern of Ethelberta's career. She plays so many superimposed parts before audiences possessed of such differing degrees of initiation into her secrets that her "true" personality proves finally elusive—perhaps even to Hardy himself, though the deliberate indirection of the final view of her seems not so much an evasion of difficulty as a conscious choice of ambiguity, a decision to rest with the enigma. (112)

Sympathetically responsive to the whole novel, Millgate also locates here Hardy's first serious attempt "to incorporate architecture more or less systematically as an element in an overall value-system." This is "an additional element in that technical adventurousness of *The Hand of Ethelberta* which seems—like the handling of contrasted rural and urban settings and of conflicting class relationships—to demand a higher place for the novel than it has customarily been accorded." Central to the novel, he argues, is its evocation of great and rapid social change: "In a world where so much was changing, manners and social attitudes must have seemed ripe for changes on a similar scale, and Hardy treats Ethelberta's career almost as a parable of social revolution."

Another view of the characterization of the heroine is expressed by John Bayley (*An Essay on Hardy*, 1978):

> Hardy is here, in fantasy and in projection, completely his own heroine. It is the most singular of his identifications, for as a man who would rather be silent than speak, an observer and not an actor, he projects an extraordinary daydream of performance, substituting for his own talent for writing the brilliance of an entertainer, and the daring wit and poise of a social beauty. Nor was that all. As a man whose relations with the world of responsibilities, however shrewd, were passive and unauthoritative, he becomes in the book the arbiter and goddess of a large family, all of whom look to Ethelberta for guidance and support in the shifts of their strange social situation. . . . And yet Ethelberta remains too much an idea and a daydream . . . to engage our interests as Hardy's real heroines can. Hardy is too dispassionate about her, and in a curious way too much in practical earnest about what she might represent for him if he had been in the position of bringing up his own family in the social scale and being responsible for what ensued. (150, 151)

Perceptively Bayley says of the novel as a whole:

> One thing which seems to me certain is that *Ethelberta* is not a failure: and that it does not show, as most Hardy critics assume, that he had no sense of how to handle a social and metropolitan theme. Rather he had too much sense of it. *Ethelberta*, like *Hamlet*, is an imaginative impression of "court life," about which the novelist is too intrigued to be sure-footed. Yet except for Shakespeare himself no English writer is more naturally a courtier than Hardy. Their attraction towards places where the role is played is a matter of feeling as well as imagination; and they have the art of pleasing both the self-appointed great, and those great by nature, without forfeiting an essential detachment and an inner

> amusement. (153)

These sympathetic studies were, as I have said, exceptional cases in the generally indifferent critical response. The situation, however, now seems to be undergoing a kind of sea change, for recently *Ethelberta* has become a focus of much serious attention from materialist and feminist critics. Representative of the former, and indeed most responsible for the current revival of interest in the novel, is Peter Widdowson, whose book, *Hardy in History: A Study in Literary Sociology* (1989), examines the ways in which the idea of "Thomas Hardy" has been ideologically constructed, first by the author himself, and then by academic criticism, education, publishing, and the mass-media. He devotes a long chapter to *Ethelberta* and discusses it in great detail along these lines:

> I shall show (while avoiding intentionalism) how *Ethelberta* self-consciously foregrounds issues of social class, gender relations, and the artifice of realist fiction writing. And I shall suggest that the exposure of the alienating lies produced by these systems is more readily perceptible in Hardy's other fiction once it has been identified in such uncompromising form in *The Hand of Ethelberta*. (157)

Widdowson shares with critics such as Millgate and Taylor the view that *Ethelberta* is not different from other Hardy novels in its critique of the class system. Yet their reading, as he sees it, has been disabled by the constraints of conventional critical discourse. Theirs is seen as a humanist-realist criticism based on liberal-bourgeois conceptions of "character" and common-sense "probabilism." According to Widdowson, what the novel is really doing is to expose the very artificiality of these conceptions, by its own artificiality and improbability, its use of coincidences, unreal characters, farcical absurdities, and other uncompromisingly fictive contrivances. What is often condemned as the awkward style of the novel is actually an effective weapon: "Certainly the novel's style is pervasively self-conscious, but its very consistency makes it more a strategic mannerism—one which intensifies the defamiliarizing ("disproportioning") effect of the whole work—than a failure of control." Widdowson regards Ethelberta as an inevitably divided character, reflecting as she does Hardy's own "recognition of the contradictory position in which he was now situated." He is very good at noticing the shared features of the author and the heroine, showing how Ethelberta's composing an epic poem corresponds to Hardy's own project of *The Dynasts* just started at the time of his writing of this novel. He also discusses, with reference to their use of Defoe, the similarity of Ethelberta's fictional theory and practice to Hardy's own, both of them highly aware of the "unreal" nature of "realism." Widdowson has a number of interesting things to say about the novel, and his is a study no serious reader of *Ethelberta* can ignore, whether to agree or disagree.

Feminist critics mainly focus on the issue of gender in the novel, in an attempt to demonstrate how the text exposes the idea of "woman" as an ideological construct. Patricia Ingham (*Thomas Hardy*, 1990), for instance, stresses elements which confound patriarchal values, such as Ethelberta's active part in giving her hand in marriage, "the startling equivalence of the two sexes" (the masculine Ethelberta and the feminine Christopher) which undermines essentialist accounts of women, and the virtual absence of the narrating voice towards the end of the novel which indicates the male narrator's appropriation by the omnicompetent heroine.

Similarly, Sarah Davies ("*The Hand of Ethelberta*: Demythologising 'Woman,'" *Critical Survey*, 1993) argues that the novel, breaking down the facile gender category, redefines the signification of "woman," in which the heroine is not an inscription by the male pen on a blank page, but a creative writer who can manipulate the "male gaze." Hardy's ultimate success lies, in her view, in showing us that "the feminine figure of the realist novel is a social and therefore male construct, a myth rather than a reality or truth."

Penny Boumelha ("A Complicated Position for a Woman: *The Hand of Ethelberta*," in *The Sense of Sex: Feminist Perspectives on Hardy*, ed. Margaret R. Higonnet, 1993) observes that

> the novel's manipulation of the plots of social mobility and marriage demonstrates how the ideas of ambition, success, family responsibility and self-fulfilment which must be negotiated in the process of such class transition are specifically inflected through ideologies of gender, in ways which in fact permeated the lives of Victorian women. And in the figure of Ethelberta as producer

> of language (writer, storyteller, coiner of aphorisms for the edification of her sister), there is in turn some interrogation of the status of those plots of mobility and stability in their relation to gender. (242-43)

These recent critics have considered some hitherto unexplored aspects of *The Hand of Ethelberta*. Their efforts are bound to attract new readers to this novel, and will no doubt send seasoned Hardyans back to it with renewed interest.

(First published in *The Hand of Etherlberta*, Ed. Toru Sasaki, Everyman Paperback, 1998)

Ch. 18 *A Laodicean* as a Novel of Ingenuity

In the General Preface to the 1912 Wessex Edition Hardy put three of his novels, *Desperate Remedies*, *The Hand of Ethelberta*, and *A Laodicean*, into the category of "Novels of Ingenuity." This, as he apologetically explains, was because they "show a not infrequent disregard of the probable in the chain of events, and depend for their interest mainly on the incidents themselves." Despite some attempts at retrieving the group from critical limbo,[1] not much attention has been paid to *A Laodicean*. I hope that attending more closely to its mode of presentation, and in particular to verbal aspects of this, we can arrive at a better appreciation of the kind of ingenuity the novel displays.

In his essay "Wilkie Collins and Dickens" (first published in 1927), T. S. Eliot considers their novels in order to "illuminate the question of the difference between the dramatic and the melodramatic in fiction"; the former makes us feel character to be "somewhat integral with plot," while the latter asks us "to accept an improbable plot, simply for the sake of seeing the thrilling situation which arises in consequence." Dickens, he says, excels in the creation of characters, and Collins is a master of plot and situation, the elements most essential to melodrama. Eliot considers *Bleak House* and *The Woman in White* the highest achievements of Dickens and of Collins, and observes that they are the novels in which the two novelists most closely approach each other. The frontier between drama and melodrama, as he sees it, is vague: "perhaps no drama has ever been greatly and permanently successful without a large melodramatic element . . . and the best melodrama partakes of the greatness of drama." When he turns from the Victorian period to the contemporary scene, Eliot wistfully notes "the dissociation of the elements of the old three-volume melodramatic novel into the various types of the modern 300-page novel." This, in his opinion, is not an ideal situation:

> Those who have lived before such terms as "high-brow fiction," "thrillers" and "detective fiction" were invented realize that melodrama is perennial and that the craving for it is perennial and must be satisfied. If we cannot get this satisfaction out of what the publishers present as "literature," then we will read . . . what we call "thrillers." But in the golden age of melodramatic fiction

> there was no such distinction. The best novels were thrilling. . . .[2]

Hardy was, surely, very much a writer of this golden age of melodramatic fiction, a worthy successor of Dickens and Collins, his best novels superbly combining "the dramatic" and "the melodramatic."

It is clear that Hardy wrote *Desperate Remedies* following the vogue for the kind of novel established by the success of *The Woman in White*. His autobiography tells us: "the powerfully not to say wildly melodramatic situations had been concocted in a style which was quite against his natural grain, through too crude an interpretation of Mr Meredith's advice. It was a sort of thing he had never contemplated writing, till, finding himself in a corner, it seemed necessary to attract public attention at all hazards."[3] Despite this dismissal, the sensation novel, with its melodrama and unorthodox morality and sexuality, was certainly not "against his natural grain."[4] To be sure, Hardy did not continue in the pure sensation vein. Nor did Collins for that matter. In fact, there is an intriguing parallel between the works of the two. When Hardy was writing *Desperate Remedies*, Collins's *Man and Wife* was running as a serial. The latter is a mixture of melodrama and social criticism (against the cult of athleticism and irregular marriage laws), combining intricate plot with sympathetic depiction of women—very much like Hardy's later fiction. Towards the end of Collins's novel, the heroine finds herself having to undergo mental torture under the same roof with her sexually attractive but brutal husband. At the climax he is killed; not by the heroine, however, but by his landlady who has lost her balance of mind because of her own husband's cruel treatment of her in the past. That is to say, Collins has the murder, which is favorable to the heroine, vicariously committed by another woman. The juxtaposition of this with Tess, where the heroine actually commits a murder yet remains a pure woman, suggests one of the ways in which Hardy continued and developed the Collinsian melodrama.

J. I. M. Stewart has an illuminating comment on Collins's fiction:

> Many of the prefaces with which [Collins] accompanied his novels render a somewhat misleading impression of his predominant concern. *No Name* is declared to evince "a resolute adherence, throughout, to the truth as it is in Nature" and to pursue "the theme of some of the greatest writers, living and dead . . . the struggle of a human creature, under those opposing

> influences of Good and Evil, which we have all felt, which we have all known." *Armadale*, which is in fact a masterpiece of intricate melodrama and nothing else, is spoken of as Thomas Hardy might have spoken of *Tess of the d'Urbervilles* or *Jude the Obscure*: "Estimated by the Clap-trap morality of the present day, this may be a very daring book. Judged by the Christian morality which is of all time, it is only a book that is daring enough to speak the truth." For *The Moonstone* itself, which is simply the best of all mystery stories, Collins writes a preface declaring that he is attempting "to trace the influence of character on circumstances"—and that it is thus unlike some of his earlier novels, which "trace the influence of circumstances upon character."[5] (Stewart's ellipsis)

Indeed, Collins's words seem to point to the future products from Hardy's pen. Collins's idea of the conflict between "circumstances and character," too, chimes with Hardy's description of his "major" works, "novels of character and environment."

Hardy's very phrase, "novels of ingenuity," may possibly have a Collinsian association. The word "ingenuity" was often used in reviews of Collins's novels, designating the intricacy of the plot—for example, The *Saturday Review* on *The Woman in White*: "[Collins's] plots are framed with artistic ingenuity"; *The North British Review* on *No Name*: "The interest of [Collins's] books is absorbing, the ingenuity of his plots marvelous . . ."; The *Spectator* on *The Moonstone*: "We are no especial admirers of the department of art to which [Collins] has devoted himself, any more than we are of double acrostics, or anagrams, or any of the many kinds of puzzle on which it pleases some minds to exercise their ingenuity."[6] This sampling clearly shows that the word "ingenuity" has both positive and negative connotations. Hardy's own usage appears to convey the latter, but one suspects that at the same time something of the former is tacit in it.

Setting judgment aside, the word could certainly be applied to a scene in *A Laodicean*. One night, caught in a severe rainstorm, Havill is forced to share a room with Dare at an inn. Dare mysteriously says, slapping his breast with his right hand, "The secret of my birth lies here."[7] (We later come to know that he has the word "de Stancy" tattooed on his breast.) Havill becomes curious and, while Dare is sleeping, unfastens the collar of his nightshirt, to see what is inscribed on his breast. But

Dare tosses about, and Havill goes back to his bed without fulfilling his intentions. Dare then wakes up, a revolver in his hand. Scared, Havill pretends to be asleep.

> A clammy dew broke out upon the face and body of [Havill] when, stepping out of bed with the weapon in his hand, Dare looked under the bed, behind the curtains, out of the window, and into a closet, as if convinced that something had occurred, but in doubt as to what it was. He then came across to where Havill was lying and still keeping up the appearance of sleep. Watching him awhile and mistrusting the reality of this semblance, Dare brought it to the test by holding the revolver within a few inches of Havill's forehead.
>
> Havill could stand no more. Crystallized with terror, he said, without however moving more than his lips, in dread of hasty action on the part of Dare: "O, good Lord, Dare, Dare, I have done nothing!" (131)

This is pure melodrama, skillfully executed. However, it is not one of the best moments in the novel, for the thrill is only momentary and the scene does not connect with the rest in any meaningful way. To use Hardy's formula, here "the interest depends on the incident itself." The case is otherwise when he is truly successful. I have referred to the murder Tess commits. That moment is clinched by the striking image of the "gigantic ace of hearts" (Ch. 56) on the ceiling. This image of the red heart is not only locally impressive but thematically related to the whole series of other red things in the novel, such as the letters "Thou, Shalt, Not, Commit—," which earlier Tess sees being painted (Ch. 12). As Tony Tanner observes, "Watching Tess's life we begin to see that her destiny is nothing more or less than the colour red."[8]

Other moments in *A Laodicean*, while "melodramatic" in the same way, have a deeper and wider resonance. Perhaps the most memorable scene in the novel is the one in which Somerset and Paula have a terrifying experience with the train near the tunnel entrance.

> Somerset looked down on the mouth of the tunnel. The popular commonplace that science, steam, and travel must always be unromantic and hideous, was not proven at this spot. On either slope of the deep cutting, green with long grass, grew drooping

> young trees of ash, beech, and other flexible varieties, their foliage almost concealing the actual railway which ran along the bottom, its thin steel rails gleaming like silver threads in the depths. The vertical front of the tunnel, faced with brick that had once been red, was now weather-stained, lichened, and mossed over in harmonious rusty-browns, pearly greys, and neutral greens, at the very base appearing a little blue-black spot like a mouse-hole—the tunnel's mouth. (85)

This description of the tunnel's mouth, "lichened, and mossed over," is highly sexualized (just like the description of "the hollow amid the ferns," the scene of Sergeant Troy's sword practice in *Far from the Madding Crowd*), covertly creating an erotic atmosphere and preparing us for what is to follow: "[The train] rushed past them, causing Paula's dress, hair, and ribbons to flutter violently, and blowing up the fallen leaves in a shower over their shoulders" (88). If I am allowed to be a trifle facetious, I confess I cannot help being reminded at this point of that famous scene in the movie, *The Seven Year Itch*, where Marilyn Monroe holds down her skirt when the passing underground train rushes up the air from beneath. Here, the skirt itself is not mentioned; "Paula's dress, hair, and ribbons" flutter violently, we are told. But the reader will visualize it, and Hardy fills in the absence here, by drawing attention to Paula's skirts later. When Somerset crosses the Channel in search of Paula, he comes to a hotel in Nice, hoping to find her there: he "turned to the large staircase . . . momentarily hoping that her figure might descend. *Her skirts* must have brushed the carpeting of those steps scores of times" (253; my italics). What happens is that the reader, with Somerset, is sent back to that tunnel entrance, and made to see Paula's skirt fluttering up once again. We have, as it were, a delayed confirmation of what we have imagined. This is the way erotic images work in the novel. Somerset first sees Paula at the baptism ceremony, peeping in from the chapel window. Although the full immersion does not take place, and therefore is not described, we imagine with Somerset Paula's clothes wet and clinging to her body. This voyeurism continues in the notorious gymnasium scene, in which Captain de Stancy gazes at Paula in the "moment of absolute abandonment to every muscular whim that could take possession of such a supple form" (158). We assume that she is wearing a very tight costume, and are told that "The white manilla ropes *clung* about the performer like snakes" (158; my italics).

At this point we are sent back to the baptism ceremony, made to see once again a vision of the fully immersed Paula. The text is confirming the imagined scene.

Somerset faces another physical crisis when he gets trapped in a turret at Stancy Castle. This is carefully worked up to. Just before he finds himself there, a dispute takes place between him and Havill about the architectural history of the Castle, and Paula, who has been listening to them keenly, asks Somerset; "Now, would you really risk anything on your belief? Would you agree to be shut up in the vaults and fed upon bread and water for a week if I could prove you wrong?" "Willingly," answers Somerset (64). Sure enough, this is almost what happens to him. At "the bottom" of the turret, he perceives that "he dropped into it as into a dry well; that, owing to its being walled up below, there was no door of exit on either side of him; that he was, in short, a prisoner" (68). He finds something lying in the corner, which "on examination proved to be a dry bone" (69). It turns out later that this bone belongs to someone who years ago accidentally fell in the same place and was starved to death (76). This is Gothic enough to arouse what Eliot calls our "perennial craving" for melodrama, but there is something casual about this episode, which makes it ultimately disappointing. In the turret, in addition to the dry bone, Somerset notices that "on the stonework behind the [spider's] web sundry names and initials had been cut by explorers in years gone by. Among these antique inscriptions he observed two bright and clean ones, consisting of the words "de Stancy" and "W. Dare," crossing each other at right angles" (69). It is a compelling detail that one feels sure is to be used later. There will, however, be no further mention whatever of these inscriptions. This is very strange. At least, one would imagine that Somerset will say something about it when he sees Dare next time, for they *have* met at the Castle *before* Somerset falls in the turret—his curiosity must have been roused. So, later when Dare comes to Somerset, wishing to be employed as his assistant, naturally one expects Somerset to refer to the recent discovery of his name up in the turret. Nothing like that happens. Here is a dialogue between Somerset and Dare, shortly after his employment. Irritated by Dare's laziness, Somerset says,

> "Well, now, Mr Dare, suppose you get back to the castle?"
> "Which history dubs Castle Stancy . . . Certainly."
> "How do you get on with the measuring?" (102)

This is clearly an opportunity lost. Dare's sarcastic remark, "Which history dubs Castle Stancy"—meaning, "The castle really belongs to de Stancy and Dare"—is, as it were, prompting Somerset to remember that writing on the turret wall. But what he says is: "How do you get on with the measuring?" How can he be so dull-witted? Or should one blame Hardy for this vapidity?

Hardy's handling of Dare is puzzling. Later in the novel there is a melodramatic confrontation between him and Paula's uncle Abner, each pointing a gun at the other in a church vestry. Dare has the upper hand, because he knows everything, in intimate detail, about Abner's past involvement with terrorist activities. His knowledge—he claims that he had "a singular dream" (331)—extends to what presumably happened when Abner was by himself. How is that possible? Or consider the turret once again. If it is impossible for Somerset to get out of the turret without opportune help from a servant, how can it be that Dare, having secretly written these words, should have been able to get out of there by himself? J. O. Bailey argues that "Undoubtedly Hardy had in mind some preternatural, Mephistophelian origin and function for William Dare."[9] To be sure, Dare describes himself as "going to and fro in the earth, and walking up and down in it, as Satan said to his Maker" (143) and Captain de Stancy calls him "quite a Mephistopheles" (149). But if he has supernatural power, why does he have to resort to his falsified photo and his theory of chances at the gaming table? It does not seem consistent at all. Or is this to do with the novel's concern with the conflict between the romantic and the modern,[10] the presentation of Dare itself incarnating such a struggle?

There is another notable inconsistency. At one point, Somerset, aware of Paula's yearning for ancient lineage, wants to find out about his own family pedigree, hoping that his is as old a family as de Stancy's. His father informing him that there is a family pedigree deposited in their London bank, he goes there and examines it. While he is about it, Paula happens to come to the very same bank, to take out from her safety deposit a diamond necklace for the Ball that evening. He digs up the pedigree, but his attention is then wholly occupied by his relationship with Paula, and the business of the pedigree is totally forgotten. Is this again Hardy's carelessness? Or is he making a point in an oblique fashion (it is love that matters, not ancient lineage)? Might the phrasing "he had *mechanically* unearthed the pedigree" (198) possibly point in that direction?

In Hardy's novels, "The narrative provides action in time. The poetic underpattern, with its accumulation of echoes, parallels, and contrasts, shows the significance of that action." The observation, made by Jean Brooks in her admirable study of Hardy, is apt. She suggests that although there are poetic symptoms which "light up at rare moments the daemonic energies that disturb the surface of modern life," in *A Laodicean* they are in general buried under inorganic incidents; in particular, "Somerset's fall down the turret staircase, unlike Knight's down the Cliff without a Name, leads nowhere in plot or poetic vision."[11] I would qualify this slightly. As I have said, with Dare's inscriptions on the wall completely forgotten, this moment is not developed in terms of plot. We can, however, find something of a "poetic underpattern" here. Somerset's fall is clearly related to his burgeoning romantic feelings towards Paula. Immediately before this near disaster, he has been working at the top of the great tower. Then, "Finding after a while that his drawing progressed but slowly, by reason of infinite joyful thoughts more allied to his nature than to his art, he relinquished rule and compass, and entered one of the two turrets opening on the roof" (68). The next moment he is trapped at the bottom of it. This image of Somerset's imprisonment functions as a prefiguration of his later predicament, where he has passively to observe the progress of the relationship between de Stancy and Paula: at one point we are told that "he was so well walled in by circumstances that he was absolutely helpless" (184). There is a variation of this metaphor when Somerset later writes complainingly to Paula of "our shut-up feelings" (244). These metaphors of "being walled in" and "shut up" are, in turn, echoed in the description of Captain de Stancy's self-suppression (which may be compared with Boldwood's in *Far from the Madding Crowd*):

> Throughout a long space he had persevered in his system of rigidly *incarcerating* within himself all instincts towards the opposite sex, with a resolution that would not have disgraced a much stronger man. By this habit, maintained with fair success, a *chamber* of his nature had been preserved intact during many later years, like the *one solitary sealed-up cell* occasionally retained by bees in a lobe of drained honey-comb. (163; italics mine)

This defense de Stancy has put up is to be broken down by Dare. The above passage leads to the scene in which he finally decides to shake off his resolutions, and having gone through a kind of ceremony of drinking the wine that Dare has sent him, looks out at the moonlit barrack-yard and says, "A man again after eighteen years" (164). I have compared de Stancy with Boldwood. In the case of the latter, there is the clinching metaphor of Boldwood's gaze at the Valentine Bathsheba has sent, till "the large red seal became as a blot of blood on the retina of his eye" (Ch. 14).[12] There should be a poetic detail, related to something de Stancy sees in the moonlight perhaps, that fixes the moment for us. The same can be said of Somerset's entrapment in the turret. The incident itself is striking enough, and though there is a poetic underpattern that links this with the rest of the novel, there is no clinching metaphor that would have made it a truly Hardyan moment.

Hardy's imaginative engagement with Dare, de Stancy, and Somerset can hardly be called satisfactory. Paula, however, is another matter. Hardy himself was rather pleased with the heroine. In 1912 he added a postscript to the Preface of the novel, where he says he finds compensation in the character of Paula, "who, on renewed acquaintance, leads me to think her individualized with some clearness, and really lovable, though she is of that reserved disposition which is the most difficult of all dispositions to depict, and tantalized the writer by eluding his grasp for some time." The operative word here is "tantalize"; she does just that. The word "tantalize" appears several times in the novel. If she tantalized Hardy, she certainly tantalizes Somerset; and the reader, too. Paula's elusiveness is precisely what makes her interesting.

This leading quality of the heroine is related to the novel's narrative method. In the first section of the novel Hardy uses Somerset as a point-of-view character: the reader follows him and sees what he sees. Basically, the narrative events are conveyed to us filtered through Somerset's consciousness only, so that we do not know what is going on in the minds of other characters. The novel is divided into six Books which bear the names of characters: Book the First, "George Somerset"; Book the Second, "Dare and Havill"; Book the Third, "de Stancy"; and so on. Accordingly, we experience events by following Dare and Havill in Book the Second, and following de Stancy in Book the Third. In Book the First, the point of view is maintained with rigorous consistency throughout.[13] As the novel progresses, however, the control of the narrative point of view is loosened. Book the Fifth and Book the Sixth, the final two Books, are titled "de Stancy and Paula," and "Paula." But we are scarcely allowed to see the inside of Paula's mind. All we know about her derives from what she does and what she says in her dealings with other characters.

Some of the moments involving Paula and Somerset are given greater intensity by the verbal liveliness in Hardy's presentation. In the incident with the train, where they instinctively seize each other, they make their first, very brief, physical contact. They come close to each other again when Somerset is taking measurements in the Castle—Paula offers help, and their hands almost touch. Soon afterwards Paula asks to be enlightened about the early Gothic work, which, according to Somerset, is known by the undercutting. Somerset agrees to take her to the part of the Castle where this undercutting is, and suggests that she touch it and see it for herself. She does so, but confesses that she still does not understand what he means. Then,

> Somerset placed his own hand in the cavity. Now their two hands were close together again. They had been close together half-an-hour earlier, and he had sedulously avoided touching hers. He dared not let such an accident happen now. And yet—surely she saw the situation! Was the inscrutable seriousness with which she applied herself to his lesson a mockery? There was such a *bottomless depth* in her eyes that it was impossible to guess truly. Let it be that destiny alone had ruled that their hands should be together a second time. (81; italics mine)

The "bottomless depth" is a hackneyed, dead metaphor, but given the poetic underpattern we have observed in relation to Somerset's entrapment at the bottom of the turret, even this cliché is energized, reverberating with other similar metaphors.

I have said that in Book the First Somerset is consistently employed as the point-of-view character. This does not mean that we know only what Somerset knows. There is always Hardy the narrator looking over Somerset's shoulder, and he sometimes makes ironic comments, as he does in the quotation above: "Let it be that destiny alone had ruled that their hands should be together a second time." The narrative intervention is clumsy here, but it is not always so, as we shall presently see. Somerset cannot fathom Paula's mind, and then,

> All rumination was cut short by an impulse. He seized her *forefinger* between his own finger and thumb, and drew it along

> the hollow, saying, "That is the curve I mean."
> Somerset's hand was hot and trembling; Paula's, on the contrary, was cool and soft as an infant's.
> "Now the arch-mould," continued he. "There—the depth of that cavity is tremendous, and it is not geometrical, as in later work." He drew her unresisting *fingers* from the capital to the arch, and laid them in the little trench as before.
> She allowed them to rest quietly there till he relinquished them. "Thank you," she then said, withdrawing her hand, brushing the dust from her finger-tips, and putting on her glove.
> Her imperception of his feeling was the very sublimity of maiden innocence if it were real; if not, well, the coquetry was no great sin. (82; italics mine)

The "finger" somehow becomes "fingers"—is it merely yet another instance of carelessness on Hardy's part, or what? At any rate, this time the narrator's ironical comment at the end is potent. It is almost as if Hardy is siding with Paula, and teasing Somerset, and by extension, the reader. This "coquetry" of Paula's is going to be a torment to Somerset.

A few chapters later, at Paula's garden party, Somerset asks her to dance with him, but she does not readily acquiesce.

> "You will just once?" said he.
> Another silence. "If you like," she venturesomely answered at last.
> Somerset closed the hand which was hanging by his side, and *somehow* hers was in it. The dance was nearly formed, and he led her forward. Several persons looked at them significantly, but he did not notice it then, and plunged into the maze.
> Never had *Mr* Somerset passed through such an experience before. Had he not felt her actual weight and warmth, he might have fancied the whole episode a figment of the imagination. (107; italics mine)

"Somehow her hand was in Somerset's" is a delicate touch, particularly when one recalls the way Somerset has *somehow* caught her *fingers* in the previous quotation. Notice also the sentence, "Never had *Mr* Somerset passed through such an experience before." Hardy always refers to him as Somerset, except on three or four occasions; and on these exceptional occasions the effect is invariably ironic. For example, there is the instance earlier in the novel when Somerset explores the Castle in Paula's absence, and finding that the door of Paula's sleeping-room is open, looks in and observes the interior. Then he notices that a dressing-room lies beyond. But, "becoming conscious that his study of ancient architecture would hardly bear stretching further in that direction, *Mr* Somerset retreated to the outside, obliviously passing by the gem of Renaissance that had led him in" (35; italics mine). These instances of ironic distancing from Somerset appear to emphasize the dreamy world of romantic fantasy he inhabits, as is suggested by the final sentence of the passage quoted above; "Had he not felt her actual weight and warmth, he might have fancied the whole episode a figment of the imagination." This impression is beautifully developed in the following scene. Somerset and Paula go out of the tent where the dance is taking place, and walk to "a little wooden tea-house that [stands] on the lawn a few yards off" (108). When they are there, a storm suddenly breaks out.

> In a moment the storm poured down with sudden violence, and from which they drew further back into the summer-house. The side of the tent from which they had emerged still remained open, the rain streaming down between their eyes and the lighted interior of the marquee like a tissue of glass threads, the brilliant forms of the dancers passing and repassing behind the watery screen, as if they were people in an enchanted submarine palace.
> "How happy they are!" said Paula. (109)

This passage is arresting, for one thing, because of the exquisite image of the "enchanted submarine palace behind the watery screen," perhaps the single most beautiful image of the whole book. It is, however, not just impressive in itself. The word "submarine" evokes a sense of depth, which, as we have been observing, is connected with Somerset's position in relation to Paula. Combined with this, the rain running "like a tissue of glass threads" curiously recalls the description (already quoted) of the tunnel's mouth, near which these two had their first physical contact; the "foliage almost concealing the actual railway which ran along the *bottom*, its thin steel rails gleaming like silver *threads* in the *depths*" (my italics).

Another reason why the above passage is remarkable is that

this is the very first moment in the novel where Somerset and Paula are significantly presented as seeing something together—"the rain streaming down between *their* eyes and the lighted interior of the marquee." It stands out because, as I have said, everything else so far has been strictly reported to us from Somerset's point of view only. Since this beautiful image is filtered through the minds of both Somerset and Paula, it may lead us to suppose that they are sharing the same feeling of elation. But then, maybe not. For Paula's exclamation—"How happy they are!"—recalls an interesting exchange that has taken place immediately before, just after their dance:

> Somerset's feelings burst from his lips. "This is the *happiest* moment I have ever known," he said. "Do you know why?"
> "I think I saw a flash of lightening through the opening of the tent," said Paula, with roguish abruptness. (108; italics mine)

Clearly Paula is uninvolved, and Somerset seems trapped in that "submarine depth" by himself. Imagining that they are sharing this dreamy vision and that the moment of mutual understanding has arrived, he takes a step forward and confesses his love for her. But, "I love you to love me" (109) is all he can get out of her. The narrator comments:

> Poor Somerset had reached a *perfectly intelligible depth*—one which had a single blissful way out of it, and nine calamitous ones; but Paula remained an *enigma* throughout the scene. (119; italics mine)

An "enigma" indeed. Even at the end of the novel, Paula says, "I know every fibre of [Somerset's] character; and he knows a good many fibres of mine; so . . . there is nothing more to be learnt" (373). Paula will remain elusive, and Somerset still has to suffer for another two hundred pages in his "pleasing agonies and painful delights" (111). (In the quotation above the phrase "a perfectly intelligible depth" once again recalls the poetic underpattern that connects this with Somerset's fall into the bottom of the turret.)

Eventually, Paula comes to Somerset, and with characteristic haughtiness says to him; "I am here to be asked" (372). Shortly afterwards, in her hotel room she is passively "watching the sleeping flies on the ceiling" (373). The "sleeping flies" on the ceiling are certainly not as striking as the "gigantic ace of hearts," but this detail does go some way towards defining Paula for us. The distance between the trivial flies and her final resolution to get married seems to indicate her own detachment from romantic involvements with Somerset.[14] As the novel's very last words—Paula to Somerset, "I wish you were a de Stancy!" (385)—suggest, she may still somehow fly away from Somerset's grasp.

Not surprisingly, some of the early reviews expressed doubts about Paula: *St James Gazette* (4 February 1882), "We have every inclination to believe her charming, but we cannot quite understand her"; and The *Critic*, a New York paper (25 February 1882), "Had this young lady been an American we fear her conduct would have been severely criticized. . . . [F]or ourselves, we prefer the frank little American flirts."

Of late, an extreme attempt to find consistency in the novel has been made by Peter Widdowson, who proposes that "*A Laodicean* . . . becomes a parodic attack—by way of its own performative anti-realist textuality—on the (mis)representations passed off as "telling things as they really are" by fictional Realism."[15] That is to say, by thwarting the reader's expectations based on the conventions of realism, the novel reveals that such notions as realism, or character, or female sexuality are merely ideological constructs. He points out, for example, that characters repeatedly say things like "the plot thickens," or "'by the merest chance' I did so and so," as if the text is aware of its own contrivance. He gives a detailed analysis of the passage describing de Stancy's peeping, where, in his opinion, the novel's own representation of the scene is self-consciously mocked (107-11).[16] He also emphasizes the text's persistent foregrounding of misrepresentation, like a fake telegram and a distorted photo Dare uses.

I offer a different view. As I have observed, Hardy seems to relish Paula's coquetry. By steadily introducing irony where he describes Somerset's courtship of Paula, Hardy emphasizes her elusiveness. Much as Paula tantalizes Somerset, Hardy tantalizes the reader. Perhaps the novel's very inconsistencies we have noted reinforce this effect. In the review in The *Nation* (5 January 1882), it is said with felicity that "Mr Hardy is an *ingenious* novelist, and . . . by applying the term 'Laodicean' to his heroine, he has managed to convey to the mind of the reader a subtle doubt with regard to her character which pervades the book almost to the end" (italics mine). If the novel holds interest, it does so not so much by supplying melodramatic complications as by emulating its heroine's elusive charm. By this curious turn, *A Laodicean* indeed becomes a "Novel of Ingenuity."

> (Originally a lecture delivered at the International Thomas Hardy Conference, Dorchester, 2000; first published in *Thomas Hardy: Texts and Contexts*, Ed. Phillip Mallett, Palgrave Macmillan, 2002)

NOTES

1 For example, Richard H. Taylor, *The Neglected Hardy* (London: Macmillan, 1982); Peter Widdowson, *Hardy in History* (London: Routledge, 1989), Roger Ebbatson, *Hardy: The Margin of the Unexpressed* (Sheffield; Sheffield Academic Press, 1993).

2 T. S. Eliot, *Selected Essays*, 2nd ed. (London: Faber and Faber, 1934), 461, 467, 460.

3 *The Life and Work of Thomas Hardy by Thomas Hardy*, Ed. Michael Millgate (London: Macmillan, 1985), 87.

4 See Taylor, Ch. 1 and Winifred Hughes, *The Maniac in the Cellar: Sensation Novels of the 1860s* (Princeton: Princeton University Press, 1980), Ch. 6.

5 Introduction to *The Moonstone* (Harmondsworth: Penguin, 1966), 14-15.

6 *Wilkie Collins: The Critical Heritage*, Ed. Norman Page (London: Routledge, 1974), 83, 140, 171.

7 J. H. Stape's Everyman Paperback edition (London: Dent, 1997), 129. All subsequent references to the novel are to this edition. Hereafter, page references are in parentheses.

8 "Colour and Movement in Hardy's *Tess of the d'Urbervilles*", rpt. in *The Victorian Novel: Modern Essays in Criticism*, Ed. Ian Watt (Oxford: Oxford University Press, 1971), 409.

9 "Hardy's 'Mephistophelian Visitants'," *PMLA* 61 (1946), 1159. Bailey does not take into account Dare's supernatural exit from the turret.

10 This theme is ably discussed by J. B. Bullen, *The Expressive Eye: Fiction and Perception in the Works of Thomas Hardy* (Oxford: Oxford University Press, 1986), Ch. 5, esp. 123-24.

11 Jean Brooks, *Thomas Hardy: The Poetic Structure* (Ithaca: Cornell University Press, 1971), 143, 153, 152.

12 I discuss the significance of this passage in Ch. 19 of this book.

13 That is, except for just one paragraph at the end of Ch. 12, in which Dare's secret activity is revealed behind Somerset's back (91).

14 Paula's "detachment" perhaps resonates with that of Ethelberta, another heroine of Hardy's "novel of ingenuity." See Ch. 16 of this book, esp. pp. 164-70.

15 Peter Widdowson, *On Thomas Hardy: Late Essays and Earlier* (Basingstoke and London: Macmillan, 1998), 113.

16 Widdowson, too, connects this scene with Paula's baptism ceremony, noting Somerset's imagined view of her wet, clinging clothes.

Ch. 19 On Boldwood's Retina: A "Moment of Vision" in *Far from the Madding Crowd* and its Possible Relation to *Middlemarch*

When Hardy died in 1928, Virginia Woolf published a remarkably perceptive appreciation of his novels in *The Times Literary Supplement*:

> [Hardy's] own word, "moments of vision," exactly describes those passages of astonishing beauty and force which are to be found in every book that he wrote. With a sudden quickening of power which we cannot foretell, nor he, it seems, control, a single scene breaks off from the rest. We see, as if it existed alone and for all time, the waggon with Fanny's dead body inside travelling along the road under the dripping trees; we see the bloated sheep struggling among the clover; we see Troy flashing his sword round Bathsheba where she stands motionless, cutting the lock off her head and spitting the caterpillar on her breast. Vivid to the eye, but not the eye alone, for every sense participates, such scenes dawn upon us and their splendour remains.[1]

Indeed, Woolf's instancing of *Far from the Madding Crowd* is appropriate, for this novel particularly abounds in these "moments of vision." Although these moments may seem to be, as she suggests, detachable set pieces ("a single scene breaks off from the rest"), most of them are not only visually compelling, but also organically integrated into the text and thematically highly charged. Woolf's phrase, "moments of vision," of course derives from the title of a Hardy poem, and it precisely points to where Hardy's gift as a poet most happily combines with his novelistic talent.

A case in point is the scene where Oak fights the storm (Ch. 37). It is often said that Hardy lifted this from Ainsworth's *Rockwood*, a romance recounting the adventures of Dick Turpin, to which he had been attached as a boy (the inclusion of Troy's performance as the highwayman might be a further indication of this influence). This may be so, but sensory details and the thematic richness packed into this scene are uniquely Hardy's own: Oak's stepping on a large toad, the hot breeze fanning him, the flash leaping out with the "shout of a fiend," and the silver-colored lightening gleaming "like a mailed army"—together with all this, there is a sense of cosmological magnitude against futile mortal activities; everything human "seemed small and trifling in such close juxtaposition with an infuriated universe." The humans, however, are not entirely helpless. As Roy Morrell points out, "Nature is one of Gabriel's resources; but he is never controlled by her, nor, in any Wordsworthian sense, does he ever trust her."[2] The able shepherd studies the workings of Nature, and lives in accordance with them. Oak sees a female form in the flash of the thunder, and realizes that it is Bathsheba. The silhouette, made by the lightening, of the two atop the haystack is visually striking. Emphasizing the virtue of work, this tableau, more than anything else, prepares for the union of the couple at the end.

No moment, however, has more "astonishing force" than Boldwood gazing at the Valentine Bathsheba has sent him:

> Upon the mantelshelf before him was a time-piece, surmounted by a spread eagle, and upon the eagle's wings was the letter Bathsheba had sent. Here the bachelor's gaze was continually fastening itself, till the large red seal became as a blot of blood on the retina of his eye. . . . (132)[3]

What is remarkable about this passage is not only its striking image (the words "Marry Me" of the seal becoming a blot of blood on the retina) as such, but also the way in which Hardy's language operates so that this "moment of vision," far from "breaking off from the rest," becomes instead a knot of various threads that run throughout the text as a whole.[4]

First of all, this image of imprinted letters is beautifully reinforced in the very next chapter (Ch. 15), which moves the action to Warren's malthouse on the following morning. It must immediately be said that what Hardy is doing with this malthouse scene is not mere copying of the famous Rainbow in *Silas Marner* (I shall come back to the George Eliot question later).[5] There is much more to it than that.

To summarize what happens in Ch. 15: the farm hands who have gathered here are talking about their new mistress Bathsheba, when Oak comes in with four lambs under his arms; the conversation now turns to how, in the time of Bathsheba's uncle, Joseph Poorgrass branded the letters J and E the wrong way round; Oak puts the marking iron to the lambs—the initials "B. E.," signifying "to all the region round that henceforth the lambs belonged to Farmer Bathsheba Everdene, and to no one else" (p. 144); then Boldwood, who has stopped by, asks him to identify the handwriting of the letter he received the day before; Oak answers that it is Bathsheba's.

Notice how the motif of branding is repeated in this sequence, which has started with the Valentine seal imprinted on Boldwood's retina. The act of branding, imprinting letters, is nothing but a way of marking one's property, and this idea of property, or "possession," is, in fact, a very important thread in the portrayal of Bathsheba's relationship with male characters. For instance, early in the novel Bathesheba, declining his marriage proposal, says to Oak:

> "What I meant to tell you was only this . . . that nobody has got me yet as a sweetheart, instead of my having a dozen, as my aunt said: I hate to be thought men's property in that way, though possibly I shall be had some day. . . . (pp. 65-66)

Marriage, for Bathsheba, means being possessed by the husband, therefore she rejects it, at least at this stage. Consider also the following passage, which comes towards the end of the novel, when Oak writes to her, after Troy's death and Boldwood's imprisonment, informing her of his decision to leave the country:

> Bathsheba actually sat and cried over this letter most bitterly. She was aggrieved and wounded that the possession of hopeless love from Gabriel, which she had grown to regard as her inalienable right for life, should have been withdrawn just at his own pleasure in this way. (p. 415)

Bathsheba, then, hates to be possessed, but at the same time she relishes the idea of possessing Oak. In addition, simultaneously at work here is the sexual implication of the word "possession":

> It appears that ordinary men take wives because possession is not possible without marriage, and that ordinary women accept husbands because marriage is not possible without possession; with totally differing aims the method is the same on both sides. (p. 163)

Thus the imprinting of the Valentine seal on Boldwood's retina signifies that he "belongs to Bathseba Everdene and to no one else." Hereafter he is "possessed" by Bathsheba, which also means that he is sexually obsessed with her. The sequence of chapters 14, 15 is essential to this overall design of the novel.

Moreover, we should also be alert to the fact that this fatal seal is red in color. What is operative here is not merely the connection with blood. For the color "red" is also rich in sexual associations, most importantly represented by Troy's army uniform. Even when Bathsheba first meets with him in the dark: "The man to whom she was hooked was brilliant in brass and scarlet" (p. 193). Again, in that sword practice scene, he appears as "a dim spot of artificial red" (p. 214). This encounter in "the hollow amid the ferns" will, in turn, lead to Bathsheba, in "the beautiful yellowing ferns with feathery arms," seeing some fungi "red as arterial blood" (the anatomical language once again recalls "the retina") in a "hollow" (p. 329), right after she has found out about Troy's previous sexual relationship with Fanny.

Indeed, the accumulated energy of these effects we have been examining is fully felt in the description of Troy leaving after the sword exercise; "his scarlet form disappear[ing] . . . almost in a flash, like a brand swiftly waved" (p. 218). Here Hardy's language does far more than just making us see a burning torch. The real beauty of the figure of the "brand" lies precisely in the fact that, aside from poetically invoking the image of a sword, it perfectly resonates with, and thereby strengthens, the imprinting and "possession" theme: it is now Bathsheba's turn to be "possessed."

Seen in this light, the Boldwood passage is a truly astonishing "moment of vision," which spins some of the more important threads of the novel, namely those of branding, possession, and the color red. Surely one of Hardy's strengths as a novelist can be found in the complex play of his figurative language, which this "moment of vision" admirably demonstrates.

Let us now turn to the question of the relation between Hardy and George Eliot, which we have touched upon. When *Far from the Madding Crowd* was published, it was on the whole favorably received. That here was a new talent was broadly recognized, and Hardy's vivid depiction of rural surroundings was unanimously praised. The *Guardian*, the *Times*, and the *Saturday Review* seized on the novel's "idyllic," or "pastoral" quality with enthusiasm, and, not surprisingly reviewers often evoked the name of George Eliot. The *Spectator*, after the appearance of the first instalment, went so far as to suggest that the novel was written by Eliot (they corrected their misattribution in February 1874, and this is where the author's identity was first made public). The *Westminster Review* made the laudatory remark that the novel stood to all contemporary fiction precisely as *Adam Bede* had done to other novels of its period. Reviewers pointed out various common elements in their artistic make-up: rural settings, portrayal of the farming class, extended use of rustic speech, inclination to analytic comments and philosophical generalizations, penchant for a scientific vocabulary, and so on.[6] Here I should like to draw attention to one particular instance of this last point.[7]

As far as I am aware, there is no concrete evidence that Hardy had ever read *Middlemarch*. It is, however, difficult to believe that when it came out in 1871-72, the young Hardy, then a newly-fledged novelist, did not read this important work by a major novelist. In view of the present discussion, there is in this novel a passage which we are tempted to speculate could not have failed to catch Hardy's fancy: the passage describing Dorothea's disillusioned state of mind during the honeymoon trip to Italy:

> Our moods are apt to bring with them images which succeed each other like the magic-lantern pictures of a doze; and in certain states of dull forlornness Dorothea all her life continued to see the vastness of St. Peter's, the huge bronze canopy . . . and the *red* drapery which was being hung for Christmas spreading itself everywhere like a disease of the *retina*. (Ch. 20; italics mine)

In fact, immediately after the appearance of Eliot's novel, in *A Pair of Blue Eyes* (1872-73), we find the following passage where Knight (who is, incidentally, in some respects rather like Casaubon), having heard about her past relationship with Stephen, decides to terminate his engagement with Elfride:

> The scene was engraved for years on the *retina* of Knight's eye: the dead and brown stubble, the weeds among it, the distant belt of beeches shutting out the view of the house, the leaves of which were now *red* and sick to death. (Ch. 34; italics mine)

There is a curious echo of Dorothea in Rome here: the retina, the color red, and the idea of long-lasting visual impressions in association with bitter emotional experience.

Was Hardy, then, influenced by George Eliot on this point?[8] "Influence," or "debt," seems to me too strong and simple a word. For Hardy might well have found in Eliot what was already present in himself. What is beyond dispute, however, is the fact that Hardy was sufficiently keen about this retina image to employ it once again in the very next novel *Far from the Madding Crowd* (1874), and that this time, as opposed to the one in *A Pair of Blue Eyes* where the effect is only locally striking, it is brilliantly related to the design of the novel as a whole, thus making the Boldwood passage a "moment of vision" of extraordinary force.

(First published in *The Thomas Hardy Journal*, 1994; this version incorporates some material from the entry on *Far from Madding Crowd* that I contributed to *Oxford Reader's Companion to Hardy*, Ed. Norman Page, 2000)

Addendum

Nicola Harris, in her discussion of the different attitudes of Hardy and George Eliot to "moral perception," refers to my above argument, in which I deal with the same passages that she considers.[9] Essentially, I am arguing against critics who speak of Hardy's debt to Eliot in a rather facile fashion. Harris, however, summarizes my contention thus: "Sasaki suggests that one of Eliot's own moments of vision, that pertaining to Dorothea's dissatisfaction with her honey-moon, ingrained itself into Hardy's own inner eye" (55). This sounds as if Hardy had become a Boldwood, and her phrasing unfortunately seems to imply Hardy's indebtedness to Eliot, quite contrary to my intention.

Harris wishes to stress the difference between the two writers: while Eliot has faith in the idea of objective reality, Hardy emphasizes the subjective, "idiosyncratic mode of regard." I would go along with this as a broad generalization, but I have difficulty in accepting superiority in Eliot's novelistic art. Regarding the two passages in question, Harris observes that while in *Middlemarch* "the formal fragmentariness is only just held back from total disintegration by the masterly skills of the omnicompetent narrator," Hardy is "neither as controlled nor as successful in preventing such formal incongruities" (55) in *Far from the Madding Crowd.* She goes on to talk about Eliot's "formal coherence" (56) and the successful combination of telling and showing. One wonders, however, where the line is to be drawn between success and failure in this respect. She speaks of Hardy's "incongruous and incompatible scientific analogy," and his "cold precision" that threatens to "undermine the autonomy of experience" (56). Again, this gives me pause. I do not think Hardy's language is incongruous here. What is locally odd could be part of a larger design and, as I tried to show in my article, there is a unique kind of "coherence" in a Hardy novel. Harris maintains that the indeterminacy of Hardy's vision generates its own "drawbacks" (52), but the truth of the matter is that Hardy and Eliot are employing different narrative techniques, with different purposes. A drawback in one kind of novel may be an advantage in another.

It should be pointed out, however, that Harris argues convincingly for the importance of Ruskin as a common source of inspiration for Hardy and Eliot. She pinpoints various key passages in *Modern Painters*, and the use she makes of Ruskin's phrase, "moral retina," is telling. In my article I suggested the possibility that the retina image (or its germ) might have been already present in Hardy's mind when he encountered the passage in *Middlemarch*. Harris has made a very good case for the likelihood that Hardy derived it from Ruskin. This, of course, is a speculation, and a most attractive one, in my view.

(First published in *George Eliot Review*, 1998)

NOTES

1 Virginia Woolf, "The Novels of Thomas Hardy" in *The Essays of Virginia Woolf*, Vol. 4, Ed. Andrew McNeillie, (1994).
2 Roy Morrell, *Thomas Hardy: The Will and the Way* (Kuala Lumpur: University of Malaya Press, 1965), 63.
3 This and subsequent references are to the New Wessex (paperback) edition of the novel (London: Macmillan, 1974).
4 For other important discussions of this passage see, for instance, Ian Gregor, *The Great Web: The Form of Hardy's Major Fiction* (London: Faber and

Faber, 1974), 54; Jean Brooks, *Thomas Hardy: The Poetic Structure* (New York: Cornell University Press, 1971), 171.

5 Although he is talking about Ch. 9, Lawrence Jones argues that the malthouse passage "reads like an imitation of the Rainbow scene." "George Eliot and Pastoral Tragicomedy in Hardy's *Far from the Madding Crowd*," *Studies in Philology* 77 (1980), 411.

6 See *Thomas Hardy: The Critical Heritage*, Ed. R. G. Cox (London: Routledge & Kegan Paul, 1970), 19-45.

7 For Hardy's "stylistic debt" to George Eliot, including the scientific language, see Lawrence Jones, "'Infected by a Vein of Mimeticism': George Eliot and the Technique of *Far from the Madding Crowd*," *The Journal of Narrative Technique* 8 (1978), 67-70.

8 Jones thinks he was. See "Infected by a Vein of Mimeticism," 58, 69.

9 Nicola Harris, "Hardy and Eliot: the Eye of Narcissus' Looking-Glass," *George Eliot Review*, 28 (1997), 49-58.

Ch. 20 John Schlesinger's *Far from the Madding Crowd*: A Reassessment

Two recent studies of the cinematic adaptation of Hardy have strengthened my feeling that an important aspect of John Schlesinger's *Far from the Madding Crowd* (1967) has not received due attention. Paul J. Niemeyer, though praising the performances (except that of Julie Christie) and Nicolas Roeg's beautiful cinematography, argues that the film is merely a comfortable pastoral which does not reflect Hardy's intention of showing how Nature lies outside the realm of human understanding:

> [I]t is in his very desire to be faithful to Hardy (or at least Hardy as he is generally perceived) as well as to the Victorian era, and in his effort to find *realistic* film images to visualize Hardy's metaphoric treatment of Nature, that Schlesinger winds up creating both a safe, contained version of Hardy as pastoralist, and a familiar picture of Hardy's world as a place where Nature blesses those who live according to its dictates.[1]

Keith Wilson, in his exploration of the problem of textual fidelity, submits that "in its pursuit of a certain surface kind of, primarily visual, atmospheric fidelity, this film, successful in many ways though it is, sacrifices the book's imaginative logic without adequately substituting an alternative cinematic one of its own."[2] He is particularly critical of the way Troy is presented, maintaining that his characterization is "opaque almost to the point of impenetrability" (100). It seems to me, however, that neither of these critics—nor, indeed, as far as I know, any previous commentator[3]—adequately responds to the film's notable achievement: an expressive style that is worthy of Hardy.

"The narrative provides action in time. The poetic underpattern, with its accumulation of echoes, parallels, and contrasts, shows the significance of that action."[4] Thus Jean Brooks succinctly describes the way Hardy's fiction works. A Hardy novel, as I see it, is highly cohesive in that this "accumulation" results in remarkably tight connections between key words, and between events. Consider the sequence dealing with the valentine Bathsheba sends to Boldwood. In Ch. 14 we have an unforgettable moment when Boldwood intently gazes at it, "till the large red seal became as a blot of blood on the retina of his eye"—an astonishing conceit. Hardy reiterates this image of "impressing" in the very next chapter. Ch. 15 shows a gathering of farmhands at Warren's malthouse next morning. They are talking about their headstrong mistress, Bathsheba, whereupon Oak enters and silences them. Then, with a marking iron, he imprints Bathsheba's initials on the lambs he has brought with him. Boldwood stops by to enquire about the handwriting of the valentine. Oak replies it is Bathsheba's. In this sequence we have two images of "impressing"—the seal on the retina; the brand on the sheep. This is thematically pregnant. Imprinting the initials has to do with the idea of possession, and so, Hardy suggests, does the relationship between man and woman: Bathsheba says, "I hate to be thought men's property . . . though possibly I shall be had some day" (Ch. 4), while Boldwood is clearly "possessed" by her. Thus Hardy's novel creates its meaning through the recurrent motifs and vigorous semantic action of its language.[5]

Schlesinger manages to find a similarly effective style. The film realizes Boldwood's gazing at the valentine in an atmosphere of extraordinary intensity. The gentleman-farmer (magnificently played by Peter Finch) is eating alone in his dining room, with the exception of two big Dalmatians. The valentine is placed on the mantelpiece, opposite him, and he casts a nervous glance at it a few times. In the quiet of the room the sound of the clocks (we see three of them on the mantelpiece) echoes with inordinate loudness, and the film shows them twice (one at a time) in close-up. The mise-en-scène links this to a later moment when Boldwood draws from Bathsheba a reluctant promise to marry him if Troy, who has disappeared, does not come back in six years' time. The action takes place in the very same room, and the two are talking to each other right in front of the mantelpiece. The camera

captures Boldwood in the same frame with one of the clocks, both in clear focus (and the part of his face around his eyes is lit to show his intensity), whereas when the camera moves to Bathsheba, the clock behind her is, by contrast, blurred. Here, too, the sound of the clocks is distinctly heard throughout. In these scenes clocks are apparently intended to symbolize the farmer's impatient desire.[6] To get back to Boldwood in the dining room: while he is eating, the dogs seem restless, as if sensing the master's inner turbulence. At some sound outside they rise up, but Boldwood stops them by interjecting in a strained voice, "Stay"—this action seems to reflect the repression of his own agitated feelings.[7] After a few moments, however, no longer capable of holding himself, he abruptly moves over to the mantelpiece, throwing the card into the fire. The consuming flame dissolves into the figure of Bathsheba on horseback, who is supervising her laborers washing the sheep in a pond, while the crackling sound of the fire transmutes itself into the splashes. Here Bathsheba is presented upside-down as reflected on the water, which suggests the distorted vision Boldwood's desire has created.

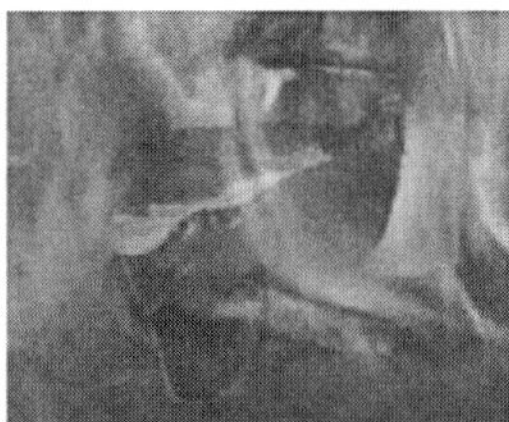
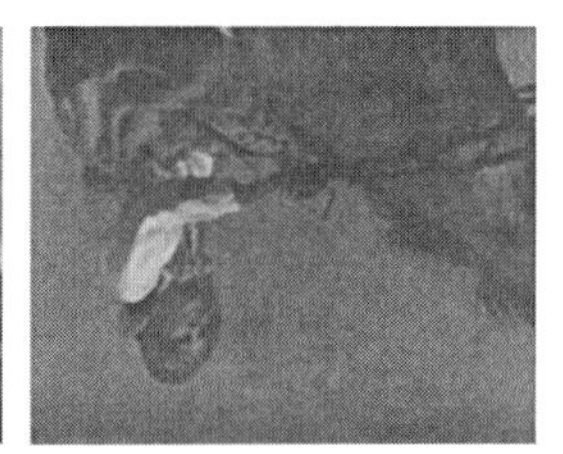

As in the above instance, Schlesinger often makes a transition from one scene to another with an interesting sense of continuity. He uses a dissolve again when moving from the water-soaked grave of Fanny Robin to the sea in which Troy has an apparently fatal swim. An effective cut is employed in the transition from Bathsheba's writing the words "Marry Me" on the valentine to Fanny and Troy on the eve of their abortive marriage ceremony. Most notable, however, is the sequence that comes immediately after the sword exercise. In her house Bathsheba declares to the women servants that she is not in love with Troy. Next we see the Sergeant traveling in a reddleman's cart (a knowing reference to Diggory Venn of *The Return of the Native*). As the cart disappears, the screen is for a moment filled with the color red, which vanishes in another moment to show a farm laborer walking outside the window; we do not immediately know what is happening, but soon realize that it was Bathsheba quickly drawing a red curtain. She is changing curtains with her servant Lydia, to whom she confesses her desperate love for Troy. The series of red objects in this sequence—Troy's uniform, the reddleman and his cart, and the curtain—make a strong impression on us, and the association of the color with Troy is intensified. We are reminded of this when the identical curtain reappears as Boldwood tries to persuade Bathsheba to accept his suit soon after Troy's disappearance.[8] This scene begins with a close-up of him in front of it. (In an earlier scene—before the Sergeant comes into the story—where the farmer courts Bathsheba after the sheep shearing supper, the color of the curtains in the background is light brown.) Thus Troy's ever-powerful presence and the consequent futility of Boldwood's attempt are hinted at with meticulous care.

Neil Sinyard has rightly observed that the difficulty of realizing a cinematic version of Hardy lies in his "peculiar combination of realism and symbolism," but his verdict on this film is unjustly harsh: "a pedestrian director like Schlesinger, grounded in British documentary, cannot rise to this extra poetic dimension."[9] One wonders why he is not attentive to the rendering of a particularly symbolic scene in the novel, Troy's sword practice. The way Schlesinger handles this and related scenes shows that he has certainly added his own poetic dimension to his film. True, some elements are blatantly obvious; above all the "phallic" sword, with which Troy seems to penetrate Bathsheba. At the end of the exercise Troy sticks it into the ground, and it calls attention to itself by catching the sunlight whilst they are embracing each other. The

sexual symbolism is repeated when Oak uses his trocar in the curing of the sheep; after casting a glance at Bathsheba who stands nearby, he sticks it perpendicularly (thus miming Troy's sword) into one of the

ailing sheep. But what is praiseworthy here as imaginative adaptation is that in the sword-practice scene Schlesinger has Troy say to her, "This is usually done on horseback," and then step back in the imitation of horseback riding, while emitting some curious metallic sound.

Significantly, in this film Troy makes his first appearance on horseback (Fanny accosts him on the road on a cloudy day; not in the snow, over the river outside his barracks, as in the novel),[10] and his association with the horse, strengthened at the sword-practice—the cavalry charge towards Bathsheba that she imagines, slightly ridiculous though it may be, is part of the deliberately prepared design—continues in a delightful reproduction of Victorian entertainment, an equestrian drama about Dick Turpin, where he displays his dexterity with the sword once more. At the end of the play (which Bathsheba and Boldwood are watching) when he mourns the death of his beloved mare, Black Bess, Troy again emits the metallic sound, thereby bringing us back to the scene of his sexual conquest.

By connecting it with the Turpin drama (where he shows Troy put on makeup), Schlesinger gives the sword practice a stronger tint of "performance." This brings to relief the actual emptiness of Troy's feelings for Bashtheba. The same point is made when, coming to woo

her while she is tending her bees, he attracts her attention by emitting the "bzzzzz" sound—another mimetic action on his part—and more strikingly when Bathsheba goes to see Troy in Weymouth (originally in Bath). She finds him in the small crowd of people watching a picture-story show about Captain Cook.[11] When she leaves the crowd with him, the showman is saying to the audience that on the barbaric island the Captain visited human sacrifices were made, and presents a graphic picture depicting such a scene, pointing it with a sword—a reminder of Troy's exercise (a little too insistent perhaps, but so is Hardy very often). The camera then follows them to the beach, and whilst they are talking we see their mouths move, but all we hear is the sound of the waves. Of this directorial decision Sinyard observes: "The sound

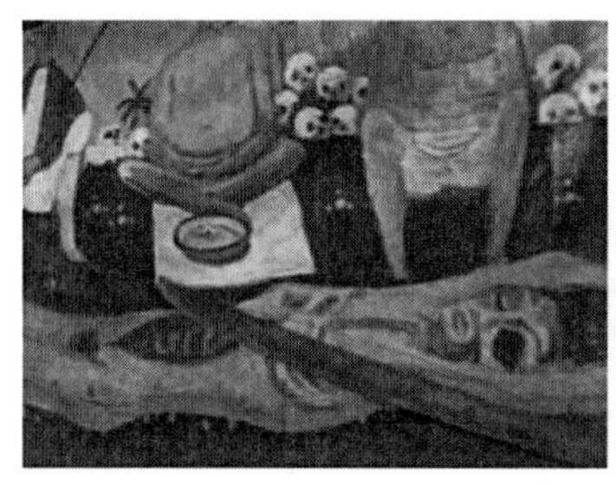

of the sea drowns out a crucial conversation between Bathsheba and Troy at Weymouth for no discernible reason, other than an inability on screenwriter Frederic Raphael's part to imagine what they might be saying to each other" (48). Against this extremely critical view, some defense has been offered. T. R. Wright argues that the scene is genuinely Hardyesque in that "[w]e are forced to imagine what the two lovers are saying to each other, just as in the novel itself we have to piece together what must have happened from the frequently interrupted and altogether incoherent narrative of Cainy Ball."[12] Niemeyer, in the course of his analysis of the relationship between men and nature as portrayed in the film, notes that "it is as if the waves are trying to silence an act—Troy's social union with Bathsheba—that should be *literally* unspeakable" (88). My view is that the film, by obliterating their speech, calls attention to the fact that what we are experiencing is cinematic story-telling. This is to emphasize, with the help of the showman who is also telling a story, that Troy is obviously concocting some sweet fiction (look at his shifty expression). In contrast with the kind of elaborately cinematic treatment of Troy's—and Boldwood's—wooing of Bathsheba, the film deals with Oak's courtship in a markedly straightforward fashion, suggesting its unaffected, genuine quality.

Troy's words may be sham, but his hold over Bathsheba is real, as the film goes on to show. After their marriage she is not at all pleased with her husband, who has got the workers into a drunken stupor, making them useless against the storm on the night of the nuptial celebration. Therefore she greets Troy in a state of pique the morning after, when he comes back home. But once he picks up a stick that was lying in the hall, handles it like a sword, and says, "I'm Sorry, Mrs

Troy," she is immediately mollified and in a shy but clearly glad fashion follows him to their bedroom.

Even at the very end (which is reached only several minutes after Bathsheba has fervently kissed Troy's dead body, bloodying her own face) we are left with the same impression. The newly wed Bathsheba and Oak are in their sitting room, the former reading a newspaper, and the latter standing by the window. It is raining very hard outside. This is a significant mise-en-scène, for the locus of their true union is not inside, but outside in the rain, as the trial of the rainstorm has attested. Then comes the sound of a musical clock, which has been given by Troy to Bathsheba. One part of its mechanism is a soldier in red uniform,

and the camera zooms in on it, until the frame freezes with its close-up. Thus the film suggests that Bathsheba is, deep down, still under the sway of Troy.[13] This is another notable departure from the novel, in which an essentially unproblematic happy ending is provided, if with a modicum of sad, chastened note: Bathsheba "never laughed readily now" and Joseph Poorgrass, the moralizing farmhand, comments that "it might have been worse" (Ch. 57).

Clearly Schlesinger is interested in, or rather fascinated by Troy, in the way D. H. Lawrence was, for whom he "is the only man in the book who knows anything about [Bathsheba]," and he can, like Alec d'Urberville, "draw from the depth of [a woman's] being."[14] To be sure, in this film characterization on the whole is simplified, but that rather sharpens the action of a ballad-like melodrama, and I do not think Troy's character is as unfathomable as Wilson claims. In my view he is consistently portrayed as a performer. He plays the parts of a lover and a husband. His rejection of Bathsheba with an outburst of love for Fanny at the side of her coffin—"This woman is more to me, dead as she is, than you ever were, or are, or could be"—is sudden and unbelievable, but the point is that *he* believes he has to act like that. The part of a grief-stricken lover is short-lived, however. It comes to an end when he has planted the bulbs for Fanny at her grave. Note that in the film the water spouting from the gargoyle washes them away *after* he has left the churchyard. In the novel Troy finds his labor of love wasted, which precipitates his departure. Schlesinger has removed this cause and can thereby suggest that, having done with the memory of Fanny, he leaves the place for another act. "[F]ar from disablingly careworn, idly slashing at the grass with a switch and galloping down the cliff pathway"—so Wilson describes Troy's descent to the sea coast in the immediately following scene. He says this in order to point out the obscurity or inconsistency of his behavior: why does he seem light-hearted? is he trying to commit suicide? why is he deserting Bathsheba "who is after all still his meal-ticket" (105)? I would answer: he is not intending to destroy himself; he has simply grown sick of playing the role of Bathsheba's husband, and is aiming to make a fresh start; to have a swim seems a fitting ceremony for that.

In his creative adaptation of *Far from the Madding Crowd* John Schlesinger has managed to produce what can be regarded as a cinematic equivalent of the cohesive texture of Hardy's fiction, while making an intriguing presentation of Sergeant Troy. This is surely quite an artistic feat and deserves proper recognition.

(First published in *Literature/Film Quarterly*, 2009)

NOTES

1 Paul J. Niemeyer, *Seeing Hardy* (Jefferson, North Carolina: McFarland, 2003).

2 Keith Wilson, "*Far from the Madding Crowd* in the Cinema: the Problem of Textual Fidelity," *Thomas Hardy on Screen*, ed. T. R. Wright (Cambridge: Cambridge University Press, 2005) 100.

3 In addition to the critics mentioned in the body of the text and the notes, I

have consulted Gene D. Philips, *John Schlesinger* (Boston: Twayne, 1981); James M. Welsh, "Hardy and the Pastoral, Schlesinger and Shepherds: *Far from the Madding Crowd*," *Literature/Film Quarterly* 9 (1981) 79-84; Fran E. Chalfont, "From Strength to Strength: John Schlesinger's Film of *Far from the Madding Crowd*," *The Thomas Hardy Annual* 5 (1987) 63-74.

4 Jean Brooks, *Thomas Hardy: The Poetic Structure* (Ithaca: Cornell University Press, 1971) 143.

5 See Ch. 19 of this book.

6 The motif of "time" is present in the novel, and each character is defined by his or her relation to it. Oak has a defective watch (Ch. 1) but he can tell the right time by looking at stars (Ch. 2). Bathsheba meets Troy for the first time in the fir plantation at night, when she is "[s]lipping along here covertly as Time" (Ch. 24). Troy's "outlook upon time was as a transient flash of the eye now and then" (Ch. 25) and he later gives her his watch which has a motto, *Cedit amor rebus*; "Love yields to circumstance" (Ch. 26). Boldwood "would annihilate the six years of his life as if they were minutes—so little did he value his time on earth beside her love" (Ch. 49).

7 The inclusion of the dogs in this scene is a brilliant stroke (they are not in the novel), in that it prompts us to recall an earlier sequence in which Oak's dog frantically chases his flock of sheep down the cliff. If Boldwood's struggle with his desire for Bathsheba is expressed in terms of the interaction between him and the Dalmatians, we may, in connection with this, find significance in the unexplained action of Oak's dog (attributed, in the novel, to the bad meat it has eaten): as the accident occurs just after Oak's abortive courting of Bathsheba, one might view the dog's wild behavior as a metaphor of his aroused, but frustrated, sexual desire for her (he has to shoot the dog in the end).

8 As Niemeyer notes, here, too, the clock sound is audible (91). It is, however, not as loud as in the other scenes I have alluded to.

9 Neil Sinyard, *Filming Literature* (London: Croom Helm, 1986) 48.

10 Rita Costabile simply regards this as a symptom of Schlesinger's insensitivity to Hardy's depiction of Nature. See her article, "Hardy in Soft Focus," *The English Novel and the Movies*, Ed. Michael Klein and Gillian Parker (New York: Frederick Ungar, 1981) 158.

11 In the crowd Troy is standing next to a soldier, apparently his acquaintance. I feel this person should have been a woman, as in the novel, a potential rival for Bathsheba.

12 T. R. Wright, "'Hardy as a Cinematic Novelist': Three Aspects of Narrative Technique," *Thomas Hardy on Screen* 17.

13 Wilson declares that as opposed to Troy's watch in the novel, this clock in the film "makes no contribution . . . to an understanding of what makes these characters act as they do." He even adds that the cutting, forced by the MGM executives who thought the film was too long, of this terminal image from American prints is "almost appropriate" (102). Niemeyer, who is more observant, argues that "Schlesinger associates Troy with images of light and springtime" (86), and says of the ending: "in spite of the gaiety that was seen at Bathsheba and Gabriel's wedding, the forces of Nature—darkness, rain, the rapid ticking away of time—will serve to quash the couple's happiness, and a new springtime—perhaps a new lover—will emerge to take its place" (92).

14 D. H. Lawrence, "Study of Thomas Hardy," *Study of Thomas Hardy and Other Essays*, Ed. Bruce Steele (Cambridge: Cambridge University Press, 1988) 23, 96.

III. OTHERS

Ch. 21 *John Marchmont's Legacy*: An Introduction

1. Sensation Novels of the 1860s

Wilkie Collins's *The Woman in White* was a tremendous publishing event of 1859-60. The circulation of *All the Year Round* in which it was serialized rose even higher than during the run of Dickens's *A Tale of Two Cities*, the novel that immediately preceded it as a leading serial; people thronged the street outside the magazine's office waiting for the appearance of a new instalment. When it was published in book form the entire first edition of one thousand copies were sold out on the very first day, and the fourth impression was printed within a month. It was even a social phenomenon. White became a popular color for feminine dress, and a number of commodities named after the novel were produced; "The Woman in White" bonnet, "The Woman in White" perfume, and so on. This monumental success triggered the vogue of "sensation novels." Mrs Henry Wood quickly followed with *East Lynne* (1861), and Mary Elizabeth Braddon with *Lady Audley's Secret* (1862).

Such novels, of which these three writers were the chief exponents, were characterized by their ample use of elements of crime, such as bigamy, fraud, blackmail, and murder, in addition to various "sensational" ingredients like insanity, adultery, and illegitimacy. Specifically, they dealt with crime within the family, secrets behind the façade of middle-class respectability. In this regard, the sensation novel may be thought of as modernized and domesticated Gothic fiction, of the kind represented by Ann Radcliffe's *The Mysteries of Udolpho* (1794) which treats of horrors in sixteenth-century Italy. In a review of Braddon's *Aurora Floyd* (1863), the young Henry James astutely observed:

> To Mr Collins belongs the credit of having introduced into fiction those most mysterious of mysteries, the mysteries which are at our own doors. This innovation gave a new impetus to the literature of horrors. It was fatal to the authority of Mrs Radcliffe and her everlasting castle in the Apennines. What are the Apennines to us, or we to the Apennines? Instead of the terrors of *Udolpho*, we were treated to the terrors of the cheerful country-house and the busy London lodgings. And there is no doubt that these were

> infinitely the more terrible.[1]

These novels, supposedly appealing to physical sensations of terror rather than to higher rational faculties, were deemed not only inferior in aesthetic terms—Collins and Braddon create their effects, according to James, "without any imagination at all"—but also morally corrupt and corrupting.

Sensation fiction drew censorious remarks from various quarters, and one of the most vehement (as well as most comprehensive) attacks, published in a notably conservative magazine, was penned by an Oxford don Henry Mansel, later Dean of St Paul's. Deploring these "morbid phenomena of literature," he characterized sensation novels as

> indications of a wide-spread corruption, of which they are in part both the effect and the cause; called into existence to supply the cravings of a diseased appetite, and contributing themselves to foster the disease, and to stimulate the want which they supply.[2]

Clearly Mansel sees a vicious circle that involves the "morally corrupt" public and the "morally corrupt" novels. He is particularly distressed by "Bigamy Novels," of which Braddon's *Lady Audley* was the quintessential example. Noting that "It is astonishing how many of our modern writers have selected this interesting breach of morality and law as the peg on which to hang a mystery and a dénouement" (490), he declares:

> [T]o what does such a story naturally lead, but to the conclusion that, whatever a censorious world may say to the contrary, female virtue has really very little to do with the Seventh Commandment? Novelists of this school do their best to inculcate as a duty the first two of the three stages towards vice—"we first endure, then pity, then embrace"; and, in so doing, they have assisted in no small degree to prepare the way for the third. (495)

Mansel is also concerned about the rise of what he calls the "Newspaper Novel," which reflects the fact that the vogue of these "corrupt" novels was aided by actual crimes and the sensational reporting of these events. After the abolition of the stamp duty on paper in 1855, newspapers had become cheap enough for a wider readership, and they covered, in lurid detail and with melodramatic exaggerations, the Yelverton bigamy-divorce trial of 1857-61, the Madeleine Smith murder trial of 1857, and various other notorious cases. The public was hungry for every little clue—there is "something unspeakably disgusting in this ravenous appetite for carrion" (502), remarks Mansel—and as the *Times* reviewer of *Lady Audley* puts it, "the police and the newspaper offices are besieged by correspondents eager to propose new lines of inquiry. The secret which baffles the detectives, it is the province of the novelist to unravel" (18 November 1862).

These attacks on moral grounds, however, can be seen as reaction on the part of the dominant conservative ideology against the threats that were posed by sensation novels. This was the period when there had been urgent debates about the laws governing marriage and divorce in England, which culminated in the Divorce and Matrimonial Causes Act of 1857 and the establishment of England's first Divorce Court in 1858. This law made divorce considerably easier where it had been extremely hard to obtain. Although it was still not equally available to both sexes (for wives were allowed to divorce their husbands on the ground of adultery only when that was compounded by other offenses such as cruelty and desertion), this was something of a minor social revolution, and the "Bigamy Novels" palpably reflected these social changes for the betterment of women's position. Indeed, the threats were most keenly felt where women were involved. As Elaine Showalter points out, "The prominence of women, not just as consumers but also as creators of sensation fiction, was one of its most disturbing elements."[3] In this connection, we might recall that the defendants in notorious trials of the period were frequently female, and that the courts were crowded by female spectators. The trial of Madeleine Smith, who poisoned her lover, fascinated middle-class women, and Mary S. Hartman suggests that they "most probably found in the trial a kind of vicarious outlet for their own frustrations."[4] And, just as women conspicuously figured in these cases, so they did in sensation novels. There were a number of female characters of strong determination, whether good like Marian Halcombe in *The Woman in White*, or evil like Lucy Graham in *Lady Audley*, who cannot be simply ruled by male domination. Although too much emphasis on their subversive quality may be misleading (for transgressions of women of powerful will were usually punished and contained), these novels certainly destabilized the traditional view of women.

This has a significant bearing upon James's comment on "the most mysterious of mysteries, the mysteries which are at our own doors." When Mansel makes a similar observation—"Proximity is, indeed, one great element of sensation"[5]—there is an underlying fear: facing tremendous changes in matters religious, social, and economic, unsettled Victorians turned to their home for security, and when that was threatened, the anxiety must have been all the stronger. No doubt orthodoxy was worried, for the undermining of the conventional idea of femininity was tantamount to the destruction of the sacred home. As Showalter observes, "[Lady Audley's] career and the careers of other sensation heroines of the 1860s make a strong statement about the way women confined to the home would take out their frustrations upon the family itself."[6] It is, therefore—aside from their exciting narrative interests that "electrify the nerves"—as representations of the women of the period that sensation novels draw our attention today; and *John Marchmont's Legacy* is no exception to this generalization.

2. Braddon's Novels up to *John Marchmont's Legacy*

Mary Elizabeth Braddon (1835-1915) was the youngest daughter of a London solicitor, Henry Braddon. Besides being unfaithful to his wife, Fanny, he was financially irresponsible and went bankrupt. Fanny Braddon started to live with her three children, separately from him in about 1840. After her brother Edward went to India and her older sister Maggie was married, Mary Elizabeth, in her attempt to support herself and her mother, first tried a career on the stage in Yorkshire as an actress (1857-60), then sought to earn a living by her pen. She wrote a comedietta called *The Loves of Arcadia*, which was successfully staged at a London theatre in March 1860. Another break presented itself when C. H. Empson, a Yorkshire printer, who had read her verse in a local paper, offered her ten pounds for a serial story. This became her first novel, *Three Times Dead, or the Secret of the Heath* (1860). Later, Braddon the successful author reminisced about this apprentice work: "I gave loose to all my leanings to the violent in melodrama. Death stalked in ghastliest form across my pages; and villainy reigned triumphant till the Nemesis of the last chapter."[7] Indeed, broadly melodramatic and filled with improbable coincidences, the novel traces the career of the villain, Ephraim East, who commits two murders and abets an aristocratic lady in another, then blackmails her into marrying him. The writing is very uneven, and half-successful attempts at Dickensian irony show that Braddon still has not found a true voice of her own.

At about that time she formed a relationship with John Maxwell, an energetic magazine-publisher, whom she had met in March 1860. They lived together from 1861, but were not able to marry until Maxwell's mentally disturbed wife died in 1874. Braddon's "irregular" life, just like George Eliot's, was often attacked when her books were reviewed. In February 1861, at the beginning of their partnership, Maxwell republished Braddon's first novel under the title of *The Trail of the Serpent*, with most of the places and characters renamed (for example, the protagonist, formerly Ephraim East, is here called Jebez North). This was something of a winner. Maxwell wrote to her, reporting triumphantly that it had sold one thousand copies in the first week after publication.[8] Interestingly, about this novel George Eliot was later to complain in a letter of 11 September 1866, shortly after the publication of her own *Felix Holt*:

> I sicken again with despondency under the sense that the most carefully written books lie, both outside and inside people's minds, deep undermost in a heap of trash. I suppose the reason my 6/- editions are never on the railway bookstalls is partly of the same kind that hinders the free distribution of Felix. They are not so attractive to the majority as "The Trail of the Serpent." . . .

In the context of our examination of the sensation novel this letter commands our attention in two respects. First, despite her denigrating comment ("a heap of trash"), in *Felix Holt* Eliot herself incorporated sensational elements in the form of the guilty secret of Mrs Transome, which reveals the powerful influence of this popular genre. Secondly, it reminds us that the railway stall was also a target of Mansel's attack: "keepers of bookstalls, as well as of refreshment-rooms, find an advantage in offering their customers something hot and strong."[9]

Braddon started contributing a number of works to Maxwell's magazines: her second novel, *The Lady Lisle*, to *The Welcome Guest* (April-August 1861); stories, mostly subliterary hackwork, to *Halfpenny Journal*; and her third novel, *Lady Audley's Secret*, to *Robin Goodfellow* from July 1861. It was the signal success of the last that instantly placed her in the literary market as the rival of Wilkie Collins. Braddon's debt to Collins is clear, as she herself later admitted at an interview:

> I always say that I owe "Lady Audley's Secret" to "The Woman in White." Wilkie Collins is assuredly my literary father. My admiration for "The Woman in White" inspired me with the idea of "Lady Audley" as a novel of construction and character.[10]

An exhaustive enumeration of the similarities between *The Woman in White* and *Lady Audley* would be tedious, but it may be noted that Braddon reverses the main situation, choosing a female, instead of a male, perpetrator of crime, and that while in the former work Anne Catherick and Laura Fairlie are rescued out of asylums, in the latter Lucy Graham is put into one. Braddon, however, was not just cleverly imitating Collins; she was also expressing opposition to him. Lucy Graham, or Lady Audley, was clearly meant as a protest against the passive and angelic type of heroines of the period, such as Laura Fairlie. In a sense, here was a feminist rewriting of that famous precursor text. Meanwhile, there is no doubt that Braddon learned her lesson from Collins very well, for certainly *Lady Audley* is much more tightly constructed than *Three Times Dead* or *The Lady Lisle*.

In January 1860, the publishers Smith & Elder had launched a high-quality literary monthly, *The Cornhill Magazine*, under the editorship of Thackeray. Its first issue contained, among other items, instalments of *Lovel the Widower* by the editor himself, *Roundabout Papers*, again by Thackeray, and *Framley Parsonage* by Trollope. The public keenly welcomed this publishing venture, which offered a serial of a novel, short stories, poetry, and articles, all for one shilling—the same price as a single monthly part of a serialized novel published separately. Maxwell was eager to imitate the *Cornhill's* popular success, and having secured George Augustus Sala as editor, started *Temple Bar* in December of the same year. Braddon was asked to contribute to this, and after publishing some poems and stories, she started *Aurora Floyd*, which ran from January 1862 to January 1863, overlapping the serialization of *Lady Audley* which finished in the *Sixpenny Magazine* in December 1862 (*Robin Goodfellow* having been discontinued in September 1861). *Aurora Floyd*, another bigamy novel, was, again, a great success, and before this novel came to its end, Braddon started *John Marchmont's Legacy* in *Temple Bar* in December 1862, which, astonishingly enough, from March 1863 ran concurrently with *Eleanor's Victory*, serialized in *Once A Week*.

3. *John Marchmont's Legacy*

In order to understand Braddon's intention in writing this novel, it is instructive to turn to her correspondence with Edward Bulwer-Lytton, whom she admired enormously and placed along with Dickens at the very top of the profession. Bulwer-Lytton, politician and writer, had achieved great popularity with such historical novels as *The Last Days of Pompeii* (1834), and had also worked hard to improve the lot of authors. With Dickens he had established a charitable scheme for needy authors, the Guild of Literature and Art, which Dickens believed would "entirely change the status of the literary man in England" (Letter to Bulwer-Lytton, 5 January 1851). Braddon sought guidance on the art of fictional writing, and her surviving letters to him amply show how much she treasured his advice. (Charles Reade was another prominent writer of the period who gave her encouragement and counsel.) Braddon had no illusions about the commercial aspect of her imaginative creations; she was writing sensation novels, she admits, because that was what the reading public wanted. That, however, was not all she cared about: "I want to serve two masters. I want to be artistic & please *you*. I want to be sensational, & to please Mudie's subscribers" (May 1863). She expressed hopes that *John Marchmont* was "better written" (13 April 1863) than *Lady Audley* or *Aurora Floyd*. And it is not simply the matter of style that she was talking about, for Braddon was also seriously ambitious as regards characterization:

> I have thought very much over what you said in your last letter with regard to a novel in which the story arises naturally out of the characters of the actors in it, as contrasted with a novel in which the actors are only marionettes, the slaves of the story. I fancied that in "John Marchmont" the story was made subordinate to the characters but even my kindest reviewers tell me that it is not so and that the characters break down when the story begins. (17 January 1864)

The critic in the *Times* (2 January 1864) must be one of those Braddon had in mind, for this reviewer states that *John Marchmont* "may be pronounced the best" of her novels so far published, but goes on to add that here, as in other sensation novels, "when . . . the story begins . . . the force of character must give way to the exigencies of plot." Indeed, criticism of this sort—that in the sensation novel the emphasis is always on plot at the expense of character—was frequently accorded to the fiction of Collins and Braddon.

Behind this argument lay what James in "The Art of Fiction" (1884) called "an old-fashioned distinction between the novel of character and the novel of incident." The use of this division in the critical discussion of fiction, which survives even to the present time, became increasingly evident as sensation novels made their presence felt. Mansel, of course, had something to say about this:

> A sensation novel, as a matter of course, abounds in incident. Indeed, as a general rule, it consists of nothing else. Deep knowledge of human nature, graphic delineations of individual character . . . would be a hindrance rather than a help to a work of this kind.[11]

George Henry Lewes was also irritated by the sensation novelists' abuse of "striking incidents," which in his opinion only disturbs "the natural evolution of their story" unless they "serve to bring into focus the diffused rays of character and emotion."[12] Lewes's view presumably parallels what Bulwer, whose letters to Braddon are almost totally lost, said to her.

Braddon was aware that her characterization in earlier novels had been weak, and she tried to make it stronger this time. She wrote to Bulwer: "I am in hopes you will like 'John Marchmont,' the story I am now doing in 'Temple Bar' better than 'Aurora.' I have tried to draw more original characters, or at least one character more original than any of my usual run of heroes & heroines" (May 1863).

When she says "at least one character," Braddon no doubt has Olivia Arundel (later Olivia Marchmont) in mind. Mary Marchmont or Belinda Crawford are no more than conventional heroines, well qualified to become, successively, the wives of the upright, manly, and fairly conventional hero, but the portrait of Olivia is powerful and original, and it is no exaggeration to say that she dominates the novel, calling forth from the reader a complex reaction that blends sympathy and repulsion. Concisely informing us that "the life of this woman is told in these few words: she did her duty" (57),[13] Braddon explores Olivia's inner and outer worlds in a remarkable passage, as follows:

> It was a fearfully monotonous, narrow, and uneventful life which Olivia Arundel led at Swampington Rectory. . . . The world outside that dull Lincolnshire town might be shaken by convulsions . . . but all those outer changes and revolutions made themselves but little felt in the quiet grass-grown streets, and the flat surrounding swamps, within whose narrow boundary Olivia Arundel had lived from infancy to womanhood; performing and repeating the same duties from day to day, with no other progress to mark the lapse of her existence than the slow alternation of the seasons, or the dark hollow circles which had lately deepened beneath her grey eyes, and the depressed lines about the corners of her firm lower-lip.
>
> These outward tokens, beyond her own control, alone betrayed this woman's secret. She was weary of her life. She sickened under the dull burden which she had borne so long, and carried so patiently. The slow round of duty was loathsome to her. The horrible, narrow, unchanging existence, shut in by cruel walls, which bounded her on every side and kept her prisoner to herself, was odious to her. The powerful intellect revolted against the fetters that bound and galled it. The proud heart beat with murderous violence against the bonds that kept it captive. (68)

This is a strong evocation of a painfully dull life, where the flatness of Olivia's daily activity is matched by the flat landscape. Her frustration and repression, the novel's imaginative core, are clearly expressed here, and Braddon goes on to show that Olivia's plight ultimately arises from the fact that she is a woman, and as such has not been given a role in life in which she can utilize and develop her talents: "She ought to have been a great man," but the "fetters that had bound Olivia's narrow life had eaten into her very soul, and cankered there" (356). To be sure, Braddon's portrayal of Olivia may at times seem excessively melodramatic, at least by the canons of fictional realism:

> Olivia Marchmont grasped the trembling hands uplifted entreatingly to her, and held them in her own,—held them as if in a vice. She stood thus, with her stepdaughter pinioned in her grasp, and her eyes fixed upon the girl's face. Two streams of lurid light seemed to emanate from those dilated grey eyes; two spots of crimson blazed in the widow's hollow cheeks. (161)

One contemporary critic remarks of the latter portion of this passage that "We doubt if, even at the Surrey Theatre, anything like it was ever delivered," but this reviewer is surely misguided in his observation about the characterization of Olivia that "she is but a creature of Miss Braddon's imagination, and that such a personage is as unreal as a hobgoblin."[14]

Braddon did not like insincere philanthropy. She looked down upon the pomposity and affectations of her day, and was to show a marked dislike for self-righteous do-gooders in some of her later novels, most notably in *Rough Justice* (1898). But here Olivia is not the target of a clear-cut satire. Braddon's presentation of this character's moral nature is interesting in its complication. On the one hand she tells us that Olivia's tragedy is that "for all her goodness" (67) or rather "even by reason of her goodness" (68) she is not loved. On the other hand, Olivia is "not a good woman, in the commoner sense we attach to the phrase" (69), or she is "a woman with a wicked heart steadfastly trying to do good, and to be good" (83). The novel is clearly troubled about the question, what really is "a good woman"? Consider, then, Olivia's essential predicament; the torment she undergoes by virtue of her own uncontrollable passion for Edward, the man who appears to her to be foolish and frivolous, "so little worthy of [her] sacrifice" (165). The novelist takes pains to tell us that Olivia is in the wrong:

> She was for ever weighing Edward Arundel against all the tortures she had endured for his sake, and for ever finding him wanting. He must have been a demigod if his perfections could have outweighed so much misery; and for this reason she was unjust to her cousin, and could not accept him for that which he really was,—a generous-hearted, candid, honourable young man (not a great man or a wonderful man),—a brave and honest-minded soldier, very well worthy of a good woman's love. (147)

Apparently this authorial comment is meant to be taken straight. But given the very power of the portrait of Olivia, and the worries about the idea of a "good woman," one is reluctant to make an easy judgment. Perhaps Edward is worthy of a good (but uninteresting) woman like Mary or Belinda, but not meant for a complicated person like Olivia? If Braddon is seen to be showing sympathetic understanding towards Olivia, might it not be possible that the novelist, who must have shared with Olivia "the powerful intellect" and the "proud heart," was putting much of herself into this character (hence sympathy), and then offering a kind of self-criticism (hence the authorial comment quoted above)?

Here it is tempting to hazard a biographical speculation. At one point in 1863, Bulwer must have criticized Braddon, as Robert Lee Wolff surmises, "specifically for not taking seriously enough the jealous torments of Aurora's disappointed lover Bulstrode and her deceived husband Mellish."[15] Braddon, in her reply, tries to explain why she "failed to reach a higher tone" in these characters:

> I have begun to question the expediency of very deep emotion, & I think when one does that one must have pretty well passed beyond the power of feeling it. It is this feeling, or rather this incapacity for any strong feeling, that, I believe, causes the flippancy of tone which jars upon your sense of the dignity of art. I can't help looking down upon my heroes when they suffer, because I always have in my mind the memory of wasted suffering of my own.

She concludes that "the faculty of writing a love story must die out with the first death of love" (May 1863).[16] Wolff suggests that this feeling "must have stemmed from some earlier passionate love affair."[17] Braddon obviously felt that she knew the pains of jealousy, and she deliberately did not elaborate them in the male characters. Her treatment of Olivia, however, is an entirely different matter. Could it be that in her serious attempt at characterization she had probed the depths of her own feelings and then came up with this impressive portrait of Olivia? What Braddon hit upon might very well have been a feeling of an intellectually acute woman hopelessly in love with a man of apparently unequal abilities. Olivia's "wasted love" (142) for Edward does seem to echo the novelist's own "wasted suffering" (the phrase used in the letter quoted above).

Olivia is not understood by anyone, not even by her widowed father, who is "afraid of his daughter" (70)—except, that is, for Paul Marchmont, who takes advantage of her secret passion for Edward, and thus is able to involve her in his wicked scheme. This is the crux of the plot development of the novel, and Braddon handles this part very well. Here "the story arises naturally out of the character," as Bulwer recommended. But she is on the less sure ground with imaginative creation of a villain: she has not been successful with a line of criminals from Ephraim East of *Three Times Dead* to Paul of this novel. She tries hard, particularly in the chapters dealing with Paul's last hours, but cannot quite bring it off. This section is by no means weak, but it lacks the psychological penetration Dickens displayed with Bill Sikes or Jonas Chuzzlewit.

Braddon, however, does better with the simple soldier-hero, Edward Arundel. It is clear from what he says to Mary—"You must never grow any older or more womanly. . . . Remember that I always love you best when I think of you as the little girl in the shabby pinafore. . . ." (15)—that he cannot face mature sexuality. He is not sensitive and cannot understand why Mary does not like the idea of her father's remarriage: he is "dumbfounded by Mary's passionate sorrow" (70). These two elements make it thoroughly convincing that Edward cannot comprehend, or even imagine, Olivia's sexual yearning for him. Probably the most sensational incident of the novel occurs in the scene where Edward hears the cry of a baby in the boathouse that Paul uses as his studio. He is with Olivia, and when she tries to stop him violently, he attributes her wild behavior to her madness, and thinks the child is hers. All this is psychologically credible, and again shows that the action of the story "arises naturally out of the characters."

The action of the novel covers a period of some seventeen years, from 1838 to 1855; in other words, though it begins a generation before the date at which the work was written and first published, it concludes within a few years of that time. This time-span is a necessary element in the structure because Edward first encounters Mary when she is no more than a child; like Jane Eyre, Maggie Tulliver, and many another Victorian heroine, Mary grows up as the narrative proceeds, and in due course marries and bears a child herself. But she remains, like Dickens's Amy Dorrit half-a-dozen years earlier, a child-woman—not least in the eyes of her husband, who tells her at one point, "My own childish pet. . . . You shall be sheltered, and protected, and hedged in on every side by your husband's love. . . . How strange it seems to me . . . that you should have been so womanly when you were a child, and yet are so childlike now that you are a woman!" (208).

Before dismissing Edward as an unenlightened representative of a patriarchal society, however, we should bear in mind that the narrator endorses Edward's attitude towards Mary—or at least does not appear to call it seriously into question. Consider the final sentence of the novel: "I leave him, above all, with the serene lamp of faith for ever burning in his soul, lighting the image of that other world . . . where his dead wife will smile upon him. . . ." In this as in so many other respects Mary stands at the opposite pole from Olivia, who, for all her infatuation with Edward, would hardly have desired or accepted this kind of love. Nevertheless, Mary and Olivia share one thing, in both being motherless. As Lyn Pykett points out, all of Braddon's heroines share this lack of a mother; Pykett goes on to claim that "As in so many nineteenth-century novels by women, the motherless heroine is both more vulnerable and more assertive than was the norm for a properly socialised woman."[18]

Edward himself is not only the very model of an English gentleman but a professional soldier of the officer class, and the dating of the action enables Braddon to dispatch him to India in the service of the East India Company for active service in the Afghan Wars of 1838-42. (It may be more than coincidence that Braddon's brother, another Edward, had gone to India.) His absence is also a convenience to the narrative, since it allows Mary to grow up and her father to come into his inheritance. Both this absence and the one near the end of the novel take him to pre-Mutiny India: the conclusion of the story in 1855 is within a couple of years of the outbreak of the Mutiny, with the ensuing transfer of the Company's powers to the British Crown—events that would still be fresh in the minds of readers when serialization of the novel began at the end of 1862.

Though such off-stage events as the Afghan Wars, reinforced by references to such heroes of the day as Napier and Outram, are reminders of a larger public world, the action of the novel takes place in England, and very largely in the relatively isolated county of Lincolnshire. Marchmont Towers belongs in many respects to the tradition, derived by the sensation novel from Gothic fiction, of the ancient, lonely and rather inaccessible mansion behind whose thick walls and heavy doors mysteries can be concealed and alarming events may take place. The introductory description of the house ("a little too dismal in its lonely grandeur") near the beginning of Ch. 5 associates it with "Ancient tales of enchantment, dark German legends, wild Scottish fantasies, grim fragments of half-forgotten demonology, strange stories of murder, violence, mystery, and wrong," while a later passage refers to it as "this grim enchanted castle, where evil spirits seemed to hold possession" (270).

As for the surrounding landscape, its desolation mirrors or objectifies the desolation of Olivia's inner life. Swampington Rectory (a loaded place-name) in the "bleak horrid county" (121) of Lincolnshire, "fenny, misty, and flat always" (54), offers no consoling natural beauty, no external solace for inner torment. Happier scenes, like Edward's childhood home in Devon and the pretty surroundings of Edward and Mary's brief honeymoon in Hampshire, are significantly located in other parts of England, more climatically favoured and more conventionally picturesque.

But the main action demands a severer setting, hostile as well as isolated. Two keywords in this novel are "bleak" and "dreary," and between them they may suggest the influence of two of the most celebrated of Braddon's contemporaries. Dickens's *Bleak House* (1853), ten years earlier, had been a precursor and almost a prototype of the sensation novel, and the plot hinges on events taking place in a lonely mansion in Lincolnshire. In Chesney Wold, as in Marchmont Towers, a proud and gifted woman compelled to suppress her passions lives a life of quiet despair, and the description of the Towers at the beginning of Ch. 6 of *John Marchmont* ("The rain beats down . . .") is strikingly reminiscent of a passage near the beginning of the second chapter of Dickens's novel ("The waters are out in Lincolnshire . . ."). Arguably, though, Olivia offers a more convincing study of feminine psychology, more inward and more felt, than Dickens's glacial and rather stagey Lady Dedlock.

Tennyson, at the height of his fame in the 1860s, is an even more obvious presence. The epithet "dreary," used so often in the novel, echoes throughout his well-known poem "Mariana," and it is interesting to note that between the serial and volume versions of this novel a rather banal chapter-title was changed in order to incorporate a clear allusion to Tennyson's poem—"Temptation" turned into "My Life is dreary" (Ch. 8). (Mariana, like the same poet's Lady of Shalott, and like Braddon's Olivia, eats her heart out in physical and emotional isolation from the world of action and self-fulfillment.) The changed title of Ch. 9 echoes a line in Tennyson's later companion-poem "Mariana in the South" ("When I shall cease to be all alone")—a quotation that in the original source appositely continues "To live forgotten, and love forlorn." Braddon's free adaptations suggest that she was quoting from memory, and she has clearly absorbed, and evidently wishes to reproduce in her own work, the spirit of these Tennysonian models. When Edward goes to Britanny in order to pick up the pieces of his shattered life, he follows in the footsteps of the hero of Tennyson's *Maud* (1855). And near the end of the novel, two more chapter-titles (41 and 43) allude respectively to Tennyson's "The Deserted House" and "The Lotos-Eaters."[19]

Such poetic elements, like the Gothic strain, have a generalizing and distancing effect, but this is also a novel resolutely of its own time: this tale of wickedness, crime and madness is set not in the barbarous past or away from the centers of civilization but in a highly organized and technologically advanced society. There are, for example, many references to the railways (and to the text that reflected their complex and minutely-planned operations, Bradshaw's railway timetable), to newspapers (advertisements are placed in the *Times*), to the postal service. An important plot-device involves the receipt of a letter which sends the hero on a journey and causes him to be seriously injured in a collision between a mail train to Exeter and a goods train carrying produce to London—powerful symbols of a highly organized modern society in which, as in the novels of Thomas Hardy, the patterns and rhythms of older modes of existence are rapidly being destroyed.

In *John Marchmont* Braddon continues, and develops, the themes and motifs which she dealt with in her previous novels. Like *Lady Audley* and *Aurora Floyd*, *John Marchmont* is a "bigamy novel," using the "dead-but-not-dead" formula. (*Three Times Dead* and *The Lady Lisle* also contain these elements.) And just as the secret of Lady Audley is madness, so is that of Olivia—"My madness has been my love" (429). Drawing attention to the connection of *Lady Audley* with *John Marchmont*, Lyn Pykett observes that "In each of these novels madness is used as a way of figuring the dangerous, improper feminine, which is both formed by and resists the management and control of the middle-class family and the self-regulation which is the internalisation of those broader social forms of control." She goes on to remark that Olivia is "in some ways an even more interesting representation [than Lady Audley] of the feminine and of madness, or indeed of the feminine as madness, since her insanity seems to be actively produced by the norms of respectable femininity."[20] If *Aurora Floyd* is a story of jealousy, *John Marchmont* offers a variation on the theme: while Aurora is an object of jealousy, Olivia is motivated by that emotion. Moreover, Braddon seems to suggest that Olivia's sexual repression is even more dangerous than Aurora's abandonment.

There are also interesting similarities between *John Marchmont* and *Eleanor's Victory*, which was running simultaneously with this novel. The latter, also, has a theatrical background (no doubt reflecting the novelist's own career), with its hero as a scene-painter, and it contains an artist-villain. There is also the situation of a very young motherless girl deeply caring for her ineffectual father. In this novel, one of the characters facetiously says, "He might come in for the title himself, my dear, if seventeen of his first cousins, and first cousins once removed, would die" (Ch. 53). This idea, foreshadowing the great Ealing film *Kind Hearts and Coronets*, is treated more seriously in *John Marchmont*. Indeed, problems pertaining to inheritance figure often in other Victorian novels: Dickens had treated them comically with Dick Swiveller in *The Old Curiosity Shop* (1841), and seriously in *Bleak House* (1853); in the period nearer Braddon's time, Collins used them in *The Woman in White* (1860) and *No Name* (1862), Meredith in *Evan Harrington* (1860), Trollope in *Orley Farm* (1862). *John Marchmont's Legacy* belongs to this group of novels, but we should be alert to the fact that the title of the novel refers not only to the property John Marchmont inherits, but also to the girl he bequeaths to Edward Arundel, as the novelist reminds us on several occasions (30, 151, 256, etc.).

Braddon knew how to tell a good story. Here she keeps the action going at an excellent pace. It slows down a little, perhaps, with Edward's courting of Belinda, but soon picks up with Olivia's emotional explosion. She had already mastered the art of writing a serial, and especially the divisions at the end of Ch. 14, and Ch. 28 (which respectively form the end of Vol. 1 and Vol. 2) hold the reader in genuine suspense. Although there is no murder in this novel, it satisfies the generic requirements with kidnapping, blackmail, and other sensational elements. These Braddon uses well, and she is capable of remarkable restraint where one might expect melodramatic excess. The description of the railway accident is a case in point (perhaps with a nod towards Ch. 32 of *Vanity Fair*):

> She prayed for him, hoping and believing everything; though at the hour in which she knelt, with the faint starlight shimmering upon her upturned face and clasped hands, Edward Arundel was lying, maimed and senseless, in the wretched waiting-room of a little railway-station in Dorsetshire. . . . (216)

Braddon always wrote fast, and she was by no means a conscious stylist, but there is energy, vitality, and a remarkable individuality in her prose; Arnold Bennett calls this "the sound vigour of the writing" in her fiction,[21] which is present in the above passage as in many other places in this novel.

"It is a fact that there are thousands of tolerably educated English people who have never heard of Meredith, Hardy, Ibsen, Maeterlinck, Kipling, Barrie, Crockett; but you would travel far before you reached the zone where the name of Braddon failed of its recognition" (24-25), wrote Bennett at the very end of Queen Victoria's reign. Braddon was an extremely popular writer with the general reading public, but her novels also fascinated a number of distinguished men of letters of the period. In 1868 Tennyson himself said to a guest that "I am simply steeped in Miss Braddon—I am reading every word she ever wrote."[22] Even Henry James, years after he published that perceptive but condescending review, wrote to her and confessed that "I used to follow you ardently, and track you close, taking from your hands deep draughts of the happiest of anodynes."[23] Indeed, there does seem to be every reason why the reader of the present day will share the enjoyment of these great Victorians.

(First published in *John Marchmont's Legacy*, Ed. Toru Sasaki and Norman Page, Oxford World's Classics, 1999)

NOTES

1 *Nation*, November 9, 1865, rpt. in *Wilkie Collins: The Critical Heritage*, Ed. Norman Page (London: Routledge & Kegan Paul, 1974), 122-23.
2 H. L. Mansel, "Sensation Novels", *Quarterly Review* 113 (April 1863), 482-83.
3 Elaine Showalter, "Desperate Remedies: Sensation Novels of the 1860s", *Victorian Newsletter*, 49 (Spring 1976), 3.
4 Mary S. Hartman, "Murder for Respectability: The Case of Madeleine Smith," *Victorian Studies*, 16 (June 1973), 399.
5 Mansel, 488.
6 Showalter, 5.
7 Braddon, "My First Novel," *The Idler Magazine*, 3 (Februrary 1893), 25.
8 See Robert Lee Wolff, *Nineteenth-Century Fiction; A Bibiliographical Catalogue Based on the Collection Formed by Robert Lee Wolff* (5 vols, New York: Garland, 1981-86), vol. 1., 145. Maxwell's letter is dated 22

February, 1861.

9 Mansel, 485.

10 Joseph Hatton, "Miss Braddon at Home: A Sketch and an Interview," *London Society*, 53 (January 1888), 28.

11 Mansel, 486.

12 *Fortnightly Review*, 6 (December 1, 1866), 893.

13 All page references are to the World's Classics edition, Ed. Toru Sasaki and Norman Page (Oxford UP, 1999).

14 "Sensation Novelists: Miss Braddon," *North British Review*, 43 (1865), 195.

15 Wolff, *Sensational Victorian: The Life and Fiction of Mary Elizabeth Braddon* (New York: Garland, 1979), 156.

16 The source of all the quotations from Braddon letters is Robert Lee Wolff, "Devoted Disciple: The Letters of Mary Elizabeth Braddon to Sir Edward Bulwer-Lytton, 1862-1873," *Harvard Library Bulletin*, 22 (1974), 5-35, 129-61.

17 Wolff, *Sensational Victorian*, 57.

18 Lyn Pykett, *The Improper Feminine: The Women's Sensation Novel and the New Woman Writing* (London: Routledge, 1992), 87.

19 I owe this paragraph to Norman Page.

20 Pykett, 95.

21 Arnold Bennett, *Fame and Fiction: An Enquiry into Certain Popularities* (London: Grant Richards, 1901), 27.

22 Charles Tennyson, *Alfred Tennyson* (London: Macmillan, 1950), 377.

23 In a letter dated August 2, 1911, quoted in *Sensational Victorian*, 10.

Ch. 22 *Praeterita* and *Mrs Dalloway*: A Hypothetical Note

"The Victorians are . . . *in* Virginia Woolf," Gillian Beer observes; they are "internalized, inseparable, as well as held at arm's length" (139). Of Ruskin, in particular, Beer states that he attracted Woolf "because of his antagonistic relationship to the powers of his society" and "his capacity for self-contradiction" (146). Beer goes on to say:

> But another reason for her responsiveness to Ruskin [in spite of his teachery tone] is his countervailing immersion in the specific: his joyous zeal in particularizing gives life to his writing in the modernist era, particularly to Virginia Woolf in her search for the "moment," both evanescent and fully known. (146)

Beer's discussion of the two writers centers round *Orlando* and *Modern Painters*. This is very natural, for there is a fairly explicit reference to Ruskin in *Orlando*, and it has been a standard practice to study that novel when the association of Woolf and Ruskin is brought up.[1] The present chapter, however, seeks to explore the relationship between these two writers through Ruskin's unfinished autobiography, *Praeterita*, and *Mrs Dalloway*.[2]

Woolf speaks, in an essay titled "Ruskin," of the Victorian writer's "force which is not to be suppressed by a whole pyramid of faults." Although "so much of his force" has gone into "satire and attempts at reformation," she suggests that "if we want to get unalloyed good from Ruskin, we take down not *Modern Painters*, or the *Stones of Venice*, or *Sesame and Lilies*, but *Praeterita*." Here Ruskin has ceased to preach, she says, and he is "unfailingly benignant":

> Compared with much of his writing, it is extremely simple in style; but the simplicity is the flower of perfect skill. The words lie like a transparent veil upon his meaning. And the passage with which the book ends, though it was written when he could hardly write, is surely more beautiful than those more elaborate and gilded ones which we are apt to cut out and admire. (462)

She then quotes a passage from the autobiography which we shall examine later.

Woolf also wrote a review of *Praeterita*, "Ruskin Looks Back on Life," subtitled "Serene Thoughts with the Echoes of Thunder."[3] Again she commends the book's plain, unadorned style: if one wishes to feel for oneself "the true temper of his genius, these pages, though much less eloquent and elaborate than many others, preserve it with exquisite simplicity and spirit" (503). She then talks about the ending of the book, but this time with a subtly different accent:

> Before the book is finished the beautiful stream wanders out of his control and loses itself in the sands. Limpid as it looks, that pure water was distilled from turmoil; and serenely as the pages run, they resound with the echoes of thunder and are lit with the reflections of lightning. For the old man who sits now babbling of his past, was a prophet once and had suffered greatly. (505)

Woolf seems to emphasize what lies behind the serenity of the prose. Of course she knew about Ruskin's madness, and suggested it by mentioning the disruptive "thunder" and "lightning." I suspect that one of the things that aroused Woolf's interest in Ruskin was his madness, and I wish to advance a hypothesis that Ruskin's autobiography served as a possible inspiration for Woolf's elaboration, if not creation, of Septimus Warren Smith in *Mrs Dalloway*.[4] I must emphasize the word "hypothesis," for what I am going to offer cannot go beyond that. Of the two essays I have quoted, the date of the first is unknown. Stuart N. Clarke says that "the style suggests a later work" (463). The latter was published in December 1927. That is to say, I have no empirical proof to show that Woolf knew *Praeterita* before she wrote *Mrs Dalloway*.[5] My speculation, however, is not groundless. In her letter to Vanessa Bell (5 April 1916) Woolf spoke of a review assignment on Ruskin,[6] and another letter (to George Rylands, 30 September 1923)—"I see Desmond [MacCarthy] has returned to his vomit this week, without bringing up anything that convinces me about Ruskin"—shows some familiarity with Ruskin. It is not altogether surprising that by the period of the composition of *Mrs Dalloway* (1922-24), the familiarity should have included *Praeterita*, given her voracious reading habit.

My hypothesis is built upon verbal echoes between the two texts. Consider the final paragraph of Ruskin's autobiography (Woolf quotes from "Fonte Branda" to "the stars" in her essay, "Ruskin"):

> How *things bind and blend themselves together*! The last time I saw the Fountain of Trevi, it was from Arthur's father's room—Joseph Severn's, where we both took Joanie to see him in 1872, and the old man made a sweet drawing of his pretty daughter-in-law, now in her schoolroom; he himself then eager in finishing his last picture of the Marriage in Cana, which he had caused to take place under a vine trellis, and delighted himself by painting the crystal and ruby glittering of the changing rivulet of water out of the Greek vase, glowing into wine. Fonte Branda I last saw with Charles Norton, under the same arches where Dante saw it. We drank of it together, and walked together that evening on the hills above, where the *fireflies* among the scented thickets shone fitfully in the still undarkened air. How they shone! moving like fine-broken starlight through the purple leaves. How they shone! through the sunset that faded into thunderous night as I entered Siena three days before, the white edges of the mountainous clouds still lighted from the west, and the openly golden sky calm behind the Gate of Siena's heart, with its still golden words, "Cor magis tibi Sena pandit," and the *fireflies* everywhere in sky and cloud *rising and falling*, mixed with the lightning, and more intense than the stars. (526-27; italics mine)

William Arrowsmith, one of the most astute commentators on *Praeterita*, makes a suggestive remark that here Ruskin must have been remembering Dante's "great metaphor . . . of the peasant and the fireflies, who stand for the fire-enveloped sinners" in the *Inferno* (219-20).[7] Significantly, Septimus is reading this very book—"Septimus, do put down your book," said Rezia, gently shutting the *Inferno*" (79)—whilst thinking about "the sin for which human nature had condemned him to death" (81). The allusions to Dante in this novel have been examined, most notably, by Beverly Ann Schlack. She argues that the name Septimus can be understood fully only in this connection. In Dante's world, "the seventh sin in the seventh terrace is sexual (lust) and it is punished in flames" (70). Septimus's chief sin is his homosexual love for Evans, and as we shall shortly see, he is in fear of being burnt. Schlack also notes: "Because Septimus is mad, he is quite literally one Dante's 'fallen people, / souls who have lost the good of intellect'" (69).[8] Of course Woolf could have conjured up these associations directly from her own reading, but her use of the Italian poet in this novel, I submit, may have had Ruskinian inflections.

Bearing in mind the ending of Ruskin's autobiography, let us examine the following passage, describing Septimus's agitated mind:

> A marvellous discovery indeed—that the human voice in certain atmospheric conditions (for one must be scientific, above all scientific) can quicken trees into life! Happily Rezia put her hand with a tremendous weight on his knee so that he was weighted down, transfixed, or the excitement of the elm trees *rising and falling*, *rising and falling* with all their leaves alight and the colour thinning and thickening from blue to the green of a hollow wave, like plumes on horses' heads, feathers on ladies', so proudly they rose and fell, so superbly, would have sent him mad. But he would not go mad. He would shut his eyes; he would see no more.
>
> But they beckoned; leaves were alive; trees were alive. And the leaves being connected by millions of fibres with his own body, there on the seat, fanned it up and down; when the branch stretched he, too, made that statement. The sparrows fluttering, *rising*, and *falling* in jagged *fountains* were part of the pattern; the white and blue, barred with black branches. (20; italics mine)

Here the trees and sparrows are "rising and falling," and they almost drive Septimus to madness. He imagines that the leaves of the "rising and falling" elm trees are "alight" and they are "connected by millions of fibres with his own body." The identification with a tree and the sense of being alight (with the latter in an intensified form) also appear in an earlier passage:

> Traffic accumulated. And there the motor car stood, with drawn blinds, and upon them a curious pattern like a tree, Septimus thought, and this gradual *drawing together of everything* to one centre before his eyes, as if some horror had come almost to the surface and was about to *burst into flames*, terrified him.[9] (13-14; italics mine)

Here I cannot help feeling the relevance of Arrowsmith's perceptive comment— though he is talking about the workings of memory—on Ruskin's "things bind and blend themselves together," which triggers the final paragraph of *Praeterita* (quoted above):

> The intricacy of binding here, whether these concinnities are deliberate or the work of "dream-gifted" association in a mind nearing madness, is close to miraculous. Ruskin's *things* ("How *things* bind and blend . . .") suggests that here *things*—active memories—*are* in control; that the narrator's mind is merely a chain on which these memories thread themselves and collect, imposing their own apparently adventitious unity on the musing mind whose past they casually glean. (208)

Similarly, things get hold of Septimus's mind, and in another passage where Woolf depicts it, she again seems to recollect Ruskin:

> Up in the sky swallows swooping, swerving, flinging themselves in and out, round and round, yet always with perfect control as if elastics held them; and the *flies rising and falling*; and the sun spotting now this leaf, now that, in mockery, dazzling it with soft gold in pure good temper; and now and again some chime (it might be a motor horn) tinkling divinely on the grass stalks—all of this, calm and reasonable as it was, made out of ordinary things as it was, was the truth now; *beauty, that was the truth now. Beauty was everywhere.* (62-63; italics mine)

When she had Septimus think of "beauty" and the "truth," it is likely that Woolf had Keats in mind, as Anne E. Fernald suggests.[10] But, since these matters can be overdetermined, it is tempting to imagine that Woolf was also thinking about Ruskin as a theorist of beauty, seeing that her phrase, the "flies rising and falling," resonates with Ruskin's "fireflies rising and falling."[11] Behind this, perhaps we hear an echo of Dante, where the fly and fireflies are placed in close proximity; in the translation of Charles Eliot Norton (a friend of Ruskin's, mentioned in the *Praeterita* quotation above): "As the rustic who rests him on the bill in the season when he that brightens the world keepeth his face least hidden from us, what time the fly yieldeth to the gnat, sees many fireflies down in the valley. . . ." (Canto XXVI).

I have premised the foregoing speculation on the possibility that Woolf read *Praeterita* before she wrote *Mrs Dalloway*. If she did not, the above findings will lead us, somewhat less excitingly, to imagine that when she turned the final page of Ruskin's autobiography she must have discovered a remarkable literary affinity with its author.

(First published in *Virginia Woolf Miscellany*, 2015)

References

Alighieri, Dante. *The Divine Comedy*. Trans. Charles Eliot Norton. Web. Accessed 2 April 2015.

Arrowsmith, William. "Ruskin's Fireflies." *The Ruskin Polygon*. Eds. John Dixon Hunt and Faith Holland. Manchester: Manchester UP, 1982. 198-235.

Beer, Gillian. "The Victorians in Virginia Woolf: 1832-1941." *Arguing with the Past*. London: Routledge, 1989. 138-58.

de Gay, Jane. *Virginia Woolf's Novels and the Literary Past*. Edinburgh: Edinburgh UP, 2006.

Ellis, Steve. *Virginia Woolf and the Victorians*. Cambridge: CUP, 2007.

Kirkpatrick, B. J. and Stuart N. Clarke. *A Bibliography of Virginia Woolf*, 4th edn, Oxford: OUP, 1997.

Landow, George P. *Ruskin*. Oxford: OUP, 1985.

Poole, Roger. *The Unknown Virginia Woolf.* Cambridge: CUP, 1978.

Ruskin, John. *Praeterita*. Oxford: OUP, 1989.

Schlack, Beverly Ann. *Continuing Presences*. University Park: Pennsylvania State UP, 1979.

Silver, Brenda R. *Virginia Woolf's Reading Notebooks*. Princeton: Princeton UP, 1983.

Webb, Caroline. "'All Was Dark; All Was Doubt; All Was Confusion': Nature, Culture, and Orlando's Ruskinian Storm-Cloud." *Virginia Woolf Out of Bounds*. Ed. Jessica Berman and Jane Goldman. New York: Pace UP, 2001. 243-49.

Woolf, Virginia. *Mrs Dalloway*. Ed. Anne E. Fernald. Cambridge: CUP, 2015.

Woolf, Virginia. "Ruskin Looks Back on Life." *The Essays of Virginia Woolf*, Vol. 4. Ed. Andrew McNeillie. London: Hogarth Press, 1994. 502-06.

Woolf, Virginia. "Ruskin." *The Essays of Virginia Woolf*, Vol. 6. Ed. Stuart N. Clarke. London: Hogarth Press, 2011. 460-64.

NOTES

1 See studies by de Gay, Ellis, and Webb.

2 Landow, pointing out the diffuse, unconventional narrative mode of *Praeterita*, has speculated about its influence on modernist writers such as "Conrad, Faulkner, and Woolf" (84).

3 Kirkpatrick and Clarke, 284.

4 For the connection between this character and Woolf's own "madness," see Poole.

5 I have consulted Silver's study of Woolf's reading.

6 Kirkpatrick and Clarke note that this review, possibly of *A Sketch of John Ruskin* by Peggy Webling, has not been traced (302).

7 Arrowsmith, it must be noted, is not arguing that Ruskin sees himself as a sinner here; he is quick to add that "not all Ruskin's fireflies are infernal or funereal" (221). The fireflies in question appear in Canto XXVI, depicting the eighth circle.

8 Fernald, in the note to her edition of the novel, states that Woolf "read Dante throughout her life, including during the composition of *Mrs Dalloway* although her most intense study of his poetry was in the 1930s" (266).

9 We have long known that Septimus is the double of Mrs Dalloway, and that they seem to communicate with each other with shared images and motifs ("Fear no more," etc.). In this connection it is interesting to note that Septimus's fear of things burning and his feeling of the "leaves alight" bring to mind Mrs Dalloway's thought when she visits a flower shop, where she finds "every flower . . . glows . . . ; every flower seems to burn by itself" (12).

10 See her note on this passage in the Cambridge edition, 252.

11 Ruskin discusses the connection of "beauty" and "truth" in his *Modern Paitners*, Vol. 2, Ch. 4, "Of False Opinions Held Concerning Beauty."

Ch. 23 Towards a Systematic Description of Narrative "Point of View": An Examination of Chatman's Theory with an Analysis of "The Blind Man"

1. Chatman's Theory of "Point of View"

The main source of the confusion surrounding the concept of "point of view" can be located in the fact that the phrase itself has at least three important meanings:

[1]
(a)Here, from this point of view, you can see my house.
[One sees a physical object from a certain spatial position.]

(b)From my point of view, she is wrong.
[One considers something from a certain ideological position.]

(c)From Japan's point of view, this is a disaster.
[One considers something with somebody's interest in mind.]

Consider, then, the following simple "story" as an example of the ways in which the term "point of view" is actually used in the critical discussion of narrative discourse:

[2]
(1)Tom worked in partnership with Dick. (2)One day he saw Dick talking to Harry, president of the rival company. (3)He thought Dick was disloyal to him. (4)Childishly he shouted at him.

It would usually be said that this "story" is written from Tom's "point of view." But only in the sense of [1c]—putting ourselves in his position, we read the story with Tom's interest uppermost in our mind—can this narrative be said consistently to employ Tom's "point of view." (Note that in this sense there is no "viewing" involved on Tom's part.) We do have Tom's "point of view" in sentences (2) and (3), corresponding to the sense of [1a] and [1b] respectively, but sentence (4) reflects the narrator's "point of view," whereby Tom's conduct is "seen" as childish. (Note, again, that strictly speaking, the narrator who does not inhabit the same world as the characters cannot literally "see"—in the sense of [1-

a]—the same things as they do.)

Thus "point of view" in the discussion of fiction could mean several different things at one and the same time. Therefore, if we want our critical argument to be precise and systematic, it is better not to let the single term "point of view" cover three separate narrative functions. Hence Chatman's sensible proposition of introducing three different terms, one for each function (1990: 143-49).[1]

"Slant" refers to the narrator's attitudes and other mental nuances appropriate to the report function of discourse (e.g. There is an ironic "slant" here.) "Filter" denotes the mental activity experienced by characters in the story world (Narrative information may be "filtered" through Tom, and when the inner world of his mind is described in any manner he becomes the "filter," or he is "infiltrated"). "Interest-focus" is related to the character in whose interest the reader is invited to read the narrative (Tom is the "interest-focus" here).

I believe that this three-way division is not only useful, but also necessary. There are, however, a few things to be pointed out, before we go ahead and put Chatman's proposition to practical use.

1.1 Filter, Slant

A very important part in the process of reading a narrative is the way in which the status of each sentence is determined: in other words, the way in which we make a decision about the source of its force: is it a factual statement of the narrator? or does it describe a particular character's thought? The question of "filter" has a direct bearing on this. Banfield (1982) has probed into this particular aspect of the fictional narration, what she calls Represented Thought, with an unparalleled theoretical vigor. Her sentence-based approach, however, is seriously limited in its disregard of contextual considerations, which hold the crucial key to our reading. Take, for example, a variation on [2]:

> [2′]
> (1)Tom worked in partnership with Dick. (2)One day Tom saw Dick talking to Harry, president of the rival company. (3)He thought Dick was disloyal to him. (4)He was untrustworthy, after all. (5)It was unforgivable. (6)He shouted at him.

The status of sentences like (4) and (5) depends on the neighboring narrative situation. When placed, as in this case, in a situation where a "filter" character is established and the "slant" in the form of commentary is absent, they are more likely to be read as representing Tom's thought. There will, however, be less likelihood of that reading, if they are placed where the narrator's commentary predominates. This is a fascinating area of narratological investigations, about which Banfield's grammar has nothing to say.[2]

The act of determining the status of a narrative sentence is called "attribution" by Ross (1976), and Toolan (1988). We should, however, take care to be explicit as to what exactly we are attributing. It is important to distinguish the content of a narrative sentence from its form, for there are cases where the former is attributed to a character whilst the latter to the narrator. A good example is James's *What Maisie Knew*. This is a narrative in which basically Maisie is the "filter" character, and the narrator reports in an elaborate language what goes on in the mind of this six-year-old girl.

With this distinction, it becomes apparent that the attribution of the language of narrative sentences, the question of linguistic responsibility, is nothing other than what has loosely been called the "voice" of the narrative.[3] I wish to point out that when this responsibility belongs to the narrator, we are dealing with the narratorial "slant." Note also that the linguistic responsibility can change from sentence to sentence, or even within a sentence. For instance, a word like "papa" in a Jamesian sentence in *What Maisie Knew* is a clear sign of this shift: in this case the linguistic responsibility momentarily shifts from the narrator's to Maisie's.

"Slant," it may also be noted, manifests itself most often in the form of the narrator's "modal expressions" (Fowler 1986: 131-32), such as "childishly" in sentence (4) of [2], and more subtly in the manner of character-reference, as we shall see in 2.3 below.

1.2 Interest-focus

When Chatman talks about "interest," he means a character's "interest." In the process of reading narratives the reader, he argues, usually identifies with characters in them and wishes them good comeuppance: in short, shares their "interest" (1990: 148). Yet a narrative may be about a character, of whom the narrator wants the reader to disapprove, or from whom to have some sense of distance. In this case, "identification" would not seem to be the right word. In fact, Chatman's idea of "interest-focus" is also connected with the reader's "interest" in a particular character. I think it is also important to recognize this in our definition of this concept. What happens in the latter case is that the reader is "interested" in a certain character without the feeling of identification.

As Leech and Short observe (1981: 341), "When an author chooses to represent the thoughts of a character, in whatever form, we are invited to see things from that character's point of view." Here they are talking about "filtration" and its relation to "interest-focus," and this is certainly one of the most important aspects of the fictional narration, in terms of its control over the reader's responses. To recognize this, then, will lead to another question I would like to raise regarding Chatman's thinking of "interest-focus": is it at the sentence level, or at the level of some larger unit? He provides the term "center" for the "interest-focus" of the whole narrative (1990: 148), but how about the "interest-focus" of a certain chapter when it is different from that of the whole novel? How do we describe this? I believe we can do without the term "center," by introducing a hierarchy and, to use *What Maisie Knew* again for illustration, say that Mrs. Wix is the immediate "interest-focus" of this sentence, that Sir Claude, at a higher level, is the "interest-focus" of the same chapter, and that Maisie, at the highest level, is the "interest-focus" of the whole novel, and so on.

The concept of "interest-focus," important as it is, might seem to escape a precise linguistic formulation. But when we start thinking about it at the sentence level, we could subject it to a systematic description with the help of Kuno's theory of "empathy": "the speaker's identification, which may vary in degree, with a person/thing that participates in the event or state that he describes in a sentence" (1987: 206). As an example Kuno considers various possibilities of a speaker's report of a situation in which a man named John hits his brother Bill:

(1)Then John hit Bill.
(2)Then John hit his brother.
(3)Then Bill's brother hit him.
(4)Then Bill was hit by John.
(5)Then Bill was hit by his brother.

There are, according to Kuno, several discourse principles involving "empathy": it is easiest for the speaker to empathize with the referent of the sentence subject; in a passive sentence it is easier for the speaker to empathize with the referent of the subject than with that of the by-agentive; given descriptor χ (e.g. John) and another descriptor $f(\chi)$ that is dependent upon χ (e.g. John's brother), the speaker's empathy with χ is greater than with $f(\chi)$; it is easier to empathize with the topic of the present discourse (1987: 206-16).

Now, consider yet another variation on (2):

> [2″]
> (1)Dick worked in partnership with Tom. (2)One day he was talking to Harry. (3)It so happens that Harry was president of the rival company. (4)Tom saw this. (5)He thought Dick was disloyal to him. (6)Dick was surprised when he was shouted at by his partner.

Although Tom is again the "filter" in sentences (4) and (5), this time we read these sentences with Dick as "interest-focus," wondering how this turn of events will affect him. We do so because Dick is introduced in sentence (1) as the grammatical subject, on the basis of which we will set about reading this narrative, thinking that it is his story. Sentence (6), containing the phrase "his partner" and a passive construction in which Dick is the subject, will confirm this reading.

Of course such a hypothesis on the reader's part may have to be modified later. It is possible that this narrative, if continued a little longer, should turn out to be about Tom, after all.

1.3 Uspensky, Fowler, and Genette on "Point of View"

Now that I have established the system of description based on Chatman, let us compare it with some other notable theories of "point of view."

Uspensky's (1973) quadripartite classification of "point of view" is, interesting as it is, less systematic than Chatman's. His "Phraseological Point of View" deals with the question of linguistic responsibility, but this term is, again, a misleading mixed metaphor, and I doubt if the distinction between "Ideological Point of View" and "Psychological Point of View" can be strictly and meaningfully maintained. "Spatial Point of View," however, is a useful concept, and we do need a separate term for this. I propose that we adopt Toolan's suggestion (1988: 68): if, for example, Tom is always present at the events a narrative describes, let us say that it adopts Tom's "spatial orientation".

Fowler's theory of "point of view" (1986: 127-46) derives from Uspensky. But his four-way division, from "Type A" to "Type D" is not very practical (it is not easy to remember which is which). There is a method of description which is easier to use, and gives a clearer picture. If one wants to classify the fictional narration according to the description of the characters' psychology—"internal" versus "external," with or without narratorial commentaries—one could construct a table, such as the following, utilizing Chatman's terminology:

[+ filter, − slant (modal)]

[+ filter, + slant (modal)]

[− filter, − slant (modal)]

[− filter, + slant (modal)]

Genette (1980) has introduced the term "focalization," by which he means "a selection of narrative information" (1988: 74). In other words, "focalization" is related to the question whether the narrator, in a given situation, tells the reader more than, as much as, or less than, a character knows. Although this term seems to have acquired wide currency, Bal (1983), another influential narratologist, has adopted it in a way that is different from Genette's—for instance, with new terms like "focalizer" and "focalized"—and as a result there is an element of undesirable confusion here.[4]

Finally, the one thing that can be said of all these theories is that they essentially address themselves to the question of "slant" and "filter." Chatman's theory has the distinct advantage of being more comprehensive, in that it also covers the equally important question of "interest-focus," which none of the others take into consideration.[5]

2. An Analysis of the Narration of "The Blind Man"

Lawrence's short story "The Blind Man" concerns Isabel and her husband Maurice who has lost his sight after being wounded in the war. They are leading a happily secluded life. Yet Isabel is not entirely free of worry, because sometimes Maurice feels depressed owing to his blindness. One day Bertie, Isabel's friend since childhood, visits them. Maurice has never liked him, and the intimacy between the two old friends puts him off. But finally he is convinced that he can establish a friendship with Bertie, after he, almost like a ritual, touches Bertie's face in the barn. Unbeknown to Maurice, however, Bertie is humiliated and shattered by this experience.

This curious story is interesting to look at in terms of its narrative "point of view," which moves around amongst the three characters. This aspect of the story has already received the special attention of critics such as West (1968) and Ross (1976). Furthermore, Cluysenaar (1976) and Fowler (1986) have made linguistic analyses of this text. All these preceding studies, however, lack in precision in one way or another, and I should like to show that Chatman's proposition, employed as a descriptive tool, offers a better way of coping with the narration of this story.

2.1 The Opening And Fowler's Analysis

"The Blind Man" opens with a scene in which Isabel is waiting for the arrival of Bertie and Maurice:

> [3]
> (1)Isabel Pervin was listening for two sounds—for the sound of wheels on the drive outside and for the noise of her husband's footsteps in the hall. (2)Her dearest and oldest friend, a man who seemed almost indispensable to her living, would drive up in the rainy dusk of the closing November day. (3)The trap had gone to fetch him from the station. (4)And her husband, who had been blinded in Flanders, and who had a disfiguring mark on his brow, would be coming in from the outhouses. (347)[6]

At the core of this story, there is the basic contrast between Bertie and Maurice; the former being small, quick, urban, intellectual, and Scottish, whereas the latter big, slow, rural, passionate, and English. Cluysenaar, noting the syntactic parallelism within sentence (1), and between sentences (2) and (4), argues that this first paragraph leads the reader to "suppose that Isabel favors Bertie over her husband" (1976: 96). Although he concurs in this interpretation, Fowler points out that Cluysenaar fails to explain how the text produces such an evaluation (1986: 80-81). The origin of the hinted negative evaluation of Maurice, he says, is in the contrast between the "sound" of Bertie's wheels and the "noise" of Maurice's footsteps in sentence (1). Fowler adds that the opposition continues in sentences (2) and (4), first between "Her dearest and oldest friend" and "her husband," and then between "a man who seemed almost indispensable to her living" and her husband "who had been blinded in Flanders, and who had a disfiguring mark on his brow."

So far so good, but now I should like to quote Fowler's subsequent argument (1986: 81-82) at some length, for I think his analysis needs a little modification:

> Through various subtle hints, we are told that these evaluations are in Isabel's consciousness: it is she who is named right at the beginning; she is given a verb of active perception, "was listening for"; the other characters are introduced in relation to her rather than as individuals—"her husband," "her friend." The internal *perspective* is confirmed by the mixed tenses of the first sentence of the next paragraph—"now" in a past tense sentence conventionally signals entry into a character's consciousness—and by the existence of many sentences in a style which could reasonably represent Isabel's reflective thoughts. But there is much in this continuation which indicates a troubled and complex *perspective*: (italics mine)

Fowler then goes on to quote the second paragraph of the story, which runs as follows:

> [4]
> (1)He had been home for a year now. (2)He was totally blind. (3)Yet they had been very happy. (4)The Grange was Maurice's own place. (5)The back was a farmstead, and the Wernhams, who occupied the rear premises, acted as farmers. (6)Isabel lived with her husband in the handsome rooms in front. (7)She and he had been almost entirely alone together in a wonderful and unspeakable intimacy. (8)Then she reviewed books for a Scottish newspaper, carrying on her old interest, and he occupied himself a good deal with the farm. (9)Sightless, he could still discuss everything with Wernham, and he could also do a good deal of work about the place—menial work, it is true, but it gave him satisfaction. (10)He milked the cows, carried in the pails, turned the separator, attended to the pigs and horses. (11)Life was still very full and strangely serene for the blind man, peaceful

> with the almost incomprehensible peace of immediate contact in darkness. (12)With his wife he had a whole world, rich and real and invisible. (p. 347)

Let us first examine Fowler's use of the word "perspective." Just like "point of view," this term is frequently used in the narratological literature—for instance, by Genette (1980) and Stanzel (1984)—and it, too, suffers from a similar sort of confusion caused by its ambivalence. I suspect that at one point Fowler uses it—"the internal *perspective*"—as a technical term, signifying that Isabel functions as "filter" here, but this is not the case at the other point—"a troubled and complex *perspective*"—where he probably means something like "a troubled and complex outlook." This could lead to an unnecessary confusion, and an example like this surely makes a case for adopting Chatman's terminology.

Fowler points out three indications of Isabel's "internal perspective" at the beginning: firstly, Isabel is the only character whose name is given at the outset; secondly, she is the subject of the verb "listen," lastly, other characters are introduced only in their relation to her. I believe that there is a small confusion here. If we are talking about Isabel's "filtration," only the second point is relevant. The first and the last have more to do with the fact that Isabel is the "interest-focus" (see 1.2). Also, if one wishes to connect Fowler's first point with the "filtration," one has to bear in mind the possibility that instead of giving her name, Lawrence could have started this story with "*She* was listening for two sounds," which would have been more effective in realizing her "internal perspective" (See Banfield 1982: 183-223; Stanzel 1984: 155-68).

What Fowler calls "a troubled and complex perspective" is produced by the vocabulary of extremes in [4]—"entirely alone," "unspeakable intimacy" and so on—thus giving us the impression that "Isabel's love for her husband is less secure than her affection for her old friend," which is already hinted in the opening paragraph (1986: 82-83). Fowler may be right to say that Isabel is responsible for this exaggerated vocabulary here. Yet, as he admits, the sentences of [3] are "first and foremost narrative sentences" (1986: 80), and essentially in what follows the narrator is supplying the information regarding the events leading up to the present, but not necessarily through the "filter" of Isabel. That is to say, there are things that are not likely to occur in her consciousness at this particular juncture: such as the content of sentences (4)-(6) of

[4]. Even though certain sentences may represent Isabel's thought, they may not be in the form which one would reasonably expect to be present in her consciousness. For instance, she would not think of Maurice as "the blind man," as in sentence (9). This phrase can only come from the narrator (see 2.3).

Thus, the narrator's presence is felt in one way or another, not just at the beginning, but throughout the whole story. West (1968: 117) is undoubtedly right in saying that this story is "directed by the exceptionally firm hand of the author" (though it would be more precise to say "the narrator"). Ross (1976), however, takes an entirely different view.

2.2 Ross And The Attributed Narration

Ross's idea of characters turning into narrators reminds us of that of Booth (1983: 149-65),[7] but he is more extreme in that he virtually disregards the presence of the narrator in the text. For instance, he contends that the first paragraph of *The Ambassadors* can be "attributed" to Strether. What this means is that the source of everything in that paragraph is Strether's consciousness. In other words, Ross is talking about the attribution of the content. He simply dismisses as "not substantial" a narratorial clause—"I have just mentioned"—which, in his view, is "the only problem to the tidy picture" (1976: 1232-33).

Ross makes up a chart of changing "attributions" in "The Blind Man" (1976: 1237) —from point A to point B the narration is attributable to Isabel, from point B to point C attributable to Maurice, and so on, all the way through. But this is much too "tidy." To be sure, there are places where it seems that the narrator steps back a little (that is to say, the "slant" is less tangible) and gives us characters' vivid impressions of narrative events more directly. For instance:

> [5]
> She pressed his arm close to her, as she went. But she longed to see him, to look at him. She was nervous. He walked erect, with face rather lifted, but with a curious tentative movement of his powerful muscular legs. She could feel the clever, careful, strong contact of his feet with the earth, as she balanced against him. For a moment he was a tower of darkness to her, as if he rose out of the earth. (354)

Here it does look as if the information about Maurice is "filtered" through Isabel. We see Maurice with her, through her eyes. But it is not always like this, and the narratorial "slant" is usually more visibly in front. Ross's argument is not convincing. Indeed, at one point his reading is seriously questionable:

> "The Blind Man" ends with a strange scene in the barn where Maurice forces Bertie to touch the scars on his face. Narration of these events is attributed to the confused Bertie, and the final significance of the events thereby becomes indeterminate. Because we are not privy to Maurice's thoughts or motives at this scene, we cannot know whether he sincerely tries to create a bond of "blood-awareness" with Bertie, or whether he humiliates the possible rival. . . . (1976: 1237-38)

Consider, however, the text of this crucial scene:

> [6]
> (1)Bertie could not answer. (2)He gazed mute and terror-struck, overcome by his own weakness. (3)He knew he could not answer. (4)He had an unreasonable fear, lest the other man should suddenly destroy him. (5)Whereas Maurice was actually filled with hot, poignant love, the passion of friendship. (6)Perhaps it was this very passion of friendship which Bertie shrank from most. (p. 364)

Despite Ross's cavalier dismissal, the narratorial "slant" is very much present, and we cannot "attribute" the whole passage to Bertie alone. Certainly he is the "filter" from sentence (1) through (4), but the "whereas" in sentence (5), which can only come from the narrator, indicates the change of "filter" here. This conjunction comes from the narrator, thus making this sentence a narratorial comment on Maurice's state of mind. Quite contrary to Ross's assertion, we are privy to Maurice's motives, and although we are not sure whether he wants to humiliate Bertie or not, Maurice's sincerity in offering the friendship is guaranteed by the narrator here.

2.3 Character-reference

Character-reference, the way in which characters are referred to, can be an important element of the fictional narration. It may indicate a character's "infiltration" as the word "papa" in *What Maisie Knew* (see 1.1), or the change of "interest-focus" (see 1.2). It can also be a source of narratorial "slant," as with the phrase "the blind man." Since neither Isabel, nor Bertie (least of all Maurice himself), would think of Maurice as "the blind man," this formulation can only be the narrator's (see 2.1). Lawrence could have done without this phrase in the story, using it only in the title. But it appears a dozen times in the text, forcing us to become more aware of the narrator's presence.

Consider, for instance, the following passage, in which Isabel, Maurice and Bertie find themselves in the dining room:

> [7]
> (1)Maurice was feeling, with curious little movements, almost like a cat kneading her bed, for his place, his knife and fork, his napkin. (2)He was getting the whole geography of his cover into his consciousness. (3)He sat erect and inscrutable, remote-seeming. (4)Bertie watched the static figure of the blind man, the delicate tactile discernment of the large, ruddy hands, and the curious mindless silence of the brow, above the scar. (5)With difficulty he looked away, and without knowing what he did, picked up a little crystal bowl of violets from the table, and held them to his nose. (358)

This passage seems to start with the narrator's description of Maurice. As we go on, however, we might want to revise this view, in particular when in sentence (4) we read the phrase "Bertie watched." Now we might think that it is Bertie's impressions that we have been reading. In other words, at this point we start thinking that the narrative information in sentences (1)-(3) has been "filtered" through Bertie's consciousness. But in sentence (4) there is also the telling character-reference, "the blind man." From this we infer that although he is the "filter," we have been reading not Bertie's immediate impressions as such, but the narrator's report of them. (That is to say, the situation is different from [5], where we have a more direct contact with a character's own perception.) This sense of firm narratorial control is to be confirmed in the phrase "without knowing what he did" in sentence (5).

2.4 The Words of Estrangement

In sentence (3) of [7], we have the word "remote-seeming." This is an instance of what Uspensky calls "the words of estrangement" (1973: 85).[8] The significant instances of words of estrangement in this story are almost exclusively connected with Maurice:

> (1) He was a man with . . . powerful legs that *seemed* [to Isabel] to know the earth . . . and his thighs and knees *seemed* massive. (354)
> (2) She watched him, and her heart sickened. He *seemed* to be listening to fate. (354)
> (3) He *seemed* [to the narrator] to know the presence of objects before he touched them. (355)
> (4) Life *seemed* [to the narrator] to move in him like a tide lapping, lapping, and advancing, enveloping all things darkly. (355)
> (5) "Sometimes I feel I am horrible," said Maurice, in a low voice, talking *as if* to himself. And Bertie felt a quiver of horror. (363)

What this means is that Maurice is something of a mystery, someone it is not easy to fathom. He is such a figure not only to the other characters in the story, but even to the narrator, as in instances (3) and (4). To be sure, the narrator can tell us what is going on in Maurice's mind, as in sentence (5) of [6], but the predominant impression is that the narrator, and by extension, the reader, remain "outside" him. This is an important point, to which I shall return in the next section.

2.5 The Ending

Having covered the more important elements of the narration of this story, we are now ready to examine the ending of the story. After the incident at the barn, Maurice and Bertie go back to Isabel, who notices that Bertie is curiously dejected while Maurice is triumphant:

> [8]
> (1)"I'm so glad," she said, in sheer perplexity.
> (2)"Yes," said Maurice.
> (3)He was indeed so glad. (4)Isabel took his hand with both hers, and held it fast.
> (5)"You'll be happier now, dear," she said.
> (6)But she was watching Bertie. (7)She knew that he had one

> desire—to escape from this intimacy, this friendship, which had been thrust upon him. (8)He could not bear it that he had been touched by the blind man, his insane reserve broken in. (9)He was like a mollusc whose shell is broken. (p. 365)

First, I should point out that it is not accurate to think, as Ross (1976: 1237) and West (1968: 117) do, that we are reading Isabel's thoughts—that is to say, she functions as the "filter"—here. To be sure, we have a verb of cognition "she knew" in sentence (7), but sentence (8) describes what has just happened in the barn, and there is no way she could have known this, because she was not there. Moreover, the phrase "the blind man" in sentence (8) strengthens the narratorial control. Thus it is not easy to share West's view that sentence (9)—which is a continuation of (8)—is "given as Isabel's" (1968: 117).

One might also ask for some solid textual basis for West's claim (1968: 117) that Isabel is "strangely content" at the end. Indeed, despite her seeming preference for Bertie over Maurice at the beginning (see 2.1), there is something in her that admires the blind man's power and "despise[s]" the small Scotsman (359). But I do not see any evidence that her "anxiety" (348) about Maurice has been cancelled. On the contrary, we are told that she is "in sheer perplexity" in sentence (1). In spite of his famous dictum, "Never to trust the artist" (1971: 8), we might take Lawrence fully at his word when he says that the ending of this story is "queer and ironic" (1962: 566). Consider sentence (5)—Isabel's remark, "You'll be happier now, dear." When she says this, she is not looking at Maurice, but at Bertie. The narrator makes a point of noting this in sentence (6): "*But* she was watching Bertie." The implication of this is very likely that Isabel's utterance in (5) does not carry her full conviction. Moreover, because of the syntactic similarity, one might hear an echo in this sentence of what Maurice has said to Bertie in the barn—"We shall know each other now." (p. 364) —and be reminded of its disastrous inadequacy. Thus the force of her remark is doubly reduced.

If sentence (5) is locally responsible, it is the overall structure of this story that is the ultimate source of the ironic effect. Just as at the beginning (see 2.1), here Isabel is situated at the center of the story, waiting for the arrival of the two men. And just as she was the "interest-focus" there, so she is here. Looking at the story as a whole, we might say that Isabel is as important an "interest-focus" as Maurice, the man referred to in the story's title. This is what Cluysenaar must mean by "the dual perspective" (that troublesome word again) of this story. Yet her argument that finally Isabel's "perspective" dominates because of "the sexual relevance" of her reactions is rather vague (1976: 98). Although I share Cluysenaar's conclusion, I hope I can describe more concretely how such a conclusion can be reached.

As we have observed in 1.2, an important aspect of the narrative management of "interest-focus" is that by showing characters' thoughts the narrator invites the reader to share their interest. In Chatman's words, "access to a character's consciousness is . . . the usual and quickest means by which we come to identify with him" (1978: 157). In "The Blind Man," Isabel is the character whose thoughts we know better than those of the other characters. We have more passages describing her inner world than those of either Maurice of Bertie. She is also the only character whose external appearance is not given. This contributes to an illusion that we are, as it were, "inside" her, which is in clear contrast with Maurice's case, where, as we have observed in 2.4, we are continually made aware of being "outside" him. It is through such narrative devices that Lawrence manages to place the reader closer to Isabel than to Maurice.

Probably because Maurice is the figure of power and domination, and embodies such Lawrentian principles as "darkness" and "blood-intimacy," there are critics like Spilka (1955: 29) who read Maurice's experience in a positive light:

> Through the friendship rite, [Maurice] moves toward greater fullness of being; his blindness is transcended, his unresolved blood-intimacy released, and the limited circle of marriage itself is broken by "the new delicate fulfillment of mortal friendship. . . ."

This interpretation, however, runs counter to my reading of the text. As I hope to have demonstrated, judging from the internal evidence, it is very hard not find this story ironic at the expense of the self-congratulatory Maurice.

3. Conclusion

Aside from those already mentioned in 2, there is another reason for my choice of a Lawrence story as a testing ground: it is the very fact that Lawrence's narration is particularly resistant to linguistic analysis. As Kuroda has observed apropos a passage in *Sons and Lovers*: "Lawrence's style reveals exquisite subtlety with respect to points of view; it is a style that [the communication theory of narration] will find most difficult to deal with" (1976: 112). There is also what Fowler calls Lawrence's "compositional defect":

> [Lawrence] foregrounds the vocabulary of sensation and evaluation indiscriminately, not differentiating the diction according to particular characters' points of view, and often intruding his own judgements into characters' thoughts. . . . (1986: 83)

However, by adopting Chatman's approach, even when confronted with such an intractable text, we can describe minutely and consistently how the Lawrentian narrator's "firm hand" operates, where we have an inside view of characters' mind, and how the focus of narrative attention moves. I am sure Chatman's approach will be much easier to apply to other fictional narratives. Following this methodology, I hope we can make some progress towards a systematic description of narrative "point of view."

(First published in *Language and Literature*, 1994)

References

Bal, M. (1983) "The narrating and focalizing: a theory of the agents in narrative," (tr.) J. Lewin, *Style* 17: 234-69.

Banfield, A. (1982) *Unspeakable Sentences*, Routledge and Kegan Paul, London.

Booth, W. (1983) *The Rhetoric of Fiction* (2nd ed.), U of Chicago Press, Chicago.

Chatman, S. (1975) "The structure of narrative transmission," in R. Fowler (ed.), *Style and Structure in Literature*, Blackwell, Oxford, 213-57.

Chatman, S. (1978) *Story and Discourse*, Cornell UP, Ithaca.

Chatman, S. (1990) *Coming to Terms*, Cornell UP, Ithaca.

Cluysenaar, A. (1976) *Introduction to Literary Stylistics*, Batsford, London.

Ehrlich, S. (1990) *Point of View*, Routledge, London.

Fowler, R. (1986) *Linguistic Criticism*, Oxford UP, Oxford.

Genette, G. (1980) *Narrative Discourse*, (tr.) J. Lewin, Cornell UP, Ithaca.
Genette, G. (1988) *Narrative Discourse Revisited*, (tr.) J. Lewin, Cornell UP, Ithaca.
Kuno, S. (1987) *Functional Syntax*, U of Chicago Press, Chicago.
Kuroda, S.-Y. (1976) "Reflections on the foundations of narrative theory," in T. van Dijk (ed.), *Pragmatics of Language and Literature*, North-Holland Publishing Company, Amsterdam, 107-40.
Lawrence, D. H. (1961) *The Complete Short Stories* vol. 2, Penguin, Harmondsworth.
Lawrence, D. H. (1962) *The Collected Letters of D. H. Lawrence*, (ed.) Harry Moore, Viking, New York.
Lawrence, D. H. (1971) *Studies in Classic American Literature*, Penguin, Harmondsworth.
Leech, G. and Short, M. (1981) *Style in Fiction*, Longman, London.
Ross, D. Jr. (1976) "Who's talking? how characters become narrators in fiction," *Modern Language Notes* 91: 1222-42
Spilka, M. (1955) *The Love Ethic of D. H. Lawrence*, Dennis Dobson, London.
Stanzel, F. K. (1984) *A Theory of Narrative*, (tr.) C. Goedsche, Cambridge UP, Cambridge.
Toolan, M. (1988) *Narrative*, Routledge, London.
Uspensky, B. (1973) *A Poetics of Composition*, (tr.) V. Zavarin and S. Wittig, U of California Press, Berkeley.
West, R. B. Jr. (1968) *Reading the Short Story*, Thomas Y. Crowell, New York.

NOTES

1 Chatman long ago already showed uneasiness with this term (1975: 215) and the germ of his recent thinking about "point of view" can be observed in his previous book on narratology (1978: 151-58).
2 Ehrlich (1990) tries to offer a corrective to Banfield, with a context-conscious approach. Her argument, however, is concerned only with the texts where Represent Speech and Thought is extensively employed. In this regard, though not primarily a linguistic study, Stanzel (1984) is more helpful in dealing with literary texts of wider variety.
3 "Voice" has been, again, one of the more troublesome terms in the critical discourse. See also Chatman (1978: 153; 1990: 118-19).
4 See Genette (1988: 72-78) for the points where he differs from Bal.
5 West (1968) seems to distinguish the narrator's "authority" and a character's

"point of view," which corresponds to Leech and Short's (1981) distinction between "discoursal point of view" and "fictional point of view." An approach of this kind, too, similarly fails to deal with "interest-focus."

6 All references to "The Blind Man" are to the Penguin edition (1961) and they are indicated by page numbers only.

7 As Genette (1980: 188) and Chatman (1978: 197-98) observe, Booth is not accurate in calling Strether a narrator, but there must be something in this notion, for even Chatman himself commits the same error when he speaks of Marcher, most probably from memory, as the narrator of "The Beast in the Jungle" (1978: 233).

8 Fowler seems wholly to accept Uspenksy's idea of "words of estrangement" (1986: 142), but I believe we need some caution here. I do not think phrases like "as if" and "like" necessarily produce the effect of "estrangement." Depending on the context, they can even be employed in an attempt to get close to the object of description. For example, the word "perhaps" can be used simply as a rhetorical device, without its literal sense of uncertainty.

Ch. 24 *After a Fashion*: An Appreciation

Some years ago Philip Davis made a list of what he considered Stanley Middleton's "major works": *Harris's Requiem*, *A Serious Woman*, *Him They Compelled*, *The Golden Evening*, *Cold Gradations*, *Holiday*, *Blind Understanding*, *Valley of Decision*, and *An After-Dinner's Sleep*.[1] Middleton being an amazingly even writer, it is very hard to discriminate, in terms of achieved quality, among his novels. Davis's choice is as good as another. One might, however, now add to the selection novels such as *Married Past Redemption* and *Toward the Sea*, which have been published in the last ten years, and had I been in Davis's position, I would certainly have put *After a Fashion* (1987) on that list. This may be a personal preference: the novel's protagonist is a thirty-two-year old university lecturer, and when I read it I was a lecturer myself, of exactly the same age. But upon rereading it recently, I still found it deeply satisfying. I should like to offer here my appreciation of Middleton's art as exemplified in this excellent novel.

After a Fashion deals with a period of ten months or so (more or less one academic year, from September to "summer," possibly June) in the life of Joseph Harrington. Three years earlier his marriage with an ambitious actress, Paulina Street, had collapsed. While she is now a famous TV star and remarried to a business tycoon with a title, he is still licking his emotional wounds. At his university Harrington comes to share an office with Helen Southwell, who, in contrast with Paulina, is a diffident woman but a very good scholar and teacher. She is generous with her time not only to students, but also to Professor Wainwright, helping in his recovery after a car accident. Moved by her care, Wainwright, a sixty-two-year-old bachelor, asks Helen to marry him. At this, she seeks advice from Harrington, ending up by confessing her love for him. Initially Harrington is not enthusiastic. He has a brief affair with Anne Selby ("normal, sexy, and efficient"), an unhappily-married neighbor. As Anne's domestic problems subside, she seems to lose interest in him. Harrington then reconsiders and asks Helen to marry him. She does not accept his offer, afraid of the commitment, and in the end Harrington is left in dejection.

At one point in the novel Wainwright says to Harrington, "You are far too pleased with yourself for your own good," and Helen echoes this when she declares, "We are not all as confident as you, Joe."

Though clever and well-organized, Harrington has his shortcomings. Most notably, he is very much self-absorbed and fails to put himself in others' positions; he is blind to his own faults and judges others pretty harshly. He continues to regard Wainwright as an "emotional cripple," even after he is touched by the senior professor's love for Helen. He feels that Helen "had some serious, basic flaw in her emotional make-up," and, noting her lack of confidence, thinks that "Virtue should be made of sterner stuff." Anne is "not interesting enough to him," and he "class[es] her with her father, a cunning, unsatisfactory creature, whose whims were governed equally by past rebuffs and present self-sought discomforts." These judgments may all be accurate, but there is something cold about them. Helen is not far wrong when she criticizes him, saying "I sometimes think, Joe, that you're hardly a human being."

So Harrington is a man with serious faults, but having turned the last page, the reader does not despise him. Middleton achieves this result largely through his narrative method. The entire story is told from Harrington's point of view. He is not telling the story himself, however. There is an authorial narrator who designates him as "Harrington," "he," and so on. This narrator makes no overt comment upon the protagonist, and rigorously eschews going into other characters' minds. The reader is always with Harrington in the sense that Harrington is the observing presence at every event the novel describes, and everything is filtered through his mind, and his mind only.

Middleton handles the narrative method with assurance. This comes near the beginning of the novel:

> The subordinate [Harrington] felt uncomfortable in Wainwright's presence. The man had been clever, written a brilliant doctorate . . . and then had settled into doing next to nothing. Neither idle nor malicious, he gave the appearance of both. . . . He chased Helen Southwell about Spenser because *he thought* his chaff would help her finish the book; he had no idea of her difficulties, her doubts, scruples, delicate qualifications, her fine discrimination. There was no intention to hurt, merely to spur. He clashed with Harold Morris, the senior lecturer, out of a mischievous sense of duty, but to Harrington the old man represented unprofitability; these exchanges had more of squabbles in the infant playground than of wit-combat. (italics mine)

The phrase, "he thought," appears to give us a glimpse of Wainwright's mind, but that is not quite the case. The passage continues:

> His kettle boiled; he lobbed teabags into the pot.

What has appeared between this and the sentence a few pages earlier—"Joseph Harrington pushed in home, snatched off his jacket and put on the kettle"—is not an objective description, but a recollection occurring in Harrington's mind. By the phrase "he thought," we must understand that Harrington thinks Wainwright thought so and so; we never know what Wainwright actually thinks. This standpoint is consistently maintained. For example, when Harrington reads Thomas Reeves's (Anne Selby's father's) manuscript, everything is reported in Harrington's language: we never know exactly what Reeves has written; all we get is Harrington's impression.

Wayne Booth has demonstrated that "the sustained inside view leads the reader to hope for good fortune for the character with whom he travels, quite independently of the qualities revealed."[2] Thus the reader who has "travelled" with Harrington through the whole length of the novel, immersed in his consciousness, is strongly induced to become sympathetic towards him. Middleton also manages to secure the reader's sympathy by at first presenting Harrington very much as a victim. We are led to believe that Harrington was deserted by Paulina. (But this is only his way of seeing the situation; we never know Paulina's side of the story.) The novel then reveals Harrington's flaws little by little, and eventually gives us an ironic portrait of him. What all this adds up to is that we are meant to be critical of Harrington, while maintaining a sympathy that is achieved by the narrative method. In a number of his novels Middleton chooses one character, and engages the reader solely with that character's mind. This method is effectively used, with ironic intent, as here and in the Booker-winning *Holiday*. The reader must keep a delicate balance between sympathy and critical distance, and is made to experience the difficulty (increased, because of the lack of authorial comments) of passing a moral judgment on the central character.

By means of this mode of narration, Harrington's inner world is tactfully revealed through his dealings with other characters. In a moving moment, Wainwright, an apparently dry and uninteresting man, tells Harrington that he has made a proposal of marriage to Helen

("Would you consent to become my wife?" is the phrase he has used—a very nice touch, this). He reflects:

> "She, and I use biblical language advisedly, restored my soul. I had killed a child. Oh, everyone assures me it wasn't my fault, but that makes no difference. I was lost, damned below Judas in my own mind. . . . [Helen] came and little by little lifted me from my desperation, made me capable again of life."

The motif of emotional recovery, "restoration of one's soul" in Wainwright's terminology, is central to the novel; as much so as in *Recovery*, Middleton's next novel where Job Turner, an old headmaster afflicted by a sense of loss after his wife's death goes through a similar process. There is a link with the later novel: Harrington's mentor, Henry Smith, a retired schoolmaster who has lost his wife—"what I might call the essence of life"—is reincarnated, as it were, as Turner. In *After a Fashion* the breakdown of his marriage with Paulina has had a devastating effect on Harrington, and, in a sentence that resonates with the title, we are told, "he had recovered, but only after a fashion." His feelings for Helen, it seems, are much inspired by Wainwright; perhaps he, too, wants to have his soul restored by her. Realizing that he has no hope of winning her himself, Wainwright even encourages Harrington to love Helen: "You could learn, could teach yourself to cherish her." When he is spurned by her, however, Harrington's role model is Reeves: "He set his teeth; he would bear all, shout and bawl back at the bleak world like Thomas Reeves." For this bluff man Harrington seems to feel the kind of respect he doesn't feel for Wainwright. "Respect" may not be the right word, but certainly Harrington is strangely drawn to him.

Reeves's autobiographical story, which Harrington is asked to read, contains an account of a seventeen-year-old boy's first sexual experience with an older woman; he is invited to her house, but before anything happens he has premature ejaculation. Harrington does not think that the episode has "brought the best out of the author," but admits that the narrative's literary faults and loose ends "attracted more strongly than its successes." He is impressed by the close of this account, where the boy walks the lamp-lit street, humiliated; "The final paragraph . . . had power," he feels. This, it seems to me, is a significant moment. The image of the solitary boy curiously foreshadows the very end of the novel itself, where Harrington walks to his room, his steps faltering. Indeed, Reeves has much in common with Harrington: his wife has left him and remarried (though a long time ago); he has been a teacher; and most important, he is essentially a lonely, disappointed man. Their similarity is made explicit in the following passage near the end, where Harrington is trying to compose his mind after Helen's rejection of him:

> Harrington pushed himself hard, to expel his disappointment. Again he failed, finding that unless he concentrated on movement his feet dragged, shuffled in short steps, motion petering out until he loitered, staring about him vaguely in search of bearings, a spiritless copy of himself. Now he was like Reeves, left to his own resources.

As I have said, Harrington in a way respects, or almost envies, Reeves's strength. Ironically, however, at the end of the novel, Reeves opts out of life while Wainwright, though physically weakened, seems to be coping.

Reeves's life seems to have taken a turn for the better at one point, when he becomes engaged to Melanie, the editor of a local paper, in which his story finally gets printed. The relationship, however, does not work, and eventually he commits suicide (to be precise, dies in a hospital after an abortive attempt at hanging himself). The news of his death does "not altogether surprise" Harrington, for they have met shortly before, when Reeves has said to him, "Dead. That's best," quoting from Sophocles's *Oedipus at Colonus*:

> Thy portion esteem I highest
> Who was not ever begot;
> Thine next, being born who diest
> And straightway again art not.

After a Fashion, like all Middleton novels, contains various literary quotations and allusions, and its characters often talk about literature. This is partly an indication of the novelist's predilections, but some literary references directly contribute to the novel's thematic organization. Reeves's Sophocles is a case in point, for the theme of death is a strong undercurrent in the story. (This, perhaps, reflects the fact that the author was facing his own death at the time of writing this novel; he was diagnosed erroneously, it fortunately turned out, as suffering from cancer.) Another literary reference of moment occurs where Wainwright and Harrington briefly discuss Christopher Fry's play, *The Lady's Not For Burning*. Harrington read the play once (his father had been excited about it, and his mother gave him a copy to read) but did not like it.

> "You don't think it will last, then?" Wainwright pulled at his lapels. "Not even as a literary curiosity?"
> *"No." Sharp from Harrington.* "Though you never can tell. The human race is pretty gullible."
> Wainwright rubbed his chin. (italics mine)

Fry's comedy, set in the Middle Ages, is essentially about misanthropy and a death-wish dissolved by love: Thomas Mendip, failing to find a meaning in life, claims that he is a murderer, and insists upon being hanged, until he meets and falls in love with Jennet Jourdemayne, who is convicted as a witch. When we read the novel with Fry's play in mind, as I feel the novelist is inviting us to do, we may find that Mendip's yearning for death is reflected, if in a covert and disguised manner, in Harrington. Harrington is not positively looking forward to death, to be sure. He does not even admit to Smith's kind of outlook—"I don't much want to live, I can tell you that"—but he already feels "he has lived his life." Harrington is described as a "Laodicean," which means that he is indifferent to life, he is not fully alive. Symptomatically, he thinks it is unlikely that he can produce another good book—"I'm getting staid." Here Paulina makes a perfect contrast; she is ambitious, even aggressively so, but as A. S. Byatt has shrewdly observed, Middleton treats the human desire for success "with an unusual respect."[3] Middleton would, I suspect, appreciate Paulina's vitality, against Harrington's negative attitude to life.

"He's dead"; thus Harrington on Wainwright, criticizing the latter's coldness. Harrington is characteristically blind to the very quality in himself that he finds reprehensible in others. He is himself suffering a death-in-life, but he does not quite realize this. There is a revealing dialogue between him and Helen:

> "I'm like Wainwright tottering around the margins of existence." Harrington laughed as he spoke.
> "Are you serious?" she asked.

"Never more so."

Of course he is not serious; that is his trouble. He is intelligent enough to see his own problems, but, from a misguided sense of superiority, is not humble enough to be serious about them. He dismisses Wainwright, as he would Mendip of Fry's play.

Harrington's lack of self-awareness leads to his failure to understand other people. In an intriguing moment in *The Lady's Not For Burning*, a man approaches Jennet, offering to use his influence to change her sentence if she lets him come to her cell. She rejects the offer, but not from physical revulsion; "Surely I'm not/ Mesmerized by some snake of chastity." She is provoked into self-examination, which results in her affirmation: "I am interested/ In my feelings." Faced with a life-or-death choice—"And so you see it might be better to die./ Though, on the other hand, I admit it might/ Be immensely foolish"—eventually she opts for life. Mendip's love for her leads him to make the same choice. This, to continue with our comparative reading, is the opposite of what Reeves does. An appraisal of personal integrity, as exemplified in Jennet, is precisely what Harrington could not achieve. His inability to understand Helen's plea for respect for her independent self—"I'm afraid of losing myself," says Helen when rejecting Harrington's proposal of marriage—is foreshadowed by his quick dismissal of the play. "'No.' Sharp from Harrington." is as severe a comment as can come from the authorial narrator.

Middleton often uses literary quotations for his epigraphs. The epigraph to *After a Fashion* is from Shakespeare's *Antony and Cleopatra*: "I'll set a bourn how far to be belov'd." This is its context:

> *Cleopatra*. If it be love indeed, tell me how much.
> *Antony*. There's beggary in the love that can be reckon'd.
> *Cleopatra*. I'll set a bourn how far to be belov'd.
> *Antony*. Then must thou needs find out new heaven, new earth.
> (I, i, 14-17.)

The line used for the epigraph is Cleopatra's retort to Antony; she absurdly and imperiously wants him to tell her how far his love might go; she is going to set a boundary for how much one (or, she) is to be loved. One might hear an echo of this line in Wainwright's criticism of Harrington's arrogance:

> "Has she never confessed she loves you? Come on, man, be honest now."
>
> Wainwright's fists were bunched on his desk.
>
> "Once. She said as much. It was some time ago. She may feel differently about it now. Love is a shifting, progressive matter."
>
> "Progressive. Matter. I suppose by that you mean she should have continued to say to you that she loved you. It's arrogant, on your part, and unlikely on hers. She is proud, and shy. Especially if you rebuffed her."

I think, however, it is possible to interpret the epigraph in another way; that is, to regard it as coming from Harrington's consciousness. I have said that everything in this novel is filtered through Harrington's mind. It seems to me that here even the epigraph is to be similarly understood: Helen's expression of her feelings perhaps appears to Harrington to be like Cleopatra's self-centered command.

Harrington is sorry for himself at the end: "Helen had no conception, he thought, of what she had done." This sentence, the core of the novel, conveys the difficulty of understanding other people in our lives. The fault is not Harrington's alone. It is inevitable, perhaps, given the self-absorption (underscored here by the narrative method) that we all are bound to be trapped in. *After a Fashion*, like many other Middleton novels, ends on a somber note, which is as it should be, for there is no easy solution. We shall probably fail in our attempt at understanding other people, just as Harrington does. Or, having learned from the novel, we might hope to succeed—after a fashion.

(First published in *Stanley Middleton at Eighty*, Ed. David Belbin and John Lucas, Five Leaves, 1999.)

NOTES

1 *Encounter* (July/August 1989), 63.
2 *The Rhetoric of Fiction*, 2nd ed. (University of Chicago Press, 1983), 246.
3 "The Art of Stanley Middleton," *The Fiction Magazine* (1985), 37.

Ch. 25 Back to Owl Creek Bridge: Robert Enrico's Adaptation Reconsidered

In 1978, reporting on a workshop on "Literature into Film," Harry M. Geduld spoke of Robert Enrico's adaptation of Ambrose Bierce's "The Occurrence at Owl Creek Bridge" as follows: "it was evident that if one saw Enrico's film without having read the story, one would have no sense of the author's ironic style" (56). The critical discussion of the film's style seems to have advanced little since. Geduld's observation is true enough, but it needs to be qualified; it does not do justice to the film's rich texture. Despite the general acclaim and several special studies devoted to it,[1] Enrico's adaptation has not been fully appreciated in terms of its stylistic achievement. The present chapter seeks to rectify this situation.

Bierce's "ironic style" is palpably felt from the beginning of the story.[2] In the first sentence of the third paragraph the narrator designates the protagonist as "The man who was engaged in being hanged" (41).[3] Here the crucial touch is the insertion of the phrase, "engaged in." While its formal ring is suitable for the solemn occasion, to say somebody is engaged in dying is peculiar, and it signals the narrator's distance from the event. The distance is magnified in the middle section of the story. Farquhar is revealed to be "a slave owner" (42) and his wife, we are told, is "only too happy to serve" the supposed Southern scout "with her own white hands" (43). The ironic tone in the choice of the word "white" is unmistakable. Lawrence I. Berkove makes an interesting case for this middle section of the story as "the most brilliant and underestimated part" (123). He argues that what we mainly get here is not the report of a neutral narrator, but Farquhar's mental rationalization, which shows "how completely self-deluded he is" (125-26). A good example is the sentence, "No service was too humble for him to perform in aid of the South, no adventure too perilous for him to undertake if consistent with the character of a civilian who was at heart a soldier" (43). This is "utter nonsense," according to Berkove (125), betraying as it does Farquhar's misguidedly romantic notion of heroism.[4] In Berkove's view Farquhar is arrogant, dishonest, deluded, immoral, and stupid. He goes as far as to say: "Bierce despises Farquhar. Never before or afterward did Bierce create a character upon whom he lavished such utter scorn" (129).

Although I find Berkove's reading a little extreme, I agree

with him in seeing Farquhar essentially as a foolish man.[5] For this interpretation of the character, the most telling detail is his remark, "I am a student of hanging" (43). Several views have been offered about this curious sentence, with varying degrees of persuasiveness.[6] But whatever the import of Farquhar's cryptic utterance might be, Bierce's point is, I would argue, to reveal the character's stupidity. Here, as he is trying to impress a man whom he believes to be a Southern scout, it would be natural if Farquhar said something like "I am a student of civil engineering," so as to stress his capability as a saboteur who might destroy the bridge. Instead, he says he is a student of hanging. We are made to wonder: who is this man to say such an extraordinary thing? We can imagine Bierce telegraphing to the reader, with cruelly absurd logic, that because he makes such an idiotic remark about hanging he ends up actually being hanged.

In making a film out of the story, Enrico deleted its middle section, which, as we have just seen, is where Bierce's irony is acutely present. This excision was done with deliberation. In an interview the director gives his rationale for the decision as follows:

> When I went over this draft I realized that in this episode with the scout what I had was simply plot. First of all, it supplies a reason for the death of Peyton Farquhar. . . .
>
> I found this too complicated. I think that Bierce's story is beautiful if one takes it at its most basic level—in other words, a man, a civilian, will be hanged. . . . My underlying aim was to show the rekindling of a sense of human dignity which this man appeared to be losing. (97-98)

Enrico's notion of Bierce's story being "beautiful" is related to his sense that it is "brimming with life in the face of death" (93). This is quite an unorthodox understanding. Just about the time when Enrico was making the film, Edmund Wilson authoritatively pronounced his judgment in the following terms:

> [Bierce] was constantly obsessed with death. . . . Death may perhaps be Ambrose Bierce's only real character. . . . In his comment on local California affairs, it is the murders and the hangings that interest him most. . . . There is no love of life in his writings. (621, 622, 625, 629)

Enrico was well aware that his was an unconventional view: "I believe that Ambrose Bierce, who has been always considered a 'black' nihilist author, is, at bottom, a man who loves mankind, who loves nature, and who loves life" (93). Here, to criticize Enrico for a "wrong" interpretation is beside the point. As an adapter he was free to alter the source material any way he might choose, and he chose this particular approach, omitting the middle section of the story. The result, according to Geduld, is that the film's Farquhar "became a kind of Everyman" (57). This statement, however, needs to be modified a little for the reasons indicated below.

In giving shape to his conception, Enrico inserted a song titled "A Livin' Man"— the lyrics run, "I see each tree, I read each vein, I hear each bug, upon each leaf . . . I wanna be a livin' man"—at the point where Farquhar, after freeing himself from the noose, breaks the surface of the water and looks around:

> I think that the idea of having a black voice came quite naturally. The form of the song was somewhat like a Negro spiritual—it told the story of a man's feelings—and the action took place in the South. The voice to use was obviously that of a black man. And also, appropriately, the voice would be that of an oppressed man. (110-11)

Now, following Geduld, let us imagine a viewer who has not read Bierce's story. Let us also suppose that this viewer has not read the Enrico interview and is unaware of the director's intention. Even then, the posited viewer might infer that, given the time and the place of the story (which Enrico meticulously reproduced with the help of Matthew Brady's photos), the man who faces an execution by Northern soldiers, and who lives in a sumptuous Southern mansion (see Figure 3 below), is a slave owner. Then the viewer would be puzzled by the song, for if the man is a slave owner he is perforce an oppressor, too. The viewer might go on to wonder: is the man an oppressor who by virtue of being oppressed belatedly realizes the atrocity of his own oppression? Is the song sung by a black man to emphasize this moral problem with severe irony?[7]

The participants of Geduld's workshop, had they had enough time to reflect, could have thought of such ironic complexities, which run counter to the film's overall presentation of Farquhar simply as an oppressed man. The apparent contradiction derives from the fact that the director did not pay due heed to the force of historical inference. The song could be construed ironical, although irony is not intended. This must be pointed out as a possible weakness of Enrico's film where his artistic control is somewhat unsteady. It must, however, also be pointed out that by choosing an actor who does not look like a stereotypical Southern plantation owner (see Figure 1) Enrico may have hoped to imply that here is an unusual Southern planter who has nothing to do with slaves—in which case hardly an "everyman," as Geduld asserts.

(Figure 1)

While the implication of the song "A Livin' Man" may be thus a little ambiguous, it is quite certain that, unlike Bierce, Enrico wants the viewer to feel sympathy for Farquhar. Consequently, Northern soldiers are regarded as threatening, cruel figures. There is an interesting shot (Figure 2) early in the film where Farquhar's hanging is being prepared; a soldier's head is seen to be framed by the loop:

(Figure 2)

Gerald B. Barrett comments that "Enrico wants us to consider the image as an ironic symbol—all men must die but the soldier is not aware of this" (199). The irony here works against the Northern soldier. Bierce as a Northerner might have been bemused.

Bierce would, however, have doubtless reacted differently to another scene from this part of the film. Shortly before the fatal drop, standing at the end of the plank, Farquhar thinks of his family: "He closed his eyes in order to fix his last thoughts upon his wife and children" (42). For the visualization of this moment Enrico puts on the screen the figures of Farquhar's wife and children playing in front of his mansion (Figure 3). His wife, who has been sitting in a rocking chair, moves out of it, and advances towards the camera. We see in the background a boy pushing a girl on a swing:

(Figure 3)

The choice of the plaything is apt, since Farquhar is just about to swing. His impending fate makes a striking contrast with the idyllic scene. Bierce would have approved this brilliant stroke, not only because of its compatibility with his sense of irony,[8] but also because of its accordance with one of his own stylistic devices.

The crucial point of Bierce's story lies in the striking ending: the revelation that the whole episode about the escape is an occurrence only within Farquhar's mind; he has never moved from the bridge and has been dangling from it (and swinging) all the while. Bierce carefully prepares for the surprise by providing subtle hints throughout the text. Before Farquhar hits the water, he feels "he swung through unthinkable arcs of oscillation, like a vast pendulum" (44). This oscillating motion is, shortly after, repeated in the curious action of the Northern soldiers' bullets in the water: "shining bits of metal, singularly flattened, oscillating slowly downward" (46). It is as if the movement of his body were transposed onto the bullets. The above-mentioned scene in Enrico's adaptation (Figure 3) can be thought of as a shrewd extension of this repeated motif of swinging motion.

Elsewhere Bierce subtly conveys to the reader the physical movement and condition of Farquhar's hanged body. When he is swept in the stream, Farquhar "whirled round and round" with "gyration that made him giddy and sick" (47; responding to this description, Enrico inserted a shot of the spinning sky and tree branches). Towards the end, before he reaches his home in his imagination, Farquhar feels "his neck was in pain" and that "His tongue was swollen with thirst; he relieved its fever by thrusting it forward from between his teeth into the cold air" (48). In actuality, what happens is not that he voluntarily thrusts his tongue out, but that the tongue involuntarily sticks out because of the strangulation. As Cathy N. Davidson says, "apparently naturalistic details . . . describe the physiological effects of death by hanging" (52). The terrible irony is driven home by the next sentence: "How softly the turf had carpeted the untraveled avenue—he could no longer feel the roadway beneath his feet" (48). Of course, there is nothing beneath his feet. F. J. Logan rightly perceives Bierce's "charnel wit" here: "This almost jovial description of the hanged man . . . make[s] it obvious that for Bierce [Farquhar] is negligible and expendable, and fair satiric game" (106).

Although this particular "charnel wit" does not make its way into Enrico's version, the film imaginatively re-creates the last part of Farquhar's mental journey. The relevant paragraph (the one immediately preceding the passage discussed above) must be quoted whole:

> By nightfall he was fatigued, footsore, famished. The thought of his wife and children urged him on. At last he found a road which led him in what he knew to be the right direction. It was as wide and straight as a city street, yet it seemed untraveled. No fields bordered it, no dwelling anywhere. Not so much as the barking of a dog suggested human habitation. The black bodies of the trees formed a straight wall on both sides, terminating on the horizon in a point, like a diagram in a lesson in perspective. Overhead, as he looked up through this rift in the wood, shone great golden stars

> looking unfamiliar and grouped in strange constellations. He was sure they were arranged in some order which had a secret and malign significance. The wood on either side was full of singular noises, among which—once, twice, and again—he distinctly heard whispers in an unknown tongue. (48)

Of the "marvel and mystery" of this passage, Berkove remarks that "the association of fantasy and death in this story is consistent" (131). Then, after noting Farquhar's realization of the pain in the neck, thrusting of the tongue, and feeling of the feet, he observes: "Again, diligent readers are retrospectively able to recognize these unusual reactions as attempts by his unconscious to reinterpret the grim physical symptoms of hanging for adaptation to his ongoing fantasy" (131). Thus, even eagle-eyed Berkove does not go any further than previous commentators, such as Davidson and Logan; he, like others, fails to respond to an interesting detail Bierce provides in the quoted passage above: "The black bodies of the trees formed a straight wall on both sides, terminating on the horizon in a point, like a diagram in a lesson in perspective." Enrico's adaptation will make us see what Bierce is getting at. For the filming of the scene, the director sought an appropriate location. He recalls: "As to the forest scenes, some were shot near Paris, where I found the rectilinear alleys which I needed to create the nightmare universe of Peyton's dream" (103). The Figure 4 shows how the film manages to visualize Bierce's description:

(Figure 4)

Note, however, Enrico talks about "the rectilinear alleys"; he uses the plural form. There is indeed the other "rectilinear alley" and it is a fascinating shot (Figure 5). After Farquhar gets out of the forest he comes upon this vista:

(Figure 5)

The seemingly quiet image, in fact, admirably expresses Farquhar's "nightmare universe." Enrico manages the feat by the device of visual parallelism.[9] Consider the scene where Farquhar comes back to his estate. He does so through a heavy iron gate (Figure 6). There is no counterpart in Bierce's story; it is purely a cinematic invention:

(Figure 6)

This image, we will note, parallels that of the "rectilinear alley." The visual echo assumes great significance when we realize that the alley and the gate send us back to the image of another "rectilinear" structure—the bridge:

(Figure 7)

By this visual parallelism, Enrico's film subtly makes the point, just as Bierce does, that Farquhar is in fact still at the bridge and has not moved from it at all. Thus, if we read the film carefully, we will perceive that the story's central irony is brilliantly visualized. In response to Geduld's comment, I would submit that although Enrico's film lacks Bierce's ironic tone it conveys his dramatic irony with signal success.

Enrico's adaptation is impressive not only visually, but also auditorily. Sound greatly enriches the film's semantic activities. At the beginning, we are shown on a tree trunk a notice that any civilian interfering with the railroad will be summarily hanged. Then there is a tracking shot of the woods, accompanied by hooting of owls, which is followed, as the camera nears the bridge, by diverse chirps of birds. We keep hearing birdsongs throughout the preparation for the execution, and in this sequence the chirping becomes dominant. This chirping is omnipresent: it is there at the end of the song "The Livin' Man"; immediately following it, in the commotion around the bridge; when Farquhar is at the river bank; when he has stopped running in the woods; during the journey from the woods to his home; and at the very end. By this pervasive chirping the film suggests that these sounds are aural residues in Farquhar's mind. They are what he has heard on the bridge; they do not belong to the places that he imagines he visits in his mental journey.[10] Ultimately they signify that he has not moved from the bridge.

The foregoing observation will gain strength when we note another significant use of sound to the same effect; this time the sound is extradiegetic, rather than intradiegetic as in the above example. The film begins with a drum roll lasting twelve long seconds, followed by another lasting fourteen seconds. The military resonance is appropriate; it is natural that Farquhar's execution should be attended by it. An auditorily arresting sequence occurs, however, where Farquhar keeps running in the forest. On the soundtrack we hear Kenny Clarke play an explosive drum solo. No other musical instrument is employed. The percussive music is so unusual that it immediately catches the viewer's attention. What is really striking, though, is the auditory parallelism involved here. Clarke's continuous beating on the snare drum reminds us of the drum roll that opens the film. We must also recall that a drum roll ends the film. The drum sound functions very much as the birdsongs do; by this device Enrico leads the viewer to imagine that the echo of the sound on the bridge reverberates in Farquhar's unconsciousness. The film thus adds another hint suggesting that he has not escaped.

This point is reinforced in a remarkable fashion by the film's ending, again through skillful control of the viewer's response. As far as I know, James W. Palmer is the only critic who has closely examined the opening and closing segments of the film. He argues that "Enrico's main addition to the story, the long tracking shots through the wintry landscape that frame the beginning and end of the film, alters the final impact of the work."[11] Noting that at the end the camera zooms back from Farquhar's body and stops with an extreme long shot of the bridge, he states:

> Not only does this shot give us a sense of completion, ending where we began, but it also gives us a different perspective from that given by the story. By reducing the scale and obscuring our final view of the event, Enrico makes his own comment on war and on the nature of man in general. The birdsongs on the soundtrack that ironically proclaim the sunrise and signal the hanging, the sentry's dutiful march back and forth on the bridge, the tangle of branches that nearly obscures the hanged man—all

> these elements elicit a number of possible reflections from the viewer, among them the general indifference of nature to man, the ritual efficiency of man's inhumanity to man, and the final insignificance of any one man's death. (Palmer, "From Owl Creek")

Let me offer a reading of the ending which is entirely different from that of Palmer. As we have observed, with the visual and auditory parallelism involving the rectilinear images and the sound of drums and birds, the film suggests that Farquhar has not moved though appearing to have done so. Bearing that in mind, what we must attend to is the camera movement at the ending, which carries great semantic importance. The final sequence starts with the camera capturing Farquhar's body hanging from the bridge (note where the body is located in relation to the bridge):

(Figure 8)

Then the camera slowly pans from left to right. It keeps moving in the same direction, showing a bleak riverside (Owl Creek), and a forest of bare trees, ending up with a distant view of the bridge:

(Figure 9)

Given the camera movement, we might think we have moved to the other side of the bridge. That, however, is not the case. Farquhar is still seen at the right side of the bridge. Therefore, we are looking at the bridge from the same angle as at the start. What has happened? Have we turned around 360 degrees? Actually, this is not an unbroken sequence; there are a few fade-ins and fade-outs. Enrico's film interestingly manipulates the viewer. We are tricked into feeling we have moved when we have not done so. Note that it is precisely what happens in Farquhar's mind. In this manner the ending of the film makes the viewer go through the same experience as the protagonist, thereby ingeniously emphasizing the story's crucial point.

I have begun this article by quoting Geduld's claim that Enrio's adaptation does not convey any sense of Bierce's "ironic style." Such an impression largely stems from the film's omission of the middle section of the story. Enrico dispenses with that part because he is sympathetic—not ironic, like Bierce—towards Farquhar. His filmic discourse, however, with the aid of visual and auditory devices, skillfully reinforces the story's central dramatic irony that, contrary to appearances, Farquhar has in actual fact not moved from the bridge. Enrico's cinematic style, which has not been fully appreciated, is, as I hope to have demonstrated, as versatile and expressive as Bierce's own.

(First published in *Style*, 2015)

References

Barrett, Gerald R. and Thomas L. Erskine. *From Fiction to Film: Ambrose Bierce's "An Occurrence at Owl Creek Bridge."* Encino: Dickenson, 1973.

Barret, Gerald R. "Double Feature: Two Versions of a Hanging." *From Fiction to Film: Ambrose Bierce's "An Occurrence at Owl Creek Bridge."* Ed. Gerald R. Barrett and Thomas L. Erskine. Encino: Dickenson, 1973. 189-211.

Berkove, Lawrence I. *A Prescription for Adversity: The Moral Art of Ambrose Bierce*. Columbus: Ohio UP, 2002.

Blume, Donald T. "'A Quarter of an Hour': Hanging as Ambrose Bierce and Peyton Farquhar Knew It," *American Literary Realism 1870-1910* 34 (2002): 146-57.

Bordwell, David and Kristin Thompson. *Film Art*. 3rd ed. New York: McGraw-Hill, 1990.

Conlogue, William. "Bierce's An Occurrence at Owl Creek Bridge," *Explicator* 48 (1989): 37-38.

Davidson, Cathy N. *The Experimental Fictions of Ambrose Bierce*. Lincoln: U of Nebraska P, 1984.

Enrico, Robert. "Director at Work." *Story into Film: Three Tales of the Supernatural Go from Page to Screen*. Ed. Ulrich Ruchti and Sybil Taylor. New York: Dell, 1978. 91-116.

Evans, Robert. Ambrose Bierce's "An Occurrence at Owl Creek Bridge": *An Annotated Critical Edition*. Web. Accessed 13 December 2013.

Geduld, Harry M. "Literature into Film: 'An Occurrence at Owl Creed Bridge'." *Yearbook of Comparative and General Literature* 27 (1978): 56-58.

Habibi, Don A. "The Magic Moment: The Liminal, Distended Time Flashforward of Ambrose Bierce." *The ABP Journal*. 1 (2005). Web. Accessed 11 December 2013.

Hennessey, Mike. *Klook: The Story of Kenny Clarke*. London: Quartet, 1990.

Logan, F. J. "The Wry Seriousness of 'Owl Creek Bridge.'" *American Literary Realism 1870-1910* 10 (1977): 101-13.

Palmer, James W. "From Owl Creek to *La Riviere du hibou*: The Film Adaptation of Bierce's 'An Occurrence at Owl Creek Bridge'." *Southern Humanities Review* 11 (1977): 363-371. Rpt. in *Short Story Criticism*. Ed. Joseph Palmisano. Vol. 72. Web. Accessed 2 December 2013.

Powers, James G. "Freud and Farquhar: An Occurrence at Owl Creek Bridge?" *Studies in Short Fiction* 19 (1982): 278-81.

Simonet, Thomas. "Filming Inner Life: The Works of Robert Enrico." *Cinema*

Journal 14 (1974): 51-59.
Wilson, Edmund. *Patriotic Gore*, 1962. New York: Norton, 1994.

NOTES

1 Enrico's *La rivière du hibou* (1962) won the Short Film Grand Prix at the Cannes Film Festival in 1962, and an Academy Award (Best Live-Action Short Subject) in 1963. Gerald R. Barrett and Thomas L. Erskine produced a book devoted to this adaptation in 1973.

2 Robert C. Evans's annotated critical edition, available at the website of the Ambrose Bierce Project, is a convenient guide to the past criticism of "Owl Creek Bridge." Of the numerous studies of Bierce's irony in the story, Lawrence I. Berkove's is the most thorough. Maintaining that the story is a hoax—"an intentional misrepresentation by the use of details" (118)—in which Bierce is constantly playing mind games with unwary readers and setting traps for them, he exhaustively cites important details with a keen eye.

3 All page references to Bierce's story are to Barrett and Erskine.

4 Concerning the last part of the sentence, Berkove points out that a civilian and a soldier are to Bierce mutually exclusive kinds of people, the distinction being at the heart of the title of the author's collection, *Tales of Soldiers and Civilians* (126).

5 F. J. Logan, too, expresses a view very close to Berkove's. The reader, however, may not be totally without sympathy for Farquhar. Don A. Habibi is perhaps right in commenting that, although Farquhar is negatively portrayed, "We applaud life's struggle to assert itself over death."

6 For example, Donald T. Blume, noting that readers of the *Examiner* where the story was first published were accustomed to sensational details in the newspaper's coverage of public executions, says, "This general public awareness of the horrors associated with the hanging process is perhaps what Bierce meant to suggest when he labeled Peyton Farquhar a 'student of hanging'" (147). James G. Powers thinks it suggests Farquhar's inner "expression of a pleasure principle, analogous to Freud's libido" (279-80). William Conlogue claims that Farquhar grows hemp (used in making rope), the implication of "a student of hanging" being that "he studies rope"; "His dream is the portrait of a narcotic hallucination" (37).

7 The British Film Institute's Collections Search database identifies the singer as Kenny Clarke, who plays drums on the soundtrack. If it is correct the

irony is multiplied, for Clarke was one of the African American musicians who moved to Europe because of racial discrimination. Annie Ross, a singer and Clarke's sometime girlfriend, recalls: "He used to feel that the white people had stolen his music. He was quite militant about it—militant enough to become a Muslim, change his name and get out of the country. He had a very hard time—he'd been ripped off time and time again" (Hennessey, 196).

8 Given the overall sympathy towards Farquhar in Enrico's film, however, the viewer would not interpret the inclusion of a swing as a piece of Biercean cynicism. In other words, the film audience will sense a situational irony, but not an ironic commentary on the protagonist.

9 Parallelism, as distinct from repetition (exact duplication), is explained by Bordwell and Thompson as "the process whereby the film cues the spectator to compare two or more distinct elements by highlighting some similarity (47).

10 This might lead us to regard the "whispers in an unknown tongue" Fauquhar hears in Bierce's story also as (distorted) aural residues in his mind.

11 Palmer notes the contrast between the barren trees here and the richly foliated trees in Farquhar's fantasies. Thomas Simonet makes the same point (57).

INDEX

Filmmakers

Scholars, Critics

Others

The Conspiracy of Words

Close Readings in Dickens, Hardy, and Others

2024年12月13日　初版第1刷発行

著　者　佐々木　徹
発行者　横山　哲彌
印刷所　岩岡印刷株式会社

発行所　大阪教育図書株式会社
〒530-0055　大阪市北区野崎町 1-25
TEL 06-6361-5936　FAX 06-6361-5819
振替 00940-1-115500

ISBN978-4-271-21071-9 C3097　落丁・乱丁本はお取り替え致します。